Tears of the Dragon

Tears of the Dragon

PAULA GOSLING

First published in Great Britain in 2004 by
Allison & Busby Limited
Bon Marche Centre
241-251 Ferndale Road
London SW9 8BJ
http://www.allisonandbusby.com

A catalogue record for this book is available from
the British Library.

10 9 8 7 6 5 4 3 2 1

ISBN 0 7490 8315 8

Printed and bound in Wales by
Creative Print & Design, Ebbw Vale

"A legend states that when China was invaded by the Tartar barbarians, the Imperial Dragon shed tears of sorrow, and these tears petrified into jade."

Richard Gump, *Jade: Stone of Heaven*

FOR – AND BECAUSE OF – JULIA

AUTHOR'S NOTE

This is a book of fiction, but it required a great deal of research, for which I would like to thank The Chicago Historical Society, and the many authors who have gone before me. I also owe a great debt of gratitude to Jax Lovesey, who led me through the complexities of Chinese languages. None of the mistakes in this book should be attributed to any one of the above. I made all of them myself and no doubt will continue to do so on a regular basis.

Prologue

Elodie Browne stepped forward, impatient to have this matter finished. It was very late, and the taxi was waiting downstairs. As the elevator doors started to close behind her, she found herself looking into darkness. Just before losing the band of light from the elevator itself, she noted red leather chairs, an oriental rug, a reception desk, and her shadow, cast long and thin before her. There was a soft thud of doors closing. Now the darkness was complete.

Wrong floor.

But when she turned and fumbled for the call button the elevator doors remained closed. It was already on its way up or down, summoned by someone else.

Which was odd. Not cleaners, she knew the cleaners came early in the morning. The guard downstairs? But he had been asleep when she had walked quietly past him. It was such a huge building – of course, it was someone working late. Someone, like herself, perhaps, slaving on an overdue piece of work. In her case, suggestions for the proposed Leatherlux radio programme which had been due in by five that afternoon. But she had gotten her bright idea on the trolley, after work, and it had been too good to just give up on.

She was aware of the large open space in which she stood. It was quiet, over-warm, yet strangely claustrophobic. And then, gradually, she heard a mumur of voices from far down the right-hand hallway. She turned and felt for the elevator call button again, anxious to get out of the dark, out of the building, home where she belonged.

The voices were louder, now.

What floor was this, anyway? Her floor didn't have a lobby with red leather chairs. And she didn't remember seeing any when the elevator doors had opened for others going up or down during the day. What button had she pushed in her haste? Or had someone pushed the button on this floor before . . . someone who was expecting the elevator doors to be open

13

and waiting?

Now the voices were definitely angry, arguing, shouting. There was a crash, a loud horrible cry, then silence. She stood there, frozen. Then, the sound of a door opening, a pause, a mutter, slow footsteps echoing against the marble walls and floor, accompanied by a dragging, slithering sound.

Suddenly afraid, Elodie banged the call button frantically. She didn't want to meet whoever or whatever was coming closer. She didn't want to be seen here. She didn't want to be here. The strange, shuffling sound came closer, the footsteps slower, more laboured. Someone breathing heavily.

Would the elevator never come?

**

The fog swirled between the black ship's side and the concrete jetty as the heavy-set man came down the gangplank. Fuel-slicked waves lapped gently at the dock pilings, constantly changing their irridescent pattern as they washed over one another, collided, broke apart, recombined. The traveller glanced up, but could barely see the bridge of the ship that loomed above him. He had forgotten how thick the fog could be in San Francisco, but it was nothing compared to what he had grown up with back home. London pea-soupers were legendary.

On the shore vague globes of fuzzy illumination showed where lights struggled against the fog. They edged the roofs of the warehouses, but were unable to penetrate the darkness that filled the gaps between them. There was a smell of diesel fuel, wet rope, sulphur, a stink of rotting cargoes, a sharp edge of something like vinegar in the air. Not the most salubrious welcome to the marvels of America, he thought.

He looked around, his right hand held lightly away from his side, the left encumbered by a heavy leather suitcase. No knowing what could come out of the fog at night, preferably not customs officers or police, or worse. He had hidden in the ship until the health inspectors had passed, having paid the captain well for the privilege of travelling from China in secret. He had his reasons, most of which were held in the suitcase he carried. More in there than shirts, more than a change of underwear and a book to read. Few knew of his arrival, but it was best to be ready for anything.

Three figures suddenly emerged from behind a stack of packing cases, and he stiffened, his right hand reaching toward the inside of his jacket. Then, as they came closer, he relaxed, and his hand dropped again to his side. He recognized one, Li Wing, an old friend from Edmonton. The other two, while unknown to him, were also Chinese.

"General – it is good to see you, sir," said Li Wing, in a low whisper.

The heavy-set man nodded. "Is the priest from Chicago here?"

"Yes. We will take you to him. It is not far."

One of the unknown Chinese stepped forward. "May I carry that for you?" he asked, in Cantonese, reaching toward the leather case, but Li Wing touched his sleeve and shook his head.

"No," snapped the General.

The man stepped back, eyes downcast. The General smiled. "It is my burden," he corrected himself, saving the face of the man who had offered to help him. "The danger should be mine alone."

Li Wing nodded. "We must go quickly," he said. "A security patrol is due soon. There would be questions."

"There are always questions," the General said. "And at least two answers for every one of them."

They walked down the dock, the fog flowing around them like liquid smoke. Their footsteps were oddly synchronized. Their shapes slowly blurred into the shadows. After a moment they had disappeared, and there was only the wash of the water and the sound of the foghorns like dying dragons in the dark.

1

"Hey, Deacon, we're going to bust up a party over on Jefferson. Want to come?"

"No, thanks."

Lt. Archie Deacon didn't even turn to the voice that called. He was getting damned sick and tired of the raids on clubs and private homes where liquor was being served. He didn't think people ought to be arrested for enjoying themselves. The bootleggers, now, they were legitimate targets, they were profiteering by breaking the law. An unjust law, to Deacon's way of thinking. A law that should never have been passed. As an officer of the law he was paid to enforce all laws, but he did not have to enjoy it like so many of his colleagues. Nor gain from it.

He lit a cigarette, watched the smoke spin and curl upward in the draft from the passing group of fellow officers making for the door.

The growing levels of corruption in the Chicago police department also worried him. He came from a family of police officers, men who had believed in upholding the law and doing it decently and honestly. It was even getting to the point where some of his colleagues were laughing at him for not taking advantage of the many opportunities offered to them by bootleggers for a little 'extra duty', such as riding shotgun on big deliveries. The internecine warfare between the various Syndicates was another source of trouble, arguments over territory leading to beatings or homicides nearly every week. And witnesses who wouldn't talk made things even more difficult.

There were racial tensions, too, within and between the various ethnic populations of the city and suburbs. The Italians and the Poles and the Irish each had their particular problems, and he had been hearing some impossible rumours from Chinatown, for instance, about bizarre murders. But the police left Chinatown to itself, just as they avoided the other ethnic suburbs unless forced to deal with them because of Prohibition. City centre was trouble enough.

Archie Deacon was not a goody-two-shoes by any stretch of the imagination. Especially if you included his bad habits into your evaluation. (He was stubborn, inclined to sarcasm, underweight for his six foot two height, smoked too much, liked jazz too much, and had red hair with the accompanying short temper.) It was not fear that kept him at his desk these days. He was not lacking in backbone. But he was becoming disenchanted with Chicago and what it was doing to itself. The politicians, the big businessmen, the bankers, the lawyers – they were profiting from the Volstead Act and the 18th Amendment as much as the bootleggers. Greed was everywhere. The decent people (and they were still in the majority) hadn't a chance. One by one they were getting dragged down, too.

"This one's going to be fun, Archie," somebody else shouted. "A big rich guy is throwing a 'garden party' for his kid's sweet sixteenth. Gonna bag some fancy asses, for sure."

"Fine," Deacon said. He put his feet up on the desk and picked up a sheaf of papers. "Enjoy yourselves." He could hear them muttering about him as they left. He sighed, knowing what they thought of him, and knowing at least half of them would accept bribes from the rich victims of the raid to 'look the other way' while they slipped out the garden gate. It was getting so he could name fewer and fewer honest cops.

It was enough to drive a man to drink.

**

"That was *my* floor you were on," said Bernice. "The whole foyer was redecorated last week." She stirred her coffee absent-mindedly and looked around the cafeteria to see if there was anyone she knew within waving distance. Bernice liked to see and be seen. She returned her attention to her friend. "What the heck were you doing here so late?"

Elodie had the grace to look ashamed. "I had this great idea for a new radio programme, and the deadline was five o'clock. Mr. Herschel is very fussy about people meeting deadlines. In fact, he's a pig about it."

17

"So, why didn't you just come in early, before he got there?"

"I was in the neighbourhood."

"At eleven o'clock at night?"

Elodie shrugged. "I had dinner with my cousin Hugh at the Browning," she explained. "It's not far away. I told him about the idea I had, and he thought it was good. I jotted things down as we talked – he's terrific with that kind of thing – and I was all excited. Hugh put me in a taxi, but I asked the cabbie to bring me here and wait while I ran upstairs. I just hit the wrong button in the elevator, that's all." She leaned forward. "This building is very creepy at night."

Bernice giggled. "Sometimes I think it's creepy during the day." She took a sip of her now lukewarm coffee. "So you think someone was dragging a body around up there?"

"Well..."

"Honestly, you and your imagination," Bernice scoffed. "More likely someone dragging a bag of rubbish to the chute. I worked on the tenth floor all this morning and I promise you, there were no bodies lying around." She paused. "There were a lot of people, though. I heard a lot of voices at the far end of the floor. Normally it's pretty quiet."

"Maybe he put it in a closet or something."

Bernice grinned. "You don't give up easy, do you?"

"It was just so ... scary." Elodie felt suddenly cold at the memory.

"It was dark and you were confused, that's all. Gosh, Ellie, you are some crazy kid. What the heck do you do up there on fifteen – drink shoe polish?"

"Very funny." Elodie scowled at Bernice. Here she was trying to be serious and Bernice wasn't making the right noises at all. It was very exasperating. It had been scary last night in the dark. Even now, in the brightness of the cafeteria, daytime, people all around, she felt a little shiver inside.

"Well, the way you talk. You're always seeing things nobody else sees, and being dramatic." Bernice fluffed her hair with a negligent hand.

"I can't help it if I have a lively mind," Elodie protested. "Anyway, no harm done. I got back in the elevator and went up and put my idea on Mr. Herschel's desk and went right back down again."

Bernice leaned forward, her red corkscrew curls bobbing. "Didn't make another stop on ten just to see if you were right?" The scarlet bow of her mouth quirked up on one side as she teased her friend.

Elodie was adamant. "Absolutely not. Anyway, I didn't know it was the tenth floor I had been on. I would have said something, but when I got down to the lobby, the guard was still asleep. As it was, with the waiting and all, I knew the taxi fare would be more than my cousin had given me. That's why I brought sandwiches today."

"Yeah, me too." Bernice looked around again. "As if I could afford a hot meal in this place every day. Coffee costs enough."

"And dessert," Elodie reminded her, glancing at the crumb-strewn plates before them. The Gower Cafeteria was subsidised for the building employees but was still too expensive for every day eating. These days you had to save wherever you could. Once a month she and Bernice had a hot meal together, invariably on a Friday when they had been paid. Otherwise they made do with buying either soup or dessert, which were cheap, and coffee which was even cheaper and came with free refills.

The employee cafeteria was on the lower basement floor, entered by a discreetly anonymous door in the middle of the row of shops that lined the corridor. Even though it was meant solely for the office workers in the building, little expense had been spared. It had a bold mock Aztec decor. The walls were painted in a soft orange with brown and ochre wall sconces, and large angular chandeliers hung above the tables, shedding a rather unflattering light. The chair backs and the pattern in the linoleum echoed that of the wall sconces, but the floor was beginning to blur with wear. It was unlikely to be replaced any time soon, because the men who ran the building had their priorities.

On the mezzanine, three floors above the workers canteen, was a highly fashionable (and profitable) restaurant with waitresses and tablecloths and little lamps on each table. It served more or less the same basic meals as the cafeteria, but with richer sauces and at three times the price. There the décor was more dramatic, based on the rising shapes of fountains. Elodie had peeked in once, and was impressed with the dramatic scarlet and silver colour scheme, the curving abstract murals on the walls, the flattering illumination from lighting recessed in star shapes on the ceiling, the wide spaces between the tables, and the gleaming black marble floor. Despite the tight times, both places were always busy in the middle of the day.

Elodie and Bernice felt lucky to be working in the biggest newest building in Chicago. In fact, they felt lucky to be working at all. Jobs were very hard to come by in 1931, and there were dozens of candidates for every one that came up. They were fairly lowly employees, but they accrued prestige from their surroundings. Designed by a famous architect, the Gower Building was the latest addition to Chicago's lakeshore skyline. Completed in 1928, it had been fully leased. Then the Crash came. Now there were quite a few empty offices along the corridors, blank glass doors with no names on, and far fewer footsteps echoed in the long, marble-lined halls. So many companies had folded. Executives who had formerly occupied luxurious offices were now selling apples in the street, others who had once commanded large staffs stood alongside former employees in the lines outside the soup kitchens. Schools were frequently closed because there was no pay for teachers, civic amenities were sporadic and undependable, and crime was becoming a way of life for many.

But there were some signs of hope. There was talk of Chicago mounting a World's Fair which would bring lots of business to the city, and the bigger companies were beginning to advertise again. "The Depression will bottom out," people told each other. "Things can only get better." But they were getting better very slowly for girls like Elodie and Bernice and their families.

"Say," said Bernice, as they went along to the Ladies Room to powder their noses before returning to work. "Would you like to earn some extra money?"

"Doing what?" Elodie asked, cautiously. Bernice was a little inclined toward what Ellie's mother called 'the wild life'. This offer could mean anything.

"Oh, don't be like that." Bernice sounded defensive. "It's nothing bad. My boss, Mr. Lee, is having one of his parties and they need help handing out drinks and stuff."

"Oh," Elodie said. "When?"

"On Saturday. Big party ... they say Barbara Hutton will be

there. She's one of Mr. Lee's special customers, you know." Bernice's voice was possessive – as if she and the Woolworth heiress were bosom friends. "And maybe some film stars. Mr. Lee has lots of famous clients, you know."

Elodie knew. Mr. Lee Chang was an importer of jade and other items of oriental art, and lived in one of the big houses on Lakeshore Drive, overlooking Lake Michigan. He was at the 'new' end, rather than with the old money that dwelt in the huge mansions closer to the city. Still, it would be nice to see inside his house – Bernice had often talked about how fantastic it was, because she had often 'helped out' at Mr. Lee's many parties. She had gone on at length about the 'moderne' decor, with every possible luxury and convenience in the latest style. Mr. Lee was a very very rich man.

"I hear he has a few other sorts of clients."

"Oh, Them." Bernice dismissed the people in question with a wave of her hand. "One or two – they have money to burn and no idea what to spend it all on. They think buying from Mr. Lee gives them class. They have no idea what they are buying, or what it's really worth."

"You mean he cheats them?" Elodie was amazed that anyone would take such a risk with People Like That.

"Not exactly." Bernice lowered her voice, confidentially. "But you know how it is with art objects . .. they're worth whatever anyone is willing to pay for them. And Mr. Lee only brings in the best of the best." She paused. "Mostly," she amended. "If they can't tell the difference, well, it's their lookout, isn't it? The way they earn their bucks, who cares how they spend it?"

Bernice was talking about the bosses of the Syndicates, of course. The men who had prospered from Prohibition and continued to do so, although there was word that this source of money might dry up – literally. The President was studying something called the Wickersham Report, which had come out in January. Word was that it was very contradictory. While some men on the Committee wanted Prohibition to continue, most said it wasn't working. If the Congress eventually repealed the 18th Amendment, what would the bootleggers do then, poor things?

Whatever these entrenched criminals attempted, it was unlikely to be honest. Once a person gets into the habit of killing off the opposition it sort of lingers, Elodie thought. If one day they outlawed chocolate or anything else, these men would simply sell chocolate on the sly, the way they sold liquor. Their kind would always prosper.

Supply and demand, her cousin Hugh had said last night. "That's what governs price, Ellie. Supply and demand. There were gangs in Chicago long before Prohibition came in. But they weren't organised the way Torrio and Capone have done it. Now crime is a business, run on business lines. If Prohibition is repealed, then they'll soon find other games to play, believe me, because the structure is already there, waiting to be used. They'll never go away."

Hugh was a newspaper reporter, and a hardened cynic at twenty-eight. His job on the *Tribune* gave him plenty of support for his attitude, as he mostly covered crime these days and the bootleggers were the major contributors to that particular beat. Ever since the shooting of a minor *Tribune* reporter named Jake Lingle, the *Tribune* had been on a crusade against the Syndicates, even though it later emerged that Lingle had been in their pay as well as the paper's. Crime and corruption were endemic in Chicago. The city had become famous for it. Or infamous.

Elodie loved to hear Hugh's stories – ones they couldn't or wouldn't print for fear of angering the 'wrong people'. In her eyes, Hugh was just about as glamorous as a man could get, even though she had known him all her life. Somehow in the last few years he had acquired a patina, a gloss of knowingness that fascinated her. She felt quite naive by comparison, and wasn't sure if it was natural or if Hugh deliberately made her feel that way. He did like to show off a bit, she reluctantly conceded. Still, he was fun, and he took her to places she would never see otherwise. But she sometimes wished that people would realize that Chicago was a very big city, also populated by good people, nice people, ordinary people. Not everybody was into crime, although it sometimes seemed like that. There were still legitimate businessmen, still happy families, still a reasonable life to lead without being involved with Them.

"Okay, I'll help out at Mr. Lee's party." Elodie felt suddenly brave. There was surely more to life than meatloaf twice a week and writing copy for wart removers. And it would help her to forget all about what might have happened on the tenth floor last night. "Do we have to dress up in maid's uniforms or anything?"

"No, just wear black." Bernice grinned at her friend in the mirror, and Elodie grinned back. Elodie never wore anything but black. People assumed she was trying to be mysterious and glamorous, but the fact was, black didn't show dirt, and was the cheapest material to buy because people needed it for mourning. And there had been a lot of mourning in Chicago the past few years. Her sister Marie made all the family's clothes, and all four of the sisters had a weekly dry-cleaning session in the basement that left them reeling from the gasoline fumes. But it saved a lot of money. And it meant they were always well turned-out.

She hardly minded at all that some wags in the office referred to her as 'The Widow'. In fact, she rather liked it. It made her feel special, which she definitely knew she wasn't. In contrast, Bernice's taste in clothes ran to the flamboyant and colourful. Indeed, today she was wearing a silk crepe dress in green with lots of little dots and arrows in red and purple. It had a cross-over ruffle-edged collar and long fitted sleeves. It must have cost her at least eight dollars, Elodie thought. She was a little envious because Bernice didn't really need to work. Her father was an undertaker and people would always be dying. Bernice could spend all her earnings on herself, and did. Her claims to poverty were valid solely because every cent she earned went onto her back.

Elodie Browne and Bernice Barker made an odd pair. Their friendship had begun when they ran into one another in the lobby one morning. They had attended the same high school, but had been mere nodding acquaintances there – now they each had found one friendly face in the huge population of the Gower Building. Bernice had many acquaintances, but surprisingly few friends. She seemed to find some sort of anchor in Elodie's serious outlook on life, but spent most of the time trying to tease her out of it. For Elodie, Bernice had an air of almost frenetic excitement that amused and stimulated her. This party, for instance. A little bit of wickedness was just what she needed in her life. She had always been a 'good' girl, working hard and seriously. Bernice was full of gossip and had a robust sense of humour that secretly tickled Elodie. She wished that she could be more buoyant and carefree, like her friend, but something had always held her back. Now she felt quite brave in taking on this extra job for the mysterious Mr. Lee and his rich friends. What would it be like?

They took the stairs to the lobby and waited for one of the many elevators banked on either side of the entrance hall. The elevator doors and their surrounds were one of the famous features of the Gower Building. They were of pale brass, elaborately engraved to the design of a famous French artist. They and the other golden decorations in the entrance were kept immmaculately bright, and people often snapped pictures of them.

While the upper floors of the building were relatively austere, albeit lined in the best marble, the echoing C-shaped lobby of the Gower Building was bright with expanses of glass behind which were exclusive shops offering wares far beyond the reach of the thousands of employees who actually worked in the building. Despite the Depression, there were still wealthy women who could afford to sweep in and shop in the Gower lobby and concourses. For the moment it was quite fashionable to do so.

That was why, in the central area of the main entrance, there was an electrically rotating podium that held constantly changing displays of things of interest to these high-spending visitors. Today there was a splendid white Lagonda on show, with deep red leather seats, big bug-eyed headlights, and highly polished chrome trim. A pair of equally polished and beautifully dressed models with marcelled silvery-blonde hair moved around the car, pointing out its finer features to any who enquired. Last week the display had been a stand of fine china from England watched over by a real butler in tails, and the week before that some odd shiny metal sculptures that nobody understood but which were supposed to be the latest thing on the Continent. Elodie found these displays both fascinating and annoying – they might amuse the rich, but they made her feel poorer than ever.

Bernice got off on the tenth floor (Elodie had a quick look through the open elevator doors and, sure enough, there were the dark red leather chairs she'd seen the night before. But no dead bodies). Elodie continued on up to the fifteenth floor, which was fully occupied by Adcock and Ash Advertising

Agency.

Elodie was a junior copywriter there. She mostly did 'dealer blocks' and catalogues, but had recently received kudos for naming a new brassiere and giving it a snappy slogan: THE BANDIT – LATEST THING IN HOLDUPS. Indeed, was also gaining the wary attention of senior copywriters as in meetings she exhibited a quick wit and a way with words that put them on their guard. She had ambitions, most of which presently centred on the work she had come in so late the previous evening to deliver.

She had a very small office in the back of the floor, while the Creative Group Heads and the top copywriters had big offices just off the main lobby. This carpeted area was open in the centre, with the offices lining each side. Every time she walked through to her little cubbyhole, she would make a fresh choice as to which office she would like for her own. All were panelled in dark wood with pebbled glass above on the interior side, and each had a window that looked out over the lake. Her office had no windows and no proper door. But it was hers, and she was grateful. The secretaries had to sit out in the open, outside each senior copywriter's or Group Head's office. As she walked on, the lush burgundy carpet gave way to dull grey linoleum. She was back where she belonged. She slipped into her rather unsteady typist's chair, looked at the framed picture on her desk, and sighed.

"I'm doing this for you," she said to the faces that looked back at her. "Otherwise, I swear I would run away to the circus."

Elodie Browne was the third eldest of four sisters. She was the first one to go to college – the oldest, Marie, had only finished high school, and the next oldest, Maybelle, had chosen to go to secretarial school. The youngest, Alyce, was still in high school. Their late father had left enough money in trust for them all to be educated, but only Elodie had been able to take full advantage of it. He had died in 1927, far too young, but had left them seemingly well provided for. Then the Depression hit, and there was no longer enough to send Alyce to university. Mrs. Browne was a teacher, and Marie ran the house. Maybelle worked at a fancy studio style magazine as personal assistant to a Very Important Man. Alyce mostly giggled and was adored by all of them.

Fortunately, their house on Kercheval had belonged to their grandparents, and there was no longer a mortgage on it, so they were spared that particular burden. But the running and upkeep of it was expensive. There were three sets of wages coming in now, but for a while there Mrs. Browne wasn't even being paid because the city couldn't afford to pay its teachers. She, like many of her colleagues, had gone on teaching, just the same. Maybelle and Elodie contributed all they could, but the old house was slowly deteriorating. So much needed to be done. On the outside it needed paint – on the inside it was shabby but familiar, and filled with warmth and laughter. Well, most of the time.

Elodie shook herself out of her reverie and picked up her pencil. Outside in the hall people were laughing and talking, coming back from lunch, putting off the afternoon's work just a little longer. She had half a catalogue still to finish, and was about to settle down to it, when she heard someone speaking as they passed by.

"Did you hear about the fuss on the tenth floor?" someone said. Elodie stiffened.

There was a murmur of other voices as the first one continued. "Some guy got robbed or something. Some kind of small-time importer who had one of those offices at the back? Place was a mess and there was blood on the floor. Nobody's seen him today, and they can't find him. They're covering it up, but I know one of the security guys, and he told me all about it. The police are pretending not to be there, but they're there all right, keeping their heads down. It looks pretty funny. Like maybe there's something more about the guy they want kept quiet. Damndest thing." The other voices murmured on, their tone both shocked and fascinated. Slowly the voices died away as whoever they belonged to moved down the hall.

Elodie stared at her hands. Her knuckles were white where she gripped the edge of her desk. She had been right. Something HAD happened on the tenth floor. Something terrible. If they were covering it up, that's why Bernice hadn't heard anything about it. She said she had worked in the mimeographing room all morning, printing out inventory sheets for Mr.Lee, so she wouldn't have been as privy to rumours as usual. Elodie remembered seeing the purple inkstains on her fingers at lunch. Normally Bernice, like all the

26

other secretaries in the building, was among the first to know everything that was going on. There was a reception desk opposite the elevator banks on each floor, and it was a clearing house for gossip. The Floor Receptionists were the queens of information, both accurate and inaccurate. Poor Bernice, she would be livid when she realized she had missed something.

Elodie wished *she* had missed whatever it was. She definitely had been on the tenth floor last night. She had heard angry voices, the crash of furniture, the frightened cry and then the footsteps and the dragging sound. And when the elevator doors had finally opened to her panickey summons, she had been perfectly visible in the light that poured out.

Had she been seen?

2

All the way home on the trolley, Elodie was worried. She did not know what to do. Should she tell the police what she had heard? But it was nothing, nothing at all. Just noises, a muffled word or two, a cry. They would demand to know why she had been there, maybe they would grill her like in the movies, suspecting she knew more than she did.

Maybe they would think she had something to do with it.

She would just have to pretend it had never happened. When Bernice found out, as she would eventually, Elodie would swear her to silence. Bernice would understand. One of the voices outside Elodie's office had said the missing man was an importer. That could mean anything. It certainly could mean Them. Capone, Moran and the rest. Everybody in the city was afraid of Them. Their tentacles were everywhere, nobody knew who worked for Them and who didn't, not for sure, anyway. And people died violently every day, she knew that, died for no obvious reason. Machine guns. Knives. Beatings. Secrets. Whispers.

Should she tell Hugh? Some of the stories he had told her came into her mind, terrible stories about terrible people. People who might seem very ordinary, and yet were involved in drugs, gambling, prostitution, bootlegging. It could be anyone. A neighbour, even a friend, familiar on the outside, but hiding another secret personality, greedy for easy money, willing to do anything for it in these days of deep Depression. Suddenly she felt hot, sweaty, then cold and shaky. What if someone on this very trolley was watching her? Maybe that man, or that woman. Maybe she had been seen last night, even identified. Maybe even now somebody was giving the order to –

"Kercheval, Union, and Trenton," called the conductor, ringing the bell as the trolley slowed to a stop with a screech of metal on metal. Elodie stood up and took a deep breath, lifted her chin. She was being perfectly silly. Nobody was watching her. She knew most of the people on the trolley by sight, travelling the same way as they all did most mornings and evenings. There was no sinister new face hiding behind a newspaper. Nobody looking anything but tired and worried at the end of another hard day. As she was.

She stepped down and walked across the road to the sidewalk, turning down her street and passing the familiar houses she knew so well. The Addisons, the Schmidts, the Vanderwalls, the Kloskys, the Lomaxes, the Pellinis, the Andersons. Were there secrets within? But each house had the windows open to catch the first fresh warm breezes of spring, and from every single one of them came the sound of the same radio programme. Amos and Andy. She found it hard to believe that crooks listened to that amiable pair of 'black' men who supposedly owned and mis-ran The Fresh Air Taxi Company, so called because its lone taxi had no windscreen. But hearing it meant Elodie was late – she usually got home about ten minutes before Amos and Andy came on. Like many folks, she kept time by what was on the radio.

Radio filled the air these days, gave entertainment and solace to all who listened. She loved it just as much as her little sister Alyce did. Indeed, Alyce organised her after school hours and weekends around what was on the radio, and in the Browne household it was never really off. Whether it was music with the Chase and Sanborne hour, or the adventures of Fu Manchu, the humour of the bickering Easy Aces, the scary mysteries of The Shadow, or the household tips of Aunt Sammy on the Housekeeper's Half Hour, the whole family had their favourites.

And it was free.

In 1931, all you needed to escape from the harsh reality of hard times was a radio and an imagination.

Elodie longed to get into radio. Writing advertising copy for rubber boots and headache remedies was not the height of her ambition. That was why she had been so eager to take part in the agency's in-house competition to dream up a radio programme for their biggest client, Leatherlux Luggage. And she had come up with a pip. Or, at least, she thought so. She would know on Friday, when Mr. Herschel announced the winner.

She reached their front path and turned in, mounting the

29

wooden steps to the porch slowly, trying to catch the last few minutes of Amos and Andy. The living room windows were open, and she could hear Alyce giggling beyond the curtains. Elodie opened the front door to the closing theme tune, and grinned at Alyce, who was sitting beside the radio.

"Was it good?"

"Sure. They're always good. The Widow Parker is after Andy, again. That woman is a menace, somebody ought to shoot her." Alyce took the radio very seriously.

Elodie took off her hat and coat and hung them up. Closing the closet door she looked around. The green flowered curtains, the worn blue velvet of the armchairs and sofa, the battered side tables, the lamps that Alyce was now turning on were all so wonderfully, comfortably familiar. There was singing upstairs – probably Maybelle getting ready to go out on a date. Something smelled wonderful, so Marie was making dinner, and she could see her mother, head bent over some papers as she checked essays on the dining room table under the big shaded light.

Elodie sighed. She was home. She was safe.

Everything was going to be just fine.

**

The room was dark but darker still were the shadows of the men standing around their victim, as he sat under the glare of an overhead light. The atmosphere was pungent with strange smells that penetrated every time he tried to draw breath through his bloodied nose. Before him stood the small man the others called *Junfa*.

"Where is it?"

"I don't know." For the twentieth time or more. "I don't know."

The *Junfa* struck again, hard and fast. More pain. More blood. More despair.

"You arranged it. We have confirmation."

"I made the intial contact. After that it was up to the General." The words were slurred through his swollen lips and broken front teeth.

"And where is the General now?"

30

Wearily, "I don't know."

Again and again, the blows, the pain. He was not a brave man, and he knew that if he had information for them he would by now have willingly given it just to stop this terrible beating. For it was not only the *Junfa* who struck, but others had struck the previous night in his office. His entire body ached, straining involuntarily against the ropes that tied his hands behind the chairback, pulling against them with every blow.

The *Junfa* leaned forward, every vicious word carried on foul breath, the sheen of sweat on his cheekbones gleaming under the light. His obvious pleasure in causing pain and fear was very evident. "If you know nothing, then killing you will lose us nothing."

The man in the chair closed his eyes, but did not speak.

The *Junfa* straightened. "Take him away, I am sick of the sight of him. Put Soo to guard him, he's good for nothing else. And bring me a pipe, I want to think." He turned away and stared down at the altar. Behind him he heard them dragging the now unconsious man out.

There had to be another way.

There was always another way.

**

Elodie's peace was short-lived. The next day, at lunch, Bernice was full of the excitement on the tenth floor. The rumours had finally penetrated even the seclusion of Mr. Lee Chang's offices.

"The police are all over the place," she said, unwrapping her sandwiches and taking a big gulp of hot coffee. "It's Mr. Webster who's missing, you know. Did I ever mention him?"

"I don't think so." Elodie wasn't sure she wanted to hear this.

Bernice spoke around a mouthful of baloney and mustard. "He's in import/export. Mr. Lee did business with him, sometimes. He was a funny little man. His hair was curly – what there was of it, and he had the bluest eyes I've ever seen." She pondered again. "They were the only attractive thing about him, those eyes."

31

"What was he like?"

Bernice shrugged. Today her dress was a deep pink silk crepe patterned with green leaves and little red cherries, under a draped collar with a big floppy Windsor bow. Elodie didn't know how she got away with such fancy clothes at work. Maybe Mr. Lee liked cheery girls. Or maybe Bernice didn't care what Mr. Lee thought. Elodie herself was in black, as usual, but had a fresh lace collar over it, and a red enamel brooch that Maybelle had loaned her.

Bernice considered her neatly polished nails before taking another bite of her sandwich. "Webster was just ordinary – except for the eyes. I know Mr. Lee didn't like him much, but apparently he could get things out of China that Mr. Lee wanted." She leaned forward. "Things are very difficult in China right now."

"Oh, really?" Elodie stirred her coffee, round and round.

Bernice waved a hand. "The Russians, apparently. But from what Mr. Lee says, things are always difficult in China."

"Things are difficult here, too," Elodie reminded her.

"Oh, not money. Politics."

"Is there a difference?" Elodie asked. Bernice frowned.

"What do you mean?"

"Nothing, nothing." If she went on stirring her coffee any longer it would be stone cold, Elodie thought. "So Mr. Lee did not like this ... Webster, was it?"

"Well, sometimes they had words over something Mr. Webster had gotten for Mr. Lee. Mr. Lee is a very honest man, you see. And I don't think Mr. Webster was."

Elodie had her doubts about the honesty of Mr. Lee. No man could be that rich in these times and be entirely above board. But Bernice, for all her air of pretended sophistication, was not very observant. Nor was she what anyone would call a deep thinker. She leaned forward, and spoke in a dramatic whisper.

"Anyway, there was blood, you know. On the floor of his office. And the desk was turned over, and all the drawers were pulled out and papers scattered everywhere. It was only when the cleaners went in and saw it all that they called security and they called the police. They didn't want a fuss, so all the policemen had to wear suits and pretend to be on business. It was all pretty silly, because it was bound to come out. It always does."

"What always does?"

"Murder." Bernice's voice was full of enjoyable horror. "So you were right – and you heard it all. I guess you should talk to the police, shouldn't you?"

Elodie went cold. She reached forward and grasped Bernice's wrist, causing Bernice to wince. "No! Listen, did you tell anyone what I told you? About being up there that night?"

"No – I don't think so." Bernice looked a little frightened at Elodie's intensity. "Don't you want to be part of it? You could find out all the details ..."

"No, I don't want to be part of it." Elodie sat back and released her friend's arm. Bernice rubbed her wrist and looked reproachful. "I couldn't really help the police," Elodie continued. "And I wasn't supposed to be there, remember? They might think I know more than I do, they might even think I was involved."

"Gee, I never thought of that, Ellie. I guess we should keep it quiet after all," Bernice said, looking a little less puzzled. "I mean, if Mr. Herschel found out, you could lose your job."

"Exactly," Elodie said, but it wasn't Mr. Herschel she was afraid of. It was the person who had been dragging what now seemed likely was the dead body of the missing Mr. Webster. She wanted nothing to do with whatever was going on or had happened on the tenth floor.

Bernice was thinking things over. "I'm sure I didn't mention it, Ellie. At least...I don't think I did." She drank more coffee, and then stood up to get a refill. "Do you want some more?" she asked, holding up her cup. Elodie handed over her own cup of now-cold coffee.

"Yes, please." She watched her friend go over to the urn and refill their cups, adding cream and sugar, coming back slowly so as not to spill any on her dress. Had Bernice said anything to anyone? She was such a flighty girl, so apt to speak without thinking, so eager in her love of gossip and 'being involved'. Having been left out of the story the day before, she had no doubt been eager for details, and could easily have said... well... almost anything.

"Listen, Bernice..." Elodie began.

"No, I'm sure I didn't say anything, Ellie," said Bernice, with rather more firmness than was necessary. "And I won't say anything. Gee, what would I do if you lost your job? I wouldn't have anyone so nice to have lunch with, would I?" Bernice smiled brightly. Too brightly.

She did say something, Elodie thought in despair.

But to whom?

**

Captain Brett shook his head. "Beats me," he said to Archie Deacon. "No reports of a body anywhere in the city. They usually leave them out to make their point."

"Maybe this isn't anything to do with our usual customers." Archie had been assigned that morning to the case, hours too late, in his opinion, but the original investigating officer had been hurt in a car accident on the way home from work. He'd read the first reports and was now catching up at the scene. "The guy wasn't in the liquor business, was he? Imports, the secretary said. Mostly from China."

"She was pretty hysterical." Captain Brett looked around the office that had belonged to the missing man. It was neither fancy nor particularly clean. It was obvious that Webster, and perhaps the secretary, were smokers, for the window was heavily filmed and the walls, originally white, were now a dirty tan. The secretary's desk had a small plant on it, but it was bent from landing on the floor, and most of the dirt was missing from its pot. The forensic people had finished their fingerprintings and photographs the afternoon before. The overturned furniture had been righted again and the floor swept. All the papers that had been scattered on the floor were gathered into a pile on the larger desk, waiting for the secretary to recover from her 'nerves' long enough to see if anything was missing. At present she was in the care of an older woman in another office, still upset – either at the thought of losing her boss – or her job. She had come in, but 'couldn't face' the office. Archie wondered how much of the fuss she was making was genuine.

"Do you think she knows more than she's saying?" Brett asked. He was not the sharpest of men, but apparently he, too, felt the secretary was being either foolish or clever.

Archie shrugged. "She didn't strike me as being particu-

34

larly bright," he said, slowly. "I think she's straight. Whether Webster was straight is another question. She did manage to say he mostly dealt in small stuff – silk cloth, small objects, sometimes special foods for the Chinese community that they couldn't get over here."

"Like birds' nests?" Captain Brett grimaced.

Deacon smiled to himself. Like most Americans, the Captain believed the Chinese only existed on bird's nest soup, sharks' fins and cats and dogs. Deacon knew better. He had met a few members of the Chinese community through his love of their food, which he knew to be healthy, simple, and quite free of both cats and dogs. True there were unusual spices, but that only added to the wonderful flavours. He'd grown up quite close to the area of the city where most Chinese lived, and had had a great friend in school named Lee Concetti, whose mother was Chinese and his father Italian. He had often been to Lee's home and eaten with them. His smile faded. Lee was dead, now. Another victim of the friction between the two ethnic neighborhoods that rubbed against one another. In that area you were either Italian or Chinese, but Lee had been both and therefore equally shunned by both. Archie remembered attending the homicide and seeing the face of his childhood friend as he lay dead in an alley with four others, all machine-gunned to permanent silence.

Lee had taken one route, Archie another. They had lost touch, but he had recognized him instantly. Just one more reason to hate the city that was greedily devouring itself.

"Well, as soon as the girl gets ahold of herself, we'll know a bit more," Captain Brett said, dismissively. "Meanwhile we've got other fish to fry. Have you set someone to question folks on this floor, see if they knew Webster, anything about him?"

"In the works." Archie lit a cigarette. "Bosco and Higgins should get anything that's going. They're good at it."

The Captain grunted. "I've got a meeting, now. I'll leave you to deal with this mess."

"Fine with me." When the Captain had left, Archie sat behind the desk and began looking through Webster's papers. A nice clean puzzle. It made a change from boozer hunts, hooker raids, and finding old friends cut into pieces by machine gun fire.

3

Leo Herschel looked rather like a bloodhound would look if it had been stretched tall and thin. Balding, brisk, and very demanding, he was the Creative Director of Adcock and Ash advertising agency. Everybody would have been terrified of him if, under his overtly fierce demeanour, he was not utterly fair in all his judgements and actions.

Nevertheless, dealing with him was never easy, as he had both high standards and a low tolerance for fools.

He had summoned the creative department into the main conference room to discuss the competition for the proposed Leatherlux radio programme. Not everyone in the agency had entered ideas. Of the eleven people present, two were artists, and seven were copywriters. There were even a couple of young 'suits', which was how the creative department described the men who represented various advertising accounts. To be 'creative' was to be somehow different from everyone else. Or so they told themselves. In fact, they were as aware of the business aspects of agency work as the 'suits' were, but the mock war between them was entertaining. And a way of working off frustration when an ad was turned down by a recalcitrant client.

Elodie slipped in at the back and took a seat near the door. She had never been in the main conference room before, and she was impressed with the richness of the decor. This is what the clients saw when they visited the agency. Glossy wood panelling, a deep blue carpet with a faint design, translucent pink light sconces on the walls, and a vast expanse of mahogany table running down the centre of the room. Ranged alongside it were chairs with seats upholstered in gold velvet. There were notepads and pencils at each place, and several pitchers of water and glasses spaced along the table. Her mouth was dry and she longed to pour herself a drink, but didn't think she should.

She didn't have much hope that her idea would be

adopted, but at least she had made the final cut, and she was interested to hear what others had come up with. The proposal was for a weekly hour long radio programme – an expensive undertaking for any client. A lot depended, therefore, on keeping the client happy by showing a correlating rise in sales.

Mr. Herschel waited until everybody seemed to be present, then stood up and surveyed his people. "I'm glad to see you all so interested in this project," he began. His voice was deep and resonant, surprisingly so for emanating from such a thin chest. "As you know, Leatherlux is one of our most valued clients, and we want to do well for them." He looked down at a sheaf of papers before him on the table. "There were 23 ideas offered for the programme, some unfortunately rather frivolous. These were weeded out. In the interests of fairness we asked that no names were attached, simply a code of any four letters. That was in keeping with our policy that a good idea doesn't care who has it." He harumphed, slightly. That slogan was his own, and he used it whenever possible.

"I admit I have been surprised by the range of imagination shown – but many of the ideas were more suited to the theatre than radio, which is a very specific medium, both new and difficult. I was not the only judge of these ideas, of course, but was joined by the client and the two experienced radio writers who will be working on the programmes along with whoever's idea is chosen. It will mean losing a member of staff because we will want the winner to be wholly committed to the project. In some cases this will be quite a sacrifice." He beamed at the one or two top copywriters in the group, then picked up the sheaf of papers. "At any rate, the winner is the author of "MMEA." He looked up. "Who might that be?"

There was a silence as everyone looked around.

Elodie was stunned. It was her entry, marked with the initials of the four Browne sisters. She raised her hand. "It's me," she said, in a small voice.

Mr. Herschel looked at her with a slightly puzzled expression, then his face cleared. "Miss Browne?" he asked, rather surprised.

"Yes, sir." Elodie looked at all the faces around her – every one of them as startled as hers must have seemed. She stood up. "Me."

"Well, well," Mr. Herschel said. He looked both pleased and definitely relieved. He wouldn't be losing any of his best copywriters after all, but a lowly beginner who happened to have a good idea. Perfect example of his philosophy. And an excellent solution to what might have been a difficult situation. Anybody could take over Elodie's work. He might even promote a secretary to fill the vacancy.

"What's your idea, then?" asked one of the other senior copywriters, looking a bit put out. Mr. Herschel might be pleased that the good idea hadn't cared who had it, but *he* obviously wasn't.

Elodie cleared her throat and looked at Mr. Herschel. "It's called Imp... "

"Now, now, no need to give it away," Mr. Herschel said, quickly. "Suffice it to say it is an excellent way to integrate the client's interests with a good story every week. I think we should all look forward to hearing the programme when it is actually broadcast."

"But we could help," protested the copywriter whose creative *amour propre* had been seriously offended. He was a plump young man with thinning hair, the son of a client, and not particularly well-liked at the agency. He knew his idea had been magnificent, and here was this little upstart getting the prize. It was so unfair!

"No, no," said Mr. Herschel, rather grandly. "This idea is good enough to stand on its own feet, and Miss Browne and the two professional radio writers she will be working with must have full responsibility." He paused. "Full creative control," he amended. In other words, Elodie immediately realized, if it failed it would be entirely her fault, and not that of the agency.

Slowly the room cleared, with not a few resentful glances from some of the others. Elodie felt herself blushing, knowing they all thought she had gotten above herself and stolen their thunder. It was a competitive world, she knew that. But she was disappointed that none of them stopped to congratulate her, not even one or two she had thought quite liked her. Finally only she and Mr. Herschel remained. He came down the room and smiled at her.

"Well done, Miss Browne," he said. "I think Imperial Hotel will be a great success."

"I hope so," Elodie said. She recollected her sister Maybelle's admonition to always seem positive and sure of herself in every situation and to never show fear of a superior. Respect, yes, but fear – never. "I mean, I know it will be," she added, firmly. "I'm very excited. Who will I be working with? When do I start? Where?"

Mr. Herschel now displayed avuncular interest along with a certain detachment. Leatherlux Luggage was a very very difficult client to please, and they had made the final decision on the concept of 'Imperial Hotel', not he. He was a little worried that Miss Browne was not up to the job, but took comfort from the fact that the two experienced radio writers would be in charge. He could liaise with them from time to time – she needn't know about that. It would have been too big a risk to take, otherwise. He believed firmly in encouraging young talent, as long as it didn't become a threat to him or the agency. And Miss Browne was a very pretty girl – she hid her intelligence rather well, he thought.

"You will start immediately, my dear. Time is of the essence as the client is eager to get on the air as soon as possible. You will be working with two professional radio writers, as I said earlier. You do understand why that is necessary?"

"Oh, of course . .. I will need to learn so much."

"Exactly. But both of the writers were enthusiastic about your idea, and said it was perfectly suited to radio, so that is very encouraging. They thought it showed you understood the medium much better than many of the others."

"I listen to the radio a good deal," Elodie said.

"Yes, well, that's fine." He was guiding her toward the door, neither touching her nor saying anything, but making it clear he, at least, was now finished with the situation. "My secretary will supply you with all details – it will mean a raise in your salary of course..."

"Oh," Elodie gasped. So that was why the others had been so cross. "I didn't realize that."

He looked at her, surprised. "You didn't?"

"No." She longed to ask how much, but restrained herself in the interest of appearing 'professional'. He, in his turn, looked momentarily regretful, apparently realizing he could have gotten away with giving her no raise at all. He allowed himself a small sigh. "You will not be working here at the agency, in fact, although we will be paying your salary as before. I believe an office has been reserved down on the tenth floor."

Elodie went cold.

The tenth floor?

Her sudden good luck had thrilled her. Now she was not so sure. It had landed her right in the middle of the investigation into the missing Mr. Webster.

Oh, well. Maybe nobody would notice her.

Or maybe she should consider wearing a disguise.

Because whoever had been shouting at Mr. Webster, whoever had killed him, might very well work right there on the tenth floor.

And she would be passing him every day.

**

Elodie's cousin Hugh Murphy was tall and fair, his hair close-cropped in an effort to control its natural curl. He often came to Elodie's house for dinner, and so was present when she made the announcement concerning her new job.

Alyce was overwhelmed. "You mean you will be working in *radio*?" she asked in a hushed voice. For her it was as if Elodie had announced she was taking the veil in a new religion.

"Well, I'll be working with two professonal writers." Elodie took another bite of Marie's wonderful apple pie, and glanced around at her family. "It means a raise."

Her mother beamed at her over the top of her spectacles. "I'm so pleased for you, darling. I'm sure you will make a success of it."

"How much?" asked the ever-practical Maybelle. She was the beauty of the family, and usually had a date on Friday nights. Indeed, on most nights, but as it happened this time she was home.

Elodie giggled. "I was afraid to ask Mr. Herschel," she admitted. "But I could see the others were cross not to have it."

"Oh, for heaven's sake," said Maybelle, exasperated at this lack of business sense. "You must know."

"Actually, it will be another ten dollars a week." Elodie spoke over-casually. There were gasps around the table. Even Hugh looked impressed.

"Good Lord," Maybelle said. "That will be nearly as much as I earn!" Maybelle worked as an assistant to the editor of a very expensive magazine called STYLE.

"It will be very welcome." Marie stood and began clearing the plates from the table. "Well done, Ellie. You should be proud of yourself."

"A radio writer," Alyce breathed to herself. She twisted one of her braids dreamily. "A real radio writer."

"Mr. Herschel's secretary gave me all the details. I will be working with a Miss Schultz and Mr. Drew Wilson."

"Drew Wilson," Alyce whispered. "He sounds handsome."

"I don't think you should get your hopes up." Hugh was amused by Alyce's obvious rapture. "That name might suit a movie star, but most writers I know are pretty ugly."

"Well, thank you very much, Hugh," Elodie said, in mock offense.

He grinned. "Let's just say good looks are not a require-ment for writers. Just good brains."

"Well, Ellie has those," her mother said, with confidence.

"We *all* have brains," Maybelle said, defensively. Then her expression softened. "But Ellie has imagination, and that's what will be important."

"Tell us your idea." Marie gathered more dishes onto her tray, but slowly, wanting to hear everything before she went to the kitchen. She was the domestic one in the family. Sewing and cooking were her delight. She had brains, yes, and imagi-nation, and some of Maybelle's business sense, too, but she was content to stay at home and look after them all. She was engaged to a very nice Scotsman named Bill, but it was expected to be a long engagement because Marie insisted they must save enough make a deposit on their own home.

"Well, it's called Imperial Hotel," Elodie began. "It will have two themes – a continuing story about staff in the hotel, from the manager right down to the lowliest maid, and a weekly story complete in itself, about one of the guests at the hotel. The two strands will sort of be . . . woven together." Even now she was not entirely certain how this would be achieved, but hoped that Miss Schultz and Mr. Wilson would be able to work it out. "It ties right in with luggage, you see. With travelling people and so on. I think that's why the client liked it."

"Very good." Hugh had heard most of this the night Ellie had thought it up. "I think it sounds fine."

Elodie was pleased because Hugh was a fairly severe critic of radio drama. "It has lots of possibilities," she murmured, hoping she sounded properly modest. She was actually so excited and scared she felt almost ill. First the terrifying moments the other night at the Gower Building, and now this incredible opportunity. And tomorrow night she would be attending a fancy high class party, albeit in a lowly capacity. Still, she now had a good reason for wanting to see how the rich lived – the radio show. She needed background, she needed ideas. She felt like all her bones were hollow, and her mind seemed somehow to flutter within her skull. Was this really Elodie Browne?

"Oooh, you could have a murder ..." Alyce began. Her eyes sparkled and she clasped her hands together in her excitement. "Something really gruesome..."

"Oh dear," said their mother. Mrs. Browne loved her girls, and worried about them constantly. She badly felt the loss of her husband, and having to make decisions on their behalf often kept her up at night. She tried to be a strong woman, but work was wearying, her pay so low, the many needs of the family so great, that sometimes she despaired. She didn't want to stifle Alyce's imagination, but with things the way they were in the city, she felt like she was trying to keep a door closed against an implacable foe.

Alyce turned to her. "But Mumma, you have to have excitement and something to keep people interested."

"It needn't be murder," Elodie said, nervously. That was a little too close for comfort.

"No, indeed." Mrs. Browne was firm. "There is far too much violence already on your precious radio, young lady," she said to Alyce. "I declare, that Fu Manchu person, and the Shadow . . . why even on your Little Orphan Annie there was a kidnapping the other week. You couldn't sleep that night, as I recall."

"They're perfectly fine," Alyce said, crossly. "They're exciting. A lot more exciting than those drips Mary and Bob."

42

Marie looked a little affronted. She was very fond of the serial Mary and Bob, and also of Moonshine and Honeysuckle which told stories of the town of Lonesome Hollow. It brightened her afternoon as she washed up the Sunday dinner dishes.

"Not a murder." Elodie folded her napkin and slipped it into her own special silver napkin ring – the one shaped like a little sleigh. It had been her father's when he was a boy. "Just stories of people, ordinary people..."

"They can't be very ordinary if they can afford Leatherlux luggage," Maybelle pointed out with some asperity.

"Well, maybe a little excitement now and again..."

"A robbery?" Alyce suggested with a little less eagerness.

"I'll have to see what the others say." Elodie was cautious. If Alyce had her way there would be corpses every floor of her lovely, elegant Imperial Hotel.

Rather like the Gower Building.

She shivered.

"Are you coming down with a cold, darling?" asked her mother. "You look a little pale."

"No, I'm fine, Mumma," Elodie said. "Just kind of excited."

"Quite understandable." Hugh wiped the corners of his mouth and put his napkin on the table. "You're entering a whole new world. I hear it's a tough world, Ellie. Lots of pressure to produce. You'll find it very tiring at first."

"Oh, dear." Mrs. Browne had very much wished Elodie would follow her into teaching rather than into the very odd world of advertising. "You're not very strong, Ellie."

"I'm as strong as a horse. This is what I want to do, and I'm going to be very very good at it."

"Bravo," Hugh said, clapping.

"Well, I have to wash my hair." Maybelle got up to carry some of the dishes out to the kitchen.

"Oh, gosh – it's almost time for —," Alyce stood up so quickly her chair nearly went over. "Ellie..."

"Go on, then." Elodie smiled as Alyce ran off into the sitting room, braids flying out behind her. Her moment of glory had passed.

Hugh looked at Ellie as the others scattered to their various after-supper occupations. "Scared?" he asked, gently.

"Why do you say that?" Her voice cracked slightly.

He raised an eyebrow. He knew her well. "What's up?" he asked. "You're not just excited ... there's something more, isn't there?"

Elodie sighed. "Something happened the other night."

"Go on."

"You mustn't tell Mumma, or the others. Or anybody."

"Good Lord, what is it?" Hugh's reporting antennae were up.

Slowly she told him about what had happened the other night on the tenth floor of the Gower building – the sounds she had heard, the subsequent investigation into the missing Mr. Webster, her fear of being involved. "And now I have to work on the tenth floor, starting Monday," she finished.

Hugh had lit a cigarette as she talked, and looked seriously at her over the rising smoke. "That's rough," he said. "You really should tell the police."

"But what can I tell them? Only sounds, only... nothing."

He nodded. "I take your point, but you can set the time of the thing for them and that might be important."

"Oh, I never thought of that."

"Well, you should consider it. I'm not saying you have to, I really understand that you're scared and don't want to be suspected of anything, but if it might help – "

"I should be a good citizen," Elodie finished. He nodded. She toyed with the corner of her napkin rolled into the little silver sleigh. "I might lose my job."

"Oh, come on ... why should it make any difference?"

"Because I was supposed to have my idea in by five o'clock. Mr. Herschel is very..."

"Oh, for crying out loud, Ellie. Be sensible. Herschel need never know anything about it."

"But what if they catch the person, and there's a trial, and I have to testify... "

"I doubt if it would come to that. If they catch him they would have to have a lot more evidence to take to court than the word of a frightened girl. Time might be important to catch the guy, but it wouldn't convict him because you didn't actually see him." He paused. "Or did you?"

"No – but he might have seen me. And if it's someone who works on the tenth floor every day, and he sees me ..."

"Ah," said Hugh. He was silent.

Elodie brightened. "Maybe it was someone from outside."

"Very probably was." He saw the risk, but really didn't think it very great. The last person to murder someone on the tenth floor was someone who actually worked on or was connected with the tenth floor, he thought. Unless it had been a spur of the moment thing. Someone intent on cold blooded murder would take care to do it well away from his own territory. Only the bootleggers didn't give a damn where they left the bodies. Indeed, they wanted them found as an example of what happened to people who cheated or displeased them. So it was bound to be an outsider. It stood to reason. Why else take the body away?

Elodie thought further. "I won't say anything myself, but if they ask me, I'll tell them." She turned to him, laid her hand on his arm. "Or you could tell them. Say you can't reveal your source but tell them the time. That would take care of it all."

"It's not on my beat," Hugh protested.

"It's a crime, isn't it?"

"Only a missing person, so far," Hugh pointed out. "I'm pretty much a homicide guy, Ellie."

"You don't want to get involved, either."

"Look, tell you what. If they find a body, I'll get involved, okay?"

"Okay." Elodie was relieved.

"But if the guy has any sense, they won't find the body," Hugh said. "Plenty of places to hide a body in Chicago."

He was wrong, of course.

4

When the long sleek black Cadillac limousine drove down Kercheval Street and stopped in front of the Browne house, a sort of tremor went through the neighbourhood. Curtains flicked, doors were gently pulled ajar, people waited to see who was inside. Had Maybelle Browne finally found a millionaire to marry? Or had she gotten involved with one of Them? 'They' were well-known to favour Cadillac limousines. And hearses. What was the neighbourhood coming to? Was someone going to open a speakeasy?

The limousine was for Elodie.

She came slowly down the steps, amazed. Bernice had told her she would be picked up, but she had assumed it would be a taxi. Even that seemed extravagant to her. She could easily have taken a trolley, she thought. But no, here it was, chrome gleaming, white sidewalls without a mark, and a uniformed chaffeur at the wheel who stared straight ahead, obviously accustomed to better neighbourhoods. And there was Bernice, hanging out of the rear window, beckoning to her.

"Come on, Ellie, we have to get there before it starts."

Elodie went to the curb and Bernice opened the door. When she did Elodie saw that she was not alone in the car – there were two other girls in there, too. All, like herself, were dressed in black. She got in, and settled herself next to Bernice.

"My goodness." The others giggled.

"Isn't it a hoot?" said one of them, an ice-blonde with pale grey eyes. "I've never been in one of these before."

"Neither have I." Elodie looked at Bernice. "You never said."

Bernice shrugged elaborately. "Mr. Lee knows how to do things. He's always been good to his staff. This is only the second or third limousine, anyway. The one he uses for things like this." 'This', presumably, being the collecting of oddments, such as groceries, dry cleaning, or girls to serve at his parties. "The other cars are much newer."

All the girls were very pretty, Elodie saw. And they were perfectly assorted – Bernice had red curls, another girl had a sleek black cap of hair cut close to her skull in strong contrast to her very white complexion, the ice-blonde had marcelled waves, and Elodie had a brown bob. A varied choice. She began to have doubts about exactly what her 'duties' might be. "Listen, Bernice...."

"Mr. Lee's parties are very dignified." Bernice obviously knew exactly what Elodie was thinking. "We just have to carry trays of drinks and canapes, and help with the buffet, that's all." She looked at Elodie. "That's ALL," she said, apparently slightly offended that anyone should think anything else.

"She's right." The dark-haired girl, whose named proved to be Betty Ann, nodded. "I've done two of these already. And he pays us well, too. We even sometimes get tips from the guests. Last time I took home almost twelve dollars!"

The others looked impressed.

"Mr. Lee just likes pretty girls," Bernice continued. "He is a connoisseur of beautiful things." She pronounced it 'connosewer', and Elodie tried not to smile. Her mother spoke beautiful French, and had taught it to all her daughters. (Their grandmother had been French, and Mrs. Browne liked to keep up their cultural heritage. "You never know who you will meet," she liked to say. She meant 'marry'.)

The limousine had pulled smoothly and quietly away from the curb in front of the Browne house, and now was turning in the direction of Lake Michigan and the Golden Mile, so-called because of all the mansions there that looked out over the vast expanse of water. The lake was so huge it had ocean-like storms, but on good days offered a glorious blue-green vista that stretched to a horizon every bit as distant as that of a sea.

Elodie sank back against the soft chestnut brown leather upholstery. She was determined to enjoy the evening, watching how the rich and famous lived and moved and talked. It would be excellent preparation for working on Imperial Hotel, which was supposed to be a luxury establishment in the heart of New York City. She was sure it would be glamorous and exciting. And it would help her to temporarily forget the tenth floor, and Monday.

**

The home of Mr. Lee Chang was enormous, newly built in the moderne style. White as a wedding cake, it was set behind a long lawn that stretched down to Lakeshore Drive. Beyond the road there was a narrow beach and what looked to be a private jetty. A rather large motorboat was moored at the far end.

As the limousine moved up the long gravelled drive Elodie took in the stark lines and the many glass-brick expanses of the house itself. It seemed to glow in the dusk, and golden light was behind every window. There were uniformed men standing at the end of the drive, apparently waiting for the guests to arrive. The double front door stood open, and as the car passed by she glimpsed a wide hall with a floor of huge black and white squares, and side tables with enormous flower arrangements in red and gold. Then the car continued around the back, and all the glory of the front was lost in the very workaday appearance of the rear face, which was plain but not unattractive. The one strange thing was an enclosed passage about sixty feet in length and made totally of glass, which stretched from french doors across the rear lawn to a small windowless building that stood against a background of trees and shadows. The passage also glowed with a golden light, and appeared to be carpeted in an unusual pale green.

The girls decamped and the limousine drove away, purring like a big cat in the silence of the evening. No – not silence, but a hush, as if waiting for a curtain to arise. There were crickets, a breeze from Lake Michigan, the distant wash of small waves on the shoreline. An owl hooted suddenly in the trees, making Elodie jump. She followed the others into what proved to be an enormous kitchen, where she met the housekeeper who looked them over with a sharp eye. Seemingly satisfied, she handed out frilly white aprons, and began to instruct them in their duties. She explained the general lay-out of the house, in case any of the guests required directions or information, but they were not to speak unless spoken to. She told them where the cloakrooms were for men and women, and what to do if any of the guests became ill. Or drunk, Elodie thought to herself, looking at the ranks of wine and champagne bottles on a table in the centre of the gleaming kitchen. Mr. Lee Chang must have a very very good bootlegger, she thought. As far as she could see, all the labels were French or British, the real thing.

White-coated men were moving quietly and efficiently around the kitchen, preparing the food. Almost all of them were oriental, and had closed, expressionless faces. The smells of the various dishes were strange and rather wonderful to Elodie. Hugh had taken her to a Chinese restaurant once, but it was not like this. She didn't recognize any of the things being prepared. The housekeeper, a Mrs. Logie, paused in her instructions and asked if there were any questions.

"Is Barbara Hutton really going to be here?" asked Betty Ann, eagerly.

Mrs. Logie frowned. "Mr. Lee has many well known friends and clients, but there is to be no gawking whatsoever, is that understood? Even if you recognize a face, you must not do or say anything that would make the guest uncomfortable in any way. They are here privately. That is of the utmost importance." Betty Ann looked a little sulky, but said no more.

Mrs. Logie continued. "Before dinner we will be serving dim sum, which is a Chinese delicacy. This is made up of many small items along with a dipping sauce. As we give you each tray, we will tell you what is on it, in case a guest asks. As each tray is emptied, you will return immediately to the kitchen for the next tray. This will continue until 8:30, at which time the dining room will be opened for the buffet, which will continue to be offered throughout the rest of the evening. You will stand behind the buffet tables and serve the guests as they come along. Is that clear?" Everyone nodded. "Very well. I suggest you now go out into the house and get your bearings. Be back here in fifteen minutes. You may use the staff cloak-room there, off the kitchen. I suggest you make yourselves comfortable before you begin serving. And wash your hands thoroughly." She glanced down. "I see Bernice has informed you of Mr. Lee's dislike of nail polish. Well done, Bernice."

Elodie almost giggled. Mrs. Logie meant they were to pee, she supposed. They'd also been told not to wear any scent or jewelry whatsoever. Nuns at the feast, she thought. Discreet, subservient, silent. Ghosts in black. She wondered if this was how all wealthy people were served, or whether it was just the private fancy of Mr. Lee Chang, whom she had yet to see.

The interior of the house was as impressive as the exterior. Much chrome and glass, and all the walls were of the very palest grey. There were, in contrast, many large modern paint-

ings on the walls. The subjects were distorted and barely recognizable, the colours were violent and unreal. Bernice
thought they were ugly, as did the other girls. Elodie quite
liked them. Maybelle had taught her a lot about art because
her magazine featured it. Sisters had their uses.

The Lee house was carpeted throughout in the same pale
green she had glimpsed in the long glass passage that led to
that odd little building in back. The furniture was all ebony,
square in outline and oriental in style, but did not look very
comfortable, despite the thick cushions of raw silk in dark
grey and straw-gold. She had the feeling they were rarely
occupied, except on occasions like this. The whole house
looked like something out of Maybelle's magazine and not a
place anybody really lived in from day to day. The main rooms
were very large, as was the reception hall. Big double doors at
the back of the main room led to the dining room, which had
a massive ebony table in the centre, and a line of small tables
against the far wall which held stacks of plates and so on for
the buffet. A fantastic chandelier hung over the table in a most
extraordinary design that reminded her of the weird sculptures that had been on display a few weeks back in the Gower
Building lobby. Could it have been fashioned by the same
artist? If so, it must have been incredibly expensive and
certainly unique.

There was a soft footstep behind them. They turned and
saw, at last, Mr. Lee Chang himself.

He was short and as round as a ball. He wore a long crimson oriental robe of thickly embroidered silk. Small black felt
shoes just showed under the hem of this extraordinary gar-
ment. He was completely bald, and had two eyes like black
currants sunk in the golden bun of his face. He gestured to
Bernice, who hurried over to him. He spoke briefly to her, then
came over to inspect the girls who would be serving his
guests. For a long moment he stared at each one, and then
suddenly he smiled. He had a wonderful smile, broad, white,
and very unexpected.

"Beautiful," he said, beaming at them. "I like beautiful
things." He gestured around. "And beautiful women. You are
welcome in my home. I am sure you will do as Mrs. Logie has
told you. If you have any questions you must go to her. I shall
be busy with my guests." He had a very slight accent, notice-

able only in his attempts to get around the letter 'l', but otherwise sounded completely American. Bernice had told Elodie that Lee Chang had been born in China and had been very poor. His parents brought him to America when his was only four, his father being employed on the railways going West. He had been orphaned by the time he was fifteen, and had worked very hard all his life. He was clearly poor no more.

He bowed, very slightly, and left them, trailing a faint aroma of jasmine.

"Whew," said the blonde standing next to Elodie. "Is he fat or is he fat?"

Bernice spoke softly. "Not all of that is Mr. Lee. He is wearing a padded vest for protection. He has many enemies – or thinks he has."

"I think he's wonderful." Elodie had been very impressed with Mr. Lee Chang. "So different. I don't imagine many wealthy men speak to servants like that."

"Mr. Lee is a very unusual man." It was plain Bernice was very proud to be working for Mr. Lee.

"I thought his name was Chang." Betty Ann looked puzzled. "That's what it says on his office door, Lee Chang Enterprises." So Betty Ann worked in the Gower Building too, Elodie thought. She wondered why she hadn't seen her before, as the jet-black cap of shiny hair and pale skin were very memorable. Betty Ann obviously considered herself a Vamp.

"In China, what we call the last name comes first," explained Bernice, as they headed back toward the kitchen. "If it was said the American way he would be Mr. Chang Lee, but he prefers the Chinese way. In fact, he insists on it." She spoke as if from a great height of superior knowledge, and Elodie could have slapped her. As they entered the kitchen, they heard cars outside, and voices. The guests were arriving. She could hardly wait to see what the rich and famous were really like.

**

Elodie was rather shocked.

Never having encountered so-called High Society outside of the newspapers before, she had actually expected them to have a flawless glow, like in the movies.

The rich and famous were, in fact, rather ordinary, save for two things – their money, and their manners. They wore their money on their backs, for the women's dresses were spectacular, the men's dinner clothes immaculately tailored. They expected to be waited on, and therefore took no notice of those who waited upon them. But under the expensive clothing the women had freckles, wrinkles, and the occasional pimple skillfully but inadequately covered with makeup. Many of the men were going bald or had dandruff. Some had bad breath. The women were either as thin as rakes, or wore flamboyantly draped dresses to distract from their bulk. Some of them smelled wonderful, and some of them definitely did not. One of the women was actually rather grubby around the neck, but wore a fabulous diamond necklace to cover it. All of them ignored her and the other girls completely, and seemed only to notice the trays. They helped themselves greedily and talked to one another, never once raising their eyes to the pretty faces behind the food.

We really are invisible, thought Elodie, as she stood in the living room holding her first tray of 'dim sum'. She had been given a tray of tiny shrimp dumplings, pale and fat, with a small porcelain bowl of murky but pungent sauce. It smelled like good old vinegar to her, and she wrinkled her nose. There was something more there, she decided, so it was probably flavoured with some exotic Chinese spices even Marie had never heard of.

Elodie's family was not wealthy, nor were they poverty stricken. They were a working family, but what she had heard referred to as 'white collar' rather than labouring. She had an education. She had good manners. She had self respect. And she had an almost overwhelming impulse to shout at the gathering crowd, like Alice, 'You're nothing but a pack of cards!'. Of course she did not, but it almost choked her. She glanced over at Bernice, who caught her eye and somehow detected the glint there. She scowled and shook her head. Elodie didn't want to upset Bernice, and she liked Mr. Lee. It was difficult, though, and as soon as her tray was emptied, she fled to the kitchen. Unfortunately Mrs. Logie saw her return and quickly snapped her fingers, summoning up another loaded tray – this time crisp little fishy-smelling toasts with no dipping sauce, for which Elodie was grateful. The fumes of the dipping sauce had made her want to sneeze.

She returned to the large main room and began to walk among the guests, offering her tray, trying to catch the conversations going on around her. She had expected hoity-toity accents and was again disappointed. Indeed, some of the guests sounded very ordinary indeed, especially some of the younger women. She wondered if they were high-class prostitutes. The thought didn't shock her. People in Chicago were getting all too accustomed to crime and loosening morals. Between Prohibition and the Depression, things were sliding fast. Maybe we should have a prostitute at Imperial Hotel, Elodie suddenly thought. But of course we couldn't actually call her that. She moved on, automatically offering her tray and thinking about her precious radio show. Now that she was over the first shock, her brain had begun working on its own, returning her to her own interests. She was only there to do a menial job. Her brain was free to roam.

She began looking at the gathering with new eyes.

There were some foreign accents among the guests – she detected French, German, and, of course, Chinese. It was the Chinese who were most fascinating. Small men, smaller women, their voices high and light, speaking their own language quick as birdchirps, but speaking English slowly, and with great care. She liked them for respecting her language. And almost all the women wore Western clothing, in the very latest styles. She found herself staying nearer to them than other guests, until again she caught Bernice's eye, and had to move in wider circles. She thought there could be at least one Chinese person working or passing through the portals of Imperial Hotel. And that woman over there, the one with the grubby neck – she would be an interesting character, too.

As for the man in the corner – Elodie looked again and nearly dropped her tray. She knew that face from the pages of the *Tribune*. Arnold Ryan. One of the top men in the Capone organisation. So Their tentacles reached even here. Hugh had told her that Ryan was known to be a cultured man; perhaps he was a collector. Bernice had said Mr. Lee sold to anyone. It was apparently true.

There was an abrupt instant of silence, then a kind of rustling murmur ran through the crowd as people turned and whispered. Elodie turned, too.

A tall, slender girl with dark blonde hair and a gown of peacock blue silk stood in the entrance, and Elodie recognized her immediately. Barbara Hutton, one of the richest young women in the world, heiress to the Woolworth millions. Her 'coming out' party in New York the year before had been a fabulously lavish affair, pictures in all the papers and magazines. Next to her stood a bored looking man with bloodshot eyes. Maybelle would know who he was, Elodie thought. She reads all the society columns. Didn't she say that Miss Hutton's father hated her current boyfriend? He didn't look like much, next to the glowing young Woolworth heiresss. Plant, that was it, Phil Plant. Elodie didn't think any more of him than she did a lot of the other guests, but Miss Hutton was special, she thought. She lived up to expectations all right. There was a kind of vibrant heat in her that radiated over the room. Everyone seemed momentarily spellbound. Then the talking began again, louder than ever, and Miss Hutton and her escort moved into the crowd. Behind her came – good heavens! – was that really Conrad Nagle – impossible! Behind the Hollywood actor came some kind of Indian prince in full regalia, a peacock feather in his turban, and a small woman who looked alarmingly like Helen Twelvetrees. All followed Miss Hutton, like some kind of retinue.

Still transfixed, Elodie got a bump on the arm by Betty Ann. "You're gawking, and your tray is empty. Don't let that old battleaxe catch you." Mrs. Logie was standing in the doorway, surveying the party and her minions.

"Guest stars," said Elodie, dreamily.

"What?" Betty Ann stared at her.

"We could have guest stars. After all, it's a very good hotel."

Betty Ann leaned forward slightly and sniffed. "Have you been sneaking cocktails?" she asked.

Elodie snapped out of it. "Sorry," she said, and made for the kitchen to get another tray. As she slipped past Mrs. Logie the older woman frowned, but said nothing. Elodie's reward for staring was another tray with a dipping sauce, this one even more pungent than the last.

The evening went on, and Elodie's feet began to hurt. Back and forth she went to the kitchen, bringing out heavily loaded trays and returning with empty or near-empty ones. All the sense of glamour engendered by the wealth on display wore away, until all she could think about was sitting down. She longed for paper and pencil to make notes about the people she was seeing and hearing. Bits of conversation suggested stories, it was all here, if she could only remember and harvest it for Monday's meeting with the writers. She had to have something to offer them. She had to be prepared. Because all she had before was the basic idea for Imperial Hotel. And that was not enough.

Finally the cocktails were finished. The heat in the main room was intense, and when the doors to the dining room were thrown open, a welcome fresh breeze came through. Someone had had the sense to open the french windows on the far side of the dining room. Framed in them was the long glowing line of the narrow glass passage. Now she could see there was someone in it, seated at the far end beside a plain door. He was a policeman, she thought. At any rate, he was in uniform and wore a gun.

"Get behind the table, miss, and start handing out the plates," Mrs. Logie hissed into her ear. Startled, Elodie went across and did as she was told. She smiled at everyone, but only one or two smiled back, invariably a man. And invariably with an assessing eye. Again, she wondered if their duties started and ended with the party. Her hand shook a little, and the man opposite her took firm hold of the plate and her hand.

It was Arnold Ryan. He smiled, quite a nice smile, really, considering the fact that he regularly had people killed. "Thank you," he said, politely. He was the only one that did.

**

Around eleven o'clock, when Elodie could have screamed with fatigue, she finally learned about the glass passage and the little building at the end of it. They were ferrying dirty dishes to the kitchen, and she asked Bernice about it.

"Oh, that's Mr. Lee's treasure house." Bernice set down the stack of dirty plates and picked up a fresh supply. "He keeps his jade there, and all his special items. That's why Miss Hutton is here tonight – he has something very rare to show her. She is a big jade collector. Mr. Lee says she was taught about jade by a blind man in San Francisco and can tell quality just by touch. She has never been here in Chicago before, I think she has come here especially to see this special stuff he's got. He was very secretive about it, even I don't know what it is, and I type up the inventories."

Elodie looked out at the glowing passage as they returned to the dining room. Most of the guests had left, and nobody was interested in the buffet now. There were just 8 guests remaining: Miss Hutton and her escort, who was by now rather drunk. He kept saying he wanted to leave and go to some club or other. She kept telling him to be quiet. With them were Mr. Ryan, a married couple of middle age, an elderly woman with masses of white hair coiled elaborately on her head, a very plump and excited woman, and a funny little man called Blick. They seemed to be waiting for something. Finally Mr. Lee walked over to the french windows. He still looked splendid in his crimson robes, but he had seemed tired earlier. Now he was full of a new energy.

"And now we shall view the jade," he said. He beamed around at the few remaining guests, and nodded to Miss Hutton. Plant was still beside her, but he looked rather vexed, and tired, too. Elodie found herself feeling sorry for him. She would have gladly taken his place to see the jade. She had never seen jade before, or oriental treasures of any kind. But nobody was going to ask her to walk down the glass passage. She sighed and stepped back to lean surreptitiously against the wall, easing one shoe off and wriggling her toes.

Suddenly, just as Mr. Lee turned to start down the passage, there was a crash from the kitchen, and shouting. The kitchen door flew open, and a man, his face covered in blood, came staggering through. At first Elodie thought one of the servants had cut himself, or another had gone berserk and used one of the big choppers on a colleague, but although the man's face was very battered and blood-streaked, she could see he was not Chinese.

"Lee!" shouted the man, lurching forward. "Don't take them in!" His words were slurred, but his warning was clear.

Mr. Lee was frozen in the act of turning, off-balance, and shocked. Everyone in the room stood gaping at the apparition before them. The man grabbed hold of the back of one of the chairs now ranged haphazardly around the ebony table. He pushed himself away and went toward Lee in a desperate, stumbling run, reaching out with both hands. Mr. Lee stepped back, but the man came on. Elodie saw, at the far end of the passage, the uniformed man with the gun was running toward the house, his gun in his hand. He looked furious, and wild. He was Chinese, like Mr. Lee, but his features were coarser.

"Mingdow," panted the stranger. "Mingdow... got me after all..." He was panting, forcing the words out. One of the cooks tried to drag him back into the kitchen, but he shrugged him off. "I got away, but I overheard them planning ... take hostages ... force you..." He gasped. "Look out!". He reached out and grabbed a large knife that lay beside a tray of sliced meats, and continued to move forward.

The uniformed guard burst out of the glass passage and without even a moment's hesitation, fired past Mr. Lee at the stranger, who cried out and fell with a great crash against one of the buffet tables, bringing the white cloth that covered it down on top of himself, along with several serving dishes.

The marcelled blonde waitress screamed at the loudness of the gun but nobody else moved or spoke, all seemed frozen in shock. Mr. Lee, who had gone pale, was the first to move. He grabbed the guard. "Why did you do that?"

"I thought he going to kill you." The guard's English was heavily accented. "I doing duty."

"No," Mr. Lee was visibly shaking, his voice sorrowful. "No," he repeated. He stared down at the white cloth that covered the fallen man. Blood was staining it, spreading and oozing through the cloth. Mr. Lee turned quickly and snatched the gun from the guard. "You didn't need to shoot," he said, furious.

The guard looked truculent. "My duty," he repeated.

"Somebody had better call the police." It was Phil Plant, now looking not at all bored, but really rather excited. "You're supposed to call the police when someone is shot, I believe."

Mr. Lee kept the gun pointed at the guard as with one foot he moved aside the white tablecloth, revealing the bloodied face of the fallen man. "Please – is he dead?" he asked. Still nobody moved.

Beside Elodie, Bernice gasped.

"Holy smoke," she said. "It's Mr. Webster!"

5

The *Junfa* was wakened from a pleasant sleep to find that their prisoner had escaped. His fury rose quickly as he spat questions at his underlings.

"Who was guarding him?" he demanded.

"Soo," was the answer.

The *Junfa* cursed. "Was he asleep?"

There was a shuffling of feet. Finally one of the men spoke. "He had a pipe."

This enraged the *Junfa* even more. "Only I may have pipes, I have told you that. Only me. Where did he get it?"

"Upstairs."

The *Junfa* closed his eyes. "Bring him."

The unfortunate Soo was produced. He gazed blearily at the *Junfa*, a foolish grin on his rough features. Whatever intelligence he normally possessed had clearly fled.

"You fool!" screamed the *Junfa*. "You ugly, stupid, hopeless fool! How did you ever become a member?" There was no reply. If anyone knew, they were not going to volunteer the information.

The *Junfa* began to pace in front of the altar. He looked up at the symbols on the wall above it. Another example had to be made. And this time he would make sure the blood did not stain his expensive suit.

**

Apparently it was Mrs. Logie who'd had the sense to ring the police. While they were waiting, Mr. Lee spoke quietly.

"That man died to protect you. Whatever was going to happen has not happened, but the danger remains. The police can only make it worse. Your names are obviously known and... I am still..." He paused, shook himself. When he went on his voice broke oddly. "Say nothing, I beg you. Say nothing." He turned to the waitresses. "I will pay you double for this terrible night. But say only that he tried to warn me. Mention nothing else, no other words, or your lives could be in danger, too."

Elodie felt a thrill of fear. Could he be serious? She could see the other girls were terrified, as she was, but was amazed to sense something else within her that she had never felt before.

Delight.

How dramatic it all was. Horrifying, to see a man shot dead in front of her, the blood, the noise, all made her feel sick inside. And yet, she was stunned to hear a little cold voice within her say 'I can use this'.

Dear God, what kind of person am I to think like that? she asked herself. But it was undeniably there, within her – the need to record and remember people's faces and reactions, as well as her own.

She looked carefully at Lee's wealthy guests. They appeared outwardly calm, all except the little plump woman, who could not stop shaking and sobbing. Miss Hutton reached over and put her hand on the older woman's arm.

"Mr. Lee is right, my dear. We must simply say this poor crazed man came in and seemed to threaten Mr. Lee and the guard shot him. As for the other things he said ..." She glanced at Mr. Lee, who nodded. "The other has nothing to do with us, as long as we remain quiet. We must promise, for Mr. Lee's sake."

After that everyone was very quiet, and Elodie longed to know what they were thinking and feeling. She herself was consumed with curiosity, but she was determined to do as Mr. Lee said. She liked him instinctively, and could see he was deeply upset and frightened.

The police arrived about fifteen minutes later, and through the french windows Elodie could see uniformed patrolmen with flashlights swarming over the grounds. Inside, they were treated to a more elegant perusal.

Because of the address, and presumably the reputation of Mr. Lee, they were attended by no less than a Captain and a Lieutenant of Police, who introduced themselves as Brett and Deacon respectively. Both wore suits, the Captain's very expensive looking, the Lieutenant's rather wrinkled.

Captain Brett was small and red-faced, with steel-grey hair

that sat in ridges close to his scalp. He was all business, brisk, and without humour. His manner was a combination of conciliatory and peremptory. It was clear he was in charge.

Lieutenant Deacon, on the other hand, was tall and angular, with amused eyebrows, and a thick thatch of dark red hair that seemed to have a life of its own, so electric was his presence. And yet he said very little. Just looked, just listened, just appeared as if the whole tableau before him was a play designed for his pleasure. He leaned against the doorway, lit a cigarette, and blew a smoke ring.

He made Elodie very nervous.

Captain Brett went straight to Mr. Lee, who was by now sitting at the head of the ebony table. The others were ranged below him in the chairs, all of the guests on the side away from the body. Miss Hutton sat beside Mr. Lee, the man Plant slumped beside her, followed by the plump woman who was a Mrs. Weatherbee, then Mr. Ryan, then an elderly married couple named Clayton, and finally little Mr. Blick. The serving girls, all of whom, like Elodie, had been in the dining room at the time of the shooting, had been allowed to sit down, but were forced to sit on the side nearest the body. The blonde looked quite ill. Bernice and Betty Ann still looked frightened. Elodie didn't know how she looked, but she felt very peculiar. She caught the eye of Lieutenant Deacon and, to her amazement, he winked at her.

"I'm very sorry this had to happen, Mr. Lee," Captain Brett was saying. "You know we've been looking for this man for almost a week, now."

Mr. Lee nodded wearily. "I spoke to the police the other day. I have no idea where he has been. I had feared he was dead. And now he is." He cast an angry glance at the guard, who was seated well away from the table on a chair in the corner. He wore a blank expression and seemed to be in shock.

"He was a friend?" Captain Brett asked.

Mr. Lee shook his head. "A colleague. A business colleague. But we have known one another for many years. He seemed concerned for my well-being . . . it was very strange."

"He gave no indication where he had been? Or what had happened to him?"

Mr. Lee glanced around the table, looking at each one in turn. "No," he said. It sounded more like an order than an answer.

61

Miss Hutton looked down at her hands and twisted the magnificent ring on her right hand. Mrs. Clayton opened her mouth as if to speak, then seemed to think better of it. Mrs. Weatherbee just whimpered.

"He...." Elodie began, and then stopped because Bernice had kicked her, very hard, under the table.

The Captain turned to Elodie. "Yes?"

Elodie shook her head. "He ... worked in the Gower Building."

The Captain looked slightly annoyed. "Yes," he said. "We know that. We know who he is."

"Sorry," said Elodie, feeling both foolish and puzzled. Again she found the Lieutenant looking at her, and again, he winked. He really was a very odd policeman. Not that she had met many policemen, but she was sure most of them were serious about things like murder. Maybe he's drunk, she thought, suddenly. But his eyes were very clear, very focused ... and very green.

Suddenly he spoke. "We'd like to speak to each of you separately," he said. His voice was a little hoarse, as if he didn't use it very often.

"We had nothing to do with this," Phil Plant said, arrogantly, slurring his words slightly. Miss Hutton reached out a hand and laid it on his sleeve. He subsided.

"It will help us if we get everybody's version of events." Captain Brett looked at each of them in turn. "Not everybody sees the same thing. Or remembers the same thing, because ... "

"Because it happened so fast," Bernice burst out. Her face was flushed, and there was a glint in her eye as she looked down the table at Mr. Lee. No wonder he pays her so well, Elodie thought. She's backing him up. She's reminding us we have an excuse not to speak fully.

The Captain scowled. "Exactly."

"My guests are very tired," Mr.Lee said. "Will this take long?"

"Not at all, not at all." Captain Brett's manner was soothing. "We know you are all upset and shocked, but really it is only a matter of corroboration, to give us a clear idea of the circumstances." He looked around. "Is there some other room we could use?"

Mrs. Logie, who had been standing in the kitchen doorway, stirred. "Mr. Lee?" she asked.

Lee waved a weary hand. "The library," he said.

"This way," Mrs. Logie said, and the two policemen followed her out. A little while later, several men arrived and swarmed over the dining room. One kept taking photographs, the light flashes upsetting everyone. One knelt by the body of Mr. Webster and seemed to be examining him. After a little while he stood up and indicated that someone could take the body away. Two men arrived with a stretcher and did that, to everyone's great relief. For ten minutes the room had seemed filled with men doing things while the people around the table sat and watched like so many wax statues.

The examining people left as suddenly as they had arrived, and a uniformed officer appeared in the doorway, glaring. "No talking," he said, and folded his arms across his chest. Nobody paid any attention to him.

Mrs. Weatherbee began to cry. Again. She had been sniffing and gasping ever since Webster had been shot. "I don't know what Mr. Weatherbee will say," she whimpered. "He doesn't approve of this kind of thing at all." She had announced earlier that Mr. Weatherbee was presently in Hong Kong and had no idea she had come out to see Mr. Lee's treasures. Elodie thought Mr. Weatherbee sounded like a tyrant.

The uniformed officer spoke up. "Hey! I said you aren't supposed to discuss anything until you talk to the Captain," he said, reprovingly. "Orders."

"Your orders, not ours," Arnold Ryan observed.

The officer bristled. "Especially you."

Mr. Ryan smiled to himself. Mrs. Clayton looked startled. "Why does he speak to you like that?" she demanded. Elodie decided the couple must be from out of town.

Mr. Ryan leaned back in his chair. "He thinks I am a very very bad man." He inspected his fingernails. "He thinks I had something to do with it."

"Do you?" asked Mr. Clayton, with keen interest.

"Absolutely not," said Mr. Ryan easily. "I came to see the jade, just as you have. I have no idea what all this is about."

"Now listen," said the uniformed officer, coming to the foot of the table. "You just stop all that gabbing, the bunch of you."

Mr. Blick, so small, so self-effacing, suddenly poked the

uniformed policeman in the side. "You should be nice," he said. "We are innocent bystanders."

"Yeah, well, I don't know about that." The officer was clearly not the brightest of lights. "I only know you ain't supposed to be talking, that's all."

"We shall refrain from further conversation," Mr. Lee announced.

So they did.

Time seemed to drag. Miss Hutton lit up cigarette after cigarette, Plant dutifully lighting them with a large gold lighter. Bernice and Betty Ann twitched and wriggled in their chairs, but the blonde girl (whose name Elodie later learned was Dawn) just slumped and stared at the floor. Mr. Blick was immobile, Mrs. Weatherbee continued to snivel into her handkerchief, and Mr. and Mrs. Clayton held hands. Mr. Ryan played with a few pieces of cutlery that lay before him on the table, left behind by an earlier diner. Mr. Lee sat in his chair and closed his eyes, sliding his hands into the sleeves of his red gown. He looks like a Chinese emperor, Elodie thought. And we are lined up along this big black table as if we were his courtiers.

She didn't know what she would say when Captain Brett or that Lieutenant talked to her. She was fairly clear in her mind about what had happened, but Mr. Lee didn't want them to say too much. How much should she say, then? She thought back and tried hard to remember what Mr. Webster had actually said. Something like 'mingdow', whatever that was. It sounded like some kind of dance. Maybe that was what Mr. Lee wanted kept secret.

But what was a *mingdow*?

It was very confusing. The whole question of what she had heard on the tenth floor the night Mr. Webster disappeared was now probably quite unimportant. She hoped so. She was determined not to mention it, unless they asked her directly if she knew anything else. She tried to escape the tension by thinking about what she would be doing in the weeks ahead. Two days from now, she thought, I will be going to the Gower building to start a whole new life, full of drama and excitement. She smiled ruefully to herself – her present life seemed to have a lot of that too. Had she wished for too much? Had she done or said something in the past few days that had brought all these changes and upsets down on her head? She wished she was back at the agency, writing catalogue entries for corn plasters. She wished –

Another uniformed officer came into the room. He gestured at the guard. "He wants to talk to you, first." The guard slowly got up and followed the officer, his head slumped, for all the world as if on his way to be hanged. Maybe he thought he was.

**

Archie wished that Captain Brett had left this to him, but he knew that was impossible, considering the status of the people involved. Brett was reputed to have a socially ambitious wife, who wanted him to become Commissioner one day, or even Mayor. He seized any opportunity to 'get in good' with people who mattered in the city. The thought of Fred Brett as Police Commissioner was frightening, as Mayor absolutely disgusting. The one they had was bad enough.

"Why did you shoot the man?" demanded Brett of the Chinese guard.

"Thought he going to kill Mr. Lee with knife." His tone was sullen, his face a mask of indifference.

"How long have you worked for Mr. Lee?"

"Three weeks. Friend send me."

"What friend?"

"Chi'en Pu Yi," said the guard.

Archie knew a few Chinese people, but had never heard of any local Chi'en Pu Yi, but that proved nothing. So many Chinese names sounded similar. The Chinese community in Chicago was not large, and was extremely tight-knit. But new members arrived frequently, mostly from Canton, relatives brought over by uncles, brothers, sons who had come to the States and earned enough to start transferring family from the old country.

"Where does he live?" asked Brett.

The guard shrugged.

"Where does he work?"

Again, the shrug.

"How did you meet him, then?"

The guard sighed heavily. "Milton Street Tong," he said.

"What's that?" Brett turned to Archie.

"Tongs are business and social organisations. Kind of like Rotary, but very localized, by area or profession." Archie explained. "They exist to help their members, and also any newcomers."

"And this Tong person recommended you to Mr. Lee just like that?" Brett demanded.

"I in police. He knew."

"Ah," said Brett, expansively. "A fellow officer."

The guard looked puzzled. "In Canton," he said. "Two years."

"When did you arrive in Chicago?" Archie asked.

"Five weeks now."

"Your English is pretty good."

"Yes."

"Where did you learn it?"

"Mission school."

It was like pulling teeth. "You understand that there will have to be an investigation," Captain Brett said. When the guard frowned again, he continued. "We have to find out just what happened."

"I did my job." The truculent guard had given his name as Sammy Chou.

"You will have to come down to the station and sign a statement. The District Attorney may want to talk to you."

Chou stood up. "Now?"

"Soon," Archie said. "For now, just wait outside with Sgt. Casey." The guard frowned. "The big man with the moustache," Archie amplified, indicating his own upper lip. Chou nodded and went out, closing the door behind him.

Brett snorted. "Either he's very dumb or very smart. And I don't think he's smart. He sure doesn't seem very upset to have shot a man. Do you think he's used to it?"

"I don't know," Archie said. "Things have been rough over there. They don't value life so much, you know. Maybe it's just as he said – he thought he was doing his job."

"What does he expect, a goddamn medal?"

Archie grinned. "Probably," he said.

Next up was Miss Hutton, mostly because Brett couldn't wait to make himself known to the famous heiress. She came in quietly and sat down without any fuss. She regarded them with her amazing blue eyes, and waited.

"I'm sorry this had to happen during your visit, Miss Hutton," Brett began. "Are you a friend of Mr. Lee's?"

"I have purchased a few pieces from him," came the soft reply. "But only through an intermediary. This is the first time I have actually met him face to face. He has an excellent reputation. This is a terrible thing for him."

"Yes," Brett agreed. "Did you know Mr. Webster?"

"Is that the name of the dead man? No, I have neither heard of nor met him. I have never seen anyone killed before." If it disturbed her, it didn't show. She had complete control of herself, her hands neither shook nor twisted in her lap. She was, in fact, utterly still.

"Few people have," Brett sympathized. He meant few people of her social status, of course. "Could you just briefly tell us what you remember?"

She closed her eyes, apparently gathering her thoughts. "We were about to go out to see the jade when the man burst into the dining room shouting at Mr. Lee not to take us to the strongroom."

"Can you remember what he said?"

"Just 'no!' or 'don't take them in', something like that. Then he picked up the knife from the buffet and said 'look out' and then the guard came through the french doors and shot him. He was very close to Mr. Lee and might have hit him instead of the man with the knife, but it was a very accurate shot." She opened her eyes. "Very accurate."

"He is an ex-police officer," Brett explained.

"I see."

"Can you remember anything else, Miss Hutton?"

She shook her head. "One of the waitresses seemed to recognize him," she offered. "But I can't remember what she said exactly."

"Something like 'It's Mr. Webster'?" suggested Archie.

She looked at him and smiled. "I believe it was more like 'Holy Smoke, it's Mr. Webster."

"That's pretty exact," Archie said, pointedly. "Are you sure you can't remember anything else anyone said?"

"She's doing her best." Brett obviously felt Miss Hutton needed protection from his over-zealous lieutenant. "What happened after that, Miss Hutton?"

"Mr. Lee was cross with the guard. He seemed to think he acted too quickly. And then that fat woman, Mrs. Weatherbee, started to scream and weep . ... it all became rather confused."

"I see," Brett said. "Of course, it was a very frightening experience."

"Of course. Very." Miss Hutton spoke calmly.

You wouldn't know it to look at her, Archie thought to himself. She's as cool as my Aunt Mary's icebox. But the eyes – there was fire there. The effect was very sexual, very attractive, and not lost on Captain Brett, either.

"I think that's all, Miss Hutton. I'll have someone come to your hotel to take down a statement, if that's all right."

"Fine." She rose gracefully. "We're at the Parker House."

"Of course. Thank you."

Archie opened his mouth to speak, but caught a sideways glance from Brett, and subsided. There were other witnesses, and Brett obviously wanted this one to be as little disturbed as possible.

"Thank you – Captain Brett, is it?" She seemed anxious to get it right.

He expanded visibly. "Yes, that's right."

"I'll remember your kindness." She turned and went out, leaving the officer outside to close the door behind her.

Brett gave a huge sigh. "What a lady," he said.

And what a performance, Archie thought.

They got much the same information from Mrs. Weatherbee, still snuffling, and the Claytons. Phil Plant had obviously been drinking heavily, both during the party and since the killing of Webster. He was both insolent and useless. Brett handled him with kid gloves, however, because of his relationship with Barbara Hutton.

The most accurate description of events seemed to come from Mr. Blick. The little man had a keen eye and clear recall. He represented a museum in New York, and had come west specifically to view and perhaps purchase the jade Mr. Lee had on offer. However, despite Blick's apparent precision, it seemed to Archie there was something not being said, something held back by them all.

By the time they were ready for Mr. Lee they found Mrs. Logie had summoned his doctor, who had advised immediate bed rest and a sedative. Brett was annoyed with himself for not calling on Lee first, but they would have to come back anyway the following day, so contented himself with that.

"Now that bastard Ryan." He rubbed his hands together. "He'll be good and annoyed by having to wait. Might trip himself up."

Archie said nothing, but doubted Ryan's vulnerability, and he was right. Ryan was as cool as Barbara Hutton had been, and added nothing to what they had already learned.

"Nothing to do with me," he said, when Brett openly accused him of complicity. "I'm here as a private citizen. I collect oriental art."

"You come to buy some of this jade stuff?"

Ryan waved a hand. "A little beyond my means, Captain. I just wanted to see it before it disappeared from the market. The supply of jade from China is rapidly diminishing, due to the civil wars there. I asked Lee to let me know when anything particularly nice came along. And, of course, I always attend his parties. He's a good customer."

"Customer?"

"Of a client," Ryan said, smoothly.

"Anybody we know?" Brett said, with heavy humour, but Archie sensed some withdrawal in him.

"I have no idea whom you know, Captain Brett. If you would give me a list . . . "

"Very funny." Brett looked less than amused.

Ryan stood. "If there's nothing else?"

"We'll need you to sign a statement in the morning."

"You know where my office is."

"In the Gower Building, isn't it?" Archie said.

"That's correct."

"So maybe you knew Webster?"

"Not at all. My office is on the twentieth floor."

"But you do collect oriental art. You presumably went to the tenth floor to see Mr. Lee from time to time."

"But not to see anyone else. I buy through Mr. Lee only." Ryan glanced around the room. "He has excellent taste, as you can see. And so do I."

"How nice for you," Brett murmured.

Ryan gave a wide smile to them both. "I am a very lucky man," he said, and left them.

Archie turned to Captain Brett. "Why didn't you push him harder?"

Brett looked embarrassed. "He has too many connections. You have to watch it these days."

"He's a crooked lawyer, he works for Capone and Nitti," Archie said, in disgust. "Is that what you mean?"

Brett ignored that, turned a page of his notebook, and said, "We'll do the maids next. Go pick one out."

Archie stood up, annoyed with Brett's cowardice and general bootlicking. He wondered how much of the well-known ambition was his wife's and how much was his own. And how crooked he really was, because it was obvious he was afraid of Ryan and the organisation behind him. Another cop gone down, he thought as he went into the dining room. He looked at the serving girls one at a time, and knew just how he wanted to see them, and which one he wanted to save for last. The cocky one with the red curls, first – she worked for Lee, and might know something more than the others. Then the icy blonde. Then the poor man's Pola Negri. He wanted to keep the little brown-haired one for last. There was something about her he liked. She looked intelligent and a little better than the others, somehow. He couldn't help wondering why.

**

Elodie's turn came at last. She had sat there patiently while the annoying Lt. Deacon called all the other girls ahead of her. It gave her time to think about what she should say, and what she should not. The officer led her to a room she hadn't seen on their earlier exploration before the party began.

Mr. Lee's library was very different from the rest of the house and she suspected this was where he spent most of his time when at home. Lined with dark wood bookshelves, all well filled, it was carpeted in red, and had deep comfortable armchairs with little tables beside them placed around the room. A larger table had been moved to the centre, and behind this sat Captain Brett and Lieutenant Deacon. The Lieutenant had a notepad in front of him, and a large sheet of paper with some kind of drawing on it. From where she sat Elodie thought it looked like an architect's drawing – probably a layout of the house and grounds. The Lieutenant had scribbled all over it. Mr. Lee wouldn't like that.

"You are?" The Captain sounded and looked very bored.

"My name is Elodie Browne. I am a writer and I work in the Gower Building. I am a friend of Bernice Barker and she asked me if I wanted to earn some extra money by helping out at Mr. Lee's party and I said yes, and that's why I'm here. I'm not a regular waitress or servant or anything." She had been waiting so long to say it that it all came out in a gush.

"A writer?" The Lieutenant seemed surprised.

"A copywriter," Elodie explained. "I work for the advertising agency Adcock and Ash. They're on the fifteenth floor." She emphasized the number.

"And you agreed to serve at a party?"

"Yes." She looked from one to the other. "I wanted some extra money, like anyone else." She paused. "And I was curious to see what rich people are like. I am going to be writing about high society on the radio, you see."

"I thought you said you were a copywriter," the Lieutenant said.

"Yes, but the agency – "   •

"Never mind all that," interrupted the Captain. "Tell us what happened tonight."

"From the beginning?"

"From where the dead man came into the room."

"He wasn't dead when he came in," Elodie said, and could have kicked herself, never mind Bernice. What a stupid thing to say, she thought, then she saw the Lieutenant was trying not to laugh. "I mean, there was a kind of crash in the kitchen and then he just . . . .burst in."

"And?"

"He shouted at Mr. Lee to stop."

"Stop what?"

"Taking the people out to see the jade?"

"Did he say anything else?"

"He told Mr. Lee to look out. He picked up a knife from the table and said 'Look out!' . . as if he was warning Mr. Lee about the guard with the gun."

"Why should he do that?"

Elodie shrugged. "I don't know. He wasn't making much sense, his face was all bruised and bleeding ... I think he was

71

dying or something. He looked like he was."

"Why do you say that?" asked the Lieutenant, leaning forward. "Nobody else said that."

"Imagination," barked the Captain. "You couldn't have known whether he was dying or not."

"He looked terrible, then," Elodie amended. "Sick and weak and . . . terrible. And frightened."

"Frightened of what?"

"I don't know. Mr. Lee? The guard with the gun? I don't know."

"Did he say anything else?" Captain Brett was persistent. Elodie wondered if one of the others had said that odd name or word that Mr. Lee didn't seem to want said.

"Not that I could understand," Elodie said, which was more or less the truth. She sat there, willing them not to ask any more questions. So, of course, the annoying Lieutenant did just that.

"Did you know Mr. Webster? You both work in the same building."

"I had never seen him. I work on a different floor. I had no reason to have any contact with him."

"Hadn't seen him around the building?"

"Not that I knew of. This was the first time I saw him. I did not know who he was until Bernice said he was Mr. Webster."

"You are good friends with Miss Barker?"

"We have lunch together every day," Elodie said. "We went to the same high school."

"And have you ever been in Mr. Lee's office, where Miss Barker works?"

"No, never."

"Have you ever been on the tenth floor?"

Damn, Elodie thought. Damn, damn, damn.

"Well...." she said, slowly.

They both looked at her expectantly.

"I think I was," she told them.

"What the devil does that mean?" demanded the Captain, who obviously didn't like her or anything about her. Writing about high society indeed, he seemed to think. Above herself, that's what she was.

Elodie felt a prickling behind her eyes, and blinked rapidly. "It was on last Thursday night," she began. The two detectives looked at one another, then back at her.

"You were on the tenth floor of the Gower Building last Thursday night?" asked the Lieutenant.

"I'm not absolutely sure," said Elodie, although of course she was. Seeing their impatience, she sighed, and reluctantly told them about the elevator stopping on the wrong floor, and the shouting, and the dragging sound, and how frightened she was.

"Why the devil didn't you tell someone?" Captain Brett looked very exasperated.

"Well, when I got down to the lobby the guard was asleep. And the taxi was waiting with the meter running and there wasn't anything I could do – "

"And you were afraid you had been seen," finished Lieutenant Deacon, who seemed to grasp even more of the sitation than she had at the time.

"Yes," she admitted. "The light from the elevator – "

Deacon nodded and leaned back, assessing her. "Can you tell us exactly what you heard?" he asked.

Elodie shrugged. "Not really. Just . . .shouting. It was all sort of a gabble. And then someone cried out – I guess that was Mr. Webster – and I kept punching the button for the elevator to come, and then a door opened and there was this dragging sound coming toward me ... " It all came back, and she gave a convulsive shiver. "Then the elevator came."

"A gabble?" asked Brett.

"Yes."

"You couldn't make out any words?"

Elodie shook her head.

"Why do you suppose that was?" asked the Lieutenant.

"Well, it was far away down the hall and the door was closed and ... " she paused, frowned. "I don't really know," she admitted, puzzled. "It didn't seem to make any sense, some-how."

"Were they speaking in English?" asked Deacon, his eyes narrowed.

"Oh." She hadn't thought of that. "Oh."

He was leaning forward now. "Could they have been speaking Italian, for instance?"

She shook her head. The Pellini family lived right behind them on Trenton, and they were often shouting. "No," she

73

said. "I know those words."

"German? French?" asked Brett.

"Not German. And I speak French. It wasn't French."

"Chinese?" Deacon suggested.

"I don't know what Chinese sounds like."

Deacon stood up and went to the door, opened it, spoke to somone outside, then returned to his seat behind the big table. After a few minutes, there was a knock and the door opened.

"Yes, sir?" came a voice behind her.

"Do you speak Chinese?" Deacon asked.

"Yes, sir." Soft footsteps padded toward Elodie and then a man went past her to the table. He stood with his back to her, but she recognized the white clothing of one of the cooks.

"I want you to go outside, close the door, and begin shouting in Chinese, something aggressive or threatening. Can you do that?"

She could see by the set of the man's shoulders that he was startled and possibly offended. "I don't understand."

"It's an experiment," Captain Brett said, authoratively. "You're an American citizen, aren't you?"

The man drew himself up proudly. "Yes, sir."

"Then it's your duty to help the police," Brett said. "Do as I say."

"Please." Deacon smiled.

That seemed to make all the difference. The man turned and walked past her without meeting her eyes. He closed the door behind him. After a minute she heard the sound of shouting . . . loud shouting . . . and it was a gabble.

"Yes," she said, in excitement. "Yes ... it sounded just like that."

Deacon leaned back in his chair. "Ah," he said. He seemed pleased.

6

"And then they said I could go home," Elodie said to the Browne family, who had all gotten out of bed to hear about what had kept her out so late. They knew where she had gone, and her mother had been particularly worried. She had never much trusted Bernice, and had been convinced her daughter was being led to an orgy of some kind.

Murder had been almost a relief.

"What was the house like?" asked Marie.

"What was Miss Hutton wearing?" asked Maybelle.

"Was there a lot of blood?" asked Alyce, who had been particularly thrilled by Elodie's narrative.

"Girls, girls, can't you see Ellie is exhausted?" Mrs. Browne stood up. "We should all go to bed."

"Oh, not yet, Mumma," pleaded Alyce. "I want to hear everything. They made Orphan Annie talk about the burglars so she wouldn't have nightmares. Elodie should tell us everything, to ease her mind."

Mrs. Browne looked at her youngest daughter. "Sometimes you worry me, Alyce."

"But that's what they said . . . " Alyce began.

"That's quite enough." Mrs. Browne considered her younger daughter for a moment, then sat down and turned back to Elodie. "Go on, then. Start from the beginning, but more slowly."

Elodie again went over the evening, this time answering everyone's questions as she went along. It took almost an hour, and it was after three in the morning when everybody was satisfied that they had heard every horrible and exciting detail.

Mrs. Browne made hot chocolate, and when it was gone, she shooed them all up to bed. "A good thing tomorrow is Sunday," she said. "We can all sleep late."

But it was a long time before Elodie fell asleep.

The next day she searched the papers for the story, but there was nothing. Not even in the *Tribune*. Perhaps it had all taken place too late to make the Sunday editions. On Monday morning, before leaving the house, she looked again, twice.

Still nothing.

How strange, she thought. I'm sure I didn't dream it.

Marie, who was cleaning up the kitchen after breakfast, agreed it was odd. "It's being hushed up," she said, darkly.

"I wonder why?" Elodie hadn't been able to eat anything more than toast. She had spent Sunday afternoon and evening trying to write down as many of the ideas for Imperial Hotel she could think of, so as to be ready for Monday morning. Now she was delaying her departure. She was eager to begin, and also nervous. Ever since Friday her new job had been on her mind. And the excitement of Saturday night had only made it worse. How could she capture something like the events at the Lee house? What if she couldn't write for radio after all? What if she failed? Would she have to go back to writing about soap and cake flour forever?

Marie ran hot water into the sink. "Probably you should ask 'who' is hushing it up. Didn't you say that mob lawyer Arnold Ryan was there? And Mr. Lee is very rich, isn't he? He knows a lot of people, I expect. People who will do what he wishes."

Elodie sighed. "I suppose so. But I'm beginning to think it was all a nightmare after all." She stood up. "I tried to call Bernice, but her mother said she wasn't home all day yesterday. I don't know what to think."

"Don't," advised Marie.

"Don't what?" Elodie was pulling on her jacket.

"Don't think about it," Marie said. She was the oldest of the Browne sisters, with softly curling hair and a wonderful posture. She looked like a duchess who was pretending to be a kitchen maid, and enjoying the experience. She scrubbed at the frying pan. "Just put your mind to your new job, and forget all about everything else. There are people to sort out things like that."

"The police," Elodie said, settling her hat using her reflection in the glass of the cupboard door. It was one Maybelle had passed on to her the day before – an 'Angel-face' cloche in pale grey that matched her coat, with a darker grey ribbon and a small jet decoration in the centre of the turned-back brim. Maybelle was right – it gave her confidence.

"Of course the police."

"I didn't think much of them," Elodie said, picking up her handbag and her father's old briefcase in which she had placed all the ideas she had scribbled down. "Especially that Lieutenant Deacon. He seemed to think it was all a big joke."

"I doubt that," said Marie. "You must have misunderstood."

"He winked at me. Twice." She paused in the kitchen door. "But he was the one who figured out about the men shouting in Chinese," she said, slowly. "So maybe he has a brain. I'm not so sure about Captain Brett, though."

"Well, I'm sure you're going to be late if you don't get a move on," Marie pointed out, waving a dripping spatula. "Goodbye, Miss Radio Writer. And good luck, by the way."

Impulsively, Elodie darted over and hugged her older sister, then went out to catch the trolley. When it pulled away and its bell rang, she decided it was celebrating her brand new start. Everything else was going to be left behind her, including dead men and odd police lieutenants.

**

It was the usual Monday morning meeting. Capone and Nitti sat at the head and foot of the table respectively, and the various lieutenants made their reports on the weekend takings. All were up, particularly prostitution, no doubt because spring was in the air. A good end to the week, and all were satisfied.

Except Capone, who was never satisfied.

"That mick bastard Moran is trying to move in on us again, Ryan. What do you say about that?"

"I haven't heard anything specific, Mr. Capone. I'll give my usual sources a check."

"You do that. Only advantage to having a mick lawyer is he knows the micks, right?"

"I do my best." Ryan's modesty was patently insincere. "But they know I work for you, so it's not easy."

"Moran doesn't seem to learn very fast, does he?" Nitti growled. "Maybe he needs another lesson in manners."

"I'll leave that to you, Frank." Capone's thick eyebrows drew together as he looked around the table. "All I got to say to you lunkheads is – do better."

One by one they slunk away, leaving only Arnold Ryan and Nitti. Capone stared down the table, his black eyes suspicious as always, his mouth a loose red slash in his pudgy face. "Arnold. I hear you were at a party on Saturday night, is that right?"

Ryan shifted in his chair slightly. "Why, yes."

"At some Chink's house out by the Lake?"

"Yes. How did you know that?"

Capone waved a hand. "It don't matter how I know, the point is, what were you doing there?"

Ryan smiled easily. "As you know I collect oriental art objects. Mr. Lee is an importer and he had something to show his special customers."

"You're a 'special customer'?"

"I like to think so."

"And what did you see?"

"Nothing, as it happens. I had been told it would be jade, but no more than that. I was hoping there would be something small that I could afford." Ryan looked down at the table and then back up. "As you know, I am not a wealthy man."

Nitti grunted and Capone barked a laugh, extracting a fresh cigar from an inner pocket and turning it around in his fat fingers. "You lawyers are all alike. You got plenty of money, you Irish bastard."

Ryan smiled. "I have enough."

Capone's laugh had been brief. Now he leaned forward and stabbed the air with his unlit cigar. "I know what happened out there, Arnold. I know a guy was bumped off, I know some fancy people were there who maybe shouldn't have been there. I know it's a mess and so do you. It's been kept out of the papers, but it won't stay quiet forever. I don't want you doing business with no Chinks from now on. Is that clear?"

"But why?" Ryan was confused. Capone had a great many

prejudices but he had never heard him speak against the Chinese before.

"I got my reasons and maybe one day they'll be your reasons, but for now, stay away from Chinks."

"Even Mr. Lee?"

"Even your goddamn Chink laundryman if you got one." It was now apparent that Capone was very angry indeed, his famous temper catching fire behind the flame as he lit his cigar. "Do I make myself clear, Mr. Art Collector Ryan?"

Arnold Ryan managed a smile. "Of course."

Capone leaned back and looked down the table at Nitti, who looked back imperturbably. "He understands, Frank. Mr. Art Collector Ryan is a smart man."

"You wouldn't employ him otherwise, Al," was Nitti's reply.

"Damn right." He looked back at Ryan. "Despite he's a goddamn mick." He took a long drag on the cigar and blew smoke down the length of the table. As always it was a cheap cigar but Ryan managed not to wince as the stink of it reached him.

"Is there anything else, Mr. Capone?" he asked.

"Naw – you got them papers I signed, so that's all." As Ryan stood Capone jabbed with his cigar again. "And no Chinks."

"No ... Chinks," Ryan agreed, dutifully, and left the room.

Capone looked at Nitti and grinned. "Did he buy it? Did I scare him?"

Nitti smiled narrowly. "You scare everybody, Al."

Capone looked pleased. "Yeah. I do, don't I? Only way to do business."

"With Ryan?"

"With anybody. Including Chinks."

**

Elodie stood across the street from the Gower Building and looked up at its strong perpendicular lines. Built in the shape of the letter C, its rows of windows glittered, reflecting the light from the Lake which lay before it. She had been coming here every morning for over a year and riding up to the fifteenth floor to work on bunion ads for Adcock and Ashe, but suddenly the building had a new glamour about it. She knew it was firmly anchored to the ground, but somehow it had acquired a glowing halo of wonderful possibilities, a new kind of promise. The carved white marble trim seemed to glow in the sun, and the elaborate brass work around the entrance shimmered like gold. Diamond reflections glinted off the glass in the revolving doors as the many workers entered the high, airy entrance hall. She had always been glad to work there, but now it seemed like an entry to another world. Stepping into the lobby this morning, she would be a different person from the little copywriter who had walked out of it the Friday before.

Between her and the entrance flowed a river of cars, shiny black, with the occasional flash of colour from some sports model or other. On bumper after bumper she saw the orange and blue stickers that read 'Repeal the Eighteenth Amendment'. More and more of them every day. Ordinary people were getting so fed up with Prohibition and the crime that had grown from it. Against them were ranged all the evil men who profited from it, many seemingly respectable, and many with the kind of authority that could keep the staus quo, no matter how many bumper stickers that appeared.

She was not going to worry about that anymore. Ahead of her waited a new world, and she was going to enter it with all flags flying. When the light changed, she walked across the boulevard with her head high and her step light.

But when the elevator door opened onto the tenth floor, and she saw the red leather chairs, the oriental rug, and the wide mahogany reception desk in the middle, she felt her stomach lurch. Now the lobby was entirely different. Bright with morning light, there were people passing through, and a pretty girl at the reception desk. I'll be fine, Elodie told herself. Then she realized the girl at the reception desk was Betty Ann, and the memory of Saturday night's events momentarily eclipsed everything else. How strange, she thought, to cover one upsetting thing with another and feel better about it.

One disaster at a time, she told herself, and turned toward the left-hand hall before Betty Ann could catch her eye. Mr. Herschel's secretary had written the number of her new office down – 1054. Well, that was something. On Mumma's next birthday she would be fifty-four, and her birthday was in October. Rather thin comfort, but it was all she had. Her heels clacked on the cold marble floor, as she counted off the odd-numbered offices on the left hand side.

1054 was just a number on a door, no name of any kind. The glass in the door was pebbled, and soft light lay beyond with no movement or anything to indicate there was anyone inside.

Elodie tried the knob and found the door was unlocked. It swung wide and she saw her new home. It was not like any office she had ever worked in before.

For a start, there were no desks. Just a couple of couches, a couple of armchairs, and a low table in the centre of the room. Another long narrow table stood against the far wall with a typewriter at one end and cups, plates, an electric hot plate, and a baker's box, half-open, at the other. On the windowsill sat a bottle of milk and a tin of Red Circle coffee. That was encouraging – Marie would only buy Eight O'Clock brand, because it was the cheapest.

Otherwise the room was empty.

Elodie went over to the window and looked out. Not much of a view – just the opposite arm of the building, and below the little figures of people hurrying in and out of the building like so many beetles. If she leaned forward and pressed her forehead against the glass, she could just glimpse the glitter of the Lake, an expanse of blue blending into the sky.

She heard the door open, and turned to see who was coming in.

It was a man of about forty or so, carrying the bottom half of the coffee pot, slopping water over the edge. He looked haggard and hungry. He was pale, with straw-coloured hair, and wore quite thick wire framed glasses, under which his nose was very red, as if he had a cold. His suit was rumpled, and his tie was askew below a loosened collar.

"Yes?" he asked, closing the door behind him. He didn't wait for an answer but slouched across the room, slammed the pot onto the table, and threw himself onto one of the couches. "Well?" he demanded.

"I'm Elodie Browne," she said.

"Oh." He closed his eyes. "The idea girl."

"Yes." She stood there waiting. He seemed to be falling

asleep. Then his eyes opened again. "Coat and hat over there – " he indicated a hatrack in the corner which was already occupied by what was obviously his own hat and coat. She put hers on the other side of the rack. "Sit down. Tell me all about it."

Elodie did as he said, but had no idea what he wanted her to say. "All about what?" she finally asked. The couch was of leather, and she could feel her legs sticking to the front of it. It also squeaked every time she moved.

"Imperial Hotel," came the answer. Again his eyes were closed.

"Are you Mr. Wilson?" Elodie asked, pretty certain he was.

"No, I'm Fu Manchu," came the growled answer. "Of course I'm Drew Wilson. Why the devil would I be here, otherwise?"

She felt like crossing the room and kicking him. He was rude and he was trying to make her feel stupid. People often made that mistake.

"Well, that's nice," she said. "Because I'm Mary Pickford, and I've always wanted to meet you, Mr. Fu."

His eyes opened. "You know all about the Chinese name business."

"I know about a lot of things." Elodie put her briefcase down beside her.

"I didn't think much of your last picture, Miss Pickford."

"The director was an idiot," Elodie snapped.

He nodded, his eyes closing again. "Same old excuse."

"Would it bother you if I screamed?" Elodie asked, sweetly.

"Feel free, I often scream myself," Wilson said. "I find it clears the lungs remarkably well. One hates to have clogged lungs."

"One does," Elodie agreed.

The office door swung inward and a woman stood in the opening – middle-aged, plump, wearing a purple dress that was obviously expensive but far too young for her. The band around the hips was already wrinkled and taut, and the short full sleeves fluttered around husky upper arms. Pale orange hair sprang out from around a small furry angora beret, and her face was pink with exertion. In one hand she clutched a huge leather bag so stuffed that it looked in danger of exploding, and a red coat was folded over her elbow. She glanced from Elodie to the sprawled form of Wilson on the couch opposite, and sighed.

"Is he hungover?" she asked.

"I have no idea," Elodie said. "I have never seen him before, drunk or sober. He says his name is Wilson."

The woman came in and slammed the door behind her, then dumped her coat and satchel onto the low table. "If he claims his name is Wilson, then he's hung over. I've never seen him any other way. He claims it's insomnia and lots of reading, but I know differently. Good morning, Drew, dear."

Wilson mumbled something under his breath. The woman turned to Elodie and approached, holding out one hand and pulling off the fuzzy beret with the other. "I'm Sal Schultz," she said. "You must be Elodie Browne. Welcome."

Elodie smiled at her. "Thanks." Miss Schultz seemed much nicer than the disagreeable Drew Wilson.

"Anybody started the coffee yet?" Sal wanted to know. Freed from the confines of the fuzzy beret, her hair seemed more like an orange dandelion clock than actual hair. She tried to pat it down, but it sprang back out again, and she gave up the unequal struggle. "No?"

"I'm sorry," Elodie said, starting to rise. "I didn't realize – "

"Of course you didn't," Sal said, going over to the table and hefting the pot. She glanced at Wilson. "I see you managed to get the water."

"And the doughnuts," Wilson said. "You do the rest."

"Such a kind man, such a sweet man." Sal opened the tin of coffee and spooned some into the basket, then put all the parts together and placed it on the hot plate, which she flicked on. "No wonder I love working with you so much."

"And you do." Wilson still didn't open his eyes. "You know you do. It's my sparkling mind and witty repartee."

"No," Sal disagreed. "It's your filthy temper, your whiskey breath, and the fact that you know more words than I do." She glanced at Elodie. "Do you know a lot of words? We're going to need a hell of a lot of words every week to fill an hour."

"I own a dictionary," Elodie offered. "I could bring it in with me tomorrow."

Sal regarded her for a moment, then chuckled. "Okay," she said. "Okay." She checked the coffeepot then came over to sit beside Elodie on the couch. "I loved your idea," she said, set-

tling herself down and holding her feet out before her like a
little child. Her shoes were also purple, but the flesh bulged
up around the strap that went over her instep. "I think we're
going to have a good time writing it. Have you written anything for radio before?"

"No," admitted Elodie.

"But you listen a lot, right?" Sal sighed.

"Same old excuse," muttered Wilson.

"I've been writing advertising copy for almost two years,
now," Elodie said, in her own defense. "I finished two years of
college before the money ran out, and I read all the time. I am
perfectly willing to steal anybody's ideas, including
Shakespeare's, and I speak French so we could always throw
in a few of those words to confuse everyone and make them
think we're smarter than we really are."

Sal looked at her with fresh respect, and laughed out loud.
She had a rich laugh that made her large bosom bounce freely.
"Okay," she said again, with approval. "Here's how we work."

"Oh, God," moaned Wilson. "Not before the coffee."

**

Writing for radio seemed to be mainly about talking, Elodie
found. She was glad Maybelle had taught her shorthand for
taking notes at college. Now she used it to write down what
each of them said. She was pretty sure she would be the one
who had to type everything up.

"You want to start every program with a set-up statement,"
Wilson said, after he had three cups of coffee, two doughnuts,
and was able to keep his eyes open continuously. "Every week
you'll get new listeners – "

"We hope," put in Sal. "But even so, it's for establishing the
setting. I thought of something like this – " Her voice changed
immediately to that of a rather pompous announcer.
"Welcome to Imperial Hotel, New York's finest hostelry."

"Hostelry?" Wilson asked.

"Whatever," Sal said, in her normal voice, then resumed
her 'radio' tones. "This is where only the best people stay, and
are served by the most highly-trained staff in the world. At the
Imperial Hotel, there is a story behind every door." She turned

to Elodie and was herself again. "Or something like that. It needs work." Wilson snorted. Sal ignored him. "You say you thought of two themes running side by side?"

"Yes," said Elodie. "We gradually get to know the staff of the hotel – they'll be leading their own lives behind the scenes – but every week there will be a main story about one of the guests."

"Too complicated," Wilson objected.

Elodie stiffened. "I don't think so. I think it can be done."

"So do I," said Sal. "I've been thinking about it ever since we chose the idea. Seems to me the first one or two programmes should be all about the staff, then we gradually cut that back and introduce the single stories."

"Who cares about bellboys and maids?" Wilson was full of objections.

"I do," Elodie said. "Ordinary people listen to the radio and they like to hear about other ordinary people sometimes."

"Like Fu Manchu?" Wilson managed a smile.

Elodie brought out one of her late father's favourite sayings. "Even Fu Manchu has to put on his trousers one leg at a time."

"Doesn't wear trousers."

"Stop it, Drew," Sal said. "I think she's right."

Wilson shrugged. "Prove it."

"Well – " Sal turned and rummaged in the big handbag she had brought with her. She withdrew a thick sheaf of type-written paper. "Let's start with the manager. I thought we could call him Mr. Dunning."

"Because he duns the guests for payment?" Wilson was obviously feeling better.

Sal ignored him. "And he has a receptionist called Molly Pritchett," she continued. "She has a crush on Mr. Dunning..."

"Who doesn't know it because he's too busy running the hotel," put in Elodie.

Sal grinned and pointed to a paragraph on the second page. "You got it."

The morning continued like this, and Elodie found that she could think in radio terms. She even impressed Drew Wilson with some of the things she brought out. It was wonderful. She liked Sal and thought she might even eventually like Wilson. They worked steadily for three hours. And then she made the mistake of mentioning the murder at the Lee house.

"I heard about that," Wilson said.

"But it wasn't in the papers." Elodie was surprised.

Wilson looked vague. "I heard it someplace."

"But you can't remember where or when." Sal obviously knew Wilson of old. She turned to Elodie and sank back against the leather of the couch, her eyes alight. "Tell."

So Elodie told.

"Must have been Fu Manchu," Wilson muttered, when she had finished. He seemed rather fond of Fu Manchu.

"Do you know what the word *mingdow* means?" Elodie asked them.

Sal shook her head, but Wilson mused half to himself, "Sounds familiar."

"Everything sounds familiar to you." Sal was exasperated. "To hear you tell it, you know everyone and have been everywhere and nothing is a mystery to you."

"About sums it up." Wilson grinned at Elodie. "She's jealous because she never reads a book and never goes anywhere. Lives at home with her old mother and sixteen cats."

"I live at home, too," Elodie said, before Sal could defend herself. "But we only have two cats. Do you really have sixteen?" she asked Sal in amazement.

"Of course not." Sal went over to the pencil sharpener and began to wind it so hard she broke the lead. "And my mother isn't that old, she's just in her sixties and she's a doctor, so there."

"My mother's a teacher," Elodie said, proudly.

"Mine is a bootlegger." Wilson was perfectly serious. "She runs a blind pig in her basement."

Sal sighed. "It's true."

"My goodness," Elodie said.

"I never drink there, of course," Wilson continued. "She makes it herself, and it would take the shine off anybody's linoleum, believe me."

Despite Sal's endorsement, Elodie wasn't certain whether to believe him or not. She knew there were literally thousands of speakeasies and so-called 'blind pigs' in Chicago now. She knew that quite ordinary girls like Bernice were quite capable of making bathtub gin for a party, although she had never been to one herself. Maybelle had. Maybelle went to a lot of parties and sometimes quite scandalized their mother with her tales. Mrs. Browne was convinced you couldn't touch pitch without it sticking to you, but Maybelle was neither a drinker nor was she 'fast'. She was just a young woman who led a busy social life in one of the most corrupt and hedonistic cities in the world. Most of the parties she attended were connected with her boss and his business, which was magazine publishing. Elodie was pretty sure that though the liquor flowed freely at them, his parties were quite respectable, and that the literary and artistic guests were perfectly respectable, too. Otherwise Maybelle wouldn't go, because Maybelle, for all her vanity and beauty, was an extremely sensible young woman. And she was Mrs. Browne's daughter.

Nevertheless, you couldn't live in Chicago without being aware of the immorality and shameless breaking of the Prohibition everywhere. There were stories every day in the papers, and then there was Hugh, who told her even more. There were killings and beatings, there was blatant prostitution, doping with hashish and cocaine, and gambling. The politicians were involved, the police, too. A lot of people were out for anything they could get in these very hard times. All because of Them. She hated Them, and yet They fascinated her.

She had brought up the party at Mr. Lee's because of Mr. Ryan being there. "He had the loveliest manners you ever saw," she had told Sal and Drew. "If I didn't know otherwise, I would never have suspected him of being what he is. We need someone like that staying at the hotel."

That was what had brought the work to a standstill. Elodie wished she had kept her mouth shut, but it was too late.

"Chinamen shooting each other," Sal mused, when Elodie had finished. "Makes a change from the names we usually see in the papers. They're mostly Italian and Irish these days."

"Plus a few Slovaks." Wilson almost sat up. "Especially out in Cicero."

"Still, I don't suppose it's anything we could use in our show," Sal continued regretfully. "Too exotic. Too strange."

"Seems a shame to waste it. You say you know this Lee guy's secretary?"

"Yes."

"Maybe you could find out more from her. Maybe it would

be a whole new series we could develop." Wilson was actually sitting upright, now, a little flushed with excitement. "Don't they call them Tongs or something?"

"What?"

"Chinese gangsters," Wilson said. "Something that begins with a T, anyway."

"It would never play," Sal said, firmly. "And nobody would sponsor it."

"Maybe a Chinese laundry?" Wilson said, subsiding.

"Very funny." Sal was not amused. "We've got enough on our plate with Imperial Hotel, we don't need to add Chinamen to the mix."

"Not yet, anyway," Wilson said. "Somebody must wash the sheets and towels at the hotel. Why not a Chinese laundryman?"

"He doesn't give up easily," Sal said to Elodie. "Now, what about this bellboy – what did we call him? Spike?"

Elodie took a surreptitious glance at her watch and thought she would faint from hunger if they didn't stop soon. "I have to meet my friend for lunch."

But Sal shook her head, and rummaged in her huge bag again. "I brought sandwiches," she said. "I hope you like pastrami."

"But Bernice . . ."

Sal leaned over and spoke *sotto voce*. "If Drew leaves this room for lunch we won't see him for the rest of the day."

"Not true," protested Drew.

"Absolutely true." Sal glanced at Elodie. "Tell you what, you go down and meet your friend today, and we'll go on working, all right? But after this..."

"I understand." Elodie rose quickly. She didn't want to upset Sal, and she certainly didn't want Wilson to disappear. Sal had impressed upon her how much work lay ahead, and though he was sarcastic and easily distracted, she had quickly seen that Wilson was a wonderful writer. He 'knew a lot of words'.

She was impatient in the elevator down to the basement staff cafeteria. She couldn't wait to hear what Bernice had to say about Saturday night, and she wanted to tell her all about Sal and Drew. To celebrate her new job, today was to be one of their rare hot meal days. Elodie chose corned beef and cabbage, something they never had at home. She had loved it ever since Hugh had taken her to an Irish speakeasy where they served food in front, and booze in back. Elodie liked beer although she never touched hard liquor, and at this particular speak they had the most amazing black beer, which the proprietor brought in through Canada especially. Nobody else had that beer, which he called 'stout'. She wished she had a glass of it to accompany her lunch, and smiled at the thought of such a thing being served in the ultra-respectable Gower Building Staff Cafeteria. She kept watching the door, expecting Bernice any minute.

But though she ate slowly, and lingered over her dessert and coffee, Bernice never appeared.

7

Archie Deacon was furious.

"Who kept it out of the papers? Who sat on it?"

Captain Brett looked out of the window. "Does it matter?"

"Of course it does. Who's interested in this, all of a sudden? Webster's disappearance got covered – why not his murder?"

Brett turned his chair back and stared at him. "Murder?"

"Of course. It's perfectly clear – that guard shot Webster to shut him up. It was the guard he was afraid of, the sight of him coming with his gun out made him grab that knife – he told Lee 'Look out!', didn't he?"

"We can't be sure what he said," Brett pointed out. "Nobody exactly agreed on anything that happened in those few minutes."

"That girl Elodie Browne was clear."

"She was the only one. Why believe her?"

"Because she's afraid we'll think she was involved," Archie said, surprising himself.

"I wondered about that. You think she is?"

"I don't know for sure. But she was on that floor in the Gower Building when Webster was kidnapped, and there she was again when he was shot. We could make a case, I suppose. But we'd need more evidence."

"You got her statement?"

"Not yet. She was supposed to come down and give it, but she hasn't appeared."

"Find her. Get it. We want this thing wrapped up and put away." Brett looked uncomfortable. "Pressure all the way from New York, because of Miss Hutton's being there. And from the Mayor's office, because of Ryan. And from the Chinese consul, because of Lee. Nobody wants it talked about."

"Or dealt with?"

"Same thing," Brett said.

"I want to talk to that guard again." Archie stood up and went toward the door.

"Can't."

Archie turned and stared at Brett. "Why not?"

"Gone. Chinese consul got a lawyer, sprung him."

"Where's he living?"

"I have no idea," Brett said, looking embarrassed. "There seem to have been some oversights when he was being booked and released."

Archie stared at him. "You mean he's disappeared?"

"Something like that."

"Damn it, Captain, he killed Webster on purpose, I'm sure of it. We have to talk to him again, maybe with an interpreter to get things absolutely straight."

"He was doing his job," Brett said, stubbornly. "Guarding Lee and the stuff in that strong room."

"For three weeks! What if he was put there . . . "

"Who by?"

"How the hell should I know? But he was there at the right minute to shut Webster up."

"Coincidence."

Archie stared at his captain for a long time. "You bastard," he said, quietly.

Brett took the insult with surprising equanimity. "I'm only a captain, Deacon. Go talk to the Commissioner. Go talk to the Mayor. Go talk to whoever you damn well please but leave me out of it." Brett turned his chair back toward the window. "I don't want to know."

**

On her way back from her solitary lunch, Elodie went to Mr. Lee's office, which took up almost all of the far end of the southern corridor. The door marked Reception had no glass in it – it was very solid-looking wood, quite out of keeping with the general style of the building. She tried it, but it was locked. When she knocked, it was some time before it was answered. With much clicking, it finally opened to reveal a small Chinese man in a severe black business suit.

"We closed." He began to shut the door in her face.

"I just want to see Miss Barker," she said, pressing a hand against the motion of the door. Her shoes were too flimsy to risk putting her foot between the door and jamb. "She was supposed to meet me and she didn't."

"Miss Barker not here today." The little man opened the door a bit wider. Elodie realized why the door was kept locked and solid (indeed, there seemed to be some kind of metal sheet embedded in it). Beyond his shoulder, she could see glass-fronted cabinets all around the walls. In them were small statues and bowls and carvings of pale green and translucent cream.

"Is that jade?" Elodie asked, impulsively, pointing.

The man glanced behind him. "You friend of Miss Barker?"

"Yes. My name is Elodie Browne."

He nodded. "She speak of you," he said, surprising her. He glanced over his shoulder again. "Would you like to see?"

"Oh, yes, please," Elodie breathed.

He checked his watch and stepped back. "Only for moment," he said. "We closed today."

"I understand," Elodie nodded. She walked over and slowly moved along in front of the glass cabinets while he relocked the outer door. The objects were even more impressive close up.

The little man came over to stand closely beside her, obviously slightly worried that what he was doing was against his orders. But he was kind enough to answer her questions, seemingly as proud of what Mr. Lee had on display as if it were his own.

"That jade, Han period," he said, indicating a wonderful deep green horse's head, with a graceful curving neck. "And that nephrite, much older." This was a small simply carved beaker in a extraordinary shade of pink.

"Is nephrite the same as jade?"

"All same. Different sources."

The nephrite beaker had a waxy inner glow that made the pale pink seem almost alive, while the surface of the horse's head was shinier. She longed to touch them both. "But they are different colours."

"Jade come in all colours. More colours than man can see," was the confusing answer.

Further along there was a particularly beautiful curved and graceful figure of a woman holding a fan. The figure was white with veins of brown that seemed to have been purposely highlighted by the carving. How could that be?

"Kwan Yin," the man said. "Good luck." He, too, had trouble with the letter 'l' as Mr. Lee had. It wasn't exactly an 'r' as caricaturists would have you believe, but it was a gentle difference she found delightful. She wished he would talk more.

She also was very taken with some crimson beads, heavily carved. "These are beautiful. Red jade?"

The little man almost smiled. "Carnelian," she was told. "Not jade."

"And this?" Elodie pointed to a carved box, also scarlet. "Is that carnelian, too?"

"No. That lacquer box."

Elodie wanted to ask about all the small metal objects, too. That they were of gold or silver was plain, but while some of the shapes were familiar, such as a bird or a dragon, there were others to which she couldn't give a name. There were lots of small highly decorated boxes, some combs, a long line of jade plaques she was told made up a belt, and three amazing vases covered all over with complicated designs, two in simple blue and white, the other highly coloured and gilded. She could have spent hours looking at everything, but she could see the little man was getting impatient. Regretfully she thanked him and went toward the door.

As she did it was suddenly thrown open and the most beautiful and exotic woman Ellie had ever seen stood before them, clearly annoyed.

"Who is this?" she demanded of the old man.

"Friend of Miss Barker. She liked to see the jade."

"Well you should never have let her in." The woman was Chinese, small and exquisite, but dressed in full and expensive Western style. She had glossy black hair that was cut in sharp wings that nearly met, like scimitars, beneath her chin. A tiny hat was tilted over one eye, and she wore a yellow suit of silk brocade. Her shoes and handbag were alligator, and around her slender golden throat she wore a necklace of matched dark green beads that was surely jade.

"You will leave immediately," she told Elodie imperiously. Then she walked straight past and entered an inner office, slamming the door behind her.

Elodie stood shocked for a moment. The old man looked apologetic. "Miss Chou," he said, as if that were sufficient explanation for the woman's bad manners. He obviously did not like Miss Chou. Elodie wondered if anyone did.

She started again toward the door, then stopped. "You speak Chinese, don't you?" she asked in a low voice, and then realised what a stupid question it was. He just nodded.

"Can you tell me what *mingdow* means in English?"

She had seen Caucasian people go pale, but the little man's yellowish skin went absolutely grey, and he drew his breath in between his teeth with a long hiss.

"No," he said. He moved the open door back and forth. "You go now."

She hadn't meant to upset him. How strange, she thought, just one word can do that to someone. What on earth could it mean? Was it some kind of swear word – had she shocked him by saying it? "Will you tell Miss Barker I was asking for her?" she asked.

"I tell her when she come in. Don't know when. Working for Mr. Lee at house today. Maybe more days. You go now," he urged, hurriedly.

"Oh. Well, thank you, very much."

He said no more, and shut the door quickly behind her. She stood there as all the locks clicked shut once more. After a minute she heard him dialling a telephone and then came the sound she remembered so well. The gabble. He was speaking Chinese to someone, and among all of it she heard again the strange word.

Mingdow.

He sounded desperate, frightened, angry.

Mingdow.

Slowly, she turned and headed for the reception area and beyond, to Room 1054, and the imaginary developments of the Imperial Hotel, which now seemed a bit less intriguing than they had before.

**

Mr. Lee Chang hooked the receiver back onto the telephone and stared at it for a moment as he thought. Who on earth was this girl Old Ling was gabbling about and how did she know that word? He looked over at Bernice Barker who was working quietly at a small desk in the corner. "A friend of yours just called at the office," he said, calmly.

Bernice looked up. "Oh?" Her hand went to her mouth. "Oh, dear. That must have been Elodie Browne. I forgot to ring this morning to tell her I couldn't meet her for lunch."

"Ling seemed impressed by her."

"Ling is an old devil," Bernice chuckled. "He likes a pretty face."

Lee Chang looked at her. Her cheeks were a little flushed from embarassment about her friend. It was very becoming. "Is she just a pretty face, then, this Ellie Browne?"

"Oh, no. Ellie is the smartest person I know. You've met her, Mr. Lee. She was one of the girls I brought to serve at the party." The memory of the party darkened her expression slightly. "She was the one with brown hair."

"Ah," said Mr. Lee. "She seemed interested in our jade."

"Ellie is interested in everything – she's a writer, you know." Bernice was gabbling a bit. "Writers have lots of curiosity. She's very clever."

"So." Mr. Lee arose from his desk. "I am going out to the vault, Bernice. Just carry on with those invoices, please."

"Yes, sir." Bernice obediently turned back to her stack of paperwork.

Walking slowly through to the dining room, Mr. Lee approached the glass passage. The new guard, an American with an unpronounceable Polish name, sat at the end of it, outside the vault.

That is how she learned the word, Lee thought to himself. At the party. Webster's words had been so slurred he had hoped nobody had noticed or remembered the word accurately. Obviously this Miss Browne – this very clever and curious Miss Browne – had remembered. That could be very unfortunate.

At the door of the vault he indicated that the guard should admit him and then lock up behind him, and this was done. Once in the room he looked around with pleasure, then scowled as he approached the large table in the centre, on which were stacked many old and battered cardboard boxes. He looked down at them and his left hand curled into a fist.

He was a fool. He should never have taken this chance. What right had he to try to alter the future of China? His beloved China, bright in his childhood memories, was all grace and beauty in his eyes. And he revered more than ever the old culture, now that it was under threat. With the downfall of the Manchu Empire, China had began to change and was changing still.

But to risk his life and the lives of others?

He was an American, now. It was not his concern. But oh, the General was persuasive. Wily, charming, intelligent, and a master salesman. The General had written to him, even come to Chicago the previous year, convincing him it would be easy and simple, without complications. No mention of the dangers. Perhaps the General had not known then what trouble would come.

And now this girl, this curious white girl who was asking questions.

What of Elodie Browne?

He raised his clenched fist and pressed down on the topmost box before him. The thin cardboard split slightly under the pressure. It seemed as if the evil of the original owner had travelled with it, bringing fear and desperation.

The bitter truth was, he could do nothing to protect the girl. He could barely continue protecting himself. If she persisted in asking questions, there was no telling what would happen to her.

Curiosity killed the cat.

But Miss Browne definitely did not have nine lives.

**

Sounds of a busy street.

Announcer: Welcome to the Hotel Imperial, where the rich and famous come to stay. Where the best people receive the best service in all the world – and where there's a story behind every door.

Theme music.

Announcer: Hotel Imperial is brought to you by the Leatherlux Luggage Company. Leatherlux cases are the first choice for people of taste and refinement. Only Leatherlux cases are handmade individually by experienced craftsmen, following classic designs handed down for generations. Ask for Leatherlux when you want to show you know the best.

Sounds of a busy lobby. A desk bell rings.

Dunning: Boy! Take Mrs. VanNoble's luggage up to Suite 560.

Bellboy: Yes, sir. Right away.

Dunning: It's very good to see you again, Mrs. VanNoble, and I hope you enjoy your stay with us. If there's anything you require, you have only to ask. (she is obviously moving away – Pause – then he adds, sotto voce) As long as it isn't for caviar. The delivery is late, again.

Desk bell rings again.

Dunning: Molly, put Mrs. VanNoble's jewelry case into the safe, please. She will send her maid down for what she wants later this evening. And Molly –

Molly: Yes, Mr. Dunning.

Dunning: When you've done that, go down to Chef Alexander and tell him to find out why the shipment from Ganucci's is late.

Molly: I believe there was some kind of accident -

Dunning: That's no concern of ours.

Molly: A mix-up at the wholesalers.

Dunning: Ha! They used that excuse last time.

Molly: Yes, Mr. Dunning. (she sighs, heavily)

**

"Are we sure we want to start out with something like that?" Sal asked, clicking off her stopwatch and putting it onto the table.

"Only as background," Elodie said. "To show some of the troubles a big hotel has. We could make it something else."

"Well, let's move on, we can always change it later." Sal made a note on the script. "It's getting late and I see Mr. Wilson is champing to escape to the nearest speak for a refreshing libation."

"I can stay here as long as you can." Drew did look a little desperate.

Elodie looked at her watch. "Are we going to be much longer?" she asked, diffidently. "I should phone home ..."

Sal looked at her own watch and sighed. "All right, we've made a start. Can you type up the notes you've taken before tomorrow?"

"Yes," Elodie said, slowly. "But ... "

"Maybe she has plans for the evening, Sal – did you ever think of that? Some of us have lives outside of radio," Drew said pointedly.

Sal Schultz looked angry and started to say something, and then apparently thought better of it. "Tomorrow, then. Goodnight, Elodie. Good day's work." She began to stuff things into her huge leather handbag. Elodie stood and retrieved her jacket and hat from the stand in the corner.

"I'll type up the notes at home," she said in a conciliatory voice. She didn't want Sal angry at her, although why she was cross Elodie didn't know.

"Good, good," Sal said absently as she poked around in the bag, making room.

Elodie hesitated a minute, then said "Goodnight," and went out. She was nearly to the elevator when Wilson caught up with her.

"You'll have to forgive Sal," he said. "Once she gets caught up in a project you have to set off an explosive to stop her. You'll get the hang of her soon enough. You just have to be firm."

"She seemed angry."

Wilson shook his head as he pushed the elevator button. "No – she's already thinking about tomorrow. I have the words, you see, but Sal has the focus. She pushes everybody the way she pushes herself. She's a terror, but she knows her stuff. You're lucky to have her on this. I still can't believe she asked for me – I haven't worked on a script for months."

"Is it because you drink too much?" Elodie found herself asking, impulsively. Good heavens, what was wrong with her, she wondered, saying something like that to someone she hardly knew and had to work with.

He grinned, not at all insulted. "Honey, everybody drinks too much these days. I just go along with the crowd. You want to come out for a cocktail or two?"

"No, thanks. I have to get home. But..."

"But no socializing with colleagues? I bet they told you that at the agency, didn't they?"

"Well . . ." She felt herself blushing.

Again, he seemed to take it well. "Good advice," he said, as the elevator doors opened, and he made a sweeping gesture. "Going downhill? Or is it just me?"

As she came out of the revolving door at the main entrance, Elodie saw that in the opposite compartment was Lieutenant Deacon. She lowered her head quickly, but he saw her, and completed the circuit to run after her.

"Miss Browne!"

Reluctantly, Elodie stopped and waited without turning. Then he was beside her, removing his hat. The thick dark red hair gleamed in the light of the streetlamps and passing cars. She had forgotten that he was actually quite good-looking. For a policeman. "I was hoping to catch you. Your mother said you must be working late. She seemed worried."

Elodie looked up at him in horror. "You spoke to my mother?"

"On the phone, yes. We need you to come downtown and sign your statement about Saturday night. We did mention it at the time," he added.

"Oh – I'm sorry, I forgot," Elodie stammered. "I started a new job today and..."

"So your mother said."

They were walking along now, side by side, dodging the few other pedestrians on the sidewalk. "You seem to have had quite a conversation with my mother," Elodie said, not at all pleased.

"Official business. She seems a very nice woman."

"She is." They continued to walk in silence for another half a block, but he didn't seem inclined to leave. "Can it wait until Saturday?" Elodie finally asked.

"Not really. If you like, we can go now, and then I'll arrange for you to be driven home afterward."

"In a police car?" The shame of it! The neighbourhood would be scandalized, to say nothing of her family. Maybelle would never speak to her again.

"No, of course not."

"Oh."

"I did explain this to your mother."

"Doesn't she expect me?"

"No."

"So you decided between you?"

99

"More or less." He took hold of her arm and stopped her. His eyes were very green under the streetlight, she thought. "It really is important. The guard has to be arraigned, you see, and we need all the statements in order for the District Attorney to prepare his case. Everyone else has done theirs without a problem."

"Including Bernice Barker?"

"Why, yes, I believe so. Why?" He seemed puzzled.

"I've been worried about her – I haven't seen her since last Saturday and we were supposed to meet for lunch today."

"I think someone went out to Mr. Lee's house on Sunday and took both their statements and that of various servants."

"Bernice was still there on Sunday?" Elodie was startled.

He grinned. "I believe she went home as you did, but Mr. Lee asked her to come back on Sunday for some urgent work."

"Oh. And today?"

He shrugged. "I have no idea about today."

Elodie considered. "Well, will it take very long, this statement business?"

"About half an hour, that's all."

In the end Elodie agreed rather than stand on the street arguing over it. She was past hunger and was just so tired she wanted to go home and go straight to bed. She'd had no idea writing for radio – even the way Sal and Drew did it – would be so exhausting.

Lt. Deacon led her to a plain sedan which was parked a little way down the street. She got into the back seat and he sat in front with the driver, who was uniformed. Even though the car was unmarked she was sure it looked like she had been arrested for something. She leaned her head against the back of the seat and closed her eyes. A headache was beginning to grow upward from the back of her neck, and the lights of the shops they passed were making it worse. It seemed only minutes before they stopped.

The car door beside her opened and Lt. Deacon bent down to look in. "Are you asleep?" He seemed amused.

"No," Elodie snapped, and got out, a little dazed. Despite the few minutes of rest, the headache was really digging in now.

"This way." He led her up some steps and into a foyer. She looked around her in amazement. She had never been in a police station, had no idea what they looked like. Chaos would have been a good description.

The noise was deafening, people shouting, a woman crying, another singing, two uniformed officers struggling with a very drunk but otherwise respectable looking older man, other officers milling around, talking and laughing. Against one wall a line of chairs contained the most varied collection of people she had ever seen. Girls dressed so outrageously she could only assume they were entertainers or even prostitutes, others in sombre business clothing much like her own. There was one very well-dressed woman who sat upright and appeared outraged at the company she was forced to endure. There were men of every size and shape, truculent, sheepish, sad, defiant, arrogant, beaten. They all turned their heads to stare at her. She felt like crying – did they think she was a criminal, too?

"Not much further," said Lt. Deacon in her ear, and taking her arm moved her gently along and toward some stairs. "Up we go."

"I'm not a child," Elodie said, crossly.

"I realize that, but you're not used to this kind of thing, are you?" His voice was kind, and her tears came closer. She hated him for forcing her down there like this, but on the other hand it would have been easier to bear if he hadn't been nice about it. She wanted to hang onto her irritation – it was a kind of shield.

Upstairs was quiet and orderly, with closed doors to offices and people in the hall who walked quickly and seemed pre-occupied. Many carried papers. None were in uniform. There were even a few women busy at desks. Elodie began to relax.

"Is it always like . . . like it was downstairs?"

He chuckled. "You caught us at a bad moment – there was a raid earlier on a speak. Looks like they took in quite a haul this time." They stopped at an open door and he gestured for her to precede him. Inside there was a very nice motherly looking woman seated behind a desk, typing.

"Evening, Maggie," Deacon said. "This is Miss Browne – we need to take her statement about Saturday night at the Lee house."

"Okay," said Maggie, cheerily. She reached across her desk and picked up a pad and pencil.

Deacon brought a chair over for Elodie and she sank onto it with a long sigh. Maggie looked at her sympathetically, put down her pad and pencil, rummaged in a desk and produced a small bottle of aspirin. "Get her some water," she ordered Deacon. "Can't you see she's exhausted?"

Deacon peered down at Elodie. "She looks fine to me," he said, but he went out to do Maggie's bidding.

"Men," Maggie said, shaking out a couple of white tablets and handing them over to Elodie. "You look like a nice girl, you shouldn't be here. Why on earth didn't he take you to the District Attorney's office?"

"I have no idea," Elodie said. "Maybe it's closed or something."

Maggie gave a derisory snort. "Not likely, these days."

Deacon returned with the water, and Elodie swallowed down the aspirin. She handed back the empty paper cup, and he looked at it in confusion, then tossed it into a wastebasket. Maggie picked up her pad and pencil again. "Shoot," she said.

Elodie looked at Deacon. "Where shall I start?"

"Start with when you got to the house," he suggested. And so she did. It took no more than ten minutes because she merely stated the facts and left out all her feelings. He seemed unsatisfied.

"Are you sure that's everything?" he asked, raising an eyebrow. No winking, now.

"Yes. Everything I can remember," Elodie said.

"Are you certain you don't remember Webster saying more than that?"

She shook her head. She had purposely not said the mysterious Chinese word, partly because Mr. Lee hadn't wanted anyone to say it, but mostly because Deacon had made her come down here the way he had. "Just 'they got me – I got away – look out behind you.' Why, has anyone else said more?" she asked.

"What makes you think that?" he demanded, abruptly.

Elodie shrugged. "What did the others say?"

He was leaning against Maggie's desk, his long legs outstretched, his arms folded across his chest. "It doesn't matter about the others. All I want is what you say," he told her, reprovingly.

The aspirin was beginning to take effect, and she suddenly

102

felt more angry than tired. "Did you make Miss Hutton come down here to this place?" she demanded. "Did you make her walk through all that downstairs, make her feel like a criminal?"

"Is that what you felt like?" he asked, quietly.

"Yes." She wanted to slap his face.

"Interesting," he said. He glanced over his shoulder. "Just type that up so Miss Browne can sign it, Maggie, and we'll be done."

Maggie looked at him in exasperation. "Why did you bring her down here and not to the DA?" she asked. "Are you trying to frighten her or something?"

"No," Deacon said, evenly. "This was closer, that's all. I'm not a monster, Maggie. You know that." He spoke over his shoulder, keeping his eyes on Elodie. She lifted her chin and stared right back.

"You could have fooled me," Maggie muttered to herself as she rolled fresh paper into her machine and began to type. Elodie watched her fingers flying over the keys and wished she could achieve that kind of speed. Even with Maybelle's help, she was still very slow. It had taken her ages to do her essays for college, but typing them pleased the professors, and Maybelle said it was all good practice. It was Maybelle's belief that every woman should be able to take shorthand and type so as to always be able to support herself. She was already trying to teach Alyce.

It only took a few minutes for the statement to be finished. Elodie read it carefully at Deacon's insistance, then signed it at the bottom. "I want to go home, now," she said, wearily.

**

He drove her himself this time. When they went out he took her another way, avoiding the front lobby, and she wondered why he hadn't done that before. The car was a small sedan, unmarked like the other, but she had a feeling it was his own, because there was a St. Christopher medal swinging from the mirror.

"Are you Catholic?" she asked.

His eyes followed hers briefly then returned to the road. "I believe St. Christopher watches over everyone, even sinners. You don't have to go to Mass to qualify." Which wasn't really an answer, she realized, but she had only asked out of idle curiosity. She had been brought up in the faith, but in the past few years it had meant less and less to her. Her sisters were more devout than she, but she wasn't sure about Mumma anymore. Sometimes she recognized a flash of defiance in Mumma's eyes when they returned from church on Sundays. Mumma had been to college, too. In many ways it made believing very difficult, as did the times they lived in.

It was a few minutes before she realized they were not going in the direction of her home. She felt sudden panic. "Where are you taking me? You said you'd take me home."

He kept his eyes on the road. "You missed your dinner. The least I can do is get you something decent to eat."

Trapped, she thought. Trapped like a rat in a trap.

The man was impossible.

And he was much bigger than she was.

8

Archie Deacon took Elodie to a small Chinese restaurant in an area of the city she had never seen. It was very different from the places Hugh had taken her – they had all been sophisticated and fairly pricey as he was on an expense account. This one was small, the tables and floor were rough and unpolished, and it was full of Chinese people, mostly families as far as she could tell. The walls were plain except for a large calendar with a gaudy picture of a dragon.

"If you want the best Chinese food, go where the Chinese themselves eat," Archie said. He seemed easy and familiar with the place, and indeed they were greeted with great friendliness – he was obviously a regular customer.

When they were seated, she challenged him." Why did you bring me here?"

He seemed surprised. "I like it," he said. "I thought you would, too."

"I do, but that isn't the point."

He raised an eyebrow. "What is the point, then?"

"Mr. Lee. The killing. All Chinese."

"And?"

"Well... maybe you thought I would be intimidated by more Chinese things ... " Even as she said it she knew that wasn't exactly what she meant. "I mean, that it would make it more ... " She faltered.

He grinned. "More familiar?"

"I don't know." She didn't want to like him, she was determined not to like him, he was a terrible horrible smart-alecky cop and he had no business treating her to a meal. "I don't know anything about China," she confessed.

"Neither do I, except that I like the food." He shrugged. "I grew up near here, and I like the few Chinese people I've met. I think that's why Brett put me on this case. He heard me talking about Chinese cooking to one of the secretaries once and so now he thinks I'm some kind of oriental expert, but I'm not."

She had to be satisfied with that, because he was obviously not going to say anything more. When the waiter came up, Deacon looked at her. "Do you have any favourites?"

"I've only ever had chop suey," she admitted.

He glanced at the waiter, who rolled his eyes, and Deacon laughed. "Chop suey isn't Chinese at all. It's American. Would you trust me to order for you?"

"Well – I don't want anything ... weird."

"Like what?"

She glanced at the waiter, embarrassed. "You know what people say .... " She lowered her voice. "About dogs and cats."

He laughed aloud, making both Elodie and the waiter jump. "All right," Deacon said. He ordered several things, which the waiter wrote down quickly, bowed, and left them. In a moment he returned carrying a teapot and two small cups, bowed again, and departed for the kitchen.

"Do you speak Chinese?" Elodie asked, in amazement, for she had recognized none of the words Deacon had used to order the food.

"Menu Chinese only," Deacon said, pouring tea into her cup. She assumed it was tea, but it had no colour at all. "This is jasmine tea. Try it."

She picked up the little cup and sipped. It had more taste than she expected, flowery and refreshing. "It's nice."

"Best thing to drink with Chinese food. Except beer – but of course, no beer here."

"Are you sure?" she asked. There was beer everywhere else, or so it seemed these days.

"Would you prefer beer?"

"No! No, not at all, this tea is fine," Elodie assured him. He made her very nervous. And all the Chinese people seemed to be looking at them – they were the only Caucasians in the place. She hoped they could get through the meal quickly – she didn't want to be here at all.

Except something smelled wonderful.

She hoped it wasn't octopus. She'd noticed on Saturday night that Bernice had had something on her tray that Mrs. Logie said was octopus. Elodie had only ever seen an octopus in an Aquarium, and it was definitely not something she wanted to see again – or eat. She shivered involuntarily at the memory of those writhing arms.

"Cold?" Deacon asked.

"No." If anything it was too warm in the little room. "What did you order?" she asked suspiciously.

"Chicken, beef, crab, pork and rice," he told her. "No cats, no dogs."

"All of that?" she said, still wary.

"You'll just have to trust me, won't you?" He drank some of his tea. "Tell me about your new job."

She didn't want to tell him about anything, but after a few false starts, she found herself going on about Sal and Drew. "They pretend to dislike one another," she concluded. "But somehow – it works. I've never worked with other people before. Not like that, anyway. They talk and talk and argue and argue and then some dialogue comes out. I write it down, and then it all starts again. It's very strange."

"Don't you like it?"

She thought about that for a moment, then decided. "Yes, I do. It's exciting. It's... fun."

"Do you like them?"

"I like Sal, she's fine, but she wants to work and work and work. Drew..." She paused. "He doesn't seem to want to be there, but she makes him stay."

"Where does he want to be?"

Elodie smiled. "At a speakeasy. I get the feeling any one would do. But he probably needs the money, like I do."

"Do you?"

"Doesn't everybody?"

"Is that why you took the job at Mr. Lee's?"

She knew it, she knew right from the start that was why he had taken her for a meal, and especially why he had taken her here. He wanted to question her about Saturday night again. Well, he wasn't going to get away with anything. She had almost begun to like him, too.

"Of course. We're all trying to save enough to get my little sister into college," Elodie said, quickly. "I have three sisters, you see, and Mumma is a teacher so she doesn't earn much, and there is the house and clothes and – "

"What are your sister's names?"

"Marie, Maybelle, and Alyce. Alyce is the youngest – she's still in high school."

"Where did the name Elodie come from?"

"It was my grandmother's name." Good, she thought, stick to the family, forget Saturday night.

"My sister's name is Louise," Deacon said.

Elodie was caught off-guard. She hadn't thought of him as having a sister, or family of any kind. He was a policeman, policemen didn't have families, they were just … cops.

"You have a sister?"

"I just said so. And a brother named Mike. My father was a cop, and my mother is a piano teacher."

"Oh." She considered this. "And what's your name?"

The green eyes crinkled at the corners. "It's Archie." He suddenly went a little red across his cheekbones. "Archibald, heaven help me. After my least favourite uncle. The sins of the father..."

She had to laugh. But it suited him.

The waiter arrived with a large tray and proceeded to cover the table with small dishes filled with exotic and quite unrecognizable things. "Oh, my," Elodie said. "All this food."

"The Chinese enjoy small amounts of lots of different flavours. We share it out," Deacon explained, as the waiter gave them each an empty bowl of their own. He also put down two sticks beside the bowls. "Do you know how to use chopsticks?"

"I've never seen them," Elodie admitted. Deacon said something to the waiter, who disappeared and returned with a fork which he laid beside Elodie's bowl with obvious disapproval. When he left, she leaned forward. "He doesn't like me."

"They think forks are barbaric," Deacon said. "Would you like to learn to use the chopsticks?"

"I don't know..."

"Here, let me show you." He proceeded with what seemed like simple instructions, but no matter how hard Elodie tried, most of the food ended up on the table outside her bowl. Deacon sighed. "It takes practice," he conceded. "I understand really skilled users can pick up the yolk of a raw egg without breaking it. Stick to the fork for now or you'll starve to death."

To Elodie's amazement and delight, the food was delicious, full of flavours she had never encountered before. She was a fairly adventurous eater – Marie liked to experiment – but she had never encountered food like this except at Mr. Lee's. And, of course, she hadn't eaten any of that, just served it.

"If you're going to eat late at night, Chinese food is ideal," Deacon told her when most of the bowls between them were empty. "It's light and easy to digest."

Was it late at night? Elodie looked down at her watch. It was almost ten!

"I need to know more about what happened Saturday night," Archie Deacon said, abruptly, again catching her off-guard in her surprise at the hour. She had been lulled by the food and the innocent conversation about families and other topics. Now here it was again, all of a sudden. It wasn't fair.

"I told you everything."

"You didn't, you know. That feeling you had when coming through the downstairs lobby at the station – that you felt like a criminal? That's guilt, Elodie."

"But ..."

"Look." He leaned forward. "Miss Hutton and the other guests are too much Mr. Lee's people, they would never do anything to upset him because they all want something from him. Mr. Ryan is interesting, but he knows very well the less he says the better. About anything. The other girls who were serving there were hopeless, not a brain between them. Even your friend Bernice was useless because she works for Mr. Lee and is loyal to him. But you – you're different than the others. You have an education, you have a brain, and if you're a writer you must be observant. You can help me, Elodie. And I need help. There is more to all this. As complicated as it seems now, there is more behind it. I think you might know what it is."

"But I don't," Elodie protested. "Really, I don't."

Archie Deacon said nothing, just kept looking at her, waiting and waiting and waiting. She suddenly realized he wasn't going to go away. If not here, then somewhere else, he would keep at her until he got what he wanted. She took a deep breath.

"M*ingdow*," she said, in a low voice.

The waiter, who had been clearing the table, gave a start and dropped his tray. Bowls smashed and scattered in all directions and he stared at her in horror, then quickly knelt down, apologising, gathering up the shards of china with shaking hands.

"Wow," Archie Deacon said, eyeing the mess on the floor.

109

"When you know something, you really know something, don't you?" Without saying anything else, he asked the waiter for the bill, paid it, and hurried her out. She could feel the waiter's eyes following them. Once back in the car, Deacon put his keys in the ignition, but didn't start the engine. He turned to face her.

"Explain."

Already sorry she had spoken, she shook her head. "That's it," she said. "Webster said '*mingdow* – got me' – and so on. It was only the one word. Or maybe two words – it was hard to tell, he said it so fast and his mouth was all … I'm not sure it's right, but that's what it sounded like."

"You said it right enough to scare the hell out of the waiter," Archie said. "What does it mean?"

Elodie stared at him. "How on earth should I know?"

"Sorry – just thought you might."

"I'd like to go home, now, please." Elodie spoke stiffly. "There isn't really anything else to say."

He sat in silence for a long while, and she could feel him watching her, but she pressed her lips together, angry at herself for giving in so easily. It wasn't that it was such a big, terrible secret, it was... what? As he started the engine and drove away from the little restaurant, she considered her emotions. All right, she resented being dragged down to the police station and being made to feel like a criminal. She was cross at Lt. Deacon – Archie – because she didn't want to like him and she did, which was of course all his fault. And then, she wanted to talk to her cousin Hugh about it. She frowned slightly. Why did she want to talk to Hugh?

Because she was curious. Because she was intrigued. Because she wanted to find out for herself what it was all about. Good heavens! Involuntarily her hand went to her mouth.

"What's wrong?" Deacon asked, looking at her sideways.

"Nothing. Indigestion." She sat back. What on earth was she thinking? A man had been kidnapped, and then killed. A man who had been very afraid of something, but more afraid for Mr. Lee, and yet was killed by a guard who was trying to protect him. Ah – that was it. That was what had been bothering her ever since Saturday night. She didn't think the guard had been protecting Mr. Lee at all. He had come running down the glass passage with his gun already out before Webster had picked up the knife from the table. And Webster had picked up the knife as soon as he saw the guard coming.

Webster had been afraid of the guard.

Which meant the guard had killed him deliberately.

She opened her mouth to say something, but shut it again. If Deacon saw it, he didn't comment. After a while, she asked about the guard. "Are they going to put him in jail?"

"I have no idea. He was doing his job, but it turns out he wasn't licensed to carry that gun. However, they let him out on bail."

"There are an awful lot of unlicensed guns around this city at the moment," Elodie said, pointedly. "I think even Mr. Ryan was carrying one under his dinner jacket."

"Oh, he was, he was. But, being Arnold Ryan, he had a license for it, all above board."

"Is he really as dangerous as they say?"

"Depends on what you call dangerous. He works for Capone. Capone gives orders, people get killed. Some people excuse that by saying most of the people who get killed deserve it because they are criminals. But sometimes innocent people die, and sometimes law enforcement officers, too."

"The way my cousin tells it, a lot of those so-called enforcement officers are criminals, too." She saw his fingers tighten on the wheel. Good, she was distracting him.

"I admit there is a lot of corruption in the police at the moment. There is a lot of corruption everywhere. But not all of us go along with it, you know."

"People are broke, people are hungry. Desperate people do desperate things. And greedy people do, too," Elodie said. "I think Prohibition is a... poisoned chalice."

He took his eyes from the road for a moment. "Wow. Is that your phrase or this cousin of yours?"

"I'm a writer, I have a way with words," Elodie said, rather primly.

"Your cousin's, then. Who is this cousin who knows so much?"

"His name is Hugh. He's a newspaper reporter."

"Not Hugh Murphy at the *Tribune*?"

She turned to look at him in surprise. "Yes. Do you know him?"

"Yes, I do." Deacon smiled to himself. "Yes, I certainly do."

"What does that mean?"

"It means I like him although a lot of my friends would like to knock his block off."

"Why?"

Deacon kept smiling as he turned into her street. "Because he mostly tells the truth, unusual in a journalist in my experience. That can get a guy enemies in this town, you know."

"Hugh is very brave."

Deacon pulled up to the curb in front of her house, turned off the engine, and turned again to look at her. "And you have a crush on him."

It was her turn to smile. "From about the age of seven."

He leaned across to open her door, putting his face close to hers. His breath smelled of Chinese spices. "Then when you've talked to him about whatever it is you've been thinking all the way home, maybe he'll advise you to tell me, too." He moved back behind the wheel and met her astonished face with grave eyes. "Good night, Miss Browne. Sleep well."

**

Wei Ching wanted very badly to become an American citizen. So much so that he had gambled with his brother for which of them would be the one to make the crossing and earn money to bring the rest of the family over in turn. Wei Ching had won. He knew his brother, who was older, was bitter about being usurped by his younger sibling, but he had managed to be graceful about it. One must always honor gambling debts, after all.

Wei Ching was a very practical person and he knew the streets of America would not be paved with gold. After all, gold is a soft metal and would never withstand the many wheels that would go to and fro on such a great nation's highways. But he had not been prepared for the ugliness of Chicago, nor, to be fair, for the beauty of the Great Lake by which it stood. It was not so much the city that was unattractive, but the people in it. So much greed and grime and trouble, so many terrible men doing terrible things, so unlike the small town from which he had come. And this thing they

112

called The Depression – a word he could hardly get his mouth around – was truly awful for all. He thought he might have been happier in other cities, but he had accepted his fate was to be in Chicago because his uncle's cousin employed him in the family restaurant, and he could quickly begin to save.

Of course, he had not counted on acquiring a wife, but Mei Mei, his cousin's youngest daughter, was a flower and a pearl, so lovely, so sweet, he could not resist. Now responsibility for her and for his family back in China weighed heavily on him. He worked very hard and tried to do all right things. He even changed his name to the more American Walter Way, but found it very hard to remember.

Which was why the girl in the booth troubled him.

She had said the word, the dreaded word they all feared. And she had been with a man that his cousin told him was a policeman. How much did the policeman know? Or the girl? He had laid awake for many hours after work, trying to decide what to do, with Mei Mei sleeping softly beside him.

The girl had looked pleasant, for a white girl, and the man, the policeman, had seemed attracted to her. But family came first, always. Always.

In the end he had left his bed and his sleeping wife and had gone out into the dark streets, to the place all men of sense avoided. It seemed to him that if he passed on this information, which could be valuable, he might keep his Chicago family safe. He would have gained some credit with the dreaded ones, credit that might stand him in good stead at some future time.

He felt sorry for the girl, and for the policeman, but it seemed to him his duty was clear.

Wei Ching was not a bad man.

He had no idea what he was doing.

9

Work on Imperial Hotel went a little more slowly on Tuesday. For a start, Drew was terribly hung over and didn't make much sense until nearly lunchtime. Lying on the couch and occasionally moaning, he made little contribution to the growing outlines and bits of dialogue that Sal and Elodie were amassing.

Neither of Elodie's new partners had smoked much the previous day, but now Sal lit cigarette after cigarette, then let them burn out in the ashtray as she became absorbed. Elodie began to think Sal was addicted to matches more than cigarettes. Drew also smoked, but he smoked each one down as far as possible before stubbing it out. Nobody in the Browne family smoked, except Hugh, and Elodie soon found her eyes smarting from the smoke and the bitter smell of the cigarette butts as they mounted up in the ashtrays. Finally she could stand it no more, and went over to open the window. A sharp cool breeze whistled in, scattering the papers on the table. After a few minutes spent capturing the errant pages and weighing them down, Elodie lowered the window to a few inches. Neither Sal nor Drew protested the influx of April breezes, and when she sat down, Elodie felt a bit better. Everything was compromise, including the scripts.

The way Sal saw it, they had to work out at least six full scripts before they even thought of presenting to the agency and then the client, much less going into production.

"Even if the agency approves, there will be complaints from the client, his lawyer, his mother-in-law and his dog," Sal said.

"Not much different from advertising, then." Elodie was smiling, but she was all too familiar with the 'client's mother-in-law' syndrome. She once had to rewrite a simple advertisement for a really ghastly tasting cough medicine five times, because the client actually said his mother didn't believe what she had written.

"But because we are going to make these the best and most compelling scripts in the whole wide world, at least some of them may be accepted and go into production." Sal was enthusiastic, and her eyes sparkled.

Ellie had never considered what actually went into producing a radio programme, and was embarrassed by her ignorance." What does that mean?"

"Choosing a producer-director, sorting out a studio, casting actors and booking time on the air," said Sal. "There's talk of combining the Red and Blue networks on NBC, but that's all wild blue yonder at the moment. Anyway, that's not our problem. Our problem is what to do about Chef Alexander's disappearance."

"I think he was kidnapped by bootleggers." Elodie shuffled through the papers on the table.

A groan came from the couch opposite. "Why?"

"Ummmm – because he was taking some money from them, of course. Charging the hotel more than they did and pocketing the difference," Sal snapped. "Common practice."

"Is it?" asked Elodie. Her ignorance on the practice of bootlegging was a good match for her ignorance of the nuts and bolts of radio.

A rustle from the couch across the room. Drew was staring at her. "Where exactly is it you live, Ellie? Cloud cuckoo land?"

"Very funny." Elodie felt herself blushing. "Not everybody is involved with the bootleggers and drunks in this city. Why should I bother to know anything about them except that they are criminal scum."

"Don't talk about my mother that way." Drew turned his head away again and closed his eyes.

"Sorry." Elodie had forgotten his mother supposedly ran a blind pig in their basement. "I might know that world exists, but I don't have to experience it myself."

"Then how are you going to write about it?" He was obviously feeling better, because he was fighting back.

"I don't have to set fire myself to know that it hurts," Elodie pointed out. "I just have to extrapolate from the pain of a burning match."

Drew snorted. "College vocabulary. Very impressive."

"Shut up, you two," Sal intervened. "Chef Alexander, remember?"

Bellboy: It's them Syndicate people, I tell ya. I saw 'em, big guys in black overcoats, with gats and everything.

Dunning: You've been reading too many comic books, Spike. I am sure Chef Alexander is just at home, too ill to send us a message.

Bellboy: Uh-uh. He's gone, he's history. Who knows, you might be next!

Molly: (bursts into tears) Spike! What a terrible thing to say!

Bellboy: (reluctantly) Well, he don't believe me. But I was there. I saw it all.

Dunning: Then why didn't you do something?

Bellboy: Are you kidding? Me?

Dunning: You could have told me.

Bellboy: Well, I'm telling you now. We have to do something before they fit him with cement galoshes –

Molly: (crying harder) Poor Chef.

Dunning: I'm going to the police. If this boy is right -

Bellboy: I'm right, all right.

Dunning: Then the hotel could be in danger, too.

Molly: (shocked) Don't you care about Chef?

Dunning: I can always get another chef, but I can't build another hotel. Haven't you ever heard of arson?

*

"Over the top," protested Drew. "Too much, too soon. And where's your hero? Dunning sounds like a pompous ass."

"You're right." Elodie reluctantly agreed. "We want people to like Dunning, even if he seems sort of starchy at first. I mean, Molly's in love with him, isn't she?"

"It worked for Mr. Rochester," Sal observed.

They thought about that for a moment, and then Drew sat up. " What time is it?"

"Lunchtime," said Sal. "What will it be, salami or egg salad?"

Drew groaned again. "Just a little milk toast, please."

Elodie stifled a giggle. "I remembered to bring sandwiches, too," she said. "I won't be lunching with my friend for a while, anyway."

"Why not?" asked Sal. "Aside from the fact that we can't spare the time?"

"Well, she's not working in the building at the moment," Elodie explained. "She's working out at Mr. Lee's."

Sal selected a sandwich and then rose to get some coffee. She found the pot empty. "Wilson! Water!"

"Get it yourself," was the snarled reply.

Sal stood her ground. "You want coffee, you get water."

Drew unfolded himself slowly from the couch and took the empty pot from Sal. "Dragon," he said.

"Boozehound," was the retort. As Drew went out sulkily carrying the empty percolator, Sal came back to sit beside Elodie. "So how's that all going?" she asked. "That stuff at the Chinaman's place?"

"I had to make a statement and sign it, yesterday." Elodie opened her own brown bag and looked to see what Marie had given her. "I hate that policeman."

"What policeman?" Sal was immediately intrigued by Elodie's intensity.

"Lieutenant Archibald Deacon," Elodie spit out. "He thinks he's so smart, he thinks he's some kind of mind-reader. And he made me eat dinner with him, too."

"Did he pay for it?" Sal was amused.

"Yes."

"Well, then, I'd say you were ahead on the deal. Wish somebody would buy me a dinner. Even a cop."

"Not this one, you wouldn't. He seems all nice, all so very pleasant, and then bang! He pounces."

"You mean he made a pass at you?"

"No, no, of course not. I meant...well..." Elodie muttered to herself.

"What?" Sal leaned forward.

"I said I don't know what I mean," Elodie repeated, miserably. "He's got me all mixed up." She opened the wax paper and found Marie had given her tomato sandwiches. And cheese.

"I don't see what you're mixed up about," Sal said, reasonably. "What's done is done, isn't it? I mean, seeing a man get killed is nasty, I agree, but once you've made your statement, that's the end of it. Even if they take that guard to court, he'll probably get off because he was just doing what he was paid to do – protect his employer."

"But he wasn't!" Elodie burst out.

"Wasn't what?" asked Drew, returning with the filled coffee pot which he thrust at Sal and then returned to his couch, lying down with a grunt.

"Wasn't protecting his employer," Elodie explained. "He killed Mr. Webster on purpose, I'm sure of it."

"Why the devil would he do that?" asked Sal as she fitted the percolator together and spooned in the coffee grounds. "He didn't even know the man, did he?"

"Well, that's just it. Maybe he did. I bet he was part of it."

"Part of what?"

"Part of the kidnapping gang that took Mr. Webster. I think Mr. Webster recognized him, and the guard shot him before Webster could say anything."

"Wow," breathed Sal.

"You think I'm right?" Elodie was encouraged.

"No – but I think we could use something like that in the script," Sal said, with enthusiasm, reaching for her pencil.

**

Before Elodie left the Gower Building that night, she took the elevator up to the fifteenth floor and used an agency telephone to ring the *Tribune*. It was just a chance, but to her relief, Hugh was still at his desk.

"It's Elodie," she said. "I need to talk to you."

"Fed up with the new job already?" Hugh sounded in a good mood.

"No, not at all. This is about Saturday night." When he did not say anything, she was puzzled. "You know about Saturday night, don't you?"

"I know a lot of things about Saturday night," Hugh said, cautiously. "Could you be more specific?"

"I need to talk to you," Elodie said again.

"Well, I'll be over for dinner on Friday night, as usual. Can't it wait?"

"No, I need to talk to you now."

Another silence. "Are you in some kind of trouble, Ellie?"

"Yes. No. I don't know."

"Are you alone?"

She frowned and looked around. There were a few people still in the office, but nobody was near her. "Yes, why?"

"Just checking. Look, can you meet me in about half an hour?"

"Oh, thanks, Hugh. It really is important."

"It better be, I have a date tonight with a new girl."

"Where should I meet you?"

They agreed on a nearby deli, and Elodie put the phone down with relief. Hugh would know what to do. Hugh always knew best.

**

"Are you nuts?" Hugh demanded, an hour later. "Forget it, leave it to the police." The delicatessen was busy with both shoppers and early diners, but Hugh's shocked voice cut through the clatter of plates, the hiss of the coffee urn and the surrounding conversations like a knife. Several people turned to look at them. Elodie lowered her voice and leant forward, nearly dipping her coat lapel into her steaming coffee cup. "But I'm sure there's some connection. I'm certain that guard meant to kill Webster before he could say anymore about mingdow."

"Are you sure that's what Webster said?" Hugh leaned back as the waiter refilled his coffee cup. He was edgy, obviously in a hurry, and had swallowed his first cup of coffee almost in a gulp. But he could see that Elodie was upset, so he was torn between listening to her and being late for his date.

Elodie thought back to Saturday night. "Positive. That is . . ."

"Well?"

"Well, it's obviously some Chinese word or other. I told you about the man in Mr. Lee's office and the waiter. It scared them, so it must be something terrible."

"Probably just some kind of Chinese swearing," Hugh said, picking up the glass dispenser and stirring sugar into his coffee. "They were probably shocked that a nice girl like you knew such words, that's all."

"Oh." She had never considered that. "No," she said after a minute. "It is something or someone, I'm sure."

"You said Arnold Ryan was there. Did he show any reaction to what Webster said?"

"No more than any of us," Elodie admitted. "Why, do you think mingdow is Chinese for the Syndicates?"

"Could be. It's a new one on me, but why not? Maybe if the guard hadn't shot Webster Mr. Ryan would have."

Elodie thought about that for a while. "But the guard was Chinese, too."

"So what?"

Elodie shook her head. "It's not Them," she said. "It's something Chinese, something about China. Something that involves Mr. Lee, otherwise why would Webster have come running to him?"

"Oh, great," Hugh said. "Do you know anything about China?"

"No."

"Neither do I." Hugh thought for a minute. "Did Mr. Lee have booze at the party?"

"Well, of course. And the real thing, too. I saw the labels. Wine from France and the liquor had British names, most of it."

"That means he has a private bootlegger, probably in Canada. And if he does, then he might have made Mr. Ryan's people angry at him and they took Webster as a warning that he should do business with them. Nothing to do with China at all, strictly local."

"Do you really think so?"

"Let's just say I'd rather think that than try to figure out some weird Chinese mystery," Hugh said, glancing at his watch and drinking up the last of his coffee. "Honey, I have to go, I told you, I have a date."

Elodie was disappointed but tried not to show it. She had been counting on Hugh to come up with answers and all he had come up with was more questions. "Somebody new?"

Hugh grinned. "Yeah. Her name is Collette, and she's a real dazzler. This might just be The One."

"Oh. That's nice."

He stood up and took his hat from the stand, then came back to look down at her. "If you are really worried about this, go back to Lieutenant Deacon."

"He said you'd say that."

"Well, I do say it. He's all right. Not like a lot of them. He's straight."

"He thinks he's so smart, I could kick him," she grumbled.

"He is smart," Hugh said. "And he knows people who know things. Maybe he knows someone who can tell him what mingdow means. And if you're so sure there is more to the shooting of Webster, you ought to tell him before the guard goes to trial, if he does. He's the man to look into it. Not you." He reached out and squeezed her shoulder. "Someone got kidnapped, someone got killed, Ellie. It's not something you should get involved in. You have this new job and you should give it everything you've got. You don't need silly distractions. You always did have too much imagination, you know."

"You think I'm being foolish," Elodie flared.

"I didn't say that. But you do have a gift for the dramatic, otherwise you wouldn't have gone into this radio writing stuff. Leave it alone, Ellie. Stick to your Imperial Hotel and let Deacon and the police take care of the rest of it. You know I'm right." He squeezed her shoulder again. "You don't want your mother to have to identify your body on a slab, do you?" he added, gruffly.

She was shocked. "That's a terrible thing to say."

"I know. I meant it to be," Hugh said. He reached into his pocket and gave her some money. "Here, take a taxi home, it's late."

"I don't want – "

"Maybe you don't, but I do," said Hugh. "Somebody has to look after you, idiot." He leaned down and winked. "Just in case the big bad *mingdow* is following you," he teased. With a quick wave, he left her and went out into the evening.

Elodie looked at her watch – dinner at home would be finished by now. When the waiter came over to clear their table, she ordered some beef and barley soup and a corned beef sandwich. It meant she would have to take the streetcar instead of a taxi, but it was worth it. Hugh wouldn't mind. He was probably right, she was just letting her imagination get away from her. It was all this writing about Imperial Hotel – she was seeing plots and mysteries everywhere. Her imagination had gotten her into trouble before, but not for a long time.

121

Her teenage years had been filled with mysteries that didn't exist and games that weren't being played. Two years of college had knocked most of that out of her, and the tough realities of working in advertising had pretty much eradicated it. Or so she had thought.

But Imperial Hotel had come out of her imagination and it was good. It was wonderful. And Hugh was right, it should be enough for her.

As it was late the trollies were less frequent and she had to wait quite a while and transfer twice. She was walking wearily up the front path when someone stepped out of the shadows behind the lilac bush, making her jump back in alarm.

It was Bernice.

"Ellie! I've been waiting and waiting," Bernice said, in a strangled whisper. In the light from the streetlamps Elodie could see she was wearing a dark blue coat and a matching cloche hat pulled well down over her ears, totally covering her red curls. Her face was very pale beneath its brim.

"Well, why on earth didn't you ring the bell and go inside to wait?" Ellie asked, startled. "Are you all right?"

"No, I'm not." Bernice glanced around, nervously. "I'm scared."

"Why?" Involuntarily, Ellie looked around, too. Nothing seemed out of place. Windows were lit in the surrounding houses, there was music playing on someone's radio – probably theirs – and she could hear cars passing on the main road a block away. A light breeze ruffled the budding branches overhead, and somewhere in the distance a dog barked. There was a haze around the moon – rain coming.

Bernice reached out and grabbed Elodie's arm, her fingers digging in through the fabric of her jacket. "Somebody is trying to kill Mr. Lee," she said dramatically. "Somebody put poison in his food this morning. He got very sick, we had to call the doctor, and the doctor said it was poison and we should call the police, but Mr. Lee wouldn't let us. Mrs. Logie was very upset..."

Elodie was horrified. She had liked the fat Chinaman. "Is Mr. Lee all right?"

"No. Yes – he's feeling better now. The doctor gave him something and he was throwing up all afternoon, poor man. When I left Mrs. Logie was looking after him. I think she's scared, too."

"But why should someone want to kill Mr. Lee?"

"Because of Suzy's jade. They want it back. I think they'll do anything to get it. Anything." She drew a ragged breath, her hand clutching Elodie even more painfully. "What should I do? I don't know what to do."

Elodie did.

10

Elodie took Bernice inside, led her to the kitchen, and quickly made some hot chocolate. One by one the other members of the Browne family appeared. Alyce had been in bed, asleep. Her eyes were a little teary from the sudden bright light of the kitchen, but she would not be left out of any excitement that might be on offer. The others had been upstairs getting ready for bed. Maybelle had her hair wound so tight in metal curlers they pulled back the skin around her eyes. It looked painful. Marie and Mrs. Browne both had their long hair in a braid down their backs. Everyone was wearing the matching bathrobes Marie had made them from a bargain bolt of flannel cloth she had found somewhere. They stood around the kitchen table looking like a gathering of some strange religious cult dedicated to wearing plaid.

"What's wrong?" Mrs. Browne demanded, viewing Bernice's chattering teeth and white face. "Are you all right, Bernice?"

"She's had a bad day," Elodie explained. "Mr. Lee was poisoned."

There were gasps all around.

"She thinks he was," Elodie amended. "It could have been just a bad bit of octopus or something."

"Octopus?" said Marie, amazed.

"No, the doctor said it was poison." Bernice managed to get the words out from between her trembling lips. She accepted the cup of hot chocolate Elodie gave her and sipped gratefully. "We all ate the same thing, but only Mr. Lee got sick." She sipped again. "He wanted to call the police."

"Mr. Lee?" Alyce asked, eagerly.

Bernice shook her head. "The doctor. He said he was obligated to notify someone, but Mr. Lee talked him out of it. I think he paid him not to say anything."

"Typical," said Maybelle, pulling out a chair and settling down to listen. The others followed suit, except for Marie, who went over to wash out the pan Elodie had used to make the hot chocolate for Bernice.

Bernice shrugged but didn't deny the bribe. Apparently Maybelle was right – money seemed to buy anything these days, Elodie thought. "Now, let's get this straight." She reached over and put her hand on Bernice's sleeve. "Who is Suzy?"

"I don't know," Bernice wailed. "But she sure is causing a lot of trouble for Mr. Lee." She looked around at their concerned faces. "Mr. Webster got it for him, you see."

"Got what for him?" Alyce asked.

"Suzy's jade," Bernice said, a little impatiently. "That's what he was going to show Miss Hutton and the others. It's worth a fortune."

"All right." Elodie kept voice steady. "And who wants it back?"

"I don't know," Bernice said.

"Did you ask Mr. Lee?"

"I'm only a secretary." Bernice seemed a little shocked at the thought. "I can't ask him things like that. I only know it's somebody."

"Mindow?" asked Elodie.

Bernice looked at her with wide eyes. "That's what Mr. Webster said, isn't it? The word Mr. Lee didn't want us to repeat."

"Yes. What does it mean?"

"I have no idea," Bernice said. "I don't speak Chinese."

"Are you sure it's Chinese?" asked Mrs. Browne.

Elodie and Bernice looked at one another. "What else could it be?" Elodie asked.

"I have no idea," said Mrs. Browne, echoing Bernice. "But without seeing it actually written down, it could be anything. Some kind of code, perhaps? Hearing a language is one thing, seeing it written down is quite another. It could be Russian or Eskimo for all we know."

"I think it is Chinese," Elodie said. "It frightened the Chinese waiter half to death."

"What Chinese waiter?" they all chorused. For Elodie had arrived home too late the night before to tell them about her 'date' with Lt. Deacon, and they had all left too quickly that morning to discuss it.

125

So Elodie had to explain about giving the statement and being taken to the funny little Chinese restaurant. "He only took me there to intimidate me. As soon as I sort of relaxed, he started questioning me again about Saturday night. I mean, I had already given my statement, but he didn't seem to believe me. He just kept asking and asking."

"He sounded very nice on the phone," said Mrs. Browne.

"Is he handsome?" demanded Alyce, ever the romantic.

"Did he make a pass?" asked Maybelle, ever the cynic.

"What did you have to eat?" asked Marie, ever the cook.

"No, yes, I have no idea," Elodie said to each in turn.

"Is he old and horrible?" Alyce persisted. "Why did you go out with him if he isn't handsome?"

"He's not bad looking at all," Bernice put in. She looked at Elodie. "If he's the one who came to Mr. Lee's house on Saturday."

"He is," Elodie said.

"You don't like him." Maybelle looked at her wisely.

"He's very pushy." Elodie looked toward the window at the end of the kitchen where they were reflected against the dark glass. They looked like some kind of bizarre jury, sat all around the table. The kitchen was normally her favourite room in the house, with its cheery red and white linoleum and the shining pans and shelves of dishes on the wall. Now it was eerie in the overhead light, and all their faces looked strangely shadowed. Marie must have been baking after dinner, for the stove was still giving off heat. She was surprised to see she still had her coat on, and began to shrug out of it.

"He winked at her on Saturday night," Bernice announced. "I saw him. He never winked at me." She sounded a little jealous.

"Oh, for goodness' sake." Elodie was exasperated. "Why are we talking about him all of a sudden?"

"Because he winked at you." Alyce was loving this – she rarely got a chance to see any of her older sisters embarrassed, especially Elodie.

"Because he makes you cross." Maybelle reached over to help her sister off with her coat. "That's a bad sign, Ellie. I think you like him more than you know."

"He sounded so nice on the telephone," Mrs. Browne said again, rather dreamily. "He really did."

126

Elodie stood up. "I think Bernice should stay here tonight," she said, firmly. "She's tired and scared."

"Of what?" Alyce wanted to know. "That word you said, that Chinese word?"

"Maybe." Elodie gathered up her coat and reached for Bernice's as well. It was very warm in the kitchen, and Bernice's previously pale face was now quite pink and there was a line of perspiration on her upper lip.

"I think you should call Lt. Deacon," Mrs. Browne said.

"No, thank you." Elodie added her own hat to Bernice's and went toward the kitchen door to hang them up in the sitting room closet.

"But Ellie..." came the family chorus again.

"Maybe in the morning." Elodie spoke over her shoulder, pushing against the kitchen door.

"Mr. Lee won't like that," Bernice protested. "I thought I could trust you, Ellie. I could lose my job if you tell the police about this."

"Why did you come to me, then?" Elodie turned and looked at her friend, a little annoyed. She was tired, and all this teasing about Archie Deacon was not sitting well with her.

Bernice's eyes filled with tears. "Because I didn't know who else to tell," she said. "And you're so clever, I thought you could tell me what the best thing to do is. But not the police."

"Oh, dear," said Mrs. Browne, looking at Elodie in despair. She always wanted her daughters to do the right thing, but what was right in this situation? Why had all this come into their lives? Not for the first time she wished her husband was still alive. She could deal with most things, but all this about Chinamen and jade, murders and policemen was beyond her. She wanted to blame Bernice, but the girl's evident distress brought out her protective instincts. And why was Elodie behaving like this? She used to be so compliant, but ever since she had been working in advertising, she had changed. And now this radio business. Mrs. Browne didn't want things to change – life was difficult enough as it was. She knew her girls had to grow up and away from her, but did it have to happen like this?

"We'll sleep on it." Elodie was decisive – she wanted all this talk to stop, now. "We're all too tired to think straight right now, especially you, Bernice. Call your mother and tell her

127

where you are, and then we're going to sleep. We can decide what to do at breakfast."

"Not the police." Bernice was very stubborn.

"We'll see," Elodie said, and went through into the dining room carrying the coats and hats before anybody could say anything else.

But later, as they were undressing for bed, Bernice again pleaded with Elodie not to go to the police. "If Mr. Lee paid the doctor not to tell, it must be really important for the police not to know. You remember he didn't want any of us to tell the police about mingpow or whatever it was on Saturday night."

"Yes, I wondered about that." Elodie handed Bernice one of her old nightgowns. It was white cotton, with long sleeves, and she could see from Bernice's expression it was probably not like the glamorous things she normally wore to bed. Nor was her bed likely to be like Elodie's battered old oak one. "Mr. Lee didn't actually say anything specific, but everybody there seemed to know automatically that they weren't supposed to repeat that word. It was like they read his mind."

"Maybe they knew what it meant," Bernice said. "Maybe they were too scared to say it."

"Mr. Webster said it," Elodie pointed out as she got under the covers.

"Yes, but he was warning Mr. Lee..."

"Listen, about the guard shooting Mr. Webster."

"What about it?"

"Had he worked for Mr. Lee for a long time?"

"No." Bernice seemed rather surprised by the question, and as she spoke it was clear she hadn't considered it before. She sat down and began to unroll her stockings. "He had only been hired a few weeks back. Normally the treasure house is kept locked but not with a guard. Come to think of it, he came after Suzy's jade arrived. And because of the party, I guess, and all the extra people being around."

"So that – what did you call it – that building at the back?"

"Mr. Lee's treasure house? That's what I call it, anyway. He just calls it the vault." Bernice straightened out her stockings and hung them over the back of the chair where she was putting the rest of her clothes. She put her shoes neatly underneath. Bernice was a very tidy girl.

"Well, isn't it normally guarded?" Ellie asked as Bernice

128

climbed into bed.

Bernice shook her head against the pillow. "No – it has all kinds of locks and alarms at both ends of the glass passage, and that glass is special, too. It's really very modern – he had it built especially by some people from New York, I think. It was already there when I started working for him."

"Have you ever been inside?"

"Oh, yes. Lots of times."

"And?"

"And what?"

"Well, what's it like in there?"

"Full of junk." Bernice was dismissive.

"What do you mean, 'junk'?"

"Well, all that Chinese stuff – jade and embroideries and so on. Statues, some painted altar things, stuff like that. It's all in glass cases, like at the office, but more . . . "

"More what?"

"More locked up," Bernice said. "I guess it's worth a lot of money but for me you could just throw it all in the Lake. It's so fussy and strange. Not like his house."

"His house is very modern."

"Exactly." Bernice gave a little bounce and the mattress creaked. "I like his house, except maybe for those paintings on the walls. But at least they're modern, not ancient and old and horrible. You should see some of the faces on those statues..."

"I thought the jade at the office was beautiful."

"I was surprised Ling let you in. He's a pain in the neck. Thinks he's the big expert on everything." Bernice dropped back down and stared up at the ceiling.

"What does he do for Mr. Lee? Is he a guard or some-thing?"

Bernice laughed. "No. He's just sort of an office boy. He's always running errands for Mr. Lee. He's in and out all the time. When he isn't running errands he just sits in the corner and reads Chinese books or stares at the secretaries."

"How many secretaries does Mr. Lee have?" Elodie was full of questions.

"Three," Bernice said. "I'm the most important, because I work for Mr. Lee himself. Maisie does bills and office stuff like ordering stationary."

"What if Mr. Lee wants to write a letter in Chinese?" Elodie asked.

Bernice sounded sulky. "The other secretary does that, a little snip named Helen Chou. She's American Chinese, she thinks she's so smart because she talks to Mr. Lee in Chinese all the time. I think she tells him lies about us . . . "

"She came in while I was there. She was very rude. And very pretty."

"And doesn't she know it? I told you, she speaks in Chinese to Mr. Lee. Lord knows what she's saying. I don't know why Mr. Lee puts up with her, sometimes you would think she was the boss, not him."

"So she takes care of all Mr. Lee's Chinese business?"

"More or less. I deal with all the American museums and collectors and stuff. You wouldn't believe what some people will pay for that junk." Bernice obviously didn't believe it herself. "In these days, when poor people are hungry, the rich spend thousands on a little piece of green stone. It's disgusting."

"Then why don't you work for someone else if it upsets you so much?"

Bernice turned her head away. "Because I like Mr. Lee and he pays me really well. And I don't want to talk about it any more. Good night."

"Good night," Elodie said. She fell asleep wondering if Helen Chou knew about Suzy's jade, where it came from, and who wanted it so badly they were prepared to kill to get it.

She dreamt that Lt. Deacon, dressed as a Chinaman, was staying at Imperial Hotel and flirting with Molly the hotel receptionist. It was all very confusing.

**

The next morning, Bernice had made up her mind. "Forget it," she said, briskly, pushing her empty breakfast plate away. "Just forget it. I was spooked, that's all."

"But Bernice – "

"No. Really, Ellie. I rang Mr. Lee this morning before you came down and he's fine, absolutely fine. He's sending his car for me, it should be here any minute." The others had left for school and work, and Marie was again busy at the sink, washing up their breakfast things. She turned and exchanged a glance with Elodie. This was an entirely different Bernice from the night before. She seemed cold and distant, and much more in control of herself.

"Are you sure you're being wise going back there?" asked Marie.

"It's Mr. Lee who's in danger, not me. If I'm there, maybe I can look after him. And I'm going to suggest that he gets some guards to patrol the grounds."

"How about an official taster?" Elodie spoke with some irony. Bernice just looked stubborn.

"That's silly. Anyway, Mrs. Logie will be looking after his food from now on, and she's okay."

"Are you sure?"

"She's been with him for years." Bernice stood up and pulled on her hat. It was covered all over in little felt flowers and there was a red silk ribbon around the brim. Another new outfit, then. No wonder Bernice stayed with Mr. Lee if he paid her enough to buy clothes like this. "If Mrs. Logie wanted to kill him she's had plenty of time to do it."

"What I don't understand is why killing Mr. Lee would make any difference," Elodie said. "These people only kidnapped Mr. Webster, it was that guard who killed him."

"Maybe they only wanted to scare Mr. Lee," Marie said.

"But why?" Elodie was puzzled.

"Because of his sons, I suppose," Bernice said.

"Mr. Lee is married?"

"He was. She's dead, but they had three sons. The first two are doctors in New York. Maybe she died giving birth to the last one – he's only about twenty. He's in China, now." Bernice's mouth twisted. "He thinks he's so wonderful, like some little prince or something. If Mr. Lee died, he'd have to come back and take over the business, and that would be a disaster. He's not at all like his father, believe me. He's a Communist, and he hates Mr. Lee because Mr. Lee has all this money. I wouldn't trust him as far as I could throw a sofa."

"What's the son's name?" asked Marie.

"Harold. Harry. I only met him a couple of times, but that was enough." Bernice was buttoning her jacket. "He was a spoiled twerp. He thought he was great, but he would never have the nerve to do anything like that."

"Maybe he's changed his spots."

Bernice laughed aloud. "That's funny."

"Why?"

"Spots," Bernice said. "Harry had terrible acne."

"I meant he might have – "

"I know what you meant," Bernice snapped. "It just struck me funny, that's all. Listen, if Harry Lee inherited any of his father's property he'd just sell it off as fast as possible, and that would kill Mr. Lee." She paused to consider what she had said. "Well, you know what I mean. Mr. Lee loves all that junk of his, really hates selling any of it. He tries to tell me all about it, but with all the Hans, Tangs, Chins and Changs, I can't understand a word of it. I do like the gold, though," she added. "The gold is okay." She looked at her watch. "The car must be here by now. I'll just go look." She went out of the room toward the front of the house.

Marie wiped her hands on her apron. "That is a very strange girl," she said. "Last night she was terrified, this morning she's as cold as ice."

"She likes the gold," Elodie said, wryly. "I gather Mr. Lee pays well."

"Is that it?" Marie seemed unconvinced. "You know, she came downstairs during the night and made a phone call."

"She did?" Elodie was astonished.

Marie nodded. "I heard her go down the stairs, and I heard her dialling the phone. Couldn't hear what she said, though – she was whispering."

Bernice stuck her head through the kitchen door. "The car's here. Thanks for letting me stay last night, Ellie. And just forget all that stuff I said. I was being silly. And thanks for that swell breakfast, Marie. 'Bye." With a wave of her hand, she was gone before Elodie could ask her about the phone call in the night.

"Curiouser and curiouser," she murmured to herself, then looked at Marie. "What do you think about all this?"

"I think two things," Marie said, opening the ice box to put away the bacon and butter. "That it's dangerous, and absolutely nothing to do with you."

"But she came to me for help," Elodie protested.

Marie opened up the top section of the ice box and checked the status of the ice block within. She seemed satisfied and slammed it shut, turning to lean against it. Her face was very serious. "You heard her, forget it. She's right, Ellie. Let it go."

But try as she might, Elodie could not.

11

Deacon had instituted a search for the elusive guard, but he was nowhere to be found. He thought someone in Chinatown must be hiding him, but breaking into their closed society was as tough as breaking into the Syndicates. Perhaps even more difficult, for the Chinese were naturally secretive and couldn't be bought. Knowing about Chinese food was not enough to understand the Chinese themselves, despite what Captain Brett thought. The other alternative was that the guard had been smuggled out of Chicago, the consul willing to forfeit his bail for the sake of secrecy. Or guilt.

He had no better luck locating the guard's Tong mentor, Chi'en Pu Yi. He went to the office of the Milton Street Tong, which was over a Chinese grocery, but could find nobody of that name, or indeed anybody who would admit to knowing anyone of that name. Perhaps the guard had made it up – so easy with Chinese names, all of which sounded the same to Western ears. He walked around the streets of Chinatown, hoping to catch a chance sighting of the guard, but to no avail. He had thought he had contacts in the community, but he quickly discovered that his nodding acquaintance with various Chinese families would be useless.

Indeed, there seemed to be a closing of ranks. All smiles, of course, all friendliness on the surface. But any mention of the odd word Elodie Browne had given him proved as disturbing as it had been to the hapless waiter in the restaurant. The usual reaction was almost like fear, followed by a very speedy profession of complete ignorance. Several insisted it wasn't even a Chinese word. The police had always pretty much left Chinatown to police its own, which it seemed to do with efficiency. Archie remembered hearing some very odd rumours now and again about unpleasant crimes in Chinatown, but nothing was ever reported officially. City policy, he supposed, not to get involved in what they could never understand in a thousand years.

He had even less luck trying to interview Mr. Lee Chang himself. Everytime he rang the Lee house, he was offered various apologies and reasons – meetings, illness, out of town on business, and so on. But he was pretty sure Lee was at home, just lying low. The men watching the house reported that the secretary, Bernice Barker, was going there every day. Other people came and went, but after the first couple of days there was no longer any excuse to demand their names or business. The Webster case was officially closed and the police had withdrawn completely from the mansion. Archie Deacon had been warned off making any further enquiries.

It was very puzzling.

Several times he had reached for the phone to talk to Elodie Browne, but stopped because he had to honestly question his motives. Was it because of the case, or because he was attracted to her? He had no idea whether she had told him everything, even now, and she could well be an accomplished liar who was up to her neck in it – although he doubted that. His instinct said she was a good and decent girl. His worry was that she seemed as fascinated by the puzzle as he was. She could cause trouble, she could get into trouble. God save us from the enthusiastic amateur, he thought.

He had little time to worry about it further. There had been a sudden rise in the homicide rate because of some fresh rivalry between the bootleggers. Ever since the St. Valentine's Day Massacre in '29 there had been intense internicine conflict between the various gangs, especially between Bugs Moran and Capone. Deacon and the other detectives were getting run off their feet in investigations as fruitless as the officially closed one into Webster's death.

Fear and greed ran Chicago now. And from Mayor Big Bill Thompson on down, there was no knowing whose toes you were stepping on, whose ego you were battering, whose bank balances were rising despite the Depression, because behind any smiling face could lurk a Connection.

Sometimes he lay in bed at night and thought about shooting Capone himself. This futile but fascinating challenge often sent him to sleep, wound up in complicated plans for ambushes and methods. And wasn't that a sign of his own corruption?

He didn't know who to trust in the Department anymore,

either. Brett was obviously compromised by his ambition and pressures from above. Other detectives seemed to be more and more affluent, judging from their shoes, their cigars, and their habits. His own partner had been shot the previous year, and so far he hadn't found anyone he could work with or confide in.

Nobody was safe anymore. Killing Capone was no answer, Archie knew that. His syndicate was too well organised not to survive his death.

But whether Deacon was in Cicero, Pilsen, the Loop or Lakeshore Drive, his mind kept on niggling about Webster, Lee, the missing guard, and that damned word.

Mingdow.

If it wasn't Chinese, what the hell was it?

And what did it mean?

**

For the rest of the week, Elodie tried to concentrate on Imperial Hotel, but her mind kept wandering back to Mr. Lee and Suzy's jade. Finally, on Friday, Sal became exasperated.

"Ellie, where is your brain today?" she demanded.

"Sorry, sorry." Elodie rubbed her eyes. Sal had had to repeat a line of dialogue three times before Elodie came out of her dream.

"Got a hangover?" Drew was obviously eager for a fellow sufferer to commiserate with.

"Of course not," Elodie snapped. "I don't drink."

"Not at all? Drew said, aghast.

"Well, sometimes," Elodie conceded. "But I never get a hangover because I never get drunk."

"My God, you must be a lonely soul these days," Drew said. "Everybody I know gets drunk at least twice a week."

"Or in your case, every night." Sal's voice was sharp and unsympathetic.

Drew shrugged. "I have an obligation to keep the liquor industry alive for the day when Prohibition is ended."

"My friend the Public Servant." Sal turned to Elodie. "Really, honey, you haven't been concentrating at all. If we don't tie this thing up tight, and fast, we'll lose it. It's your idea, remember. If it doesn't work out you'll be back writing about corn plasters. Is that what you want?"

"No, of course not." Elodie was suitably repentant. "I'm sorry, Sal. It's this Chinese business."

"Oh, that." Sal's tone was dismissive. "I thought you'd got that out of your system."

"I haven't heard from Bernice all week," Elodie explained. "Mr. Lee's office is still closed. And when I phone her at home she's never there. Her mother sounds pretty worried, said Bernice is always at Mr. Lee's, comes home late and goes straight to bed, and never says anything to anybody but hello and goodbye. That's not like Bernice – she's always been really flighty and kind of crazy. In a nice way, I mean."

"What's a nice way to be crazy?" Drew wanted to know.

"She's ... fun," Elodie said. "A little wild, a little scatty, but all right. Not the other night, though." She had told them about Bernice's scare and the change in her the following morning. Sal and Drew were sympathetic, but not really interested. Their job was Imperial Hotel. So was Elodie's.

"Imperial Hotel is your chance to come big, honey," Sal said, earnestly, lighting yet another cigarette. "There's good money in this radio writing racket, believe me. And you've got the ideas and the imagination for it, you think the right way. You could do really well if you'd just concentrate on what we're doing here."

Elodie was contrite. "You're right, I've been stupid," she said. "I won't let you down anymore."

"It's yourself you'd be letting down," Sal said, firmly. "Now, what are we going to do about the dead man in Suite 404?"

**

Dixon: I got a responsibility, Mr. Dunning.

Dunning: I know that, Dix. But bringing in the police could do the hotel's reputation untold damage.

Dixon: I ain't gonna be no part of any cover-up. Us hotel detectives have got a bad enough reputation as it is. I try to run my side of things on the up and up. That guy didn't just drop dead, he was murdered. It's clear as a bell. If you won't call the cops, I will. I have to, Mr. Dunning. It's my job.

Dunning: Are you sure he was murdered? I mean, there's no blood...

Dixon: I guess you didn't take a very close look. He was strangled with his own bathrobe belt. And by somebody he trusted.

Dunning: Why do you say that?

Dixon: He was in his pyjamas, for crying out loud. You don't let just anyone into your room when you're in your pyjamas. And he was strangled from behind, so he had his back to the killer. Do you turn your back on someone you don't trust? What did he do, anyway? What was his game?

Dunning: (uneasily) He was a salesman, that's all.

Dixon: Selling what?

Dunning: (clearing his throat) I don't really know.

Dixon: Then you'd better find out, and fast. Because the cops are going to ask questions. A LOT of questions.

**

"How about diamonds?" Elodie suggested.

"Too obvious," Sal said. "And if he was carrying diamonds he would have put them in the hotel safe and Dunning would have known about it.

"Maybe he did." Drew regarded his shoes at the far end of the sofa. He scissored his feet back and forth. "Maybe Dunning did it and that's why he's trying to get Dix to cover it up."

"Why do you keep trying to get rid of Dunning, for heaven's sake?" Sal demanded.

"He bores me." It was late and the weekend loomed ahead. Drew was getting eager to start some serious drinking.

"That's just silly." Elodie was very fond of Dunning's character, he was complex and sort of hard to figure out, but his heart was in the right place, she was sure of it. "Mr. Dunning is a pivotal character."

"Yeah, yeah." Silence. "Drugs," Drew said, suddenly. "He was a pharmaceutical salesman. Had access to all kinds of stuff, samples."

"That's good." Sal cheered up immediately. "Go on."

"Maybe he had information about some new kind of drug." Elodie, too, had caught the spark. "Maybe he wasn't selling drugs, but information to some rival company."

"And?"

"And once he'd sold the information he was no longer useful and so they killed him," Elodie finished.

"Or else he was going to confess." Drew's scissoring feet speeded up. "He found out something, knew too much, got scared and they killed him to shut him up."

Like Webster, Elodie thought. Like Webster.

Sal was writing furiously. "Go on," she demanded.

Drew was sitting up, now. "Is Suite 404 adjoining?"

"I don't remember." Sal scrabbled among the pile of notes and jottings on the table between the two couches. "I think so." To help them visualize the hotel, they had actually spent one morning doing an entire physical layout of the building, public rooms, bedrooms, suites, etc., to make it more real and to retain the logic of movements and patterns. "Yes." Sal's finger stabbed down on one of the sketches.

"We have to put someone good in the next suite, then," Drew said. "Someone absolutely too good to be true, above suspicion, all that. And he would be the killer."

"Or she," Elodie said.

"Better, better. Someone you'd never guess."

Like a guard you'd just hired to protect your treasure house, for instance, thought Elodie.

"What about a doctor?" she suggested.

"Great, doctor, drugs, nice connection," Sal muttered.

**

Doctor Manning: I didn't hear anything during the night, Inspector. I sleep very heavily.

Police Detective: Do you know the deceased?

Doctor Manning: Why should I? He was just another guest in the hotel.

Police detective: He was a drugs salesman for Lippert Pharmaceuticals. Do you know the name?

Doctor Manning: Of course, they are one of the biggest companies of their kind in the country.

Police Detective: I hear they've been having a hard time lately. Lost a lot of money in the Crash, had to lay off a lot of people.

Doctor Manning: I don't understand the connection.

Police Detective: According to my sources, they were about to

139

launch a new drug of some kind.

Doctor Manning: Yes, I heard that, too.

Police Detective: And according to these sources, another company had a similar drug almost ready.

Doctor Manning: (disinterested) Oh?

Police Detective: And this other company lists you as a consultant, Doctor Manning. The name Hadyn Chemicals mean anything to you?

Doctor Manning: Of course.

Police Detective: According to their Head of Research, a Dr. Thornberry, you have been instrumental in developing this drug of theirs which is very similar to the drug Lippert have produced. Extremely similar. Almost identical, one could say.

Doctor Manning: I don't see what you're driving at.

Police Detective: Mr. Proctor sold you information, didn't he, Manning? And Mr. Proctor thought he deserved more money for that, didn't he?

Doctor Manning: I have no idea what you're talking about.

Police Detective: We've checked the hotel records, Doctor Manning. On four previous occasions, you and Mr. Proctor have stayed at this hotel in adjoining suites. How do you explain that?

Doctor Manning: This is a very popular hotel.

Police Detective: It is also a very big hotel, Doctor. But you and Mr. Proctor always specified which rooms you wanted, and you always got them. A perfect set-up to meet without anyone seeing you. Nice long meetings where you could copy all the information you needed to help your company get in first with the new drug. There would be millions in it, wouldn't there? Millions. And Mr. Proctor wanted his share. STOP HIM! DON'T LET HIM GET AWAY!

**

"I like it," Sal said. "Needs a lot of work, much too wordy, but I think it will do very nicely for Episode Three."

"Can I go now?" asked Drew, plaintively. "Pleeeeze?"

"Oh, for Pete's sake, we're just getting hot," Sal protested.

"It's nearly eight o'clock, Sal," Elodie said, gently.

"Oh, hell." Sal looked at her watch. "I'm sorry, Ellie. And you said you wanted to get away early, didn't you? The library or something?"

"It doesn't matter," Elodie said. "I can go tomorrow."

"Looking for fresh ideas?" Drew had swung his feet to the floor, but spoke rather snidely. Obviously his craving was shortening his temper. "Running out of inspiration already?"

"Not at all." Elodie didn't bite. "I just want some information."

"A bit of information to add verisimilitude to an otherwise bald and unconvincing narrative?"

"What?" Sal asked.

"Gilbert and Sullivan." Elodie was surprised by this brief show of erudition. There was obviously more to Mr. Drew Wilson than met the eye. Indeed, she thought, as she watched him wrestling with his overcoat, there would have to be.

"My, my, I'm impressed." Sal was obviously not impressed at all. "Opera, yet."

"Goodnight, ladies." Drew doffed his hat. "I hate to leave you now."

"The hell you do," Sal said. She turned to Elodie, who was gathering up her papers. She had begun to carry a handbag almost as big as Sal's, necessary because of all the bits of script and notes they accumulated each day. "Can you type that up over the weekend? Or will you be at the library all day?"

"Yes, I'll type it up, or maybe my sister will if I ask her nicely. As for the library, I have no idea how long I'll need to be there. Stealing ideas from other people takes time, you know." She grinned at Sal, who grinned back, not entirely sincerely.

"So does learning Chinese. Am I right or am I right?"

"Oh, Sal .. ."

Sal gave her a long level look. "Get it out of your system, Ellie. I need you here Monday. All of you, brains included."

"Maybe there's a script idea in it," Elodie said, feebly.

"And maybe Caesar wore galoshes. See you Monday, kid." And she went out, leaving Elodie staring at the door.

When she left their room she crossed Reception and went down to the offices of Lee Enterprises.

Still closed.

Still locked.

Still a mystery.

**

Mei Mei Chen was very cross. She stamped her little foot and waved a finger under her husband's nose. "You did a bad thing. You made them mad at that poor girl. Who knows what they will do?"

Wei Ching was defensive. "I didn't say her name. I don't know her name. Cousin Ping said her companion was a policeman."

"And does that mean you should betray him?"

Wei Ching looked guilty but not contrite. "Policemen can look after themselves."

"This is not Canton. Denouncing is not the American way. That is what you came to America to get away from. You will not be a good American until you think like an American."

Wei Ching flared. "Just because you were born here does not stop you being Chinese in your heart."

Mei Mei, who was normally most demure, actually shouted. "It stops me being an idiot! Why draw attention to yourself? To me?"

Wei Ching hung his head. "I thought if I was helpful to them, they would remember it and ... "

"And not murder us like the others?" Mei Mei was becoming distraught. "You are a wonderful husband, Ching, you work hard, you send money back to your brother and parents, but you are a fool." She paced around the little room they shared over the restaurant. A whole room to themselves was a luxury and was due solely to Wang's love for his daughter. "We must move away."

Wei Ching was stunned. "Move away?"

"Yes." Mei Mei drew herself up. "It is the only way."

"But your father, the restaurant..."

She eyed him carefully. "Did you mention the restaurant? My father?"

"N...no. I just said I overheard a girl and a policeman talking."

"That is something, anyway."

"But where would we go?" Wei Ching was stunned by this change in his dear wife. Women in China were never disrespectful to their husbands, nor did they give orders.

"To San Francisco. My mother's people are there, we should be safe with them."

"Your father – "

"My father will agree. My mother will make him agree. I will be surprised if he does not cast us out, anyway. What you did was wrong. We are an American family now. We try to live by the things Father learned when he was becoming a citizen, and what I learned in school. I love you, Wei Ching, but I am ashamed of what you have done."

Ching felt his heart twist in his chest. "I am a fool."

Mei Mei's expression softened. "You thought you were doing right."

He looked at her in despair. "Becoming an American is very difficult."

She nodded. "Yes."

He considered. "In China family comes first, always."

"Family is important in America, too. Not everyone in this city is bad, but those who are bad are strong. I promise you it isn't so in other places. Other cities can be good and fine places to live. Small towns and villages also. There is more to America than Chicago. Do you understand?"

"I only know Chicago." He had come into America through Mexico and been taken by train right across the country to the job that was waiting for him.

"Then it is good that we leave as quickly as possible." Mei Mei drew herself up proudly. "I am an American girl. I will show you what America can be."

"You were not like this before we married." It was not so much a complaint as an expression of wonder. Who was this Mei Mei who stood before him now?

"Ah, no," Mei Mei agreed. "I wanted you to love me."

Ching slumped in his chair. "I am so confused."

Mei Mei was sorry for him. America was home to her, she had gone to American schools and had American friends. She loved her country. But to her husband it was strange and frightening. She knelt beside him. "You are strong," she said, softly. "You will learn."

12

Saturday began with rain. Elodie slept late because much of her night had been spent tossing and turning and trying to avoid more nightmares. Just before dawn she fell into a deep and grateful trough of darkness that obliterated everything, but she awoke feeling heavy and drugged. When she got downstairs Alyce was sitting with her head on the arm of her chair, listening to The Children's Hour and singing softly along with the theme.

"Oh, we just roll along, havin' our ups, havin' our downs – "

"Where did the White Rabbit Line go today?" Elodie asked.

Alyce didn't raise her head. "Lots of places," she said, dreamily. "Have you ever heard of Kachaturian?"

Elodie smiled to herself. "Didn't he run a restaurant over on Randolf Street?" she asked.

Alyce sat up. There was an imprint of the upholstery on her cheek. "No!" she said, and then had to laugh. "Very funny, Ellie."

"Gotcha." Elodie gently tugged one of Alyce's pigtails, then headed into the kitchen. Marie was there, rolling out pastry for a pie. She put down her rolling pin, and started for the icebox.

"I only have eggs left," she said.

"I don't want anything but coffee and toast." Elodie wondered if this was what a hangover felt like. If so, how could Drew stand it every day?

"That's not a very good start to the day." Marie thought Ellie was too thin and was always trying to 'build her up'.

Mrs. Browne came in, carrying a basket of apples from the storeroom in the basement. "Good afternoon, Ellie," she said, reprovingly.

"Sorry I slept so late," Elodie said. "I didn't have a very good night."

Mrs. Browne put down the basket of apples and felt

Elodie's forehead. "No fever," she pronounced.

"I feel perfectly fine." Elodie covered the lie by going over to pour out some tepid coffee from the pot on the stove.

"Oh, for goodness' sake," Marie said, exasperated. "Let me make some fresh – that's hours old."

"Where is everybody?" Elodie sank onto one of the kitchen chairs and leaned her head on one hand while sneaking a little corner of raw pastry from the other side of the table. It was sweet and slightly grainy.

"Maybelle has gone shopping for her boss," Mrs. Browne said. "Everybody else is right here as you can plainly see."

"I was hoping she would do some typing for me." Elodie snagged another bit of pastry, and Marie affectionately batted her hand away. "I have to go out."

"Where?" Mrs. Browne wanted to know, sitting down next to her. "It looks to me like you're coming down with something, young lady. I don't think you should go out in the rain."

"I'm fine, Mumma, I'm just tired – it's hard work writing scripts."

"All the more reason to stay home and rest on the weekend." Marie put a fresh cup of steaming coffee in front of her sister and another before her mother.

"Thank you, dear," said Mrs. Browne, reaching for the pitcher of fresh milk that sat at the end of the table near the window. "Marie is right, Ellie. You have shadows under your eyes." She poured the rich milk generously into both cups. Mr. Jacobs from the farm must have come by this morning, Elodie thought. It always tastes best on the first day. Mrs. Browne could have had milk from one of the new commercial dairies, but she kept to her old favourites. Nobody could match the milk from Mr. Jacob's cows.

"She looks like a racoon," said Alyce, coming in. "Can I have some coffee, too?"

"Plenty of milk, not too strong."

"Oh, for goodness' sake, Mumma, I'm nearly sixteen." Alyce was exasperated by Mrs. Browne's constant insistence on her health and wellbeing. "I think I can drink regular coffee now."

"Well," Mrs. Browne conceded. "All right, but no more after lunch. You'll never get your sleep." She turned to Elodie. "Probably what's wrong with you, my girl. Too much coffee."

"Maybe," Elodie agreed. "Sal makes really strong stuff, and we always run out of milk by three o'clock and have to toss for who goes out to get more."

"Well, there you are, then." Marie folded the pastry over the rolling pin and lifted it over into the pie dish. She pressed it gently down and left the edges overhanging while she started peeling the apples Mrs. Browne had brought up. "Everybody knows there's caffeine in coffee and that's a stimulant."

"My, my." Mrs. Browne spoke with fond indulgence. "You've been listening to Betty Crocker on the radio again." Marie smiled but said nothing. She handed a long strip of peel to Alyce.

"Throw this over your shoulder, let's see who you're going to marry," she said. Alyce complied then twisted around to look down at the red and white linoleum.

"His name begins with W," she said, horrified. "Oh, no, not Willie Straybuck, he's awful! All spots."

"Now, now," soothed Mrs. Browne. "It could be a last name, you know. What about that nice Gerry Watts down the street?"

Alyce considered. "He's not too bad, I guess." She grabbed an apple from the basket and went back into the sitting room.

Spots, Elodie thought, munching on the toast Marie had made for her. Harry Lee had spots, and was a Communist. Elodie had met a few half-hearted Communists while at college – they were always wanting money for posters and things. And parties – they were very fond of parties, as she recalled. But their kind of parties weren't much fun, mostly people giving speeches or reading bad poems and drinking wine until they threw up. And they never seemed to wash. No wonder Harry Lee had spots, if he was like that.

She finished her toast and coffee and stood up. "I'm going to the university library."

"What on earth for?" demanded Mrs. Browne.

"Information." Elodie started to explain, stopped, then went on. "For the show. I need to know stuff about architecture and elevators and plumbing. Sal wants to put a secret passage in the hotel basement, but Drew doesn't think the building is old enough. From slave times, you see. The Underground Railway," she improvised. Although thinking

146

about it...

"Couldn't you make the building old enough?" Marie asked. "Plenty of old buildings in this town, still."

"That's what I think, but Drew says no, so I have to get some facts. It's all part of the work, you see. Not nine to five anymore."

"They are certainly making you work hard for your money," Mrs. Browne said, with a degree of disapproval. She was very protective of her girls, as she was of her students. "Although the extra is welcome."

"I don't mind, I love it. It's not like work to me. It's fun." It occurred to Elodie she was protesting too much.

"I'd believe you more if you didn't look like a racoon, as Alyce said," Mrs. Browne commented, but said no more. She could see Ellie was enthusiastic, and she was never one to daunt any kind of enthusiasm in anyone. It was part of being a good teacher and a good parent, as Mr. Browne had always said. He had been a teacher, too, at the University. She sighed, missing him as always.

Elodie kissed her mother's forehead, waved to Marie, and went into the living room to get her coat and hat.

"Better take an umbrella," Alyce said, from her accustomed spot by the big radio. "They just announced it would rain all day long."

**

The late Mr. Browne had been a lay teacher at DePaul University, and Elodie had gone there for two years until the money ran thin. Even with help from the University, because of Mr. Browne's employment there, she couldn't in all conscience use up any more of the education fund her parents had so carefully set aside. There was Alyce to consider. Another wage was needed if Alyce was to attend DePaul, too. So Elodie had left and worked in several different places until she found the copywriting job at Adcock and Ash.

Now, as she took a trolley to the campus, she was glad she had retained her student identity card. It would give her access to one of the best libraries in the city, and one she knew well.

She loved the library, the smell of bindings and oak shelves and furniture polish, the way the light slanted down from the high windows with swirls of bookdust within. Many of her student hours had been spent there, and she felt right at home the minute she walked in. While it was easy to locate the section that dealt with foreign languages, following through to Chinese was less successful. She walked past it twice before she realized where it was. The librarian in charge of Language and Linguistics was doubtful he could help her at all. "What exactly do you need?" he asked.

"I want to find out the meaning of a Chinese word," Elodie said.

The librarian raised an eyebrow. "Is that Mandarin or Cantonese?" he asked.

"I beg your pardon?"

He sighed. He was a small, bald man with a scrawny neck and a habit of twisting his head sideways and pulling at his collar between sentences. "There are two languages – actually there are hundreds but only one written language – in China. Can you spell the word for me?"

"I've only heard it spoken aloud," Elodie said.

"Ah. Here in Chicago?"

"Yes." Well, where else, she thought. Do I look like a world traveller? "It sounded like '*mingdow*'."

"It is probably Cantonese," he said, with some satisfaction. "Almost all of the Chinese community here in Chicago is from the Canton province. Let us see." He bustled away and disappeared between two ceiling high lines of stacks. Elodie followed.

He was reaching up to a fairly high shelf and finally succeeded in bringing down a thick and rather dusty volume. "This should be a big help. And God Bless the missionary who wrote it over fifty years ago."

"What is it?" Elodie asked, following him again as he took the book to a large table in the corner and laid it down.

"A dictionary of Cantonese written in English – but written in two ways, spelled and spoken equivalents. So different, you see. So different." He opened the book. "Now, say the word again."

"It might be two words," Elodie pointed out.

He drew himself up a little, obviously proud of his knowledge. "I am quite aware of that. I have studied a little with Father Anselm myself, as it happens. Languages are my passion, you see," he added, rather shyly, as if imparting a great secret. She liked him the better for it.

"Father Anselm?"

"Our great orientalist," the librarian said. "He was a missionary in China for twenty years as a young man. Now he teaches here at DePaul. We are lucky to have him." He leaned a little forward. "The Oriental Institute keep trying to poach him, you see. They don't have much in the way of far eastern expertise, just near eastern." He sniffed. Apparently there was a hierarchy of 'eastern' in his view. "Mummies," he added, under his breath. "I ask you." He was thumbing through the book, pausing at a page, then moving on. "This is really very difficult."

"I'm sorry I can't tell you more,"Elodie said. "I do know saying the word aloud to a Chinese person gets quite a reaction."

He didn't seem to hear her. After a minute, he pointed to a word and raised his head. "Here's 'ming'. It can mean brilliant, shining, radiant ... depending on the pronunciation."

"And the rest of it?"

That took another five minutes. Then the little librarian straightened up." Well, I can't imagine why you would be so interested in this," he said. "Ming means brilliant or gleaming or shining. Dao could be 'sword', among other things. Ming Dao could mean 'shining sword' therefore. Or not. Most Chinese words have two or three meanings. It's a tonal language, you see, so much depends on inflection."

"Is that all?" Elodie asked, startled. "Just Shining Sword?"

"To the best of my knowledge, which I humbly admit is limited. It may be that when combined they have another meaning entirely, that sometimes happens. Especially if it is some kind of local slang or dialect. May I ask where you heard it spoken?"

Elodie could hardly say by a dead man. "At a party," she said, truthfully.

"Ah." The librarian nodded. He knew all about student

parties. "Well, I expect someone was teasing you," he said. "Is it for a game? A dare of some kind? To find it out, I mean? I haven't had any other enquiries about it."

"Yes, that's it. A bet between me and another girl," Elodie said, quickly. "She's Chinese, you see. And she bet me I could not find out what it meant without asking another Chinese person."

"Great gamblers, the Chinese. Well, you can tell her you asked me. My name is Evans, and you asked me. I am definitely not Chinese." He suddenly smiled, and Elodie was reminded of an elf or gremlin, for his mouth was wide and his teeth very large and white. He only lacked the pointed ears, she thought.

"I am very grateful," she said.

"Not at all, not at all. I love a challenging question," Mr.Evans said, twisting his head to the side again. She wondered if his laundry put too much starch in his collars. He began to walk back to the stacks.

"Is Father Anselm still here at the university?" she asked, impulsively.

"Oh, yes. But I believe he's been away." Mr. Evans spoke over his shoulder. "In California, I think. You can ask at the Department if he's back yet. But they won't be open until Monday. I'm sure he'll be able to tell you more than I can. I only do the words, you see. He knows all the rest." He glanced back. "You're Dr. Browne's daughter, aren't you?"

"Why, yes," Elodie said, taken aback at being recognized.

"A very great man. We miss him here."

"So do I," Elodie said, fervently. Papa would have been such a help in all this, she thought. He loved a mystery, too.

But would he have encouraged her in trying to solve this one?

She thought not, once he'd heard about Mr. Webster's death.

"Thank you, Mr. Evans."

"Any time, any time," came his voice from a distance, muffled by the books that surrounded them. As Elodie walked away, she could hear him humming to himself. He seemed to be quite perked up by her visit.

She only felt more confused than ever.

13

After church on Sundays was Alyce's favourite time. There was nice music on the radio, and the Sunday papers had all the comic strips she loved. She lay on the floor with the colourful pages spread out before her. Skeezix, Captain Katzenjammer and the Kids, Caspar Milquetoast, Jiggs and Maggie – they were all there for her. And, especially, Little Orphan Annie. After that, if she was very lucky, Mrs. Browne would have allowed her to buy a copy of *The American Weekly*, if the cover photo wasn't too lurid. Mrs. Browne did not really approve of Mr. Hearst or the contents of his publication but she occasionally indulged her youngest daughter's fascination with crime and the doings and romances of the rich and famous.

Today was one such day.

After absorbing all the comics, Alyce turned to the *American Weekly* and immediately announced to Elodie that Barbara Hutton was going to Europe.

"Oh, really?" Elodie asked.

"Yes. It says here that her father doesn't approve of her boyfriend Phil Morgan Plant and is sending her away to get over him." Alyce looked up, round-eyed. "Was he with her at the party?"

"Oh, yes." Elodie was filing her nails. She thought back to the rather louche Mr. Plant. If she were Miss Hutton's father, she would have recommended the same trip. "Does it say when she is leaving?"

"No, not exactly." Alyce giggled. "But it says that rumour has it Plant has booked a ticket on the same liner. Boy, I bet that makes her father wild."

"Plant has a lot of money of his own." Maybelle was on the other side of the room where she was reading a new book called *The Good Earth* which someone at work had lent her. As she read she kept twisting her hair into little tendrils. Beside her on the table was a bowl of her favourite dill pickles. "He can't be after her inheritance." She plucked up a pickle and began to gnaw the end. Sometimes she ate so many her lips turned quite white, greatly alarming her mother.

"He drinks and gambles and used to be married to Constance Bennett but now he goes out with all kinds of movie actresses," Alyce said. "Is Miss Hutton Catholic?"

"I don't think so. Why?"

"Well, then she couldn't marry this Plant man because he's divorced," Alyce seemed to think that explained everything. "So I don't know what her father is so upset about."

"Bad influence," Elodie suggested. "Miss Hutton is pretty young, you know."

"Was she nice?" Being 'nice' came high on Alyce's list of values.

"Actually, she was." Elodie thought back. "She was very . . . gracious."

There was an unlovely snort from Maybelle. "With her money she can afford to be gracious."

"Well, she could also afford to be obnoxious, and she wasn't." Elodie wondered why on earth she was defending Barbara Hutton of all people. "Did it say anything else about her in there?"

Alyce turned a page. "No. But they found three bodies out in Cicero."

"Nothing new there, then." Maybelle helped herself to another pickle and turned a page of her book.

Elodie put down her nailfile and looked out at the sunshiny day. The trees were bending in a strong breeze, and a piece of newspaper skittered down the street to wrap itself around a car tyre. It chilled her that Alyce could read so casually about three dead bodies, and Maybelle make so little of it. They were all becoming numb to the violence in the city. Was Miss Hutton 'nice', Alyce had wanted to know. Was anyone, these days? Surely accepting violence condones it in the end. So much wrong, and yet the sun comes out and the birds sing and children go to school and people get married and have babies and go to work, honest work, and grow old and die in their beds, never having been touched by crime. If it went on the way it was going, how much longer would they still have 'nice' people anywhere? What was the quote Papa always gave? Evil happens when good men do nothing? Something

152

like that. Was she going to be one of the ones who do nothing? Was she going to be one of the ones who hide behind the curtains and pretend everything bad will go away by itself?

A rich fragrance drifted in from the kitchen where Marie was making Sunday lunch – smelled like meatloaf, Elodie thought, and remembered when there was always a roast on the table on Sundays. But Marie did wonders with their limited budget, and had a vast collection of recipes copied from the magazines that were read and traded among those of her friends with a similar interest in homemaking. And then there were the programmes on the radio. Betty Crocker and Aunt Sally both had many suggestions for stretching limited funds – a problem that dominated most households these days. Marie made a small income, too, from her dressmaking, and now with Elodie's raise, there might be an occasional roast again on Sundays. Hugh wouldn't care, Hugh loved Marie's meatloaf. And her apple pie.

When Hugh arrived, he blew in like a cyclone, his hat askew and his coat flapping open. "Boy, that wind is picking up," he said, kissing each of them in turn on the cheek. Maybelle hardly looked up from her book, and Alyce blushed.

Elodie looked at him affectionately. Later on, they would talk. Hugh had to understand, now, had to see it her way.

He had to.

It *was* meatloaf, a big fat juicy one, with lots of gravy. With new potatoes and spring greens from their own garden out back, and some of the tomatoes and green beans Marie had canned last year. And apple pie with cream. They sat, full and rather stunned from their own eager consumption, and then Hugh jumped up.

"Time for a good walk," he said. "Helps pack it all down."

Maybelle gave a ladylike groan. "No thank you. If I'm going to be playing bridge later on, I need a nap."

"And I've got homework to do." Alyce did not like physical exercise of any kind whatsoever. She said walking to school and back every day was enough for her. Homework was always a good excuse to get out of anything.

Mrs. Browne looked at her. "I thought you finished your homework on Friday," she said, with a slight frown.

"All but one little tiny bit," said Alyce, evasively. Friday nights were especially good on the radio.

"Marie?" Hugh asked.

But she shook her head. "Have to wash the dishes."

"We'll help you," Elodie said, not very eagerly.

Marie laughed. "Last time you and Hugh helped me with the dishes you broke two plates and a glass and dented my best roasting pan. Thanks, but no thanks."

"It was a fair fight," Hugh protested. "Ellie ducked, that's all."

Mrs. Browne stood up. "I'll help Marie, you two go and have your walk. I can see you're dying to get going."

Without further argument, Elodie and Hugh put on their outer things and went down the front steps into the breezy April afternoon.

"Wow." Elodie grabbed her hat and jammed it down further onto her head. "You're right about the wind."

"Good for the lungs." Hugh took a huge breath and coughed violently. He wiped his eyes with a handkerchief, jammed it back into his pocket, and looked down at her solemnly. "Now, what is it you're dying to tell me?"

Elodie stared at him. "How did you know?"

"Ellie, I've known you since you were born." Hugh put his arm around her shoulders. "You were like a cat on hot bricks all during dinner, and you kept opening your mouth and then closing it without saying anything. You looked like a guppy."

"I'm turning into a zoo," Elodie said. "Yesterday Alyce said I look like a racoon, and now you say I'm like a guppy."

He glanced at her closely. "You do look a little dark around the eyes."

"Yes, all right. Maybe."

"Is it this new job? Not going well?"

"Oh, it's fine. Hard work, but so much fun ... "

"Well, then?"

"Somebody tried to poison Mr. Lee," Elodie said, abruptly.

Hugh stopped and stared at her. "That Chinese guy? The one where Webster was shot?"

"Yes." Quickly she told him about Bernice's fears and then her strange change of attitude. "And that word – that Chinese word I told you about?" He nodded. "Well, it could mean Shining Sword."

"And?"

She shrugged. "And nothing. It sounds kind of scary but but obviously means more than just that. The librarian said Chinese words often have many meanings. So he told me about Father Anselm and I want to talk to him. I think he could explain it all."

"Who the devil is Father Anselm?"

"One of the professors at DePaul. He lived in China for twenty years as a missionary, apparently. But he won't be back from California until Tuesday. I was hoping you'd go with me to talk to him. I'm sure there's a story in it, Hugh." That was her trump card – any reporter worth his salt jumps at a possible story.

But not Hugh, apparently. "I thought I told you to stay out of it, Ellie. To forget it." His voice was gruff, and he wouldn't meet her eyes. He seemed suddenly fascinated by the closed sign on the grocery store opposite.

The wind tugged at her hat and again she pulled it down to her ears. They were both leaning forward into the wind, which was surely coming straight off the Lake. Even after travelling over half the city there was a real chill in it.

Elodie looked at him suspiciously. "What do you know that I don't, Hugh?"

"What makes you say that, for goodness' sake?"

"It's for goodness' sake I want to know. What possible harm could come from talking to a priest?"

Hugh stopped walking and jammed his hands into his pockets. They were at the corner, and he looked all around while he thought what to say. "There's more to this than you know, Ellie," he finally said.

"And what might that be?"

He made a peculiar face, as if he had tasted something bitter. "The Chinese and the Italians," he finally said.

"I don't understand."

"They're fighting over boundaries again," Hugh said.

"What boundaries?"

Hugh gave a deep sigh. "Who controls the brothels, who controls the drugs. Booze too, although the Chinese aren't so interested in that. Chinatown is right next to Little Italy. The Chinese tolerate a lot of things the Italians don't like but would like the money from."

"Like what?"

"Let's not go into details."

"But I need details if I'm going to figure this out."

"Figure what out?"

"Why Webster was kidnapped and then killed. Why someone is trying to kill Mr. Lee."

"It's none of your business, Ellie. Mine, either."

She looked up at him." Are... are you scared, Hugh?"

"If you'd heard and seen some of the stuff I have, Ellie, you'd be scared, too. Nobody knows who to trust, anymore. And a lot of people think life is cheap – the Italians because they can go to confession, the Chinese because... well, because in their country, life *is* cheap. If you get nosy, if you get in between them, your life would be cheap, too. And I don't want that to happen."

"Well, neither do I. But I don't see what talking to a priest will do."

"You said he lived in China for twenty years."

"Yes, so he'll understand them."

"The Chinese can be very persuasive. They have a revolution going on over there every five minutes. People are taking sides, people who aren't Chinese at all. He could have hidden motives."

"He's a priest, Hugh. He was a missionary."

"People change. You know nothing about this Father Anselm. What's he doing out in California during term time, for example? Doesn't he have classes to teach?"

"I have no idea. I'm sure it's something . .. "

"Something what?"

"I don't know," she admitted. "Respectable."

Hugh gave a short laugh. "In this town? In this year?"

"There's more, isn't there, Hugh? More than just you being suspicious of everyone."

"I know that the big foot that slammed down on the Webster killing came from high up and flattened everything. I know Big Bill Thompson is after another term as mayor, and he's got Capone on his side, which means an Italian connection which means a Catholic connection. I know that Lee is very very rich, and nobody sells that much jade in these times. I think Lee could be selling drugs, and getting them out of China through Webster. Too much money involved for the Syndicate to ignore."

"I liked Mr. Lee," Elodie said, defensively. "I'm sure he wouldn't do anything like that."

He looked at her pityingly. "Oh, Ellie, you are so damn naive."

"No, I am so damn fed up with people ignoring all the terrible things that are going on in our city and all over the country. I am fed up with nobody caring, nobody doing anything about anything."

"Ellie – "

"And I am damn fed up with you patronizing me, Hugh Murphy," she said, literally stamping her foot. Her foot was numb and the stamp made it sting. "Ouch."

"All right, look. I'll go with you to see this Father Anselm, if you promise to be satisfied with whatever he has to say, and to leave all this alone."

"I can't promise that." She was quiet for a moment. "But I'll try. It could be something very simple, you know."

"Oh, yeah," Hugh said, turning back toward the house. "Like all the simple things that are happening in Chicago right now."

**

That evening after supper they settled down to bridge: Mrs. Browne, Elodie, Maybelle, and Hugh. Alyce was listening to the radio. Bridge had swept the nation lately. Maybelle had become a demon bridge player, matched only by Hugh. Elodie and Mrs. Browne were the weaker pair, but they gamely joined in the weekly 'tournament'.

Cheap entertainment was needed by a nation rocked back to survival level. Almost everyone could afford a deck of cards. Elaborate jigsaw puzzles were starting to appear – Alyce was wild to have one. And, best of all, the radio was free and sets were cheaper every day as the demand for them grew and grew.

"Oh, boy!" said Alyce, suddenly. She was listening to The Collier Hour and sat up in her excitement. "Fu Manchu!"

Elodie glanced over. "What?"

"Fu Manchu . . . a whole new serial. Mr. Rohmer just introduced the first episode. Sounds really gruesome." A some-

157

what unholy glee suffused Alyce's round little face. "I love Fu Manchu."

"China seems to be of the moment," Maybelle observed, laying down her hand for Hugh's dummy. "The novel I'm reading is all about China."

Hugh and Elodie exchanged a glance as Hugh selected a card from the dummy hand and laid it down, drawing Mrs. Browne's ace of hearts out of hiding.

"You should have ducked," Maybelle reproved her.

"I know, dear, but he would have gotten it eventually," sighed Mrs. Browne.

"You should have made it harder for him."

Mrs. Browne nodded and rearranged her cards. "Yes, dear. I'm sure you're right."

"Whose side are you on, anyway?" Hugh asked his partner, with a grin.

"I just like to see the game played well," Maybelle said, imperturbably.

"You're lucky to see it played at all." Elodie's patience had snapped. "I certainly didn't feel like playing bridge tonight."

"Oooh, very grouchy," said Maybelle. "Dear me."

Elodie had to laugh. She knew Maybelle didn't mean anything by correcting everyone's play. Maybelle spoke her mind freely, but she was never unkind. She had just become so good at the game that she was thinking of joining a proper bridge club. She was a very organised and precise person, which was one of the things that made her such a valuable employee for her rather scatter-brained but brilliant boss. The only annoying thing about Maybelle was that she was usually right. But she was so lovely that even being corrected by her wasn't a problem.

"Darling, turn that down, would you?" Mrs. Browne was counting under her breath as she dealt the next hand. The drama on the radio was becaming rather fraught. "It's very distracting."

Marie, who was sewing in the sideroom off the sitting room said, "Why don't you listen on my little radio in the kitchen?"

"Because by the time I get it tuned it will be all over," Alyce complained. "Besides, this one is better." She turned down the volume a tiny bit, and Mrs. Browne's mouth twitched in a smile.

"Thank you, dear." She spoke in such a telling voice that Alyce turned it down a little more, and put her head right up against the speaker so as not to miss a single thing.

"I'm not at all sure she should be listening to that," Mrs. Browne said in a quiet voice.

Hugh laughed gently. "She's just fifteen, Aunt Elizabeth. Everything is exciting when you're fifteen, but it goes in one ear and out the other."

"I'm not so sure about that." Mrs. Browne glanced toward the copy of *The American Weekly* which lay on the floor beside Alyce's chair. "These are such dreadful times – it must leave a mark on children. I know my students are far more unruly than they used to be. Some of them are downright sassy to the younger teachers."

"But surely not to you, Mumma," said Elodie.

"I should think not. I am very firm with all my students." They all laughed. Mrs. Browne had the softest heart in the city, and everybody, including her students, knew it. On the other hand, it was certainly possible her students never sassed her because they were so fond of her. She was an excellent teacher. It was respect as much as affection that kept her students in line.

"I know what you mean," said Marie. "You can't imagine how rude some people are in the shops and markets. Everybody is out for themselves these days."

"Wow." Alyce sat up as the closing theme for the programme came on. "That was terrific."

"Time you were in bed, young lady." Mrs. Browne glanced at the clock on the bookcase under the window. "School tomorrow."

"I know." Alyce sighed and turned off the radio. Very reluctantly, she went toward the door to the stairs. "Good night everybody."

They all said goodnight, and went on with the game. Hugh and Maybelle had won four rubbers and everybody was getting ready to quit, when the telephone rang.

Maybelle was closest, and got up to answer it. She then held it out to Hugh. "It's for you, Hugh. Somebody at the paper."

"Oh, thanks." Hugh got up and went to the phone. "Don't tell me, some speakeasy got raided and they found the Mayor

159

there," he said to whoever was on the other end of the line. His smile slowly faded as whoever was calling spoke. "Jesus, are they sure?"

Mrs. Browne frowned at his language, but said nothing as she gathered up the cards and began separating the two decks. Elodie and Maybelle listened unashamedly. Hugh wasn't easily shocked, but his face was getting whiter and whiter. After a minute or two of listening, he spoke again. "I'll go right down," he said, and hung up the phone. Slowly he turned and looked at the women around the card table. His eyes went to Elodie, and his expression was bleak.

"Ellie..."

"What is it?" asked Elodie, her heart tightening in her chest.

"Your friend," he said. "Your friend Bernice Barker."

"Oh, no..."

Hugh nodded. "They just found her body in an alley behind Wentworth Avenue. I'm afraid she's been murdered. I'm so sorry, Ellie."

Elodie put her hands over her face, and began to cry. Hugh came over to stand beside her. "Now do you understand why I want you to stay out of it?" he said, softly.

"Out of what?" demanded Mrs. Browne.

"Wentworth is Chinatown, isn't it?" asked Maybelle.

"Oh, no....oh, no .." wailed Elodie.

"Stay out of what?" repeated Mrs. Browne.

"Trouble," said Hugh. "Big, big trouble."

14

Deacon recognized her the minute he saw her, but it would have been easier if her head had still been attached to her body. Instead, it lay neatly next to her left shoulder. The sight was so unreal that it took him a minute or so to orientate himself. It was the red curls that made him recognize Lee Chang's secretary. Her name had come through at the station with the shout, gleaned by the first patrol on the scene from the handbag found alongside the body, but he hadn't made the connection until now.

Around him moved the photographer, his flash bulbs lighting up the scene sporadically, revealing all the filthy details. An alley behind a Chinese laundry, garbage cans, empty cardboard boxes with Chinese writing on them, baskets of squashed vegetables from a grocery further along. Puffs of steam escaped through the laundry's vents, occasionally obscuring the pathetic figure. She wore a brightly coloured print dress and a dark coat. There were runs in her stockings where they had snagged on the rough surface of the alleyway in her final death spasms. There was a great pool of blood surrounding the head and shoulders in a halo of darkening scarlet. Her entire body must have been drained of blood, he thought. The waxy white face was lax and expressionless, blank blue eyes staring up at the starry night, their life and sparkle extinguished.

He had put her down as a good-time girl.

Well, her fun was over.

"This was in her hand, Archie." The Medical Examiner handed Deacon a small piece of paper. It was a photograph of a chess piece, elaborately carved. A knight, he thought, from the shape. The crumpled photograph in black and white gave no indication of the colour, although it was pale.

"Time of death?" Deacon asked.

The Medical Examiner, a small round man with the unlikely name of Blossom, looked at him in exasperation.

161

"Some time before we got here."

"Oh, come on."

"From the rate of blood drying, I'd say no more than two hours ago," came the reluctant information. "But you know I have to do an autopsy to be sure. It's chilly out tonight, but there's heat and steam from that laundry wall, which messes up temperature. It's after midnight and they're still working in there, believe it or not."

"Oh, I believe it," Archie said. "Nobody can work as hard as the Chinese when they want to. They have relatives waiting to come over. It's kind of a very slow colonization," he said, not without affection.

"If it's any consolation, she was killed before her head was cut off." He looked down at Bernice Barker's body. "Hard to tell yet because of the decapitation cut across the throat, but maybe strangled."

"How do you know?"

Blossom gestured widely. "Blood pattern. If she was still alive when her head was cut off, the heart would have been pumping and blood would have shot everywhere. Including over the killer. But as she was dead there was no pressure. She just – drained from the large vessels in the neck." He leaned forward to inspect the base of the severed head and muttered half to himself. "Just like the others."

"The *others*?" Archie just caught the words.

Blossom realised he'd been overheard, and turned away. Busied himself with putting his instruments back into his little black bag. "Forget I spoke."

"Now, how can I forget that for crying out loud? What others?"

Blossom flushed. "It's been kept quiet because they're afraid of panic. That's what we were told."

"Go on."

Blossom uttered a low curse, then shrugged. "Last three months or so we've had five homicides here in Chinatown. Three shot, one stabbed, one poisoned. But all of them had their heads cut off afterward." He looked down at Bernice Barker's body. "She's not Chinese, though. They were all Chinese."

"Jesus wept. Why haven't I heard about this?" But, thinking back, he recalled whispers, rumours. Nothing more.

"We were told to cover up the decapitation part." Blossom was deeply embarrassed. "Somebody paid somebody, I don't know. Like since they were Chinese it was irrelevant what weird things they did to their dead folks. As if their rituals or whatever were no business of ours. You know how things are these days. People get spooked by what they don't understand. Now, I don't know what to do about this one, seeing she's not Chinese."

"I know who she is," Archie said. "She works for a Chinese importer called Lee Chang."

Blossom stared up at him in dismay. "Hell's teeth – the one where that guy Webster was shot last week?"

"The very one."

"So there's a Chinese *connection*." Blossom fancied himself a bit of a detective.

"Time will tell," Archie said. "I can't think of any other reason for her to be down here at night except on business for him." He looked around. "Rotten way to die," muttered.

"Never came across a good one." Blossom was philosophic. "Even in bed you got lumps." He snapped his bag shut. "Can I take her away now?"

Archie turned to the photographer. "You finished?"

"Yeah."

"And you?" he asked the artist who was drawing the scene.

"Just two more minutes." The artist's tongue protruded from the corner of his mouth as his pencil raced across the page of his big notebook.

"Okay," Blossom said. "I'll tell them to bring the stretcher."

Deacon watched the little medico leave. The police detectives would go over the alley with flashlights, looking for clues, but he doubted they would find anything except the occasional rat. Alleys are good places for murder – ideal from the killer's point of view. Too many clues to too many lives other than that of the victim. What might be important was usually obscured by a surfeit of information. No, the only clue was this little photograph, which he would show to Lee Chang, even if he had to drag him out of bed to look at it. He would find out what was going on or get fired trying. The death of Bernice Barker re-opened the Webster case, officially or unofficially, as far as he was concerned. And it reopened the mental wound he'd been carrying since Webster's murder. He hated things going on that made no sense. Crooks killing crooks, that made a kind of sense. But young girls full of life – no.

He turned, realizing how angry he really was, and bumped into someone standing behind him.

"What the hell are you doing here?" he demanded.

Hugh Murphy looked past him to where Bernice Barker still lay. Still forever.

"I got a call," Hugh said. He couldn't take his eyes off the dead girl. She looked like a shop dummy, but she was real. And her head …. It was ghastly, like nothing he'd ever seen before. Finally he looked at Deacon. "I was at Elodie Browne's house when it came through."

"Oh, shit."

"Exactly." Hugh fumbled in his jacket for a cigarette, offered it to Deacon, who declined, and lit it up himself. "Elodie is pretty broken up. Bernice was her closest friend and she thinks it's her fault, somehow. She told me how you pressed her for information. She wishes she'd kept her mouth shut, poor kid."

"She was the only one there with any brains," Archie said, defensively. "I wasn't about to get anything out of people like Miss Hutton or Lee Chang himself. They think they are above the police, somehow. I had no other alternative but to ask Miss Browne."

"And to take her to dinner?"

Archie felt himself flush. "You can't blame a man for trying," he said.

Hugh smiled. "I know. She's cute and smart and funny. Unfortunately she's my cousin. That means I care about her and what happens to her. Including who is interested in her."

"Understood." Archie regarded the reporter. One thing about Murphy, he thought, he talks straight and expects straight answers. Makes life a lot easier. Unless there's something you don't want to tell him. Then it makes life very difficult. Relationships between the police and the press had never been easy, nor would they ever be. Murphy was about the best of a bad bunch.

"You know she has all kinds of ideas about all this business with Webster and so on," Hugh continued. "She has too much

164

imagination, too much determination, and no common sense at all. Can you stop her?"

"It's got nothing to do with me." Even as Archie spoke he knew it wasn't true. He sighed. "Anyway, she doesn't like me, won't listen to anything I say."

"Or me," Hugh agreed. "Maybe you could arrest her for something and keep her in jail."

"Very funny." They both stepped back as the stretcher-bearers came past to collect the body. "This might stop her," Archie said, gesturing toward the pathetic small body and detached head of the late Bernice Barker.

"Is it going to stop you?"

Archie looked at the reporter, recognized a friend with common interests. "It makes everything worse, as you damn well know."

Hugh nodded. "Well, that's exactly the effect it had on Elodie. First she broke down, then she got angry. Her mother and sisters practically had to tie her down to stop her coming down here with me. They finally put her to bed with some kind of pills her mother had for her arthritis. I told them to lock the door just to make sure." They both turned to follow the oddly-laden stretcher out of the alley and around the corner to the mortuary van. "You know about this *mingdow* business?"

"She told me. I can't find anyone who knows anything about it."

Hugh nodded. "Well, she did." They came to a stop under the corner streetlight.

Archie looked at him in amazement. "She did?"

Hugh gave a very small chuckle. "Very resourceful is our Elodie. She went to her university library and got it translated by some specialist or other. It could mean several things but 'Shining Sword' seems the most likely, apparently. Ring any bells?"

Archie frowned. "No, but it sounds bad."

"I thought so, too," Hugh agreed.

"Especially since..." He stopped.

"Since what?"

"Since heads are getting chopped off. Maybe by a shining sword?"

Hugh finished his cigarette and tossed the butt into the

gutter. "Heads? Plural?"

"Apparently, according to Blossom. But it's been kept quiet. Very quiet."

"But you won't let me use that, will you?" Hugh didn't really need to ask.

"No." Archie indicated the shops that lined the street where they stood. "Look at them, all Chinese-owned, all good businesses, well-run and profitable. Owned by family men. All above board. And yet, underneath, there is a whole world we know nothing about and have no entry into. Knowing how that word translates doesn't tell us anything about what it actually means. And nobody can close you out like a Chinese who doesn't want to talk. Or tell you more lies and make you believe them if it's to protect what he wants to protect. I've been trying all week to get some response to that word. No luck at all. I like them enormously, admire them, really, but I'll never get inside their world in a thousand years."

"Elodie might," Hugh said.

Archie turned to him in surprise. "What do you mean?"

"She's got an appointment with a Catholic priest at DePaul University on Tuesday. He used to be a missionary in China. If anyone knows about the world of the Chinese people, it's him."

Archie was dumbfounded. "She did that?"

"I told you she's resourceful. And a danger to herself and everyone around her."

"Are you going with her?"

"What do you think?" Hugh said.

"You'll let me know what she finds out?"

Hugh shrugged. "Knowing Elodie as I do, she'll want to tell you herself. She did an end-run around you on this one, didn't she? Well, she'll want to rub it in. She doesn't dislike you, by the way. I wish she did." They stood watching the mortuary van drive away. "Meanwhile, what can you give me on this?"

Hugh had produced his notebook and pencil. He was all reporter again. Archie looked at him in resignation. "You know the drill. If we have anything it will come out at a press conference."

"They won't be able to shut this one down the way they did the Webster killing," Hugh agreed.

166

"You know where the pressure came from on that?" Archie asked, with interest.

"Not specifically. High up. And from the east coast. Personally I think it was La Hutton's father weighing in with his money. Wouldn't have wanted the fact that his darling daughter was anywhere near anything as nasty as murder. And he has friends in this town, you know. Including the Mayor. A word here, another there – that's all it takes up on the social mountaintops."

"It kind of makes you fond of Capone," Archie said. "At least you know his motives."

Hugh shrugged. "Not so different – money, privacy, power, freedom to do what they damn well please. That's all any of them want."

"I used to love this town," Archie said, sadly.

"Me, too," Hugh agreed. "Damn shame we both make our living from what's wrong with it." Their eyes met in mutual understanding and sadness.

"Including nice young girls getting their heads chopped off."

"Yes," Hugh agreed. "Including that."

**

"My God, what's happened to you?" Sal demanded as Elodie came through the door and stood staring at the coatrack for a moment as if it could tell her the meaning of life.

With a start, Elodie came to herself and shook off her coat, hung it up, and then took off her hat, which she realized was not hers at all but one of Maybelle's, grabbed off the hook at home as she rushed out. She held it in her hand, staring at it.

"It's a hat," Wilson said from his usual position on the couch. "Had it on your head when you came in, remember?"

"Cut it out, Drew," Sal snapped as she got up and came over to where Elodie stood. She took the hat from Elodie's grasp, put it on the rack, and then led Elodie over to their couch and pushed her down. "Coffee," she said, and brought her a cup, standing over her until Elodie had drunk it, then going back to refill it for her. She sat down next to Elodie, and waited.

"My friend," Elodie finally said. Her voice wavered.

"The one you've been worried about?" asked Sal, gently.

Elodie nodded. "She was murdered last night." Her voice broke and the tears threatened again. She ducked her head and drank the hot coffee fast.

"Dear God in Heaven," Sal gasped.

"Son of a bitch," was Drew's contribution.

The cup began to shake in the saucer and Sal took it from her, putting it on the worktable that stood between the two couches. "You should have stayed in bed," Sal said. "You could have sent a message...."

Elodie shook her head violently. "No!" She took a deep breath and slowly let it out. "I was awake in bed all night, I couldn't stay there a minute longer. And don't be nice to me, everybody is being so nice to me, and I can't stand it. It's probably my fault she's dead." Again, her voice almost betrayed her. She still couldn't believe that vibrant, funny, pretty Bernice was dead and still. Bernice had never been still in her whole life. How could someone that alive be dead? "It's my fault," she whispered.

"Horseshit," said Drew.

Elodie looked over at him, startled by his vehemence. "She came to me and was worried, frightened. I tried to help but – "

"Exactly." Sal sat back. "You tried to help and she said no thanks, if I remember right."

"Yes, but – "

"But nothing," Drew said.

"I should have told the police about Mr. Lee getting poisoned," Elodie went on.

" Obviously Mr. Lee didn't want that," Sal pointed out. "Now, what exactly happened?"

Elodie closed her eyes. "My cousin Hugh got a call from his paper saying Bernice was dead. He went down there. She . . .she was in an alley in Chinatown." She swallowed hard. "Her head was..." Her voice fell to a whisper. "Her head was cut off."

"That's interesting," Drew mused.

Elodie opened her eyes and stared at him, aghast. "*Interesting?*"

"Sorry, didn't mean to sound callous. It's just that decapitation is not the usual method of despatch in this town. You said she was in Chinatown?"

"Yes. An alley behind a Chinese laundry, Hugh said." Elodie had better control of her voice and herself, now. Drew's dispassionate tone had helped more than Sal's sympathy. "Hugh tried to get more details, but that... that Deacon was in charge and wouldn't tell him anything. They're supposed to have some kind of press conference today for all the papers, but Hugh said they won't allow them to print the cause of death. You'd think .. I mean . . Deacon knows he's my cousin."

"And should have given him an exclusive?" Drew asked. "That's not how it works. They have to keep stuff back, you know. Stuff only the killer would know." He propped himself up on one elbow. "She might have just been in the wrong place at the wrong time."

"And somebody just killed her for no reason?" Elodie's voice was hard.

"No," Drew said, evenly. "For her money."

Elodie shook her head. "Her handbag was right beside her, nothing taken as far as they could tell. Hugh did learn that much." She looked from Drew to Sal. "She must have been there for a reason. Would she be in Chinatown in the middle of the night just for a stroll? No – it's something to do with Mr. Lee and Webster and Suzy's jade. I'm sure of it."

"Whose jade?"

"Suzy. That's what Bernice said. Suzy's jade. I guess Mr. Lee has it and somebody wants it."

Drew lay back down and stared at the ceiling. "If you knew Suzy like I know Suzy," he sang softly to himself.

"Is it Barbara Hutton's nickname, maybe?" Sal suggested. "Doesn't sound right."

"What about some other collector? Maybe in Europe?"

"I wonder," murmured Drew.

Both Elodie and Sal stared at him. "Wonder what?" they asked in unison.

"Well, maybe it's another Ming Dao. I mean, another Chinese word that we aren't getting right because we don't know the right pronounciation. Suzy, Suzy. It does sound familiar."

"It does?" They were still speaking in unison.

"I got interested in China when you told us about the party

and so on. China is fascinating, you know. Very complex. Full of feuds and fights and secret societies and spies. Did you know the Chinese have had a Secret Service since 510 BC? First started by a guy named Sun Tzu. I've been reading up on Chinese history. I've nearly gotten up to the Boxer Rebellion."

"I thought they had a revolution in China, not a rebellion." Sal said. "That they were more democratic now."

Drew chuckled. "A republic is not necessarily a democracy . . . and there have been several civil wars. Still people jockeying for power – although I admit I haven't got into modern China, yet. I haven't found much written since the War. Probably because nobody can work out enough of what's going on to write about it."

The more Elodie learned about Drew Wilson, the odder he seemed. She would have been startled to discover, for example, that he was not as alcoholic as he and Sal made out. In fact, although he liked his drink, his real vice was reading late into the night – hence the thick glasses. Insomnia was the bane of his existence and the blessing of his intellect. If he hadn't had to earn a living, Drew Wilson would be reading 18 hours a day or more. He knew the theory of practically everything, but often put on two different coloured socks in the morning. As Sal had once said, he knew a lot of words, but didn't always make a lot of sense.

"How do you have time for reading when you are so busy drinking?" Ellie asked.

He smiled up at the ceiling. "I'm a secret vampire," he said. "Awake all night. Might as well fill the shining hours."

"Shining?"

He turned his head from where it rested on the arm of the sofa. "I beg your pardon?"

"Nothing," Elodie said. She stared down at her hands. She was holding them so tightly her knuckles were white. One by one she moved her fingers, forced them to open. Bernice was dead, Bernice was dead. Now her hands were open. Bernice was gone.

Sal cleared her throat. "As fascinating as this lesson has been, I think we should get to work. We can talk about Chinese history during lunch, if we must."

"Yes," Elodie agreed. She didn't want to think about Bernice or China or Suzy or whatever her name was anymore.

Better to work, better to think about the people staying at Imperial Hotel. Nice imaginary people you could make do whatever you wanted them to do. There she was in control, not pushed around by things she didn't understand.

**

Molly: Thank heaven Chef Alexander is back. This wedding would be impossible if he wasn't here.

Spike: Sounds like it's going to be impossible even with him here. Who ever heard of a wedding where the bride wears purple?

Molly: I guess she's kind of an unusual person.

Spike: Unusual? Crazy, you mean.

Molly: Somebody told me she thinks she's a witch.

Spike: A what?

Molly: Her cat is going to be maid of honour.

Spike: Okay, okay, now you're just getting silly.

Molly: I'm not. She has this cat who walks on a leash. It's supposed to walk up the aisle with her. It has a diamond collar. Its name is Nebuchadnezzar.

Spike: (nearly hysterical with laughter) Nebuchadnezzar McGillicudy? This I have got to see.

Dunning: (coming up behind Spike). And what's so funny?

Molly: We were just talking about the McGillicudy—

**

"McGillicudy what?" interrupted Sal. "Who's this nutcase going to marry?"

"Something really outrageous," Drew said. "We're playing this one for laughs, right? If her name is Mercedes McGillicudy, what would her married name be?"

They thought about that for a moment or two, then Sal started to laugh.

**

Molly: We were just talking about the McGillicudy-Benz wedding, Mr. Dunning. It sounds very . . . unusual."

Dunning: It's outrageous. When I agreed to the booking her par-

ents said nothing about all this nonsense. I thought it would be straightforward, classic ...

Spike: But it's totally nuts.

Dunning: I'm afraid the newspapers will make us a laughing stock. The McGillicudys are so wealthy the society pages are bound to cover it. Why on earth didn't they go to the Ritz?

Molly: They had her coming-out party at the Ritz, remember?

Dunning: Oh, yes, that's right. (groans) Monkeys, wasn't it? Monkeys and a tiger who attacked the bandleader?

Spike: How come – were they playing the Tiger Rag?(snickers)

Dunning: (groaning) I should have known, I should have known.

Molly: (soothingly) I'm sure it will be all right, Mr. Dunning. I'm sure it will be fine.

Chef Alexander: Mistair Dunning! Mistair Dunning! I cannot do this thing.

Dunning: What thing?

Chef Alexander: All the courses – to be in the shape of the animals. And the cake . . the cake!

Spike: (half to himself) I can hardly wait to hear this.

Chef Alexander: A pyramid! She says she wants a purple pyramid with a light on the top flashing on and off, on and off. Who can do such a thing? When they cut it they will be electrocuted!

(Spike collapses in hysterics)

**

Elodie got through the day somehow. The fact that they were trying to produce something outrageous to fit the prospective bride Mercedes Benz helped a lot to lift her spirits. It required a lot more concentration to try and produce amusing images in the minds of the listeners than it did to scare them or mystify them. Sal said drama was easy, comedy was hard. Even so, she thought as she went down in the elevator, maybe we should make it funnier. Or, at least, do more comedy episodes. People loved to laugh. Shows like Easy Aces and The Gumps were getting really popular because times were so hard. People needed to get away from the fact that there was less food on the table, no jobs, and all the rest of it.

All the rest of it being like having a friend murdered.

By the time the elevator reached street level any solace produced by creating their silly programme and the banter that went with it had evaporated.

And seeing Lt. Archie Deacon once again waiting for her in the lobby didn't help.

15

"Have you ..." Elodie began. But Deacon shook his head.

"Sorry. We haven't gotten anywhere with finding out who killed your friend or why."

"Thank you," she said, and turned away to walk briskly toward the exit, but he followed her, his hat in his hand.

"I want to talk to you."

"I'm sorry, I'm on my way home and I'm tired. I told you everything I know about what happened at Mr. Lee's house."

"Liar," he said.

She stopped so abruptly that he nearly ran into the back of her. "I beg your pardon?" Her voice was as cold as she could make it. Which was difficult because she was having trouble not bursting into tears.

"Shining Sword."

"Oh." She looked down at her shoes. "Did Hugh tell you that?"

"Yes. And about this monk you're going to go talk to tomorrow."

"Oh, for goodness' sake, he's not a monk. Well, not exactly."

"I don't care what he is, I think you should cancel your appointment and forget about all this once and for all. Leave it to us."

She raised an eyebrow. "Oh, yes? The trusty police, the incorruptable and wonderful police department of Chicago is going to solve it, are they? I think not."

"Thanks for your faith in us," Archie said, with equal sarcasm.

Elodie turned and went out the revolving door, and Deacon followed her yet again. "I don't want to talk to you," she said, over her shoulder. "Go away or I'll call a cop."

"Very funny. Listen to me – "

"No." She put her hands over her ears – not easy, with her handbag swinging wildly against her chin.

He moved around in front of her and tried to force her

174

hands down. "For goodness' sake, stop being so childish." He saw the tears glistening in her eyes and gentled his tone. "All right, all right. Maybe we can help one another, then."

She lowered her hands slowly. "What do you mean?"

He looked up. "It's starting to rain. Come on, I'll buy you a drink."

"What?"

"Of coffee. Or tea. Or sasparilla – whatever you like. But if we keep standing here arguing we're going to get soaked." He took her elbow and propelled her across the street and down a block to an unprepossessing entrance with placards on either side advertising The Chicago Rhythm Boys. It was a basement jazz club. Fortunately, the place was quiet – obviously the Rhythm Boys didn't come on until much later. Tables surrounded a shiny dance floor, but without customers the place felt rather damp, and the dingy walls looked bleak with the lights full on. Waiters in shirtsleeves were moving among the tables, setting them up for the evening, talking desultorily among themselves, laughing from time to time. Later on the lights would be dimmed, the music would be loud, the dance floor would be full and the glasses and coffee cups would not contain sasparilla or coffee.

Behind the bar a man was polishing a large coffee urn. He looked up and saw Deacon. His face went lax for a moment, then he spotted Elodie and he smiled. "Off-duty, Lieutenant?" he asked. His voice was odd, whispery, almost hollow.

"You got any coffee in that thing?" Archie asked.

"I could squeeze out a cup or two, but I'm not bragging on it," the man said. "It's hot, that's about it."

"Fine. Thanks." Archie led Elodie to a small table and pulled out a chair for her. "My lady," he said, indicating the seat.

Elodie glared at him, but she sat down. She didn't know if she could stand any more coffee, but she didn't have to drink it.

He sat opposite her, laid his hat on a third chair, and folded his arms onto the table, leaning forward to gaze into her face. "You are a very stubborn person."

"I'm angry." She bit off the words. "My friend has been horribly murdered. I don't like that."

"Neither do I."

"And I want to know why."

"So do I. Tell me about Shining Sword." He leaned back as the barkeep put down two coffees and a small pitcher of cream. "You want sugar?"

"No, thank you," Elodie said, and picking up the spoon, she began to stir the suspect and murky liquid.

"Please tell me what you've learned," Archie said, surprising her with all this sudden show of manners.

"I don't think it will help you."

"Try me."

Elodie sighed. "All I know about Shining Sword is that it is a possible translation of the word – the words – ming dao." She explained about the librarian at the university. "That does not explain what it might really mean – or stand for."

"It scared the hell out of the waiter at the restaurant the other night."

"I know. Drew thinks that it may be the name of a secret society."

"Drew?"

"A man I work with. He's been reading about China. He says it's full of secret societies. He's going to try to find out about Suzy."

Archie looked at her with a frown. "Who the devil is Suzy?"

Elodie sighed. "I don't know. Drew thinks it might be another Chinese word we're saying wrong."

"I think I'm getting a headache," he said, plaintively. He had come to the Gower Building to intercept her and try to stop her getting involved any further in all this, and now he was discovering she knew a lot more about it than he did. He'd had no luck finding out the meaning of the odd word that Webster had shouted out before he was killed, despite what he had thought were 'connections' with the Chinese community. He had learned quickly enough that all their bowing and smiling revealed nothing at all, which was exactly what they were intended to do. And now that he had learned of the other deaths of Chinese people by decapitation, he thought he could see why. "Would you just explain all this in simple English?"

"Why should I?"

He gazed at her, calculating. "Because if you do I'll tell you

176

all I know so far about Bernice's murder."

She pressed her lips together, then relaxed. "I was just interested in the word, and why Mr. Lee didn't want us to talk about it."

"Ah, so that was it."

"That's how it started. And the fact that I think that guard meant to kill Mr. Webster right from the start." She began to speak faster. "Mr. Webster knew something was going to happen there that night, he tried to stop it. The guard was part of it. He shot Mr. Webster to shut him up."

He realized he shouldn't have been surprised, as he had credited her with brains from the start, but he was. "That's what I think, too."

"What did the guard say?"

Archie felt himself flush, partly from embarrassment but mostly from anger. "He's disappeared." Her spoon stopped going around and around in her coffee for a moment, then continued its pointless journey. He reached across and touched her hand. "You're going to wear a hole in the cup."

Elodie put the spoon down. "Are you searching for him?"

"No."

"Why not?"

"Because until last night, the Webster case was officially closed. I was told to stay away from it."

"Why?" She saw his jaw clench.

"Because Miss Hutton was there? Because Big Bill Thompson wants to be re-elected mayor? Because Mr. Lee Chang is really Al Capone in disguise? Because nobody really gives a damn if a small time importer gets shot by some guard 'doing his duty'? I'm told we shouldn't waste time on such matters when there is so much 'real' crime in Chicago." His smile was wry. "A lot of which we contribute to ourselves in a show of brotherhood with the criminals. Common interest in the downside of humanity, you see."

"That bothers you a lot, doesn't it?" she asked, sympathetically.

"Yes, it does. It's beginning to make me ashamed of what I do, what my family has done for several generations. You have no idea how much corruption there is in this town."

"I think I do. My sister regularly reads the *American Weekly* when our mother isn't looking."

His laugh held no amusement. "Hypocrisy sells."

"I hate it, too. I really do. And don't tell me not to be angry, because I can't stop. Not now. Not after Bernice." She grimaced. "We're not getting very far, are we?"

"We might if we pooled what we know," Archie said, earnestly. "I can see no matter what Hugh or I say, you're going to keep getting into this thing, aren't you?"

She smiled. "Hugh put you up to all this?"

"He cares about you. He's afraid for you. So am I. Two murders, Elodie. And others I just found out about." He explained about the killings of Chinese victims, and the hushing up of their decapitation. "If this is being done by some secret society, it makes it even worse. Not one killer, but a group. No wonder the Chinese community has been too scared to tell anyone about Ming Dao. This is not some intellectual game. If they – whoever they are – killed Bernice, they could kill you, too. I don't want that to happen."

"You don't?" She looked up at him.

He smiled, a real smile this time. "It would look lousy on my record."

Elodie was oddly disappointed by this attempt at humour. "The only new things I've learned, thanks to Drew, are about these secret societies. They've had them for centuries now. They all have names, although not all of them are as dramatic as Shining Sword. Drew said one of the earliest ones was called The Red Eyebrows."

"Good Lord."

"I know. In the old days some of them were pretty lawless, but now most of them are benign, to do with merchants and charities and so on, sort of like men's clubs we have that do good. Drew didn't know much more than that. Except there's something called Tongs and something called Triads – I'm not clear what the difference is. I can't see Father Anselm until tomorrow. He's in Chinatown, today."

"Killing people?" Archie asked, not seriously.

She didn't dignify that with a response. "And I apparently have to see him off-campus, at his home, because he's on some kind of temporary sabbatical."

"You shouldn't go alone."

"Well, for goodness' sake, he's a priest. Anyway, Hugh is going with me. He promised."

"And will you promise to tell me everything Anselm tells you?"

"Yes," Elodie said. "I promise. Because of Bernice." She leaned back in her chair. She was past the first shock of Bernice's death. Hard, cold anger had driven out her sorrow, although she knew it would return. Now she felt only resentment that her friend had been killed so callously, and guilt . . . there would always be guilt. "You said you would tell me all you know about her death, remember?"

He nodded, reached into his pocket, and produced a glassine envelope containing the black and white photograph they'd found clutched in Bernice's dead hand. "Know anything about this?"

She took it and looked closely. "What is it?"

"It's hard to tell the size because there's nothing else in the picture, but to me it looks like some kind of chess piece."

"A Chinese chess piece?"

He shrugged. "I don't even know if it's Chinese."

"It looks a lot like some of the things in Mr. Lee's office cabinets," Elodie said, slowly. "They were carved sort of like this, but not so – "

"Fussy?"

"Intricate," she corrected him. She handed it back. "It's very beautiful. If it's as small as a chess piece, it's amazing."

He glanced at it again, then put it back into his pocket. "Other than that, and the details of the post mortem which you don't want to hear, we've drawn a blank. All we have is that she was in Chinatown at night for some reason, and she was killed. We didn't find anything in the alley that told us any more. We think she was killed there, however, not somewhere else. It was a dead end alley, so she couldn't have been taking a short cut. She must have gone in there with her killer, or met him there. The medical examiner said he was probably left-handed, from the angle of the cut, and maybe not much taller than she was." He shrugged. "That's it."

"Sherlock Holmes could have told you what he ate for breakfast," Elodie said, disappointed.

"And where is he when you need him?" Archie said.

She looked at her hands, which she was now embarrassed to see were grubby from writing with pencils all day. She moved them to her lap and looked up at him. "Bernice was

179

frightened when I last saw her. Someone had tried to poison Mr. Lee. She said it was because of Suzy's jade."

"What?" He was shocked. "Poisoned? Nobody reported that."

"No, Mr. Lee wouldn't let them. She said he was frightened, too. But Marie heard her telephoning someone during the night and the next morning she was different. Told me to forget all about it. Said it was nothing. I never saw her again."

"Maybe the guard was protecting him, then," Archie mused. "So when Webster messed up their first plan, they tried poison, and scared him into sending Bernice with a picture of . . . Suzy's jade? Is that what all this is about?"

"Maybe."

"But they killed Bernice."

She nodded, miserable again.

He stood up. "Come on, I'll drive you home. It's time Mr. Lee did some explaining."

**

After dropping Elodie off, Archie drove out along Lake Shore Drive to the Lee house. It had taken most of his afternoon, but he had finally convinced a judge, an old friend of his father's, to grant him an arrest warrant for Lee. It would help him to get into the house, at least, and finally talk to the elusive merchant. Lee would have the option of talking to Archie there, or downtown. It was the quickest way he could think of to force an interview. Deacon didn't tell Brett or anyone else about the warrant. The judge was one of his private weapons, used only in emergencies. If that meant he and the judge were corrupt, so be it. Join the crowd, Archie, old son, he told himself. Join the crowd.

Mrs. Logie, the housekeeper, answered the door.

"I want to see Mr. Lee," Archie said.

"I'm sorry, Mr. Lee is not available." She started to close the door.

"I have a warrant for his arrest," Archie said, producing it. "He can talk here at his home, or accompany me to headquarters. His choice."

She tried to stare him down, but didn't succeed. Finally she stepped back, opening the door wider. "I'll see if Mr. Lee will see you. He is not well."

"Neither is Bernice Barker," Archie said, angrily. "If he makes me wait more than ten minutes, I'll call for backup and he can be taken downtown by force. As I say, his choice." Bluff, of course, but she bought it. Strangely enough, law-abiding civilians usually did.

"Wait here." She disappeared up the angular stairway, leaving Archie to look around the entrance hall. He hadn't had much time to examine the house when he was here before. He had been surprised then that the house wasn't more 'Chinese', but rather followed the current trend toward an angular 'mod-erne' decor. On the other hand, the library where he and Brett had conducted their interviews had been more like an Englishman's castle than oriental. Lee was certainly an odd duck, if only speaking architecturally.

But, when Mrs. Logie gestured for him to come upstairs, and conducted him to a set of double doors, he was still unprepared for what lay within.

Here was China at last.

The walls were scarlet, the wood of the elaborately carved furniture was black, the carpet was heavily figured in pale colours, and the bed in the center of the room was hung with thickly embroidered golden silk. There were tables with bowls of flowers adding their fragrance to what was undoubtedly incense. The room was large, but felt somehow claustrophobic because it was so filled with furniture, and very warm. The bed, in particular, overpowered the room, it was so immense.

In the middle of the bed lay Mr. Lee, wearing bright yellow pajamas, looking like a fat Buddha at rest. His eyes were black as obsidian, set in a pale face, and his housekeeper had been right. He did not look well.

Archie had an strong impulse to throw open some win-dows and get some fresh air into the place, but he could see no windows, merely carved screens where windows might be.

"You have come to arrest me," Lee said. His voice was hoarse, as if his throat were sore.

"I have come to talk to you," Archie corrected him. He glanced behind him at the housekeeper. "Alone, if possible."

She looked at Lee. He waved a hand weakly, and she went out, closing the double doors behind her. Archie moved forward.

181

"Please sit," said Lee.

Archie chose a small chair and brought it over beside the bed. "I can see you are not well."

"A touch of indigestion."

"I was told you were poisoned."

Lee was startled. "Who told you that?"

"Bernice Barker."

The black eyes widened. "You spoke to Bernice?"

"Not exactly. She spoke to someone else. And now she's dead. Why is that, Mr. Lee?"

Lee looked away. "It is very complicated," he said.

"I have plenty of time."

Lee closed his eyes for a moment, then opened them, but not to look at Deacon. "Do you know anything about China?"

"Not really, no."

Lee smoothed the coverlet that lay across his ample middle. "I sell Chinese art objects," he said.

"I know that. So did Webster."

Again, Lee waved his hand as if motioning away an annoying fly. "No. He imported cheap everyday things. I do not. My wares are very expensive, Lieutenant Deacon. I sell only the best to the best museums and collectors. They are the only ones who can afford my wares in these hard times." He stopped.

Archie waited, and finally Lee continued.

"The political situation in China at the present time is very complex. At the moment there is a nationalist government in power, but it is under constant attack from all sides. Japan wants to invade but hesitates. Russia and Germany, also. Many Chinese people want to reinstate dynastic rule, which at least was stable if not altogether salutary, but more and more want to follow the Russians into Communism. Communism does not believe in art, especially religious art, and a great deal of Chinese art has to do with religion."

"Tell me about Suzy's jade," Deacon said, interrupting what looked like becoming a long speech about Chinese politics.

Lee was stunned. "How do you know about that?"

"I know you were planning to show your guests the other night something special in the jade line. I have learned it might have belonged to someone called Suzy."

"T'zu Hsi," Lee said, correcting his pronounciation. "The Dowager Empress. An evil, vicious and vain woman – perhaps even a murderess of her own son and others. She held the last power in the Manchu Empire and a more dreadful woman you cannot imagine. They called her the Dragon Empress, and the things she did are still whispered about. She was smart, though. Smart, sneaky, clever. She held the country together through fear and cunning. When she finally died, everything began to disintegrate."

"She had jade?"

"Of course she had access to all the Imperial jade, a vast collection accumulated over centuries. But she also had had a private collection of jade and jewels, mostly for her own adornment and pleasure, which disappeared when the Qing dynasty fell."

"Stolen?"

Lee avoided his eyes. "One presumes."

"And you have this jade?"

"I might."

"Well, you either have it or you don't."

"I have some jade which might be part of that fabulous secret collection," Lee said, carefully. "It was smuggled out of China by. . . an interested party, and conveyed to me for sale to the highest bidder."

"Smuggled out and smuggled in?"

Lee almost smiled. "Does it matter? The point is, getting it out of China was most difficult. And therefore the provenance is unproven."

"Provenance?"

"Proof of its origin or previous ownership," Lee said. "It is reputed to be part of T'zu Hsi's treasure. That aside, it is sufficiently exquisite in its own right to command a high price regardless of its lack of provenance."

"And who took it out of China? Was it Webster?"

"He had a part to play in the negotiations, yes, but it was far too much for him to handle. He came to me. Arrangements were made. The jade arrived safely and is presently in my strong room." He finally focused on Deacon. "I have new guards," he said, pointedly. "American guards."

"You think your guard shot Webster on purpose?"

"Of course he did."

183

"And was that because of Shining Sword?"

Lee said something terse in what Deacon assumed was Chinese. It didn't sound like poetry. "You know a great deal," Lee Chang snapped. "How do you know so much?"

"I do my research," Deacon told him, leaving Elodie out of it.

"You have interesting contacts, then. No Chinese told you about Shining Sword, did they?"

"No. Is it a secret society?"

Lee regarded him with interest. "I had not thought the Chicago police files to be so extensive." Deacon shrugged, and Lee gave him a little bow. "You impress me, Lieutenant. Ming Dao is indeed a secret society, as you call it. One of the most terrible and feared in all China today. It is quite new and largely made up of criminals and assassins, and is allied with the Communist cause. So far in this country it has only reared its wicked head here in Chicago, for some reason. I am sure if it is not stopped it will spread to other American cities with Chinese inhabitants. God help them if so."

"And this group kidnapped Webster?"

"They followed the trail of T'zu Hsi's jade to him, undoubtedly. They would have wanted to know where it is now. Some others have been involved in the transport of the jade. There is no knowing how much he told them of the chain – possibly up to the fact I now have it. It's worth a very great deal of money to them. Money for a Communist take-over of China. They are fanatical. I can only assume they tortured him but somehow he escaped. He came to warn me."

"About?"

"I have no precise answer for you, as the guard shot him before he could speak."

"The guard has disappeared. We can't find him anywhere. He may no longer be in the country. How did you come to hire him?"

Lee was silent for a moment, considering the question, then paled, and hissed like a snake between his teeth. "So," he whispered. Suddenly he shouted, making Deacon jump." Mrs. Logie!" The double doors opened instantly, and Archie realized the housekeeper had been standing immediately outside all the time. "Bring Helen Chou to me."

Mrs. Logie looked troubled. "She isn't here, sir. She left just after the Lieutenant arrived."

"Where did she go?"

"I have no idea. One minute she was there in the office, and the next she was gone. I saw her car go down the drive a few minutes ago."

Lee hissed again. It was quite an extraordinary sound. "So – it was she who was the snake in my bosom. She brought the guard to me, said he was a cousin, and needed the work. I wondered at the time, for I didn't like the man, but I needed someone, and Helen said he was trustworthy." He looked at Mrs. Logie with a new apprehension. "My keys..."

"I have your keys, Mr. Lee," Mrs. Logie said, quietly. "I have kept them with me ever since you fell ill. She could have taken nothing. Found nothing."

Lee sank back against his pillows, relief momentarily replacing the anger and fear, leaving him looking older, paler, and more ill than ever. "Helen wanted to go as the go-between with the Ming Dao and now I see why. But I sent Bernice thinking they would not dare harm an American. When they saw she was not Helen – " He raised his hands and let them drop limply onto the coverlet. "Now they will try again," he said, half to himself.

"Helen is of no more use to them. I must warn the General."

"The General?" Deacon was growing more and more confused.

"They are implacable. They will make a new plan. They want the jade and will strike again and again until they have what they want. It is hopeless."

"We can protect you, Mr. Lee. We can protect the jade," Deacon said, eagerly, volunteering the entire Chicago police force. "Let us help."

Lee stared at him. "But how can you?" he asked. "How will you tell the villains from the honest people? To you we all look alike." And slowly, quietly, and then with increasing despair, he began to laugh.

After Archie Deacon dropped her off, Elodie came in the front door and encountered Maybelle about to go out the same way. "Where are you off to?"

Her older sister wasn't dressed up to her usual evening standard but instead was attired in a sports outfit of sweater and slacks, which showed off her admirable figure to great effect. "I'm going to play miniature golf with Mr. Neal." Maybelle ducked her head to check her reflection in the entry mirror, and bared her teeth to check for lipstick smears.

Elodie frowned. "I thought Mr. Neal was married."

Maybelle tossed her hair and lifted her chin. "So?"

"Does Mumma know?"

Maybelle relented. "It's not just me, silly, it's the whole office. This new place has opened up near his house, and he's invited everybody along, that's all." She fixed Elodie with a sane and serious look. "I'm not an idiot, Ellie. I know what I'm doing."

"Are you sure?" Parker Neal was Maybelle's boss, and Elodie had met him once. He was handsome, charming, and very very rich. He was also very married to a well known local society girl.

"It's not Mr. Neal I have my eye on," Maybelle said. "It's Jim Beattie, from Accounting."

"Ah." Elodie was relieved.

"Anyway, we have to support Mr. Neal because his wife has left him," Maybelle tossed over her shoulder as she closed the front door.

Alyce looked up from her usual place beside the radio, and grinned. "She's just teasing you, Ellie. You know she wouldn't do anything wrong."

"I'm not so sure anymore," Elodie said, putting her hat and coat in the closet.

"Oh, Ellie..." Alyce said, appalled. "Maybelle . . . "

"It's not Maybelle who worries me. It's everything . . . people just aren't who they pretend to be these days. Archie was telling me he met the sweetest little woman last year – but he had to arrest her because she'd chopped up her husband with an axe. He says he doesn't know the honest policemen from the dishonest. Everybody seems to be wearing masks these days."

"The Shadow knows," Alyce said in a mysterious voice.

Elodie stared at her. "What?"

"What evil lurks in the minds of men. The Shadow knows."

"Oh, Lord, not another radio programme."

"But you work in radio, now." Alyce was deeply wounded at this evidence of perfidy toward her favourite form of entertainment. "I thought you were all for it."

Elodie sank down into her father's old chair, seeking its comfort. Sometimes, if you sat down hard enough, you could still catch the scent of his cigars. "Oh, honey, I am, I am. Don't pay any attention to me. I'm just so tired, I can't think straight. Even Archie said so."

Alyce surveyed her for a moment, and even turned down the jazzy music that was playing on the radio beside her. "Archie?"

Elodie felt herself flushing. "Lieutenant Deacon, I meant."

"I heard you the first time," Alyce said, with an air of amused accusation. "You called him Archie. You're sweet on him. I knew it, I really knew it."

"Well, that's more than I know." Elodie was too weary to argue the point. "He's in charge of finding out who killed Bernice."

"Oh." Alyce was instantly contrite. "I forgot. I'm sorry." Elodie shook her head and waved the apology away. Alyce went on. "I mean, it's bad that she was killed and so on, but she wasn't all that good a friend of yours, was she?"

"We went to school together," Elodie said, evasively. "We worked in the same building. We had lunch together nearly every day."

"But you didn't like her all that much, did you? Not really." Alyce, for all her youth, was very perceptive. "And Mumma didn't approve of her, either."

"Does that mean I'm not supposed to care that she had her head chopped off in some filthy alley?" Elodie realized she was more angry than she had thought. "That she laid there all alone while people walked right by only a few feet away?"

"Ellie!" Mrs. Browne came into the room and glanced at Alyce, who looked quite shocked. "There's no need to talk like that."

Elodie put her hands to her face. "I'm sorry, Mumma. I'm just so tired . . . I'm sorry, Alyce." She took her hands away. "I don't know where that came from."

"Nobody deserves to get murdered." Alyce's voice trembled only a little. "And Bernice wasn't so bad, really."

"She was a flighty little miss," Marie joined them with a brimming sewing basket. She sat down in her usual place and began sorting spools of thread. "Not to speak ill of the dead, but there's no reason to be hypocritical about it. I liked her, myself. She had spirit." This was surprising coming from Marie, who was the mildest of the Browne sisters.

"Did you really, Marie?" Elodie was grateful for the support.

"Yes, I did." Marie stabbed several pins into the fat red pincushion Alyce had made for her in her domestic science class. "But it was clear she would come to a bad end, Ellie, one way or another. Girls like that take chances. She took one too many, I guess." She looked up, her gaze kind and a little sad. "It does you credit that you care."

"Too much, perhaps." Mrs. Browne sat down beside Elodie in her own favourite chair, next to her late husband's. "You're getting all wound up in this, Ellie. I don't like it. You have a new job that needs all your attention. That alone is tiring. To go around asking questions about something that doesn't concern you, something that is obviously very dangerous, is too much. You're not that strong, you know. You never have been."

"I'm perfectly fine." Elodie knew her mother was right. "But Archie needs my help." She put up a hand. "Oh, not investigating murder, exactly. But I can do some research for him about what might lie behind it. I can do that much, anyway, to help. Tomorrow I'm going to talk to Father Anselm, and then that's the end of it for me."

"And who is Father Anselm?" Mrs. Browne's voice was wary.

"He's a missionary priest who teaches at DePaul." Elodie leaned forward to explain. "I have an appointment with him tomorrow to find out some things about China. He was there for many years." She told them about going to the library and the things that Drew Wilson had said. "It's all tied up with China, because of Mr. Lee and Mr. Webster and the guard and the jade and the secret society and . . ."

Mrs. Browne put her hand over Elodie's, which was now gripping the armrest of her father's chair so hard that the leather was creaking. "Ellie, slow down. You're babbling."

"I am?" Elodie abruptly realized she was also crying, and that they were all staring at her with worried expressions. She wiped her cheeks with the back of her hand. "I . . . I'm sorry."

"Take a deep breath in through your nose and out through your mouth," Mrs. Browne advised. It was her remedy for just about everything emotional. "And again." Elodie obeyed, and gradually felt herself relaxing. "Now then . . . I think you had better tell us all about it. I had no idea you had gone this far, and I'm not sure I want you to go any further."

"She's helping that cop she's sweet on," Alyce gave a little bounce of indignation. "So would I if I was Elodie. It's exciting. Like a story on the radio. I bet it's Fu Manchu."

"Alyce!" Mrs. Browne said, disapprovingly.

Elodie had to laugh, just a little. "She's right, Mumma. It is exciting."

"Not for Bernice." Marie pulled a stocking over her darning egg and picked up her needle.

"Well, I'm not going to walk down any dark alleys," Elodie said. "I'm just going to talk to a priest. And, anyway, Hugh is coming with me."

"And why is that?" Mrs. Browne asked, pointedly. "Because he's worried about you, too?"

"Well, there might be a story in it for him."

"But he is worried about you, isn't he?" Mrs. Browne persisted.

"I suppose so. Hugh worries about everything." It had been the source of many arguments between them as they grew up together. "But it's so interesting, Mumma." Slowly, she explained about 'Suzy' and the jade and the Ming Dao. "Father Anselm will know all about the Ming Dao and the other things, I'm sure of it. Mr. Evans said he was a great authority."

"So is Maybelle, to hear her tell it." Alyce had obviously

189

been subjected to a speech or two from Maybelle. "She's read one novel about China and so she thinks she knows everything. She said it's a terrible place for the peasants."

"Well, I'm not a peasant and I have no intention of going to China." Elodie smiled at Alyce.

"But you insist on seeing this priest?" Mrs. Browne asked.

"That's all, Mumma. Just to talk to him, to see if he knows anything that will help Archie figure this all out. Archie's own captain is making it hard for him. He closed the investigation on Mr. Webster because of some kind of pressure from over his head, and then he had to re-open it because of Bernice and he didn't like having to do that, and Archie has to work alone because he doesn't know who to trust . . ."

"Are you sure it's not this Archie who interests you more than China?" Mrs. Browne's voice was gentle.

"Bernice said he was very attractive." Marie replaced the darned stocking with another holed one and rethreaded her needle.

"No." Elodie heard her voice crack. "No. I really like Mr. Lee and I liked Bernice, too, no matter what you say. She was fun, and she was good-hearted and . . . " She realized she was weeping again.

Marie stood up. "You need something to eat." Like their mother, she had her own special remedies, and they all had to do with food. "I bet you're absolutely sloshing with coffee and nothing else since lunch. I kept your dinner warm in the oven, but it's probably dried up by now. I'll make you a sandwich."

"I'm not hungry." The very thought of food made Elodie feel quite ill.

"You will eat something." Mrs. Browne, concerned mother, turned into Mrs. Browne, stern teacher of recalcitrant children. "And then you will have a relaxing bath and go straight to bed. We can talk about all of this again in the morning."

"But – "

Mrs. Brown stood up and looked down at her miserable daughter. "Do I have to get angry, Ellie?" Her voice was kind but firm. Elodie knew the tone, they had all grown up with it, and there was no use arguing. She got up obediently, suddenly grateful to have someone take charge of her. She knew her mother was right, she was too tired, too wound up, too involved for her own good.

She also knew that whatever anybody said, she was going to see Father Anselm tomorrow. Silently she followed Marie through the dining room. Behind them, Alyce turned up the volume on the radio, where a manly voice was announcing Miss Smith would now sing 'What Is This Thing Called Love?'.

Elodie immediately thought of Archie Deacon, and was so disconcerted that she nearly walked into the swinging kitchen door.

**

The object of Elodie's mental image was not a happy man.

Archie drove away from the Lee house in some confusion, having learned both too much and too little.

Lee admitted sending Bernice to Chinatown with a picture of one of the jade chess pieces belonging to the late T'zu Hsi as evidence of his possession and willingness to negotiate.

But he refused to say – or did not know – who met Bernice and killed her. That it was some member of the dreaded Ming Dao was obvious, but Lee claimed to know no names. Helen Chou had wanted to go, made great efforts to be the one representing Lee, pointing out that she spoke Chinese and could therefore deal more effectively with whoever came to meet her. But Bernice, jealous of her position as Lee's personal secretary, had insisted. Lee, too ill to argue with two shrill women, had let Bernice take on the responsibility because he thought she was bolder than Helen and possibly safer from attack because she was an American.

And now Helen Chou, by her sudden and inexplicable disappearance, seemed likely to be the traitor in the Lee organisation. It had been Helen, after all, who had conveyed the time and place of the meeting, claiming there had been a telephone call demanding it. And she had not been at the party, having claimed to be ill on the night. Extraordinary, as she would have been expected to be Lee's hostess to those guests whose English was poor.

"The guard was named Chou," Archie had pointed out.

Lee shook his head. "Chou is as common in China as Smith is here." It had been obvious that Lee Chang was seriously affected by Helen's apparent disloyalty. He seemed convinced that Archie would be hampered because he wouldn't be able to recognize which Chinese person was good or bad. Lee himself had been fooled, after all. When his somewhat hysterical laughter had faded, he had sunk back in his pillows and closed his eyes. Although Archie went on questioning him, he only gave brief answers and was generally uncooperative. It was as if he had accepted his fate, whatever it might be. He never opened his eyes after that. He had gone somewhere far away inside himself, and eventually Archie had given up.

"The treasure is cursed," were Lee's last words. "I should never have agreed to take it. I will die for my greed."

Archie had stood, promising to have the house watched. He left Lee to the tender ministrations of Mrs. Logie, who glared at him balefully as he left.

He returned to the station, wrote out a brief report of his interview (not mentioning his method of getting into the house), and organised regular drive-bys of the Lee mansion. Lee's new guards were patrolling the grounds. Archie knew the company that employed them. They would be reliable – they ought to be, because the agency charged top dollar. Many of them were former police officers.

He frowned. Not that that guaranteed anything these days.

Back in his apartment he tried to put it all together. This treasure was more than just a chess set, that was certain. It seemed clear to him that Webster's ill-fated intervention had prevented a terrrible crime taking place. He conjectured that once Lee and his guests had entered the strongroom, the planted guard would have sealed them in, making them hostages against the handing over of the treasure to the Ming Dao.

The fact that Miss Hutton would have been among the hostages would have created tremendous pressure and a certain scandal. Lee – and whoever his seller had been – would have been pressured from all sides to hand over the jade as ransom immediately.

The identity of the seller was another secret Lee had kept to himself, along with the value and extent of the treasure itself. Who had smuggled it out of China and into the United States? Some ex-member of the Qing dynasty who had inherited it? Some thief who had stolen it? That it was apparently recognizable would have precluded its sale in China itself. Immigration from China was increasing steadily. Had it come into the hands of some wealthy Chinese who hoped to move his assets out of the homeland and into America in order to give himself a base here before the Communists totally took over?

And who was the General?

Deacon made himself scrambled eggs – more or less the height of his culinary skills – ate it with a crust of bread that hadn't gone mouldy, and went to bed. How was he to find the killer of Bernice Barker when it could be any Chinese person in Chicago? And Lee was right – the members of this Ming Dao probably looked no different than any other Chinese.

Guilty or innocent, they would bow, smile, tell lies, bow, smile, and tell more lies.

They could all be killers.

And what if all this about the Ming Dao came out to the public? Clearly this was why the powers that be feared publicity about the decapitated Chinese murder victims. There would be repugnance, a backlash against the entire Chinese community, and possibly panic. Innocent people could get hurt. Prejudice against immigrants was easily inflamed in these hard times, when every job was precious, every penny counted. Worried people turned to drink. That would please the Syndicates.

He opened his eyes suddenly and stared at the blocks of light cast from the window onto the ceiling.

The Syndicates.

There had been many conflicts between the Italian and Chinese neighbourhoods which lay side by side. Beatings, a shooting, competition for prime business sites and housing space. Could Capone or one of the others be involved in this? Was it even more complicated than it had seemed to him five minutes ago?

Was that why someone had hushed up the Webster murder? Why someone had been so reluctant to re-open the case when Bernice Barker was killed? Why he was getting no help from anyone on the Force? He'd be willing to bet a week's salary that already Brett or someone else had cancelled the drive-bys he had set up for the Lee house.

"Let 'em blame it all on the Chinks."

He could hear Capone saying it right now.

He could hear his vulgar, rasping laughter.

And he could hear his own heart start to race as from the street below there came the wail of a siren.

Who had died tonight?

Who would die tomorrow?

17

Exhaustion took Elodie deep into sleep almost immediately, for which she was grateful. Just before she dropped off she resolved that her appointment with Father Anselm would be the last thing she would do because all this stuff about China was getting very scary. Hugh and Archie were right – whoever killed Mr. Webster and Bernice (to say nothing of the five nameless Chinese) was still out there. Whether it was a group or a single person, she would be foolish to tempt fate by getting in their way. The police should and could handle it.

With that decision made, oblivion claimed her.

She slept late – or pretended to – until nearly everyone had left the house. Her mother had to teach, Maybelle had her job, Alyce had school. That left only Marie downstairs.

Would Marie try to stop her?

She dressed carefully, wanting to look serious and scholarly for Father Anselm. Since she always wore black, that was not a big problem, but she eschewed the normal accessories she used to brighten an outfit, and settled on a plain white collar and cuffs.

The smell of coffee wafted up the stairs as she descended. She knew Marie always percolated a second pot once everyone had left, so she could sip it as she listened to her favourite radio programmes. Morning was when programmes like Betty Crocker, Aunt Jemima, Housekeeper's Half Hour and The Wife Saver came on. Sure enough, she found Marie listening to some suggestions to liven up pot roast and making entries in one of the big housekeeping and recipe books she kept so carefully. "For the grandchildren," she always said, with a smile.

There had to be at least five of the blue notebooks already resting on a shelf in the pantry. Maybelle often told Marie if she would get enough of her recipes and tips together they might get published one day. But Marie was too modest to contemplate such a thing. She was optimistic about 'the

195

grandchildren' she expected them all to have one day, and Elodie had always loved her for that. Marie had a beau – Bill Matthew – but the prospect of marriage and children was still a distant one because she felt it was up to her to run the house until Mrs. Browne retired from teaching. Mrs. Browne said that was nonsense, they could manage – Marie should marry Bill and settle down in her own home. But Marie said there was time enough for that when they could afford it. Meanwhile she wrote her notes in the big blue books, and Bill saved what money he could in these hard times.

But Elodie worried that he wouldn't wait forever.

Marie looked up. "You're safe, they're all gone."

"Didn't fool you?"

"Didn't fool Mumma, either." Marie turned over a page and continued writing. "She's counting on your good sense."

"And you?"

Marie shrugged. "I cook and clean and sew. You're the one who causes trouble."

"I don't mean to." Elodie poured herself some coffee and took one of the muffins that were cooling on the cake rack. She pulled out a chair and sat down opposite Marie, who made a final entry and closed her notebook as the theme music for the programme came on.

"Are you going on with it?" Marie asked.

Elodie bit into the muffin and nearly choked on an errant crumb. "Are you going to stop me?"

Marie got up and went to the sink to rinse out her cup and pour a fresh one. "No. I wouldn't even try, Ellie. You know your own mind, and I have a feeling that nothing I say would make any difference, anyway."

"True." Elodie shoved in the last bit of muffin and chewed thoughtfully. "Anyway, Hugh is going with me, so that's all right."

But she was wrong.

As she was retrieving her coat from the closet the telephone rang, and it was Hugh himself. "Ellie, you have to cancel that appointment."

"Why?" She glanced toward the kitchen and kept her voice low.

"Because I have to go out to Cicero on another story and I can't go with you. Make it for tomorrow or something."

"I can't – I made the appointment through his department at the college, I have no way of reaching him directly."

"Call them and get them to do it. You're not to go alone."

"Phooey." She wound the phone cord around her forearm and then unwound it again, making a pattern in her flesh. She waited for the inevitable outburst, but it did not come. Only a deep, exasperated sigh.

"Dammit, I haven't time to argue, the photographer is waiting for me," Hugh said, hurriedly. "You're not to go alone, Ellie."

"I understand." She understood she would be going alone and wasn't in the least worried about it. "Thank you for calling." Elodie hung up.

Marie came into the dining room with an armful of freshly-ironed napkins which she put into the drawer of the sideboard. "Who was that?"

"The meeting to go over the new scripts has been rescheduled. We'll be glad of the extra time."

"Well, you'd better get down there and get to work, then. You're late enough as it is. I imagine they'll be glad to see you."

"I imagine so." She didn't want Marie worrying all day long. She had an impulse to call Archie Deacon and ask him to accompany her, but dismissed it as quite ridiculous. He could only confuse an issue which was probably quite straightforward. "Can I have another muffin to eat on the trolley?"

"I'll put it into your lunch bag." Marie asked no questions, and Elodie wondered if she suspected. Probably. She might stay at home all day being domestic and actually enjoying it, but she was no fool, and she knew Elodie through and through. The lie unspoken was still a lie, but somehow a little less sinful than the lie direct. And the meeting *had* been rescheduled, but she had known that yesterday. As for Sal and Drew, they thought she had a doctor's appointment this morning, so would not expect her. The lie direct was for non-family.

Elodie collected her lunch from Marie, put on her hat and coat, and went out to meet the day. It was windy, but the sky was blue and the air was fresh. By tonight she would have the whole Chinese business cleared up in her own mind. If anything Father Anselm had to say was relevant to Archie's investigation she would relay it and that would be that. She had hoped he would call and tell her about his talk with Mr. Lee, but the phone had been silent all evening and only Hugh had called this morning.

Oh well – if it had been anything really scary he would have called her, wouldn't he? Of course.

She saw the trolley coming down the street and ran to catch it. It wouldn't be polite to be late.

**

After two trolley transfers she was in the right neighborhood, but unsure exactly where to find either Addison Avenue or St. John's House. Stopping in a corner shop, she got precise directions and eventually located both.

St. John's House was a large, purpose-built edifice but neither forbidding nor institutional. In fact, it was of warm pink brick accented with white shutters, flanked by large oak trees, and had an immaculate front lawn bordered by spring flowers that tossed in the breeze as she went up the curving path to the front door.

Inside, she went to a desk marked Reception and asked for Father Anselm, stating her name and that she had an appointment. The young priest behind the desk seemed unsurprised by that – she was still young enough to pass for a student, after all. He directed her to a small, comfortable lounge, and said he would summon Father Anselm for her.

The lounge was filled with pairs of chairs covered in cheerful flower prints. Small tables sat between each pair, and it was obviously a place designed for private conversations. It smelled of lavender and furniture polish, and the carpet, though worn, glowed with rich colour.

She was standing by the window, looking out at a side garden that was clearly tended with great love, when she heard a step behind her and turned. Father Anselm stood in the doorway, and he was not at all what she had expected, if indeed she had formed any preconceptions at all.

For a start, he was black. And yet he was also, unmistakably, at least partially Chinese. The combination was extraordinary, resulting in tilted eyes and high cheekbones in a mahogany face. He stood straight, but his hair was grey and there were deep lines in his face. He noted her expression and chuckled.

"Not what you expected?" His smile was startingly white against the dark complexion. Elodie didn't know what to say, and felt herself flushing because of her inability to control her reaction. Father Anselm waved a negligent hand. "Don't worry about it. It has proved most useful to me to be . . . how shall we put it . . . unusual? It disarms people, and once they get accustomed to it, everything is fine."

"I'm sorry." Actually, she was fascinated. His accent was clearly American, and despite his unusual appearance, he was obviously from the midwest.

"Please sit down, Miss Browne." He gestured her to a comfortable chair, and took one next to it. He wore a dark blue sweater and trousers, and only the white band of his collar indicated his calling. "Mr. Evans told me you had come to him with some questions about China – most particularly 'ming dao'?"

"Yes." Elodie sat on the edge of her chair, unsure how to proceed. "It was a bet..."

Anselm gently interrupted her. "We will proceed much more quickly if you tell me how you heard the words and in what circumstances. I can't say I'm happy that an obviously respectable young woman should have those words on her lips."

"Is it so terrible, then?"

He leaned back in his chair. "It could be." But he smiled as he said it, and she was encouraged.

"They were the words of a dying man." She hadn't meant it to come out quite so dramatically. He seemed unperturbed.

"No more than I expected. Go on."

Quickly, Elodie outlined what had happened at the party when Webster had burst in. "He said the Ming Dao had 'got him' but that he'd gotten away."

"Then he was a lucky man." Anselm crossed one leg over the other and folded his hands in his lap. "Go on."

She related how the guard had shot him before he could say any more, and that the guard had claimed to be only 'doing his duty' to protect Mr. Lee, but Mr. Lee had been angry at him. The police had taken the guard away, but he had since disappeared. Anselm kept nodding as she spoke. She stopped there, not wanting to go on to Bernice's death before she knew more.

Anselm looked out the window for a moment, gathering his thoughts. Eventually he spoke, rather reflectively. "Perhaps it would be helpful if I told you a little of my own background."

"All right." Having gotten her first worries off her chest, Elodie felt herself beginning to relax, and moved back a little in the overstuffed chair.

"I was born here in Chicago. My mother was Chinese, my father black. I took the name Anselm when I was ordained, of course. I grew up in a neighborhood where I was an outsider in everyone's eyes, not like any of them. The Chinese rejected my mother for marrying out, my father's people felt the same toward him. It was a lonely life for them, too, but they had a remarkably happy marriage. My father was a fireman, and not home as much as he would have liked because of his working hours, so my mother's influence was strong. There were three children, and we all have entered the Church, perhaps because it was only there and at home that we felt accepted and comfortable. My sister is in a nursing order, my brother is a Franciscan monk in California. I chose to be a missionary and a teacher. Because I spoke Chinese, my destination was an obvious one. I was sent to China, where I taught in a mission school and was very happy there. I loved the Chinese culture, the people, everything." He paused. Sighed. "Everything." He looked down at his hands. "But things were not well in China – still are not. The last royal dynasty that ruled, the Qing, fell shortly before the Great War began. Afterward everything was and still is in a state of flux. Sun Yat Sen was a visionary who wanted democracy for China, but because he could not get proper support from the British or Americans, other influences began to try and take control. When Sun died, and things were very uncertain, the Russians were eager to move into power. Also the Japanese. Now Chiang Kai Shek has set up a nationalist government, but it is under many threats from many sides. I have tried, in my small way, to be of help to the Nationalist Kuomintang government because in them I see the best hope for a free China where their splendid culture would be respected and retained."

"Why did you leave?"

"The Communists are growing stronger and stronger. They were put down rather brutally once, but they are reforming in the countryside, and it is only a matter of time before they gather sufficient strength to challenge the present government. I had been in China for twenty years, and it was thought best that I return to Chicago to teach others who may follow. But I have remained in touch with friends I made there, and have helped where I could. Naturally I support Chiang Kai Shek, who at least respects China's cultural heritage. The Ming Dao, on the other hand, belong to the Communist faction."

"Is it a secret society?"

He glanced at her in surprise. "You know about that?"

"I have a friend – a work colleague – who thought they might be. He said there are lots of secret societies in China."

"Indeed there are, and have been for centuries. Some are new and troublesome, others are old and respected. The Ming Dao belong to the first group. They are ruthless, vicious, stop at nothing. Kidnapping is one of their specialities. As is murder."

"Why would they kidnap Mr. Webster? Was it because of Suzy's jade?"

"You seem to know a good deal more than Mr. Evans indicated, Miss Browne." Father Anselm did not look particularly pleased at this discovery. He scowled and looked around the empty room uneasily. "How did you learn about that?"

"Bernice told me. I think Mr. Lee Chang has the jade now. But I don't know where he got it."

Father Anselm gazed at her with a degree of sadness. "He got it from me." His voice was quiet. "And was this Bernice the unfortunate young woman who was found murdered in Chinatown?"

"Yes, she was."

"*Mea culpa*, I'm afraid."

"You didn't kill her!" Elodie could not believe that.

"No, but I have participated in a chain of events that may have led to her death. I am very sorry."

Elodie could hardly believe her ears. She had arrived with a simple wish to learn more about Ming Dao, what it meant, what it was. Now this quiet, unusual man was saying he was the person who brought the jade to Mr. Lee and so in some way felt responsible for Bernice's death. She thought back to the steps she had taken, one by one, that had inevitably led her to this man. Had she been directed here? It seemed incredible, incomprehensible. Especially in this small, slightly shabby, but very American room, with its flowered upholstery and holy pictures on the walls. Behind Father Anselm a painting of the Madonna looked down with sadness and infinite sympathy in her eyes. Below the painting was a vase with the dried folded palm leaves left over from Palm Sunday.

"I'm afraid I don't understand at all," Elodie said.

"Perhaps I can help." The voice came from behind them. It was a rough-edged voice with an unmistakable East London accent. Elodie turned and saw a short, stocky, balding man with a sagging face and heavy black eyebrows. He stepped into the room and closed the door behind him.

"Morris, you should have stayed in your room," Father Anselm was concerned and made as if to rise from his chair. "You aren't well."

He was waved back into his seat. "I'm fine. And I don't think you should be taking all the blame for this mess onto yourself." The man came forward, pulled a chair over, sat down and smiled benignly at them.

Father Anselm shook his head, sighed, but was apparently resigned to his presence. "Miss Browne, I want you to meet the General. General Morris Cohen, one of Chiang Kai Shek's chief aides." The priest allowed himself a brief smile. "Popularly known in China as Two-Gun Cohen."

**

Miss Desire Smith: (over dramatically) I can't go on like this!

Mr. Dunning: I assure you, Miss Desire, that the new orchestra will be ready to rehearse with you this afternoon.

Miss Desire Smith: You don't understand . . . I am sensitive to nuances . . .there may be a terrible clash . . . (stops suddenly and loses accent) –
what will they be wearing?
Dunning: I beg your pardon?

Miss Desire Smith: What colour are their outfits? Not red, are they?

Mr. Dunning: I'm afraid I don't know, but –

Miss Desire Smith: (calling for agent) Charlie! Charlie! Where's my contract?

Hugh Murphy knocked on the frosted glass of Room 1054 and a voice told him to come in. He did so, and was greeted by the sight of a stoutish woman in a tight and eye-wateringly bright green dress. She was sitting on a battered leather sofa, and opposite her, a long, thin man was stretched out on a second sofa, his head propped on one armrest, his feet on the other. The woman had frizzy hair and astonished-looking drawn-on eyebrows. The man looked decidedly unwell, with a pasty complexion and dark circles under his eyes. The big table between the two sofas was thickly covered with papers, some typewritten, some scrawled with handwriting. A typewriter was on a small wheeled table to one side, and against the far wall was another table with coffee-making equipment. The room smelled strongly of coffee, cigarettes, and – rather surprisingly – an expensive perfume he recognized. His new girlfriend wore the same scent.

"I'm looking for Elodie Browne." Hugh stepped into the room, holding the door partly open behind him.

"So are we," said the supine man. "She was due here over an hour ago. She had a doctor's appointment."

"There's nothing wrong with her, is there?" The woman seemed worried. Despite her odd appearance, her tone was motherly.

"Not as far as I know."

"Who are you?" asked the man, sounding rather like the caterpillar in *Alice in Wonderland*.

"My name is Hugh Murphy. I'm -"

"Ellie's cousin." The woman stood up and came over to shake his hand. Her grip was surprisingly strong. "How do you do. I'm Sal Schwartz and that lounge lizard over there is Drew Wilson."

"You're the writers."

"For our sins." The woman sat down again, smoothing her dress over her ample thighs. "Ellie has told us a lot about you."

Hugh smiled. "Ellie is a force unto herself. But her sister

said she had come to work as usual this morning."

Sal and Drew looked at one another and frowned. "No, she had a doctor's appointment," Drew repeated. "She told us yesterday. But she said she would be back by lunchtime, and she isn't."

"Damn." Hugh felt his anger rising. "It wasn't a doctor she was going to see. I told her not to go. That little idiot."

"Hey – that's our Ellie you're talking about. Where's she gone, then, if not to the doctor?"

"To see a man about a word." Hugh felt a little sick. She couldn't still be with Father Anselm. It was nearly two-thirty, and the appointment had been at ten.

"Uh-oh." Drew actually sat up. "Ming Dao?"

Hugh was startled. "You know about that?"

"We do." Sal looked a little cross, too. "We told her to forget about it. It was beginning to affect her work. We're up against a deadline here, and we need her full concentration. It's her idea, after all. She has a remarkable imagination. Perfect for radio."

"That imagination of hers may be perfect for radio, but it's the bane of my life." Hugh came all the way in and closed the door. "Could I cadge a cup of coffee?"

"Help yourself." Sal was expansive. "Want a sandwich? You can have the extra one I brought for Ellie in case she forgot."

Drew lay back down on the sofa and closed his eyes. "Sal would feed the nation if she could."

"Thanks." Hugh was grateful for the offer, as he had had no chance to stop for lunch on the way back from the bloodbath in Cicero. He gulped the hot coffee and stuffed the sandwich down as quickly as he could. "I have to find a phone." He spoke with difficulty around the last of the ham on rye Sal had provided.

"You can use ours," Sal said, pointing. "We finally got one put in yesterday."

Hugh rang information and got the number of St. John's House, as Ellie could have done if she had really intended to cancel her appointment with Father Anselm. He mentally cursed her stubbornness and her damned curiosity. And she had more or less lied to him on the phone that morning. What the devil was she up to?

18

Elodie looked in amazement at the man named Two-Gun Cohen. He certainly didn't look like a military man. He was short and overweight, and his rather poor complexion was pasty. With his mild expression and kind eyes he could have been a tailor, a tobacconist, a schoolteacher. She had almost laughed aloud when Father Anselm had introduced him.

The General chuckled. "Don't fit the description, do I?

"Oh, but –" Elodie began.

He chuckled again and sat down with a little grunt in one of the easy chairs. "I picked up the nickname when I was running a military school in China some years ago, and it stuck. The Chinese properly call me 'Mah Kun' which is the closest they can come to the name I was born with, Morris Cohen. Frankly, I like 'Two-gun' the best. Makes me sound quite the thing."

Elodie thought it made him sound like one of Capone's men, but didn't say so. She felt an immediate liking for the General. He and Father Anselm seemed to be good friends. They exchanged a glance and some agreement seemed to pass between them.

"Miss Browne, I think you deserve an explanation," the General said.

"I would like one." Elodie sat back a little in her chair. "But I realize it's none of my business."

"I think losing your friend makes it your business, in a way." Two-Gun reached into his jacket and withdrew a cigar, taking his time to unwrap, clip, and light it. "But where to begin?"

"With the jade, I think." Father Anselm. "I am sure Miss Browne can be discreet."

"You really don't know me," Elodie protested.

"I am a very good judge of character." Two-Gun gently tapped a bit of cigar ash into a glass dish on the little table beside his chair. "You were clever enough to get this far, so you deserve to know the facts, at least. " He took another puff of the cigar, and then laid it in the ashtray. "You've been curious about someone named Suzy?" He explained who 'Suzy' really was. "T'zu Hsi's treasure has quite a history. It has passed through many hands since her death, very few of them legitimate. A few small pieces are antique, but most of it is modern, made to her commission. Among this latter group is a chess set, a crown, and many pieces of jewelry. Traditionally jade is not mixed with other stones, but she had her own ideas and the money to indulge them. No need to go into details, my dear, but the treasure eventually came into my hands. Or, rather, into the hands of Chiang Kai Shek. While it is extremely valuable in artistic terms, he is a realist. I was commissioned to sell it and buy guns and ammnuition against the revolution which is threatening the new nationalist government."

"There are others who want it for the same reason but a different cause," Father Anselm said.

"The Ming Dao?"

"Yes."

Elodie clasped her hands in her lap. Chicago had become bad enough as it was, but here was a whole new source of conflict and cruelty, an offshoot of a far–away struggle in a strange and mysterious country most Americans knew little about. She looked at the priest. "You condone this ... purchase of arms?"

"Not Christian?" Father Anselm had the grace to look embarrassed. "You're right, of course. But at least the Nationalist Government would allow religious freedom. Communism does not. There will be time for ploughshares later on."

"I see."

Elodie was struggling to encompass it all. Last week she had been a lowly copywriter concerned with shoe polish and corn plasters. Then she had been a waitress at a party and seen a man murdered right before her eyes. Then she was a radio copywriter whose mind kept wandering to the puzzle of the word Ming Dao. People like Father Anselm and 'Two-Gun' Cohen were from another world of civil war and smuggling. Ming Dao turned out to be a ruthless group of men who kidnapped and killed people. They had killed Mr. Webster and they had killed Bernice. Before she had known nothing of China beyond chop suey. Now she felt like she was in the middle of some outrageous Saturday matinee.

Father Anselm leant forward earnestly. "It is a time of war, Miss Browne. I can't stand aside and see China tear herself apart. Such a great nation deserves to preserve its history and ensure its future. Morris and I are only a small part of it all, but if we can make a difference I, for one, am prepared to accept risks and even the disapproval of my religion. The Catholic Church has gone to war before and no doubt will again, should the threat be great enough."

"My friend the Idealist." Two-Gun was amused. "Me, I am a practical man. I do what I can and try to stay alive. If I can make a profit along the way, so be it." He leant back and picked up his cigar again, watching her through the curls of smoke.

She hardly knew what to say. Her curiosity had been satisfied. She had her answers. She knew what Ming Dao was, and she knew about Suzy's Jade. She had promised herself that would be enough. So now was the time to let it all go, time to leave the rest to Father Anselm and Two-Gun Cohen. Pulling her feet back, she prepared to stand up. As she did so, the door to the lounge opened and three Chinese men entered. They were well dressed and smiling, friends of Father Anselm, she assumed. The last one in turned to thank the young priest who had admitted them, and then firmly shut the door in his face.

The smiles disappeared.

The first man, who was wearing a grey hat and suit, drew a gun and gestured at them all with it. "You come."

"Oh, dear," said Father Anselm.

"Bloody hell," said Two-Gun Cohen.

Elodie opened her mouth, but nothing came out.

"You come now. No fuss or we shoot." Grey Hat paused, then turned the gun toward Elodie. "We shoot her."

Father Anselm stood up. "She has nothing to do with this, she is just my student. We're discussing her term paper on China . . ."

The second man scowled and spoke in rapid Chinese to Grey Hat. The third man, short and broad-chested, said nothing but his eyes were beady and black, like a snake's. He kept staring at Elodie and wetting his lips.

"She comes, too." Grey Hat was impatient. "Or I shoot her here and now. Might shoot more on way out. Your choice, priest."

They obeyed. There didn't seem to be anything else to do. As they went toward the outer door the young priest in Reception cleared his throat. "When will you be back, Father?"

Father Anselm hesitated, and Elodie could see he was weighing the chances of shouting for help and perhaps precipitating a bloodbath in this house of peace. He finally spoke. "I don't know, my son."

Grey Hat prodded Father Anselm in the back with the gun, which was now hidden in his pocket, and muttered something. Father Anselm moved forward again. Elodie knew that the General must have a gun in his back, too, because she did. Held by the man who kept licking his lips and breathing hot garlicky air down the back of her neck.

The young priest had only been at St. John's House for a few months, but had become accustomed to seeing Father Anselm with Chinese people. He smiled and nodded as they went out. "Have a nice lunch," he called after them.

Outside they were hustled down the path and then along the sidewalk to a white van with the words 'Schaeffer's Sausages' painted on it. Grey Hat opened the rear doors and they were pushed unceremoniously up into it. Obviously it was not used for meat deliveries, for there were benches along each side. As they sat, the fat thug got in, too, and slammed the doors shut. He leaned against the doors and continued to stare at Elodie. With a lurch that nearly unsettled them all, the van moved away.

Father Anselm was very distressed. "I'm sorry, Miss Browne, they should never have forced you to come with us."

"Is it the Ming Dao?" Elodie was annoyed to hear her voice quaver.

"I fear so."

The General was furious. "I should have expected this. Webster gave away more than we thought."

She felt tears start behind her eyes, and blinked fast. "Everybody told me to stop, but I wouldn't."

"Stop what?" the General wanted to know.

"Being nosy. Imagining I could find out about Ming Dao

and solve the mystery." She winced. "I've been reading too many of Alyce's Nancy Drew books."

The General looked puzzled. "Nancy Drew?"

"I believe Nancy Drew is a character in a new popular series of girl's adventure books," Father Anselm said. The General didn't seem any wiser for the explanation.

"I've been in China too long," he said, crossly. "I have no bloody idea what goes on here or in England, anymore." He looked at Elodie. "You seem a nice young woman. I apologise for the way you're being treated. I'll get them to release you as soon as we get wherever it is we're going." He seemed to be confident.

From the look on the Chinese guard's face, Elodie didn't think it would be that simple. She was absolutely terrified, her stomach was churning and her heart felt like it was trying to burst out through her ribs. Despite this, she found herself fighting to suppress wild laughter that threatened to well up in her. It was so ridiculous. Here she was in the back of a van with a dancing pig on it, being guarded by a member of some dreadful murdering Chinese secret society, in the company of a politically active Catholic priest and an English Jewish smuggler and arms buyer. Quite the ethnic cross-section, she thought, and again struggled against the hysterical laughter.

She suddenly thought of Bernice lying in an alley with her head cut off, and the rising laughter turned to rising bile. What would the Ming Dao do to her? She swallowed hard and clenched her hands together to stop their trembling.

She must be more positive. She must look around, think constructively, try to imagine a way to fight back, to escape. Think, Ellie, think.

What would Nancy Drew do?

**

An hour later Drew Wilson and Hugh Murphy left St. John's house and stood on the pavement under the oak trees.

"This is insane," Drew said. "That young idiot of a priest didn't even question it." He was apparently no fan of Catholicism, and seemed to feel the failure of the young priest in Reception to realize something was amiss was entirely due to religious fatalism.

Hugh looked up and down Addison Avenue. A peaceful semi-suburban street, nothing remarkable about it. A fairly wealthy neighbourhood, judging from the houses on either side.

"Let's ask the neighbours." He started toward the house directly opposite St. John's House.

"Let's call the police." Drew followed him, feeling in his pocket for his trusty flask. He realized that wanting to involve the police only proved how rattled he was. "That girl Bernice was murdered, and that guy – whatsisname – "

"Webster."

Drew took a swig from his flask, offered it to Hugh, who shook his head. "Yeah, Webster. I mean, Jesus, these Ming Dao people are killers."

Hugh scowled. "If it was the Ming Dao."

Drew was exasperated. "Who else could it be? The Chinese Brass Band Marching Society? The Kowloon Balloon Company?"

Hugh ignored that. "It's been almost two hours, now. Either they're already dead, in which case we can do nothing, or they aren't, in which case we have a chance. Let's get some facts for the police to go on, first. Then we'll think about calling them."

"You're as bad as Ellie about going your own way." Drew was disgusted.

Hugh stopped in the middle of the street and Drew almost walked into him. "Do you really trust the police?" Hugh demanded.

Drew stared at him, then replaced the flask in his pocket, settled his overcoat on his shoulders, and began to walk ahead. "Point taken. What do we ask these nosy neighbours?"

"If any of them saw the make of the car they left in? Perhaps a license number? "

"This is not exactly a lace-curtain neighborhood. People in these houses are not the nosy type."

"No, but their servants are." Hugh went straight up to a front door and pressed the doorbell.

**

"Let 'em blame it all on the Chinks."

The words Archie had imagined coming from Capone still haunted him. All the while he was attending the homicide scene in Cicero, he had been itching to see if he could find some link between the Syndicate and the Chinese community – or, at least, the criminal part of it. He finally left his fellow officers to deal with the latest Prohibition mess. For a moment he thought he had seen Hugh Murphy in the crowd of reporters, but knew must be with Elodie interviewing that priest. Just as well, too. She needed looking after every minute.

When he returned to headquarters he checked out the previous night's activities – four speakeasies raided, two beatings, and a collision between a truck loaded with beer and a fire engine on the way to a blaze. Seventeen arrests from the speakeasies (either a very quiet night or a great deal of money had changed hands before the 'respected citizens' disappeared into the shadows). Blind eyes turned everywhere.

He sighed and poured his first cup of coffee. Sitting at his desk he looked around the squad room. Four detectives were in, and there wasn't a single one he could talk to about his worries and suspicions. Slovensky had a handicapped kid who needed operations, he was pretty sure Morgan had a drink problem, Levy had an old mother and grandmother dependent on him, and Scott had just married an Italian girl whose father was rumoured to be a banker for the Syndicate. They all had pressures that might drive them to forget the rules. When his old partner had been killed in a warehouse shoot-out, he had lost the one man he trusted. He refused to have another partner, despite continuing pressure from Captain Brett. He knew what Brett wanted was to give Archie a partner who would keep an eye on him, report back, and in general rein him in. Well, he would have none of it. He went out with others in group situations, he did his duty when ordered (as in the Webster shooting when he had been the only man available), but he investigated on his own.

So far.

He didn't know how long it would be before Brett had his way, preaching that policy required it, and attached someone to his shoulder. "Every officer needs back-up," Brett would say. Indeed, had said many times. What he meant was every officer needed a witness to cover his actions, and what he *really* meant was that Archie was a loose cannon who needed anchoring.

The men around him weren't bad men, Archie reflected. Most of the corruption was down to the uniformed force – they had the most opportunity. But not all. He would trust most of his fellow detectives to physically back him in a difficult situation, their loyalty in that respect wasn't in question. Nor were they stupid men. But they were underpaid, like everyone these days, and had families or bad habits to support. Little by little what reservations they had started out with concerning 'blind eyes' had eroded as they saw 'everyone doing it'. First, for a price, they had overlooked little crimes, then bigger ones, until these days they actually hired out to ride shotgun on booze deliveries, to stand guard outside the famous Syndicate 'dinners' which were really business meetings (or worse), even to moonlight as 'protection' at parties, or to provide special muscle when enforcement was required at a higher level. He knew at least two of them even revelled in it, proud of their 'contacts'.

He finished his coffee and stood up. What he wanted to know was in the files. It might be recent, it might be old news. But there was only one man for the job, and he, fortunately, was another old friend of his late father's – a man he thought he could trust.

At least, he hoped so.

Archie took the stairs down to the basement and walked the gritty route to the door marked Files, his footsteps echoing in the long narrow corridors that networked beneath the building. Beyond that door were rows and rows of shelves filled with case notes, far too many for a man to just start at one end and proceed to the other. A guide was needed. And that man was Sgt. Patrick Ignatious Piper, popularly known as Pip.

Pip was in his lair, a caged-off corner containing a big desk, a table and chair, a telephone extension, several filing cabinets, and a very large picnic basket. This contained Pip's supplies for the day. Pip was just a few years off retirement, and these days his main entertainment was eating. Largely immobile in the Files, he had grown so fat his stomach hung over his invisible belt, and his uniform strained at every seam.

Nevertheless, Pip was light on his feet and swift in motion. This was because his off-duty hobby was ballroom dancing – the only exercise he got, now that he was confined to office duties. Once considered the best marksman on the Force, he had encountered someone even faster on the draw about fifteen years before, and as a result had only one ear. Considered too deaf and unsightly to go on patrol, he had been assigned to Files. Rumour was he had a celluloid ear which he attached to his spectacles and wore when he went dancing, so as not to frighten his lady partners, but nobody had ever actually seen it. On duty he never bothered, so presented a friendly if rather lopsided aspect to his fellow officers.

"Well, if it isn't the great Lt. Deacon, scourge of the underworld," Pip said, obviously delighted to have company so early in the day.

Archie sat down. "How's it going, Pip?"

Pip scratched his stomach. "Fair to middlin', thanks. What can we do for you?"

"I'm looking for a connection between Capone and the Chinese."

"The Chinese what? Laundry? Restaurant?"

"I have no idea."

"That's what I like – precise information."

"Well, it's kind of a flyer. There may be no connection at all." Briefly Archie sketched the situation.

Pip reached into his picnic basket and extracted a partially opened box of cookies. He popped one into his mouth and chewed thoughtfully. "Nothing comes to mind, except ...." He slapped the box down on his desk in case Deacon was hungry and heaved himself to his feet. "But there has been a lot of minor stuff between the Chinks and the Eyeties lately. Mostly domestic stuff about property, so on, as I recall." He went over to a file cabinet and opened the top drawer, scrabbled a while, extracted a manila folder. "This might be something. Rival applications for a limited food license over on Wentworth. You know what that means."

It meant that whoever got the license would run a blind pig operation behind the cover of the restaurant. Depending on the pull of the owner, he could do it behind a closed door or even up front, offering booze in teapots, knowing he wouldn't be busted because he paid his dues to the precinct involved.

Pip carried the file over to his desk and settled himself again with a thump and grunt. "Let's see. Oh yeah – turned into a street fight, that's why we got involved. I thought there was something. The Eyetie wanting the license was Jake Manotta – you know the name?"

"Capone Syndicate – mid-level."

"Right. Other applicant one Wu Chien. Don't know who the hell he is. They not only look alike, they all sound alike to me. He wanted it for a social club set-up, it says here. Good position, too . . . no wonder they got so het up."

"Social club?"

Pip shrugged. "Could be straight, more likely one of those places for queers they run. You know about those? Must be three or four of them down there in Chinatown."

"I know the Chinese are more tolerant about that kind of thing." Archie frowned. "Does it say the name of the club or group he represented?"

Pip looked down the page and gave a shout of laughter. "Would you believe this? It says the name of the club was to be Chih Mei – but some nut has translated that as 'Red Eyebrows'."

Archie leaned back in his chair. Hadn't Ellie said something about Red Eyebrows? He'd have to ask her. Maybe he could take her to lunch at that place in the Gower Building – the fancy one. He knew the headwaiter – he'd get a good table and a reasonable bill. Then he closed his eyes in self-disgust. That's how it started – blind eyes to little crimes, then bigger ones. So easy, so easy. Damn.

"Anything else you can think of?" He opened his eyes again to see Pip looking at him curiously.

Pip shrugged, and his glasses tilted sideways, propped as they were on only one ear. He pushed them straight automatically, as he must have done a hundred times a day.

"Neighborhood scuffles, mostly kids. Years back there was that big bust-up. I could look that up for you...it's out there somewhere." He gestured toward the lines of shelved case notes.

"Would you mind?"

Pip scowled. "Only two years to retirement, you know." He heaved himself to his feet again, slipped out of the cage and disappeared between the shelves. Archie could hear him scuffling along, muttering to himself about nosy cops. But he knew Pip was intrigued – he wouldn't have offered to look if he hadn't been. Down here, away from the action, he appreciated being included on a little inside thinking now and again. Archie had counted on that.

After about five minutes, Pip reappeared, carrying a cardboard box, which he thumped down on the desk and then dropped into his chair. "Bigger kerfuffle than I thought." He lifted the lid of the box and began to look through the contents. "Went to court . . . lots of people hurt, one died as I recall. Yeah, here." He pulled out some papers which were already going a little brown at the edges.

"Can I see?" Archie reached out.

Pip pulled back. "I can do it faster than you," he said, proprietarily. "I know how these things go. Get out your pencil."

Archie did so, knowing Pip was right. It would take him forever to go through all the forms that were so familiar to the older man. He also had a terrible feeling he knew what he was going to hear.

"Here we go. Four hospitalized, all Chinese. One Eyetie killed – name of – "

"Joe Concetti." Archie's interruption was softly spoken, but the tone brought Pip's eyes up from the page.

"You already know about this?"

"I was a patrolman at the time. Joe Concetti wasn't Italian – at least, not entirely. Chinese mother, Italian father. Nothing to do with crime, though. Decent family. I was told he just got caught up in it by accident."

"Not according to this." Pip waved the papers. "According to this, he was the one who started it. Seems he got into a fight with . . . holy shit . . . Jake Manotta." He glanced up and saw Archie's expression, and went back to the papers. "Other names here – Bugliami, Spinoza, Ricotti . . . they're all connected guys, you know. "

"Joe wasn't."

"Afraid he was. According to Ricotti the fight was about who would supply some Eyetie restaurants ... Concetti was after the run, and so were the others."

"No. Not Joe." He wouldn't believe it.

"You knew him?"

"Friend. Long-time friend. Kids together."

"Well, he wasn't a kid anymore, Archie. Apparently Manotta was 'offended' by his being crossed by what he called a 'half-breed'. According to testimony by some of the others Concetti was on the rise in the organisation and Manotta resented it."

"Did Manotta kill him?"

Pip's expression was wry. "Nobody killed him. You remember 'nobody', don't you? He's responsible for a lot of killings these days." Pip looked down at the paper. "It got out of hand because some Chinese boys saw Concetti in trouble and jumped in. He looked Chinese?"

"Yes. Like his mother." And when he had called around to give his condolences Mrs. Liu Concetti had thanked him and said nothing about what Joe had been doing. But she had looked ashamed, he remembered, now. So she must have known the truth. Even Joe had gone bad. Clever, intelligent, street-smart Joe, who was going to be a lawyer, who felt about the law the way Archie himself felt. What had happened? When had it happened? And why? He thought back to the Concetti apartment . . . and how surprised he had been at its shabbiness when in the early days it had been so beautifully kept. The Depression. Always the Depression. And so few opportunities for a 'half-breed' with no money to become a lawyer or anything else respectable.

"What was the result?" Archie had been too sad to follow the details of the case, so convinced had he been that poor Joe had just been in the wrong place at the wrong time.

Pip took his eyes away from Archie's bleak face and paged through the papers a bit further. He shrugged. "Most of 'em let go, some got six months for affray. Mostly the Eyeties."

"Including Manotta?"

"Yeah. Including Manotta. Plus he got another two for bad behaviour while he was banged up." Pip put the papers down on his desk. "He's trouble, Archie. Story on the street is he's now an enforcer with a 'teashop' as his legit front."

"I know that. And he likes the knife."

Pip nodded. "He likes the knife." Pip slowly put the papers back in order and slipped them into the box. "What are you thinking, Archie?"

"I'm thinking of Bernice Barker."

"The one with her head cut off in Chinatown?"

"On the edge of Chinatown."

"But you said this was all about some fancy jade thing and the Webster shooting out on that Chinese guy's mansion on Lakeshore."

Archie stood up. "I did, didn't I?"

Pip leaned back in his chair and gazed at Archie. "I don't like the look in your eye, son. It's personal, now, isn't it?"

Archie didn't answer that. "Thanks for your help, Pip." He left the cage and started for the door.

Pip called after him. "Regular Chinese puzzle, hey?"

Archie didn't answer that, either.

19

Elodie and the two other captives were herded out of the van, across an alley, and into the rear door of some nameless building that looked like it could be a warehouse. Elodie looked around to try and see something she could identify later, something that would reveal their location. But she was moved along too quickly for more than a quick glimpse of a long straight alley and a smell of water nearby. The Lake or the river?

Inside they were moved down a long wooden-floored corridor and into a small room. The door slammed behind them and they stood for a moment, getting their bearings. Not much to see – a small table, four chairs, overhead lamp hanging down, no windows, and just the one door.

"Sit down, Miss Browne," said Two-Gun Cohen in a kindly voice. "I'm sure we'll have this sorted out quite quickly."

Elodie didn't think so, but she sat down gratefully, for her legs felt very untrustworthy. Cohen sat down beside her, but Father Anselm stood, his head at an odd angle. He seemed to be sniffing. He glanced at the General.

"Am I wrong?"

The General looked puzzled, then took a deep breath. "No, you're not wrong. I should have guessed that would be part of it."

"What is it?" Elodie asked, as Father Anselm sat down, too.

"Opium." General Cohen looked around, then gestured toward a small vent high in the ceiling.

Elodie sniffed, but only caught a faint scent of pickles overlaid by a strong barnyard odour that reminded her of cows. Maybe they were near the stockyards, then. She was about to say as much, when the door opened and two of the men who had kidnapped them entered, followed by a young Chinese man. The two kidnappers still had their guns. They closed the door and then stood either side of it as the younger man came forward.

"Who's the girl?" His voice was honey-smooth and totally without an accent, so he was probably American, Elodie thought.

Father Anselm spoke quickly. "She's one of my students. We were discussing her thesis when your men burst in. They wouldn't listen to reason and made her come, too. She has nothing to do with this. You must let her go."

The young man smiled. It was not a nice smile, but a gloating one. "And what is this thesis about – the General, here, perhaps?"

"I have been researching a paper on ethnic communities here in Chicago." Elodie had picked up Anselm's cue and spoke boldly, even angrily. "And my mother is not going to like this one little bit. She expects me home for dinner." She thinned her voice to sound younger than she was, and put on a pout. "And I don't drink, either," she added.

"Why should that interest me?" The young man's eyes narrowed.

"Well, you're bootleggers, aren't you? Nobody else carries guns and pushes people around but bootleggers. I think you're just awful."

The young man stared at her and then began to laugh. It was not at all a pleasant sound. "Oh, yes, we are bootleggers, aren't we?" He turned to the two men beside the door and said something in Chinese. They laughed, too – but their amusement did not reach their eyes.

"I think you should let her go before this goes any further." The General sounded angry, too. "You can deal with us as you like, as you seem to have the upper hand at the moment, but let her go."

"I will consider it," the young man said. "But she might be useful, even so."

Elodie visualized one terrible thing after another that might come under the heading of 'useful' to a bunch of kidnappers and maybe killers. She wanted to ask right out if this boy-man had killed Bernice, but sensibly maintained her sulky expression. "I won't do anything for a bootlegger. My daddy says – "

"I don't give a damn what your father says or what your mother thinks." The young man had abruptly lost patience. "Just sit there and keep your silly mouth shut."

Elodie shrank down in her seat and allowed her fear to show. This seemed to please him far more than her protestations about parental disapproval. He gave her one last glare and turned his attention to the General.

"You know what we want. Hand it over and we'll let you go."

"It's not mine to give." The General spoke calmly, and folded his hands across his paunch.

"It doesn't belong to old 'Cash My Check' either. You took it from Ah Hop at Bias Bay. He got it from Lai Choi San."

"Who did she get it from?"

"The trail is long, but it doesn't matter." The young man was dismissive. "What is more interesting is how Chiang Kai Shek ended up with it. And now you."

"I haven't got it," Cohen said, with wide-eyed innocence.

"Then who does?"

"Someone else, obviously. There is a buyer . . . "

The young man drew in a sharp breath between his perfect teeth, reminding Elodie of a snake about to strike. "You stupid old man . . ." He clenched his fists and stepped forward as if to hit Cohen. The General didn't flinch. The young man turned to Father Anselm.

"You have meddled once too often in what doesn't concern you, nigger. You claim to be a holy man, but you are as guilty as he is of undermining the new China."

"Actually, I'm rather fond of the old China." The priest's eyes didn't even flicker at the boy's insult. "And I'm only half-nigger, by the way. Or didn't you know that?"

"All the worse for you."

"Oh?"

"If you don't cooperate it would give me great pleasure to spill your filthy mixed blood."

Father Anselm went fractionally paler, but kept his features calm.

Cohen, however, snapped. He half-rose and uttered a long string of Chinese words that were clearly both insults and curses. The young man stepped forward and, this time, did strike Cohen flat-handed across the face.

"Enough, you stupid old fool. I am the Junfa here. I want the jade."

Cohen stared at him, the mark of the blow livid on his

cheek. "It is out of my hands."

This enraged the young man, whose face flushed darkly, revealing a very mottled complexion. "I know who has it. You are to get it back from him and give it to me."

"Why?" Two-Gun Cohen seemed genuinely curious. He was intentionally baiting the young man, which Elodie didn't think was a very good idea, for the young man produced a gun of his own from behind his back.

"Stop playing the fool, Cohen. It gets us nowhere. If for no other reason than to stop Chiang Kai Shek profiting from it."

"You'd like the profit yourself, I suppose?"

"There is a new China coming..."

The General snorted dismissively. "Spare us the Communist rhetoric." He glanced up at the vent near the ceiling. "From what I can smell, the New China has the same stink as the old China. Aren't you satisfied with the profit from that?"

The young man smiled. He was definitely American – so what was he doing in all this? Was he some disaffected college student like those she had met at those pro-Communist parties? In fact, had she met him before? She regarded him from under her eyelids, still in her character of frightened student. There was something about him that stirred in the back of her mind, which was odd. She was discovering that for some reason, the few Chinese people she had met did not all look alike to her. She could tell them apart easily, and she was pretty certain she had never seen him before. And yet –

"It has always been a steady source of income, for you as well as for us. Chiang takes a profit, too. Enough for all. And better to come."

"What do you mean?" Father Anselm asked.

"I mean there soon will be more than one way to weaken the corrupt citizens of the Western world. Already they are far down the road to ruin due to their own foolish laws, and if Repeal comes, we are ready to offer them a new slope to slide down."

"Opium?" Anselm was dismissive. "You will never get Americans to smoke opium. That's ridiculous."

"Opium has more to offer than you think, priest. Much more."

"Such as?" Again, the General seemed curious.

"Such as something the Germans were kind enough to discover. Something called Heroin. The Bright Young Things sniff cocaine today, and they will inject heroin tomorrow. A simple progression for the simple-minded." The young man suddenly seemed to realize he was saying too much. He changed tack.

"Enough. You, girl. If I let you go, will you carry a message for me?"

Elodie shivered as he spoke to her. "No."

"Oh, I think you will. You don't want to be responsible for the death of a priest, do you?"

Elodie gasped. Father Anselm reached over and put his hand on top of hers. "Don't be afraid, my child."

"Oh, yes, be afraid, my child." The young man sneered at the priest's tone. "Your precious priest professor will be shot dead unless you take a message for me. I will exchange the priest for certain items."

Elodie put a whine into her voice. "What about this other man? Will you kill him, too?"

"This 'other man' is an enemy to China."

"Only to your China." Cohen was disgusted and made no effort to hide it.

Elodie spoke quickly to avoid another blow falling, or worse. "I don't understand – who do I take this message to? The police?"

The young man came over to the table and leaned across it so his face was only inches from hers. "Listen, Miss Student, if you were smart enough to get into college you should be smart enough to understand this. If you speak to the police the priest will die and you will die, too. I will find you, I will kill you. Clear enough?"

Elodie nodded, her eyes locked with his. Close-up his breath was foul, and his acned face was slightly oily, so his cheekbones showed under the overhead light. I know who you are, she suddenly thought. Dear God, I think I know who you are. She prayed her realization didn't show on her face.

He straightened up. "You are to take my message to a Mr. Lee Chang. If he doesn't produce the items I want in twenty-four hours, I will kill the priest and this so-called General. If he hands it over, they go free. Very simple. Can you remember that?"

"Yes," she whispered. "Twenty-four hours. What time is it now?"

He muttered in exasperated Chinese, and looked at his wristwatch. "It is three o'clock. Mr. Lee has until three o'clock tomorrow to bring me the shipment."

"Where should he bring it?"

He didn't fall for that one. He produced a piece of paper and put his gun in his belt while he scribbled a message and thrust it at her. "He will know." She looked at the note. It was in Chinese. So she couldn't lead the police to where they were being held. "Mr. Lee lives on Lakeshore Drive, number 1200. My men will drop you there. No tricks, little Miss Student. You will be followed. Deliver the message, go home, and say nothing to anyone. You will be watched day and night. My people are invisible, but they will be there in the shadows, watching you. If you do anything other than what you have been told, they have orders to kill you and your family immediately. Do you understand?"

Elodie couldn't hold back the fear any longer, and despite her best efforts to play a part and remain calm, began to cry. "You didn't have to say that." She wiped her betraying tears away with the back of her hand. "I'll take your stupid message. Why don't you take it yourself? Why don't you just telephone this Mr. Lee?"

"Stop your snivelling! I have my reasons. And he will not let me or any of my people into his house. We have tried."

"I'm sure you have," put in Two-Gun Cohen. "He's not the fool your guard thought he was, is he?"

The young man curled his lip. "No, he is not that kind of a fool, but fool he is, just the same. To think he could give you the money, do 'his part' to help your corrupt government, disgusts me. You and he are the faces of degenerate capitalistic greed." He walked over and grasped Elodie's arm, jerking her to her feet. "Go. Do as you are told. And remember, you are being watched always. Always."

He turned to the two men who had kidnapped them and gave their orders in Chinese. He pushed her toward one of them – the fat one who seemed so fascinated by Elodie. As the thug took her from the room, Father Anselm called out. "Be brave, Miss Browne. Do not be afraid."

She thought she heard the sound of a blow and a chair

falling as the door closed behind her. She stopped, but the kidnapper jerked her forward again, out to the van which still stood in the alleyway. Again she was thrust inside, alone now, and the door locked behind her. Again she was driven fast, thrown from side to side, for at least twenty minutes. She could make no sense of the pattern of twists and turns, but knew from the sound of traffic that they passed through the Loop. Now that she was out of that room, she felt the fear overwhelm her, and she sobbed quietly to herself. Faced with the animosity of their captor, she had felt more anger than anything else, because he was so unpleasant, and because she had been trying so hard to keep up her pretence of being a student and an innocent bystander. She would deliver his message, all right. Whether she was brave enough to do anything else, she didn't know. What if they did something to her, or to her family? "Always watching from the shadows," he had said. She thought of Bernice, and trembled.

The van screeched to a halt, footsteps came around from the front and the rear door was opened. She could see the Lake on her right, trees, a lawn. The driver gestured her out, and helped her roughly to the ground. "Go. Do." He pushed her ahead of him, and she found herself at the end of the long drive that led to the Lee mansion. She started slowly up the drive, her legs weak beneath her. Was the fat thug watching her now? If she waited until she got closer to the house would he see her and if she ran into the woods, would he shoot her? Step by step she approached the house. She hadn't heard the van drive away. They must still be there, waiting for her to return. And to kill her? Elodie wiped her tears away, smoothed her hair, straightened up. She would deliver her message and then she would ask Mr. Lee to help her. That's right, that's what she would do. Once she was in the house, she would be safe.

She went up to the big double front door and found the bell. After a minute one of the doors swung back, and Mrs. Logie stood there. She gave no sign of recognizing Elodie, and did not look at all welcoming. Elodie cleared her throat.

"My name is Elodie Browne. I have a message for Mr. Lee. From his son, Harry."

20

Chef Alexander: Always they want something new. I make beautiful French cuisine, and they say they want chop suey. How can I make this? I will not kill a little dog for anyone!

**

Sal looked over what she had just written and groaned. She was a team player – on her own it just didn't have the snap that Drew provided, or the freshness that came from Ellie. I am a journeyman writer, Sal thought to herself, I can turn it out, reams of the stuff, but I need help. She had few personal illusions, she was long past that adolescent dream. But this time – this time – she thought it might just happen, the magic, the excitement, the sheer pleasure of doing something well that had for so long been missing from her life.

There was a knock at the door. Hugh Murphy back again?

"Come in," Sal called, too dispirited to go to the door.

It opened, and a very tall redheaded man walked in, his hat in his hand, a smile on his face. He glanced around the room and the smile disappeared. "I was looking for Miss Browne. Is this – "

"This is where she should be," Sal said. "But she isn't, as you can see. Are you from the agency?" If he was, she would have to make up something fast to explain Ellie's absence or the girl might be in trouble. "She had a doctor's appointment."

"No, I'm not from the agency. A doctor's appointment? When for?"

"Uh . ." Sal shifted uncomfortably on the leather sofa. "Just before lunch." The sofa creaked beneath her, and she tried an encouraging smile. "She might be back any minute."

"Oh. Can I wait?"

She hadn't counted on that. "Well, she might be longer. She said something about them having to do blood tests and ...

stuff like that."

The man came in and closed the door behind him. "You're Sal, aren't you?"

"Yes. Sal Schultz. And you?" She didn't like the way he was looking at her, but he said he wasn't from the agency so – another of Ellie's 'cousins'?

"My name is Archie Deacon. I'm – "

" – the cop." She felt suddenly relieved. "Ellie has told us about you."

He sat down on Drew's couch and put his hat on top of the papers scattered over the table. "She didn't have a doctor's appointment." It wasn't a question. "She went to talk to that priest, didn't she? With her cousin?"

"No." Sal wasn't sure what to say. He was a cop, after all. "That is, she went to see a priest, but her cousin wasn't with her. He came here looking for her hours ago. He – "

Alarm crossed Archie's face. "He wasn't with her?"

How much did he know about all this? Ellie had said he was working on the case, but she also said she didn't like him. Mind you, that might have been just because he was so irritating. Sal assessed him carefully. He didn't look irritating – he was pretty good-looking, as a matter of fact, in a kind of rugged, smart-ass way.

"Well, yes . . . he was kind of worried about her, apparently. He'd told her not to go, and she went anyway."

Archie cursed under his breath. "The little idiot – that's just what he should have expected her to do."

"I think he did, really. That was why he was worried." Sal felt more and more confident about this Deacon guy. He might be a cop, but she sensed he was genuinely concerned about Ellie, which wasn't a very cop thing to be. At least, not like any cops she'd ever met. "They went to get her."

Archie had been looking down at his clenched fists, and his head came up, fast. "They?"

"Drew went with him. Drew is our writing partner. I think he just wanted to get out from under the work. Drew isn't exactly dedicated to it. More to the bottle, to tell the truth. But he has his moments."

"I know – Ellie told me about him, too. Does he always lie down on this couch and make sarcastic remarks?"

"You got it."

"And is he a nice, big, strong guy, lots of muscles and brains?"

Sal had to smile. "Afraid not. About as skinny as you and usually hung over. But he does have brains. Her cousin looked pretty strong. Why – do you think there's trouble?"

"Do you know what time her appointment was for?"

"Ten."

He looked at his watch. "Almost six hours ago?" He stood up, agitated, and grabbed his hat. "Where is this place?"

Sal scrabbled among the papers and came up with a scrap on which Hugh had written the priest's address. She handed it to Archie. "They've probably gotten her by now. Maybe she went home?"

He went to the phone and dialled. He knew Ellie's home phone number without having to look it up, Sal noted. "Hello – may I speak to Elodie, please?" Pause. "Okay, thanks." He put the phone down. "According to her sister, Elodie is still at work."

Sal leaned back wearily. "For such a bright young girl, she can be awful dumb."

"Not dumb, just stubborn and over-confident. I'm going after them. If they aren't there, I'll ring back here." He leaned over and jotted down the number on the phone dial. "If they aren't here . . . " He looked bleak.

Sal spoke encouragingly. "This could just be one of those coming and going things, you know. She leaves before they get there so they miss her. She decides to stop somewhere for lunch or to do some shopping ..."

"Have they rung back to see if she's here?"

"Well, no, but – "

Archie moved toward the door. "Miss Schultz, if she shows up, will you do something for me?"

"Sure." She liked this guy, no matter what Ellie had said about him.

"Will you tie her up to the leg of this table until I get back?" He clapped his hat onto his head and slammed the door behind him.

"Sure," Sal said faintly, to the empty room. "I was going to do that anyway. We got a script to write."

**

227

"Mr. Lee doesn't have a son." The housekeeper's expression was as dour as ever. She was a tall but bulky woman, her hair drawn back so tightly it almost gave her eyes a Chinese slant. Maybe that was what she was trying to do, Ellie thought.

"Yes, he does. Bernice told me about him. Small, nasty, with a bad case of acne. I think he killed Bernice because she recognized him."

"That's ridiculous." Mrs. Logie wasn't going to move.

"Look." Ellie produced the piece of paper from her jacket pocket and held it out so the houskeeper could see it. "I have to give this to Mr. Lee. If he doesn't do what they want, they are going to kill two perfectly nice men, one of them a priest and one a General."

Mrs. Logie's eyes widened. "The General?" she gasped.

"Yes. General Cohen his name is. Listen, there is someone watching me right this very minute. I have to come in. I have to see Mr. Lee. I have to."

After a moment, Mrs. Logie stood back and let Ellie into the entrance hall. She stood for a moment in the open door, her eyes flashing around the grounds outside. "I don't see anyone."

"He said they were invisible. He said they would be in the shadows. He said they would kill me and my family – please." Ellie heard the desperation in her voice, and apparently the housekeeper did, too. She closed the door and turned to face the frightened but oddly angry girl.

"What did he look like? This man you called Harry? Did he have – " She paused, and swallowed.

"What? Did he have what?"

"A scar on the back of his hand – almost star-shaped?"

Ellie thought back to the room and the man holding a gun almost in her face. "Yes," she said. "Like a splash."

Mrs. Logie's face went pale and she sagged a little against the door. "So," she hissed. "He's back."

"It is Harry, isn't it? I was right?"

Mrs. Logie nodded and seemed to pull herself together. "I gave him that scar. It was an accident. In return, he gave me this." She pulled down the front of her dress as far as she could, revealing a wide area of cruel scarring. "It goes all the way down." She gestured down the front of her body as far as her abdomen. "Boiling oil. I splashed a little on him while I was cooking, and he picked up the pan and threw it all over me. It was the last of many straws, and Mr. Lee disowned him. He went to China. We thought we'd seen the last of him."

"He belongs to Ming Dao. He wants Suzy's jade. Or – "

"Come with me. You'd better see Mr. Lee right away." Instead of going to her employer's private office, she led Ellie through the dining room and opened the french doors. The glass-lined passage stretched before them. Outside the light had begun to fade, and the tops of the trees beyond were lit by a pinkish glow from the setting sun. At the other end of the passage a guard sat beside a heavy door. Seeing them, he stood up, warily watching.

"Is that – " Ellie hung back.

"A new guard, don't worry."

"Is Mr. Lee in there?"

"Yes. He's packing up T'zu Hsi's jade." Mrs. Logie looked grim. "He's found a buyer."

**

"I saw your car outside." Archie Deacon stood beside the booth where Hugh Murphy and Drew Wilson were drinking whiskey out of coffee cups. Two obviously stale and untouched sandwiches sat on a plate on the table between them, further camouflage, should anyone be interested. In a place like this, nobody was. Archie knew it and knew the owners paid their dues to both the Syndicate and the police. But art for art's sake.

"How did you know my car?" Hugh was tight – it was obviously not his first cup of 'coffee'.

"I'm a cop, I'm observant," Archie said, not bothering to remind Hugh that he had seen the car many times when the reporter covered a crime scene. And after driving all over the neighborhood near St. John's House it was not difficult to see the big card on the visor marked 'PRESS'. He pulled a chair over from one of the tables and placed it in the aisle beside the booth. He glanced across. "Drew Wilson? I'm Lieutenant Archie Deacon. Where's Ellie?"

Drew looked clear-eyed and intelligent – obviously the whiskey had released him from his hangover, but he was not as far gone as Hugh. Only when he spoke could a slight whisper of a slur be heard in his words.

"Want some coffee?" he asked. "Good coffee here."

"I know all about the coffee here. Where's Ellie?"

"Gone," Hugh said, owlishly. "Little Red Riding Hood has disappeared into the woods. Like a pork chop." He drained his coffee cup and looked around for a waiter. Archie pushed his hand with the cup back down onto the table, then looked at Drew and raised an eyebrow.

"Tell me," he demanded. "Fast."

Drew told him about the Chinese men and the priest and some other man leaving with Ellie just before noon. "We talked to the neighbours. Nice neighborhood. Nice people. Ellie was taken away in a butcher's van with a pig on it."

"Oink," said Hugh.

"If they saw that why didn't they call the police?" Archie demanded. Drew eyed him.

"Nice neighborhood," he repeated. "Mind your own business, you see. Too many strange sights in this town these days. Keep your head down. Anyway, she was with a priest, right? So they thought it must have been okay. Sorry."

"Well, why didn't you call the police?"

"We did." Hugh was gazing sadly down at his empty cup. "They said you were out. We called three times and you were always out."

"Well, why didn't you speak to someone else?" Archie could hardly contain his exasperation.

"We spoke to a Captain Brett and he hung up on us. I think he thought we were pranksters. A lot of that around, you know."

Archie put his elbows on the table and covered his face with his hands. "What did you tell Brett?"

"That a girl named Elodie Browne and a priest had been kidnapped by a bunch of Chinese in a van with a pig on it," Drew explained carefully. "He didn't believe me, he didn't believe Hugh, here, either. He seemed kind of stupid for a captain, if you ask me."

Archie took his hands away. "He's not stupid. I wish he was. He's just . . . " He stopped. How bad was Brett? Ambitious? Devious? Corrupt? How far had it gone with him? Was he even now calling people he shouldn't be calling, or had he really dismissed it as nonsense?

"What? What is he?" Hugh wanted to know. "Is he Chinese, too?" Hugh shook his head slowly and sadly. "Damn Chinese are everywhere, it seems to me. Poor Ellie. All gone. My fault, my fault, my most grievous fault." He thumped himself on the chest.

Archie just managed to stop himself from slugging Hugh, and turned to Drew. "How long have you two been here?"

Drew shrugged. "Time flies when you're having fun."

"Listen – " Archie started to rise, but Drew took hold of his sleeve and pulled him back down. He was suddenly serious and his voice was flat.

"It's a dead end, Lieutenant. I looked up the name on the butcher's van in the phone book and called them. They said it had been stolen yesterday while doing deliveries."

"What did the driver say?"

"He was inside with a lamb carcass over his shoulder. When he came out, it was gone."

"Where was this?"

Drew sighed and said exactly what Archie did not expect him to say. "Cicero. Pershing Avenue."

Archie stared at him. "But that's Capone's territory."

Drew nodded. "Cheeky Chinks – you got to hand it to them."

Archie stood up. "No, we don't." He looked down at the two of them, disgusted by their failure to grasp what was going on, and by their retreat into booze instead of action. "If it turns out that Ellie is dead because you've been sitting on your asses, you have no idea how sorry I'll make you. Now, sober up and listen."

21

It was, indeed, a treasure house.

The heavy door thudded shut behind Elodie and Mrs. Logie. After a moment, they heard the guard thrust the outer lock home. Mr. Lee, who was bending over a large table littered with battered old boxes and packing materials, looked up in surprise. For a moment, Elodie could not even speak.

Like Lee's office in the Gower Building, the square room was lined with glass shelving – but here the objects were almost all either jade or gold, and the glitter was dazzling. In one corner stood a massive gold and red enamel altar of some sort, decorated all over with the most elaborate curling patterns, set off with crystals or – could they be real jewels? High on three walls, above the glass shelves, were wide-sleeved robes framed to show off their exquisite embroidery, the colours rich and warm. The glass shelves themselves held bowls of the most delicate carving, others plainer, but so thinly wrought they were translucent and seemed to glow. Closer to her were small figures that appeared to be a group of musicians in pale yellow with brown mottling, and they were certainly jade. There were other figures, animals, birds, in many colours, ranging through a deep rich green down through paler greens to a caramel shade that looked almost good enough to eat. There was a dark green cow lying down beside what looked like a solid gold dragon, an oddly shaped rectangular vase with a round centre, flat circles and half-circles of jade and others of bronze or gold and many many small boxes of varied design. Some things were simple in shape, others were elaborately carved. The room smelled of flowers and something else Elodie couldn't place, presumably some kind of incense.

"What is wrong?" Mr. Lee asked Mrs. Logie. He didn't seem angry, merely curious. "Why have you brought this girl here?"

Before Mrs. Logie could speak, Elodie held out the piece of

paper with the Chinese characters on it. "They want Suzy's jade or Father Anselm and General Cohen will be killed."

"Who are 'they'?" Still Mr. Lee did not seem particularly upset, although Elodie thought she saw his hands tremble briefly.

"Ming Dao." Elodie's voice was overlaid by Mrs. Logie's flat tones.

"It's Harry," she said, at the same time.

Mr. Lee slowly straightened up. He was wearing another Chinese robe, much plainer than those framed above him, in a deep azure blue. Its embroidery was simple and limited to the cuffs of the wide sleeves. Rather incongruously, Mr. Lee was also wearing a pair of plain white cotton gloves. They gave an almost clownlike contrast to the robe, for they were a little too big and the fingers flopped over at the ends. Mr. Lee stared at the two women and then he focused on Mrs. Logie.

"Impossible."

"She saw him. She described him perfectly." Mrs. Logie took a deep breath and almost whispered. "She saw the scar on his hand."

Mr. Lee hissed something in Chinese, and his face was a mixture of disbelief and fear. "He is a Communist? Ming Dao?"

"Apparently," Mrs. Logie said. "They are holding the General and the priest."

"You have twenty-four hours to bring the jade here." Again Elodie held out the bit of paper. Slowly Mr. Lee came around the end of the table and took the paper from her.

"I do not know this place." He looked at Elodie. "But you are familiar to me. Why?"

Elodie reminded him of the party where Webster had been killed and where she had been both waitress and witness. "This morning I was speaking to Father Anselm and General Cohen when three Chinese men came to take them away. They made me go, too, even though Father Anselm said I was just one of his students."

"And are you?" Mr. Lee reached out a gloved hand and leaned on the table behind him for support. One of the old boxes almost fell off, and Mrs. Logie stepped forward quickly to steady it. Mr. Lee ignored her, his full concentration now on Elodie.

"No. I was there because of Ming Dao. I mean, the words Ming Dao – Mr. Webster said them before he died, and I was . . . curious." She explained about going to the library and Mr. Evans' suggestion that she speak to Father Anselm if she wanted to know more about China. "So I made an appointment and went to see him."

"But . . . why should you do this?" Lee was puzzled – so much so that he seemed to have forgotten the paper in his hand.

"At first it was just curiosity. I'm a writer, you see. Words interest me."

"But surely that's not enough ... Webster was killed for those words."

"Yes, I realized that. But the guard shooting him seemed to be intentional. So at first it was just a mystery, you see. A puzzle. I couldn't stop thinking about it. It was interfering with my work – I just had to find out what it was all about. And then they killed Bernice. She was my friend, and I got very angry."

Lee was amazed. "You are a very unusual young woman."

"A very foolish young woman." Mrs. Logie's voice was harsh. "You're lucky they let you go."

Elodie would have laughed if she wasn't still so scared. "I told them they should deliver the message themselves. If they had, I wouldn't be here. But he believed I was just a silly girl student, so he used me. He threatened me, and my family, too."

"Harry could never understand women," Mr. Lee said. "Even Helen– " He paused and glanced at Mrs. Logie. "Helen."

Mrs. Logie nodded. "I always said she was in love with him. You refused to believe me."

"If I had sent Helen . . . "

"You sent Bernice. And she recognized him. I think that's why he killed her." Elodie spoke sadly, wishing she could sit down and just have a good cry. Every bone in her body ached. "He didn't want you to know he was here."

"He hates me." Mr. Lee spoke bitterly. "The feeling is mutual, but he is my son. From the beginning he was not like the others. Always cruel, always without conscience. My two older children are good children, they have made me proud.

But their mother is dead. Harry was – "

"Harry is mine." Mrs. Logie spoke softly. "God help me, he is mine."

Mr. Lee glanced toward the woman who acted as his housekeeper. His expression softened, and for a moment he seemed younger, remembering. "My first wife was an invalid for many years. Harriet was a kind and gentle nurse, and I came to love her. A child was born. Then, when my wife died, we married." Lee's eyes suddenly glittered with tears. "But for many reasons, we never made the marriage public."

"It was my choice," said Mrs. Logie. "I thought it would make business with China difficult if they knew he had a child by a white woman and married her. I was wrong. Harry always felt it was because we were ashamed of him. It ... turned him."

Mr. Lee briefly laid a white-gloved hand on her arm. His touch was gentle, affectionate. "It was not that. Something in him was bad from the very beginning." He looked back at Elodie. "My ancestors were not always . . . "

Mrs. Logie – or Mrs. Lee as she really was – put her hand over his. "He is what he is. Evil has its own life to live – it finds homes where it can."

Elodie stood listening to all this, sorry for them, sorry for everything, but there was little time for sorrow or regrets now. "He might really kill them, then?"

"Harry never made idle threats." Mrs. Logie stepped back from her husband, but spoke earnestly to him. "You have to hand over the jade."

Mr. Lee looked bleak. "That is no guarantee he won't kill them. The General works for Chiang Kai Shek and the priest supports his government. If you hadn't recognized Harry, Miss Browne, I might have believed handing over the jade to Ming Dao would save them. But now I cannot. Harry will make sure they die – to shame me."

**

It was getting late. Archie had poured enough real coffee into Hugh and Drew to sober them up. If anything, it had made them feel worse.

"What about a missing person report?" Hugh asked, his face lighting up.

Archie shook his head. "They haven't been missing long enough."

"Oh."

They were in Archie's car, watching the street lights come on. The speakeasy they had been in was on a busy street, but the rush-hour had passed. They were parked in front of a barber's shop, and within they could see an elderly man sweeping up the hair that had fallen to the floor during the day. Either he wasn't too enthusiastic about his job, or he was spinning it out to last as long as possible. Drew stared at him, fascinated.

"Do you suppose he has a method?" He spoke to no one in particular. "Like blonde hair first, then red, then brown? Or maybe – "

"Can it, Wilson." Archie was still angry at the two of them. He started the engine.

"Where are we going?" Hugh asked.

"Back to the beginning." Archie waited a moment for a car to pass, then pulled out. A few minutes later they were back on Addison Avenue.

The ground floor windows of St. John's House were alight, but only one or two on the floor above. Archie rang the bell and waited. Eventually the door opened and a priest stood there. He had a napkin in his hand. "Yes?"

Archie produced his badge and identification. "I'd like to speak to the man in charge, please."

"We're having our evening meal – " the priest began, with an apologetic smile. He was middle-aged and greying, not the young one they had spoken to earlier." This is important." Archie's smile was not apologetic. "A matter of life or death." He reached into his jacket and produced his badge.

"Oh, if it's a matter of a sick call – "

"It's not. Please – the man in charge."

The priest frowned. "This is a purely domiciliary establish-ment." When that produced only puzzlement on the three men before him, he relented. "Well, our most senior resident is Father James, and he deals with housekeeping and so on."

"He'll do." Archie stepped forward, causing the priest to step back.

"Well, you can wait in here." He indicated the lounge. "I'll get him." He started away, then turned back. "He won't like missing dessert. He's very fond of – "

"Keep it for him." Archie was on the verge of shouting but managed to keep his voice even.

Drew suddenly spoke up. "Do you know Father Anselm?"

"Why, yes, of course."

"Do you want him to be killed?"

The man's face went white. "Dear Lord – "

"Just get your Father James, please." Archie took hold of Drew's arm and dragged him into the lounge as the young priest scuttled off. He pushed Drew into a chair. "You didn't need to say that."

"Oh, yes, I did." Drew was unrepentant. "After his dessert this Father James would want his coffee, then his cigar, then a prayer or two. These people take the long view of life. All in God's good time."

"That's unfair." Hugh sounded resentful.

"It's common sense. I don't say it's wrong." Drew was still just drunk enough to be philosophical. "Just that you have to goose them to get them moving."

"It seems to have worked." Archie had seen an elderly priest hurrying toward them. White-haired and limping slightly, he leant on an black cane and looked upset. He came into the lounge and glared at them.

"What's all this about Anselm?" he demanded. "What's the damn fool gotten himself into this time?" Hugh indicated a chair and the priest sat down impatiently. "Well?"

"This morning a young woman came to see Father Anselm – " Archie began.

"One of his students. They're always taking up his free time."

Hugh spoke up. "Not quite. She was my cousin, Elodie Browne. She was interested in finding out something about China. It concerned a group called Ming Dao – "

"Means nothing to me." Father James was dismissive. "Anselm is the China expert. I myself know more about Poland. Father William was in Mexico. We house mostly priests in transit here. Father Anselm is one of our few permanent residents."

"Yes, well, while they were talking another man joined

them – "

"Probably Cohen. Go on."

"Who's Cohen?" Archie leaned forward suddenly. "Not a priest, surely, with that name."

Father James managed a smile. "No. General Cohen, from China. Two-Gun Cohen they call him. Sounds like a gangster, but a very nice man, very interesting. Anselm was very proud to have him here as a guest. Go on, go on." The elderly priest's eyes went toward the hallway down which he had arrived, obviously wondering what was happening to his dessert in his absence.

"Three Chinese men joined them, and then they all left together, rather quickly. We think they've been kidnapped."

"Nonsense."

"We don't think so. We think they are all in serious danger. We have to find them as quickly as possible."

The old man finally gave them his full attention. "You told Father Peter that Anselm could be killed."

"Yes." They all spoke at once.

Father James closed his eyes for a moment and his lips moved slightly. When he finished his prayer he clutched at the top of his cane and stared at them sadly. "The Chinese. It's the Chinese, you say."

"That's right. Possibly a secret society called Ming Dao, or Shining Sword. They have killed already, and could easily kill again."

"All right – I can see why they might want General Cohen, he might be worth a ransom. I gather he's someone quite important in China. But why Anselm? And why this young girl?"

"Wrong place, wrong time."

The old man's face went a little grey and he slumped in his chair. Hugh leapt up and went to him, but he was waved away. "I'm all right." He felt in a pocket of his cassock and produced a small box, from which he extracted a pill and placed it under his tongue. After a moment he seemed a little better. "I can't see what I can do for you. This is so bizarre . . . "

"Do you have any idea where they might have been taken?"

He shook his head. "No, no, of course not. Chinatown, presumably. But – "

238

"Yes ... but." Archie understood the 'but' only too well. Chinatown was another world within Chicago, secretive, complex. Quite beyond the big city's corruption, it had its own wars, its own crimes, its own sins, and its own innocents. Telling them apart was the problem. In both worlds.

Father James rubbed his right knee absently, then suddenly brightened. "I believe I can help you. Or, rather, I know a man who probably can help you. He's Anselm's closest friend in the Chinese community, and if anyone knows what's going on, he does. Here – give me a bit of paper." Drew produced a notebook and tore out a page, passing it with a pencil to Father James, who with some difficulty wrote down a name and address. "Dr. Tsung, his name is. I remember, because he sent me something for my arthritis. It tasted dreadful, but it did ease the pain." He handed the paper to Archie.

Staring down at the paper, Archie felt a small leap of hope. At last, a way in. Please, God, let this Dr. Tsung not be a man of polite bows, smiles, and lies. If he is Anselm's friend, let him help us. He suddenly realized he was praying, and was startled at himself. It had to be the atmosphere in this place, he thought. All these holy pictures, all these dog collars. He realized Father James was looking at him and smiling sympathetically.

"Don't worry, my son. God listens to everyone." His rheumy eyes went to Drew. "Especially to sinners."

Drew stared back at him, expressionless. "Lucky for us, then," he said.

**

"But you have to!" Elodie held out her hands in supplication. "He gave you twenty-four hours."

"He gave me nothing," Lee Chang said. "And I have a buyer, a museum in Philadelphia. If the General dies I will get the money back to China somehow. I am a man of honour. I said I would raise the money and I will. The General will understand."

"But can't you at least try?" Elodie's voice cracked. "The priest will die, too."

"The priest knew what he was doing." Lee was looking

239

more stubborn by the minute. He had gone back around the table and resumed packing, placing things carefully in correspondingly shaped pockets in the boxes.

"What is Suzy's jade? Is it so valuable? Is it worth men's lives?"

"T'zu Hsi." He corrected her pronunciation. "When the old Empire fell, many pieces were looted from the Imperial Palace. The private personal collection of the Dowager Empress completely disappeared. It was unique. See for yourself." Lee straightened and indicated the box in front of him. Elodie came around the table and stared down.

It was the chess set, one piece of which had been in the photograph held in Bernice's dead hand. It was not like anything else in the room. It was modern and it was astonishing. The pieces were either a deep gleaming black or a pale ghostly white. Each piece was set in a base of gold shaped like some strange plant with tendrils that curled up the sides of the carved jade. She reached out a tentative finger and touched the largest of the black pieces. The King seemed to draw her hand to pick it up. Next to the chess set was a set of pink jade cups with a matching larger vessel – all heavily carved in the old style, but set in silver mounts full of curls and whorls in the style called Art Nouveau.

"She took much of the old and made it new." Lee Chang spoke quietly, fingering what appeared to be an elaborate gold and dark green jade tiara. "This was to be worn to the Court of the English Queen Victoria, but the visit was never made. To create it she destroyed a perfect T'ang horse. Fine Imperial quality jade is getting more rare by the day, now. She would choose only the best." He reached into a very small box and withdrew a female figure, the lines smooth and flowing. He placed it in her hand. "Some old pieces she revered. This is one of the 'lost' Ch'ien Lung pieces. Hold it, feel it." It was cool and smooth, the colour the palest green with streaks of darker green that the carver had worked into the lines of the woman's robe. There was a barely discernable but intricate pattern incised in the robe of the figure, and Elodie thought it must be the goddess Kwan Yin again.

Her fingers involuntarily closed around the small figure, her thumb stroked the smooth graceful lines. It was cool, so cool, and so satisfying to hold. "It's so simple, and yet . . ." She couldn't find the words.

Lee Chang smiled at her. "Be careful. You could be seduced by the stone." When she looked up at him, puzzled, he nodded. "They call it 'jade madness'. In the past twenty years or so it has ensnared many Westerners. T'zu Hsi had it, too. Look." He reached for a square box, and lifted the lid. Within lay the most beautiful things Elodie had ever seen. Two butterflies. One in gold and one in silver or platinum, each with outspread wings set with many tiny cabochons of jade in different colours, and detailed in diamonds and pearls. The gold work was again in the sinuous, sensual style of Art Nouveau. It was simply incredible. She longed to see what was in the other boxes.

Mrs. Logie had been silent through all this, but now she spoke up. "Chang," she said, softly. "The General and the priest are good men. Their ghosts will not leave you. They will be waiting for you when you yourself die."

"Thousands could die if the Kuomintang government does not get its money." Lee spoke a little too loudly, a little too fast, but his voice wavered at the end. "Yet another civil war is coming."

"That would not be on your head, but on the heads of Chiang Kai Shek and others who will make decisions, wrong or right. This is in your hands. Here and now."

"The museum – "

"No, Chang." Her voice remained soft, but it seemed sharp enough to pierce him. He was silent.

Elodie had been looking at a clock on the table, and suddenly realized it was not just an ornament but was keeping what was probably the right time. Nineteen hours left. And she should have been home long ago.

"We should call the police." Mrs. Logie seemed to have come to a decision. "You have the address there in your hand. Send them there. They will release the General and the priest and you will still have your jade to sell."

Elodie agreed. She wanted to call Archie. Archie would know what to do. The man outside couldn't see what she was doing, he wouldn't know. But first she wanted to call home, to hear her mother's reassuring tones, and to warn them to be careful. In her mind echoed Harry Lee's threat to her family as well as herself. There might be people watching her house even now. "First I have to call home," she said, quickly. "Then we can call the police."

"The police will kill my son." Lee's voice rose, thin and high. "He is evil, but he is my son."

"He is my son, too, and I say let him die." Mrs. Logie's face was set. "If he lives his evil will go on and on and on. Let there be an end to it."

"Please." Elodie looked from one to the other. "Let me call home and warn them."

"We'll have to go back to the house, there's no phone here." Mrs. Logie knocked on the outer door and they heard the bolt slide back. The guard opened the door and looked in.

"We're going back to the house." She glanced back at Mr. Lee. "All of us."

He opened his mouth as if to protest, then his shoulders slumped. He came around the table with a lingering glance at the jade, then followed them down the long glass passage to the house. They heard the guard close the treasure house door and lock it.

Mrs. Logie led them straight to Lee's library and indicated the phone. She seemed, suddenly, to be in charge. Mr. Lee just slumped into a chair and stared down at his black satin slippers. Slowly, finger by finger, he drew off the white cotton gloves.

Elodie rang her home number. After a minute, Alyce answered. "Browne residence."

"Alyce, let me speak to Mumma."

"She's next door, Mrs. Morgan isn't very well. Where are you, Ellie? It's so late. We were worried..."

"I've been ... delayed." She couldn't tell Alyce any of this, she'd burst with foolish excitement, run to the neighbours, terrify everyone. It was Tuesday. Ellie took a deep breath, and thought of Maybelle, sitting in her chair and eating pickles while she read the latest novel and let her hair dry. "Is Maybelle there?"

"Yeees ... just a minute." She could tell Alyce was disappointed. After a moment, Maybelle's clear and amused tones came down the line.

"Don't tell me you're out with that policeman again."

"No. Listen – I'm at Mr. Lee's house and there's trouble. You must get Mumma back. You must all stay in the house and keep the shades drawn."

"What on earth ..."

"No. Listen. You might all be in danger. You have to believe me, May. It has to do with jade and Bernice getting killed and ... honestly, it's really true. You have to trust me and do what I say."

"All right. I believe you." Maybelle knew when to argue and when to listen. Silently, Elodie blessed her. Maybelle's voice sharpened. "What about you?"

"I'm all right at the moment, but I have to stay where I am. I'm going to hang up now, and call Archie. He's – " There was an odd sound and the phone went dead. She looked at Mr. Lee and Mrs. Logie. "The phone ..."

Mrs. Logie came across and took the phone and receiver from her. She rattled the hook on the side of the phone again and again. Then she slowly replaced the receiver and put the phone down. "It's dead. Your man outside must have cut the line."

Elodie sat down hard on the nearest chair.

Harry Lee had told the truth. She was being watched.

There was no way to get help now.

22

At the Browne residence, the doorbell rang.

Before Maybelle could stop her, Alyce went to the door and opened it. A strange woman stood there, wearing a bright orange coat and a peculiar hat with leaves and a big fake orange on it. Her shoes were orange, too, and Maybelle knew immediately that she had paid a great deal for her outfit, because looking so outrageous in these hard times was expensive. As it was, the hat, coat and shoes were wet, which did them and the woman herself no favours. It had started to rain about ten minutes before, just as Maybelle returned from fetching Mrs. Browne from next-door.

Ever since, Maybelle had been on the telephone, trying to re-establish the broken connection to Ellie. The operator said there was a fault on the line.

"Hello, dear." The woman in the doorway smiled at Alyce. "May I come in? My name is Sal Schultz. I work with your sister."

"Come in, come in." Maybelle put the phone down and came across the room. Maybe this odd-looking woman knew something about what was going on.

"Thank you." Sal came in. Behind her, Alyce stood staring.

"Alyce, close the door and lock it." Maybelle snapped.

Startled, Alyce did as she was told, then came back into the room. Remembering her manners, she spoke hesitantly. "Umm – may I take your coat?"

"Yes, thank you, I'm wet through." Sal shrugged off the coat, revealing a lime green dress that was too tight for her. Even in its stretched and distended state Maybelle recognized it – they had featured it in the January issue. Sal handed the coat to Alyce, who blinked at the clash of colours.

Maybelle held out her hand. "I'm Ellie's sister, Maybelle. That's Alyce. Please sit down – I'll get my mother. She's in the kitchen."

Sal's grip was firm but brief. "Ellie's not here, then?"

"No. I just had a telephone call from her."

Sal froze halfway down into an armchair. "She called here?"

"Yes. She – "

"Thank God, she's still alive, then." Sal completed her descent into the armchair with a thump and a grateful sigh.

"What?" demanded Alyce. "What did you say?" Her big brown eyes looked even bigger as her face grew pale. She looked from the older woman to her sister. "What does she mean, 'still alive'? May? What's going on?"

"Honey, I wish I knew. Go get Mumma and Marie, would you?"

Maybelle watched her go though the dining room, then leaned closer to Sal. "She said she was at Mr. Lee's and was going to call Archie, but then we were cut off."

"At Mr. Lee's?" Sal was startled. "Are the others with her, too?"

"What others?"

"The priest and some other man named Cohen. Drew rang me and said they had all been kidnapped together. He was going down to Chinatown with Ellie's cousin and Archie to find them."

"She didn't say anything about anyone else. Is Archie that policeman Ellie doesn't like? You mean the police already know about this?"

Sal looked evasive. "Well, not exactly. And she does like him, by the way, she just doesn't realize it yet."

"But we have to call the police right away." Maybelle started to get up.

Sal reached out to stop her. "They tried that. The police don't believe them, and Archie is afraid of calling in the police because . . ."

"But he must. They have to search . . ."

Sal shook her head. "They don't know where to start. They aren't even sure they're in Chinatown. And apparently there's some connection with .. . " Sal stopped, and eyed Maybelle, assessing her. She was beautiful but seemed to have a brain. "With the Syndicates. At least, Archie thinks so. He doesn't trust the police at the moment, and I guess he knows what he's talking about. I told Drew I would come here and explain, but you seem to know more than I do."

"Only that Ellie isn't in Chinatown." Maybelle thought for a minute. "The others might be, I suppose. But how did she get away if they were kidnapped?"

"Kidnapped!?!" Mrs. Browne had come up as they were speaking, with Alyce and Marie right behind her. "Ellie has been kidnapped?" She glared at Maybelle. "You didn't tell me?"

Maybelle looked up. "With a priest and another man."

"Drew said he's some kind of General," Sal put in. "But Ellie may not be with them anymore."

"Where is she?" Mrs. Browne was obviously torn between fear and outrage.

Maybelle cleared her throat and glanced at Sal. "She's at that Mr. Lee's house."

"Well, then, we must go and get her." Mrs. Browne was galvanized. "Alyce, Marie, get your coats, it's raining ..."

"No!" Maybelle had to shout to get through to her mother who was bustling about with great purpose. "Ellie said we must stay here. I told you. She said we were in danger."

"You never mentioned danger. You just said she was going to be late. You said something about her being worried about us. I thought you meant because of the storm warning on the radio. Now you tell me she's with that Mr. Lee. Which is it?" Mrs. Browne was not going to be dissuaded easily from her rescue mission.

"She said . . . " Maybelle swallowed. "She said it had to do with Bernice and jade or something. She was serious, Mumma. She meant us to just stay here and wait."

"But Bernice is dead!" Alyce said, in a gasp.

"Exactly." Sal looked at each one in turn. "Exactly."

"My stars, I don't know what to think." Mrs. Browne sat down on the hassock that stood in front of the late Mr. Browne's favourite chair, which Sal had inadvertently chosen. Mrs. Browne suddenly seemed to see her for the first time. "Do I know you?"

"It's Sal Schultz, Mumma," Maybelle explained. "She writes for the radio with Ellie and . . " She paused and looked at Sal.

"Drew Wilson. He's with Hugh and Archie now, looking for Ellie and the others."

"Hugh? Hugh knows about all this?" Mrs. Browne didn't

know where to put herself she was so agitated. Marie came over and put her hands on her mother's shoulders, and Mrs. Browne reached up to touch them for reassurance. Alyce was nearly beside herself with excitement.

"Wow! Kidnappers and Chinamen and . . . it's all like Fu Manchu!"

Sal looked at her with sympathy. "That's make believe, Alyce. This is real, I'm afraid."

But Alyce seemed unable to take that in. Her eyes were bright and her cheeks had red blotches on them. "It's so . . . so . . . crazy!"

"We've gotten so accustomed to crime and death and sin in this city even the children can't tell the difference. It's not healthy. You're not to listen to that kind of thing anymore, Alyce." Mrs. Browne tried to invoke the only kind of order she knew, but her voice carried little conviction. The admonition was, as always, automatic, as she tried to come to terms with the situation that had suddenly erupted into their quiet and ordinary lives. She had always felt bad things only happened to bad girls, was confident her girls were unlikely to fall prey to the sins of the big city. No illegal drink, no bad company, no wicked behaviour was ever going to touch any of them, least of all Ellie, who was so serious, who worked so hard.

Yet now, out of the blue, they were in the midst of something even more bizarre than Mr. Capone and his crooked associates had ever dreamt up. She honestly could have taken news that Ellie had been caught in a raid on a speakeasy, or in some gambling den. That was all too familiar ground these days. But this –

"She was just playing, you know," Mrs. Browne suddenly said. "Just playing detective."

"Like Nancy Drew." Alyce nodded, as if this were, in fact, what any red-blooded American girl would do, given the stimulus of a man shot dead in front of her at some weird party. Why, it was just what Alyce herself would have done, too!

"All right." Mrs. Browne drew herself up, folded her hands in her lap, and looked at Sal. "Tell me from the beginning. I want to know just how bad all this is."

It was a small shop on the corner of Wentworth and 18th Street. The elevated trains ran nearby, filling the night air with their clatter. Chinatown stayed up late, for the streets were still busy. The address was correct by number, but all the legends on the windows were solely in Chinese. They entered, and were immediately assailed by a thousand scents. The walls were covered with hundreds of little glass-fronted drawers. Behind each glass panel could be seen different coloured lumps of various substances, twisted roots, little twigs, powders, granules, even small white bones. The air was suffused with bitter and sweet, spicy and sharp, smells of all kinds both pleasant and extremely unpleasant. No one was in the shop, but strange music could be heard from the back, flutes and some plucked string instrument.

Hugh spotted a bell on the main counter and rang it. Almost immediately curtains in the rear wall parted and a small Chinese man of indeterminate age appeared. He could have been forty or four hundred and he was everbody's idea of a Chinaman – his hair was in a queue, he wore a small black cap, and was dressed in a long robe with wide sleeves that concealed his crossed hands. His face was wrinkled but benign. He bowed.

"N*in hao*." Archie spoke one of the few Chinese words he knew outside of menus. "You are Dr. Tsung?"

"I am. You require medicine?"

"No, thank you. We come on behalf of Father Anselm."

Tsung's manner immediately became more friendly. He smiled, revealing small teeth, four of them gold. "And how is the good father?" he asked.

"He is in serious trouble." Hugh's voice was impatient. "We need help for him."

Dr. Tsung frowned. "But how can I help?"

"It's Chinese trouble," Drew said. "Ming Dao trouble."

Dr. Tsung closed his eyes for a moment, then opened them. They were as dark as obsidian, and filled with pain. "I feared this." He gestured for them to follow him and went back through the curtains. Archie, Hugh and Drew exchanged glances, then followed the little man into another world.

Archie recognized it as a smaller version of Lee Chang's bedroom, but without the bed itself. The colours were blue and green rather than red, but the furniture was similar, as were the hangings and pictures on the wall, but it lacked the clutter of Lee's many personal treasures. Surfaces were plain, free of any objects save for a small blue and white porcelain bowl containing three oranges.

Tsung crossed to a modern victrola and lifted the arm from the spinning record, silencing the plaintive melody of the flutes. "Sit, please." When they had complied he, too, sat and looked at each one in turn, his gaze finally settling on Archie." Tell, please."

Archie spoke briefly and to the point, summing up what had happened as far as they understood it. Tsung nodded and nodded. When Archie had finished, Tsung sighed.

"The Ming Dao arrived in Chicago about six months ago. They immediately began pressuring our people to support the Communist cause. Many of us had relatives still in China, and they promised retribution if we did not comply. What Mr. Capone calls 'protection', I believe?"

The others nodded in turn. Mr. Capone sold protection from Mr. Capone himself. Pay up or suffer the consequences. All too familiar to anyone in Chicago these days.

"Alternatively they offered assistance in bringing family members over here – depending on how much one could pay. There was little choice between them. Either way worked. Those that resisted – " he paused.

"Had their heads cut off?" Archie supplied.

Tsung nodded. "That was one thing they did. They also have been instrumental in greatly increasing the smuggling of opium into this country. It is the other coin in which they trade."

"And what has that got to do with General Cohen and Father Anselm?"

A brief smile flickered in the corners of Dr. Tsung's mouth. "Two-Gun Cohen. A remarkable man. He was very close to Dr. Sun."

"Dr. Sun?" asked Hugh, who was not as familiar with China as he was with Cicero, Ilinois – an equally foreign country with equally complex politics.

"Sun Yat Sen," Drew said.

249

"A great man." Tsung's voice was reverent. "Sadly let down by the very countries he most admired, America and Britain. Cohen was his protector, his advisor, his go-between. Now he does the same for Chiang Kai Shek, who fights to maintain those ideals but who is being undermined by Russia, Japan, even Germany. It was Cohen who brought T'zu Hsi's jade here to sell so he could buy arms for Chiang's Kuomintang government. How Chiang and Cohen got it is a mystery, but there was talk of a raid on the pirates of Bias Bay."

"Pirates?" Hugh was astounded. "Pirates?" He could hardly believe his ears and had visions of Long John Silver in his three-cornered hat and peg leg.

"Piracy is still very much in evidence in China," Dr. Tsung explained. "We are moving very fast forward from a feudal system to modern politics, much like Russia. These things normally happen gradually, but now men like Lenin for Communism and Dr. Sun for democracy try to jump the intervening stages. Anomalies remain – things become confused."

"You're telling me," Hugh breathed.

Dr. Tsung nodded. "I am trying to, young man. As I said, the Ming Dao represent the worst aspects of Communism. When they got word that Father Anselm had brought T'zu Hsi's jade from San Francisco to Chicago, they wanted the money it would bring for their cause rather than for the cause of the republicans."

"Cohen brought it into the country but Father Anselm brought it here?"

"The General had business in Canada," Dr. Tsung said. "I had not realized he had come down to Chicago so quickly."

"How did the Ming Dao hear about the jade?" Archie asked.

Dr. Tsung gently waved his fingers. "A woman, I believe. It is often a woman. That has not changed."

"So the Ming Dao have now kidnapped Anselm and Cohen in order to force Lee to surrender the jade?"

"That would seem to be so." Dr. Tsung looked very sad. "I do not know Lee Chang very well. I do not know what he will do."

"Where would they be holding Anselm, Cohen and the girl?" asked Archie.

Tsung frowned. "I have no idea. Thery could be here in Chinatown, but equally they could be anywhere in the city – even the suburbs. You see – " He paused. "This is very hard for me to say. Not only do the Ming Dao espouse Communism. I told you about the opium." The others nodded. "There is new interest in opium outside of Chinatown, now. Great interest. Not as opium, I believe, but refined into a drug much more powerful than cocaine, which is so popular among the young at the moment. More powerful in effect and addiction, therefore more powerful in terms of social degradation, which the Ming Dao want, and much more powerful in terms of money."

"Which interests who?"

Dr. Tsung raised his hands in a gesture of despair. "Who sells cocaine to all the silly young men and women? Who deals in liquor, gambling, prostitution? Who would be corrupt enough to be prepared to enslave thousands for profit?"

"Capone."

Tsung bowed his head. "So I believe. It has started already. Just at the edge of Chinatown itself, there is a new house of opium being run by a member of that man's organisation. A tea shop, or so it would appear from outside. Just another disguise at which they have become so proficient. The police do not bother with Chinatown, and they do not bother with this teashop. But there the web begins."

"You say it's run by a member of Capone's outfit?" Archie leaned forward. "Do you know his name?"

Dr. Tsung thought for a moment. "I believe it is Jake something."

"Jake Manotta?"

Tsung nodded. "That is it. Jake Manotta. The teashop is called The Copper Kettle. In the British style. But no one drinks tea there, unless they enter by mistake."

Archie looked at Hugh and Drew.

"I suddenly feel the need of a nice cup of tea, don't you?"

"Oh, definitely, old bean." Drew's English accent was excellent. "Abso-jolly-lutely."

**

251

The Copper Kettle was not likely to have casual customers. The lace curtains in the window were yellow with smokestain, and there was dust on the display of pastries on the table just behind the glass.

Archie and Hugh stood on the opposite corner, watching. They had been there about ten minutes, and in that time several people had gone inside. One was Chinese, the others were all white and young, with slightly haunted faces. Not at all your usual teashop clientele.

Drew came back and joined them. "There's a back door to the alley," he said. "Windows are barred and blanked off from inside. Couple of vents down low. Smells weird back there. I think I read somewhere opium smoke smells sweetish, so maybe that's it."

"An opium den." Hugh shook his head. "Here, in Chicago. It's not enough they can sniff themselves silly with 'snow', booze themselves witless, gamble what little wages they get straight into Capone's pockets, now they're taking up smoking opium? I thought that went out with Sherlock Holmes."

"He took cocaine." Drew was a stickler for details.

"Yeah, yeah, but in one of those stories at least he goes into some opium den in Limehouse or somewhere ..." Hugh was still not entirely sober.

"This is 1931 and I still want a cup of tea." Archie's face was grim. "We may have to fight to get it."

"Maybe you should call for back-up?" Drew sounded nervous. He was a drinker, not a fighter. His mother told him so.

"No knowing who would come," Archie said. "That's my problem, gentlemen. Not knowing which of my fellow officers is in Capone's pocket – and that includes my Captain." He looked from one to the other. "Ellie could be in there right now. Are you with me?"

"Oh, shit," said Drew, morosely. He followed the other two across the street, lagging only a little behind, and muttering, "The game is afoot."

The sweet smell Drew had described hung heavily inside the dirty little tearoom, which was hardly big enough to hold more than three dusty tables, each set for four. They crossed the narrow room to a door in the rear wall. It resembled a swinging door but was locked. Archie banged on it, taking out his gun. "Open up."

Silence.

Archie banged harder on the wooden panels and again demanded entrance. There was a scuttling sound from behind the door, low voices arguing. Finally a key turned in the lock and the door was slightly opened. "Sorry, we're clo – "

Archie shouldered the door fully open, revealing not a kitchen full of copper kettles, but a small office with a desk, chairs, and a large fancy Chinese cupboard beside a further door at the rear. The sweetish smell was stronger, still, and indeed the two men in the office seemed slightly dazed by its presence. That suited Archie just fine. He displayed his gun.

"Evening, Jake." His voice was bitter.

The man behind the desk gazed at him as if pleasantly surprised. "Well, if it isn't little Archie Deacon."

Jake Manotta was built like a bull gone to fat. His thin black hair was greased back straight from a high forehead, and his moustache was hair-thin. He wore an expensive suit, and there was a jewelled stickpin in his silk tie. The only thing that set him apart from Hollywood's vision of a gentleman gangster were his hands, which were covered with heavy gold rings on each thick finger. Jake's version of a permanently available knuckle-duster.

Archie remembered his friend Joe Concetti's dead face. It had been battered to pieces by those hands and those rings. He remembered now some of the strange indentations in Joe's torn flesh, deep holes shaped like diamonds. His finger tightened on the trigger.

If Manotta noticed, it didn't seem to bother him. The man who had opened the door was skinny but mean looking. Hugh and Drew had come in quickly behind Archie, and they had Manotta's assistant by an arm each, preventing him from drawing the gun in his shoulder holster.

All Hugh kept thinking as he clutched the man's arm and smelled his sweat and cheap hair oil, was 'they all dress the part, they all dress the part', as if some central authority ruled appearances. He hadn't let on to Archie, but he was terrified, and he was pretty certain Drew was, too. If it hadn't been for Ellie, he could never have done this. Any of this. He looked past Manotta's sneering face. Who was behind that rear door? More gunsels? Bigger and meaner than the one he held, who seemed to be vibrating with fear or anger? Guys with machine guns? Capone's people loved machine guns, their 'Chicago typewriters'. So much noise and destruction – a lot of bang for their buck. People in Chicago automatically dropped to the floor at the first rattling fusilllade.

"I'm looking for a girl, a priest, and a Jew." Archie kept his voice and his gun level.

Marotta stared at him for a moment, apparently perplexed, then laughed out loud. "I've heard of weird sex, Deacon, but that particular combo is new even to me."

"What's in that fancy cupboard?"

Manotta kept his eyes forward, and blinked, slowly. "My underwear."

"Open it."

Manotta indicated his refusal with a stream of spat-out Italian. Archie raised his gun and fired straight bewtween the large brass handles of the cupboard. The noise was deafening in the small room and both Hugh and Drew nearly wet their pants with the shock of it. They didn't recognize Archie, suddenly. Outside, he had seemed a nice, regular guy, maybe a little grumpy. Now he looked just like Manotta, grim and mean.

After a moment, one of the splintered double doors of the Chinese cupboard swung open. Inside were shelves filled with odd paraphernalia, pipes, boxes, and syringes. Archie went around the desk and opened the other door, keeping his gun on Manotta. He examined the objects curiously, took a couple of the boxes and put them in his pocket. Then he went to the door beside it and opened it.

A pall of smoke swirled toward him and he nearly choked. Beyond he could see a neat line of cots with people on them. He turned to Manotta, who was watching him with apparent amusement. Lifting his foot, Archie knocked Manotta's chair back, leaving him sprawled on the floor. Then he went into the semi-darkened room. All of the people on the beds were Chinese, some lying staring and mumbling to themselves, some asleep. At the far end of the room sat a Chinese woman, doing something on a table littered with long pipes and other objects like those in the cupboard. He heard a step behind him. Manotta stood in the open doorway, grinning.

"Want to try it? I can give you a good price." He seemed unafraid, even unbothered by being dumped unceremoniously on the floor of his office.

"Where are the kids?"

"What kids?"

"I saw them come in myself. They weren't Chinese. I didn't see them leave."

"Oh they were just passing through, collecting supplies," Manotta said. "They went out the other way." He nodded his head toward yet another door Archie hadn't noticed in all the smoky haze. The smell was getting to him, he felt a little strange. The door was in a side wall, and he realized it led to the building next door. "Maybe what you want is in there," Jake sneered.

Manotta followed Archie to the other door. Beyond it was another room, also filled with supine bodies. But there was no smoke here. Just idiot smiles on the faces of the people sprawled around on the floor. Around them was a litter of glass ampoules and hypodermic syringes. Archie whirled to face Manotta.

"Cocaine, too?"

Manotta shook his head. "Oh, no. Not cocaine. Something new. Something much, much better. Heroin. Takes you to the moon, Deacon. Takes you high and wide. I can give you a good price there, too. I'm the sole dealer in Chicago, but I'm getting ready to expand. I can get it for you wholesale. It's quick, it's easy, it's small and no overheads like bottles and trucks and sawdust bars or nightclubs. It's the future, Archie. When Repeal comes, we'll be ready. And there's not a damn thing you can do about it."

23

After the exotic surroundings of Dr. Tsung's Chinese medicine shop, and the squalor of the Brass Kettle, Kercheval Street was a pleasant contrast. Archie parked near the Browne house and looked down at his hands. Hugh and Drew had barely restrained him from attacking Manotta, and he wished again that they hadn't, even though he would have come off second best to Manotta's weight and diamond-studded rings. They had phoned an anonymous tip to the police about the Copper Kettle, but he doubted it had been followed up. If the police took action, they would no doubt find all the evidence gone. Small and portable with no overheads, Manotta had gloated. Which meant he could move fast. But Manotta was right – the cops let Chinatown police itself. The tip wouldn't be taken seriously.

"Sal must be here by now," Drew said. He had phoned her from St. John's House. They got out of the car and walked back to the front path. As they did there was a flash of lightning and a distant crack and rumble of thunder. A sudden breeze turned the young leaves on the trees backward, their pale undersides shown in the light of the streetlamps. The lights were on inside the Browne house, but all the blinds were drawn and it was eerily silent. Hugh realized that, for once, Alyce's precious radio was turned off.

They went up the steps and along the porch. Hugh knocked. "Hey, in there. It's Hugh. Let us in."

There was a sound beside them, and the blind of the front sitting room was pulled slightly aside and a wary eye peered out at them. After a moment the front door was unlocked and Mrs. Browne stood there. "Have you found her?" she asked, eagerly.

Hugh shook his head and the three of them walked in. Mrs. Browne, very downcast, locked the door behind them. Archie was startled – three versions of Ellie sat looking at him, along with Sal Schultz. Mrs. Browne became suddenly formal and introduced her girls – Marie, Maybelle, Alyce. All the Browne women had Ellie's big dark eyes, except Maybelle, whose eyes were deep blue, but she had Ellie's mouth and chin.

Maybelle spoke up. "She's at Mr. Lee's house."

The three men stared at her. Had they been going around in circles for nothing? Had Ellie been at Lee's all along?

"Are Anselm and Cohen with her?" asked Hugh, who was the first to recover.

"We don't know," Maybelle said. "We were cut off."

"She phoned?" Drew was very taken with Maybelle.

Maybelle nodded.

"I wanted to go right out and get her, but Maybelle said she told her we were in some kind of danger." Mrs. Browne's hands twisted together, her knuckles white.

Archie frowned. Danger, here? How could that be, unless Ellie had given the Ming Dao her address, and that seemed unlikely. What's more, how had she become separated from the others, if she had, and gotten to Lee's house? Why hadn't she come home? Thunder rumbled again, far-off.

"I'll make some coffee," Marie said. "You all look absolutely terrible."

"Hugh, why has this happened? What is going on? Why don't the police do something?" Mrs. Browne's eyes went to Archie. "You have to go out there right now. You have to!"

Archie saw she was near breaking point, and understood how this sudden eruption of violence into her heretofore quiet life had shaken her deeply. For the Browne family, like most of the families in Chicago, violence was in the newspapers, only. It happened downtown, and in a few suburbs like Cicero, but never 'here'. He doubted a shot had ever been fired within their hearing, nor the snarling rattle of a machine gun, and police sirens came only from a distance. They lived on the shores of Chicago's violence and corruption, but a newspaper story didn't draw blood on Kercheval Street and hundreds of other streets like it. Reading about criminals was like hearing about a neighbour's wayward relatives. They were gossiped about and conjectured over, but never seen or heard. Therefore it was all the more shocking when they came face to face with its reality.

Archie Deacon was bone tired, and wished Mrs. Browne would sit down, so he could. Finally she did, and he, Hugh

257

and Drew almost fell into sofa and chairs. He looked at his two 'assistants' and was sorry for them. Hugh covered crime, but only from the sidelines. Drew dealt with crime, but only in his imagination from his usual position on the office sofa. He knew they had been frightened at the Copper Kettle but they had come through for him. He only hoped they could continue. If they felt as lousy as he did ...

"Coffee." Marie arrived with a tray. Hugh took a cup gratefully, and couldn't help wondering if there was any of her wonderful apple pie in the pantry. Marie wasn't as classically beautiful as Maybelle, nor as lively as Alyce, nor as exasperating as Ellie, but there was a warmth and heart to her that always soothed him. He drank his coffee down, leaned back against the sofa, and closed his eyes. If, after all this, Ellie wasn't dead, he would certainly kill her himself. If only she hadn't been so nosy, so persistent, so stubborn, so ... adorable. He'd been so pleased at her new job, sure it would absorb all her energy. Unfortunately, as so often before, she had fooled him.

Drew felt very peculiar. He was not accustomed to 'family'. He had no siblings, his mother had always been unstable, his father an absent mystery. He had grown up any old how, educated himself with omnivorous reading, found a small talent for the new medium of radio, and got through life with the aid of a bottle or two. Now here were all these women, nice women, kind and loving of one another and their cousin Hugh. He and Archie were outsiders and he felt lonlier than ever. He glanced over at Sal and saw understanding and sympathy in her eyes.

Good old Sal.

He drank his coffee and listened as Archie explained what they had been doing, and what he thought of the situation they were in. Archie was like the Browne family, just plain decent. How he had managed to avoid being touched by the tide of corruption like so many of his fellow officers had was a mystery to Drew, who usually took the easy ways out. In which case, he asked himself, what the hell am I doing here? But he knew – it was Ellie. It was all about Ellie. For all of them.

"We'll go out to Lee's place, now," Archie finished, setting his empty coffee cup down on the floor. "We'll get Ellie and then decide what to do next."

Drew and Hugh looked at him in surprise. Next? They were going to do more even after they had rescued Ellie? Looking at one another, each saw dismay.

Holy cats.

**

"Keep going! Keep going!" Hugh's voice was almost shrill. They were moving along Lakeshore Drive, looking for Lee's place.

"But that's ..." Archie protested.

"Put your damn foot down!" Hugh, in the back seat, clutched Archie's shoulder. "Go past, go past."

Archie did as he was told, only at the last moment seeing what Hugh had seen. A white van with a pig on it was parked next to the entrance of the Lee mansion's drive. Two figures were inside, hardly discernible through the heavy rain that had begun to fall. On their right faint lines of white were visible on the glittering blackness of the Lake as it churned before the wind.

He drove on along the shore until they rounded a bend, then pulled over to the side of the road. They could hear the angry thud and wash of the waves on the stony beach even through the car's closed windows.

"Do you think it's just those two, or are there more of them around?" Drew asked, nervously.

"No idea." Archie was thinking hard. He pulled a battered pack of cigarettes from inside his jacket and regarded them balefully. "I said I'd give these up. Hell with it." But every white cylinder he drew out was bent and split. Drew took pity on him and offered one of his own. Lighting up was difficult, as both of them were shaking.

"Do you think they're all in there?" Hugh asked from the darkness of the rear seat. "Anselm, the other guy, and Ellie?"

"I hope so," Archie said. "I'm tired of running around like a dog after its own tail."

Drew considered the glowing end of his own cigarette. "Getting them back won't solve much, you know. That Ming Dao bunch will go on trying. We don't even know how many there are in the whole group. Could be dozens – hundreds."

"One thing at a time." Archie coughed, glowered at his cigarette and threw it out of the window in a golden arc. It fell onto the wet grass beside the car, sizzled, and went out. "We'll have to circle around through the woods at the back. If there are more of those bastards back there, we'll pick them off as we go."

"But if you fire – " Hugh began.

Archie snorted. "Walk softly and carry a big stick," he quoted. Hugh, who was heavy-footed at the best of times, doubted he could comply, but he would try. Drew said nothing for a minute, then made an observation.

"Carry a big rock would be better."

"Carry whatever you can get your goddamn hands on." Archie was keying himself up. He liked to investigate alone, but he was more accustomed to going into a dangerous situation with trained and armed officers beside him. Not nervous amateurs. There was, however, no alternative.

He restarted the engine and rolled slowly along the edge of the road until they came to the place where the woods met the road between estates. He cut the engine and the lights. Opening his door quietly he glanced back at the other two. "Move it," he commanded in a rough whisper. The rain suddenly blew in upon them, relentless and icy.

There was a long, long pause, and then Drew got out and pushed his seat forward so Hugh could emerge. The whites of their eyes shone as they regarded one another. They were already wet through, and their hair was being beaten down onto their foreheads by the rain.

"Damn," muttered Hugh.

"What?"

"I knew I should have gone to the toilet before we left."

Archie gestured widely. "Pick a tree. And then shut up and follow me."

**

Ellie, Mrs. Logie and Lee Chang had been going back and forth to the vault, bringing in the many old boxes that held

T'zu Hsi's jade. Mr. Lee told her it was traditional to pack jade in old boxes. If they were being watched, it would seem as if they were getting ready to comply with Harry's demands, for their activity was clearly visible through the glass passage, which now was awash with the falling rain.

Ellie had gone into the kitchen with Mrs. Logie to get something to eat, when she gave a gasp and a small squeak. There was a distorted face pressed against the kitchen window. Mrs. Logie turned and drew a sharp breath.

"No, no – it's all right." Ellie's spirits soared as the face drew back a little and she was amazed to see it belonged to her cousin Hugh. What on earth was he doing here? "It's my cousin." Ellie hurried to the rear door and unlocked it. Hugh blew in with the rain, followed by Archie and – "Drew?" Ellie was dumbfounded.

"Are you okay?" Hugh came over and grabbed her by the upper arms. His grasp was painful, his clothes and hair were dripping wet.

"Ouch, yes. I'm fine." Ellie pulled away, rubbing her arms. "How did you – "

"Are the others here?" Archie demanded, pushing his hair back from his gleaming forehead. This only resulted in his hair standing up in spikes.

"No." Mrs. Logie regarded them suspiciously. "How did you get past all those men outside?"

"There are only two at the foot of the drive."

"Oh."

"We had a hell of a time getting across the back lawn – the light from that damn glass passage reaches nearly all the way to the woods." Hugh was looking around curiously. "But we didn't see anyone else, and I don't think anyone saw us."

"They cut off the phone. They brought me here. Mr. Lee has to give up the jade to Harry or he'll kill General Cohen and Father Anselm." Ellie's words tumbled over one another in her haste to explain. "And I think they're near the stockyards because I could smell manure." She frowned. "And ether . . . and pickles."

"Who the hell is Harry?" Drew interrupted.

"Oh, dear." Ellie looked at Mrs. Logie, who had resumed her usual blank expression in the face of these strangers. "It's kind of a long story."

"Oh, swell," said Hugh, taking off his wet jacket. "There's nothing I like better than a nice long story in the middle of the night. We've been all over Hell's Half Acre looking for you, Ellie. We're half drowned. What the devil is going on?"

The kitchen door swung back, and Lee Chang stood looking at them in astonishment, then recognized Archie. "You have brought the police?" He seemed upset by this.

"No. Just me." Archie looked around. "Can we sit down and talk about all this? My back is killing me." He had fallen twice in the woods while the other two 'amateurs' had stepped lightly along as if sneaking up on houses was something they did every day of their lives. He was relieved to see Ellie, but growing more exasperated by the minute. "I seem to remember there are no windows in your library, Mr. Lee. It would be better if we weren't seen to be with you for the moment. We were lucky. Those two out front must be making regular tours of the grounds. We came across two of your own guards in the woods."

"Fell over them." Hugh still felt sick at the sight of all that blood.

Mr. Lee clutched at the doorframe as if to keep himself from falling. "Dead?"

"Very." Archie moved toward him. "This is getting uglier by the minute. And I want to know why, Mr. Lee."

24

It took a while for everyone to tell what they knew. At the end of it, Archie looked bleak. The storm was directly overhead, now, and he had to raise his voice to be heard over the thunder and wind. "I don't know what the hell to do," he admitted. "I really don't." He turned to Ellie. "You say the place they're being held is a large building?" She nodded. "How many men did you actually see?"

"Five. But I could hear others in the building, shouting amd moving things around. General Cohen said he smelled opium. I could only smell manure and pickles. And something like ether."

"A lot of opium in Chinese history," Drew said.

"A lot of opium in China today." Lee was as weary as the rest of them.

Archie turned to Ellie. "But you said you smelled ether?" She nodded, and he swore under his breath.

"I thought we were in the basement of a hospital until the General said he smelled opium." Ellie was close to tears. Time was passing, and nobody seemed to be doing anything but talk. She thought of Father Anselm and Two-Gun Cohen and Harry Lee's vicious sneers. Right after she had been taken from that room to come here, she had heard the sound of a blow and a chair falling. She thought of the big sullen men with Harry. Were they beating the priest and the General for more information, as they had beaten Webster? For pleasure? Were the two of them even still alive?

"You've got to do something!" she cried. "Stop talking and do something. Take the jade out to the men in the van – they'll take it to Harry and he'll let the General and Father Anselm go."

"I doubt that." Archie's voice was flat. "That address he sent to Mr. Lee is on the riverfront. You said it was a big building – but not a hospital, Ellie, most likely a warehouse. Ether in a warehouse tells me just one thing. They're using a cocaine lab's facilities to process opium into heroin. And the people who process cocaine work for Capone." He looked around at them in despair. "Don't you see? They're combining forces, using people like Manotta to get what heroin they've made so far to hook people on the street, moving them from opium and cocaine to heroin. It's not a little Chinese operation. It's big business. Dr. Tsung said they were anticipating Repeal, and I think he's right. Torrio set up the Syndicate, organised it on business lines, before he handed over to Capone. Why let a good outfit go to waste just because liquor becomes legal again? If we contact the police on this, word will get straight back to Capone. We don't need the police, we need an army!"

Mrs. Logie covered her face and moaned. "Harry. Harry."

Mr. Lee's face had been changing as Archie spoke. He went from hopelessness to shock to anger to resolve. "Do any of you men know how to reconnect the telephone wires that were cut?"

"I do," said Drew. "As long as they just cut them and didn't take out a section."

"Do you know how a combustion engine works?" Hugh's question was in jest, but Drew nodded.

"In theory."

Hugh just shook his head. Was there nothing this Drew guy didn't know – in theory? He resolved there and then to renew his library card when all this was over. If he was still alive, that is.

"I told you, calling the police is useless," Archie snapped.

Mr. Lee shook his head. "Not the police." He looked suddenly sly and almost mischievous. "I have an idea," he said.

**

"Where do you want these guys?" Arnold Ryan indicated the two Chinese thugs his own men had dragged out of the van at the foot of the drive and trussed up like a pair of turkeys. Forewarned by Lee, they had had no trouble sneaking up on them under cover of the storm. It had taken Drew less than ten minutes to reconnect the cut phone wires outside the house, although he returned wetter than ever and nursing a cut hand. Ryan shook the rain off his hat and began to unbuckle his raincoat.

"Living room. But they need watching," Archie said.

Ryan looked at him, then turned to look at Lee. "Odd company you're keeping, these days, Lee. Or have you got another body on the premises?"

"I have need of help from all available sources," Lee Chang said, calmly. He gestured and they followed him into the library, leaving Ryan's two 'friends' to guard the Chinamen.

It took quite a while to explain everything. As they each spoke, Ryan regarded them in turn, lively interest on his face. He did not seem surprised by any of it, just interested. Elodie supposed nothing would surprise him these days. Not even jade from a dead Empress and people with their heads cut off. Mr. Lee finished up by explaining what he wanted from Ryan.

"I think I can get you what you need." Ryan leaned back in his chair. "Ever since the Valentine's Day thing, Bugs Moran looks for ways to knock Capone's legs out from under him."

"I thought you worked for Capone," Archie said.

"So does Capone." Arnold Ryan smiled. "Because he has an Irish wife, he is prepared to overlook the fact that I am Irish as well. In fact, I occasionally give him useful information about the Moran outfit – when Bugs says it's okay, that is."

"You're working both ends against the middle." Drew's expression bordered on admiration.

"I'm a lawyer." Ryan took a drag on his cigar. "I work for myself."

"Isn't that dangerous?" Even as she said it, Ellie knew her question was naive.

"My dear, walking across the street in Chicago is dangerous." Ryan smiled his charming alligator smile. "If it pleases me to take money from fools on both sides, so be it. Their day is ending."

"Yours could be, too." Hugh knew none of this could be reported, and it peeved him. A great, great story was being enacted in front of him, and he couldn't say a word. It might make his career, and he would have to let it go. He glanced at Ellie, who almost smiled. She could sense his frustration.

"Oh, my day is nearly over." Ryan glanced at Lee Chang. "My doctor says a year or eighteen months if I'm lucky." His tone was informative, and totally without self-pity.

"Oh." Ellie's cry of sympathy was involuntary. By Lee Chang's expression, she saw that he had already known of

Ryan's prognosis, but the others were as surprised as she was. Ryan looked perfectly fit and healthy.

"That is why Mr. Lee's offer of a jade piece in exchange for my assistance is so satisfactory. I will end my days possessing something of inestimable beauty I could not othewise afford – not even with Mob money." He glanced at Lee. "You have it here?"

Lee stood up and walked over to where the boxes containing T'zu Hsi's treasure were piled on his desk. He opened one or two, then found what he was looking for. He came back and handed the small box to Ryan, who put his cigar carefully into the ashtray beside him, and took the box in his hands. "What will the General Two-Gun Cohen say when he knows I have this?"

"If he lives, he will say 'Thank you' Mr. Ryan." Lee managed a smile. "If he does not live, no one will know. There is no inventory except in here." He lightly touched his forehead.

"And when I die?"

Lee shrugged. "It is yours to do with as you wish."

Ryan nodded, satisfied. Slowly he lifted off the cover of the box and drew a sharp breath. "Holy Mary, Mother of God." He stared into the box for a long moment, then looked up at Lee who still stood beside him. "They're incredible."

Ellie realized Lee had given him the butterflies. Ryan would obviously recognize their worth immediately, but it was not their value that filled his eyes. Just their incomparable beauty. In that moment she would have forgiven him anything.

"I want my son to live." Lee's voice was soft.

"No." Mrs. Logie's voice was harsh. "Disown him. Leave him."

Lee turned to her, his face sad. "Do you really want that?"

"Yes, yes!" Mrs. Logie's voice trembled. She covered her face with her hands and tears ran out between her fingers. "No," she whispered.

Ryan was still staring into the box. Finally he spoke. "How many men do you need?"

Archie stood up. "That depends on what we can get out of those two in the other room."

Ryan glanced up at the clock face opposite him. "You'd better be quick. We'll have to move before dawn, and that's not so

266

far away now."

**

Ryan had spoken directly to Moran on the phone, explaining that he needed about twenty well-armed men immediately. They could hear Moran's rasping voice clear across the room but not what he said. Ryan simplified the situation but made it clear it was an opportunity to do serious damage to Capone. That brought forth a loud guffaw from the other end of the line.

"I just need muscle and bullets, Bugs. No brains required on this one. You understand?"

Moran's voice softened. He understood.

When he had finished making arrangements, Ryan put the phone down, and turned to Archie. "Half an hour. Six cars and a couple of vans. We can brief them outside." He turned to Ellie.

"Now – draw what you can remember seeing."

"But I'm going, too."

"The hell you are." Hugh was suddenly overwhelmed by anger. "You started all this – "

"I did not!"

" – and now that we've got you out of it we're damn well not going to let you back in. This is going to be ugly, Ellie. You stay here."

"I will not! And you didn't get me out of it, I got myself out by convincing Harry Lee that I was just a dumb little student. If I go in first, maybe carrying some of the jade, he'll think he's won. He'll be off his guard."

Archie turned from where he was getting paper and pencil from Lee's desk. "For five minutes. A lot of bullets can be fired in five minutes. Once you've brought the jade you're no more use to him. You've seen him, you can identify him, you know something of what is going on. Why should he let you live any more than the priest or Cohen? Don't be stupid."

"I am not stupid!" Ellie flared. "I'll take in something small and say the rest is out in the van and I'll go back out to get it."

"And he'll shoot you in the back." Ryan's voice was flat. "He'll expect his men to bring back the jade, not you. Archie

267

here is wrong. You're not stupid, Miss Browne. You've proved that, from what I hear. But neither are you expendable. There will be shooting. People will die. Their men, even some of Moran's men, I expect. He knows that, we know that." He glanced at Lee and Mrs. Logie. "She stays."

Lee nodded. "But my son – "

"Have you a picture of your son?" Archie interrupted. Lee looked at Mrs. Logie, who nodded and went out of the room. Archie continued. "There will be a lot of Chinese men, Mr. Lee."

"And we all look alike." Lee's voice was bitter, resigned. "I understand."

"We'll do our best, Mr. Lee." Drew heard himself speak, and realized he had just volunteered for the operation. What the devil was happening to him? he wondered. Bravery was all very well in books and on the radio, but he was a dreamer, a drinker – not a fighter. "I mean – I'm sure they'll make every effort – "

"I heard you the first time, Wilson." Archie grinned at him. "Ever fired a gun?"

"Good God, no!"

"It's easy," said Ellie, her face filled with resentment. "You just point and pull, right?" She glared at Archie. "Even a woman can do that."

"Ever see a man go down with his intestines pouring out of a big hole in his gut?" Ryan's voice was a slap in the face. "Ever hear a man with shattered legs begging you to kill him so the pain will stop? Ever see what a machine gun can to to a watermelon, much less a man?"

Ellie went pale.

"I think you get my drift." Ryan handed her the paper and pencil. "Draw, Miss Browne. Just draw."

25

Drew had begun drinking while they waited for Moran's thugs to arrive. When they appeared, they were even more frightening than he expected. They weren't all big, or tough, or particularly unattractive in any way save one.

Their eyes were dead.

He knew instinctively that every one of them had killed at one time or another, and were perfectly prepared to kill again. It was their job, and like the baker and the candlestick maker, they did it carefully and well.

As they stood in the driveway in front of Lee's house, he exchanged a glance with Hugh. The reporter in Hugh was awake and interested, but the man within was as frightened as Drew was by these silent, obedient men who carried guns as casually as they might carry a cane or roll a hoop.

The night was tapering, the storm had passed, but there still fell a soft, filmy rain. Hat brims, cars and even Drew's spectacles glittered. Archie and Ryan were explaining what the men were to do. Lee Chang stood beside them, his face impassive. Harry Lee's picture was passed from hand to hand, illuminated by flashlights.

Drew tried to pretend it was a movie.

It wasn't.

He had filled his flask from Lee's supply, and took another swig. The gun they had given him was heavy in his jacket pocket, and banged against his side when he raised his arm to drink. He knew he would not be able to use it. Indeed, he was not at all sure he could put one foot in front of the other when they got where they were going.

He was assigned a car, and sat in the back seat between two of Moran's men. When he offered his flask, they shook their heads.

"After," the one on the right said.

Neither he, his companion, nor the two men in the front seat spoke again.

Drew could smell their sweat, but knew it was not from fear but excitement, as soldiers sweat before battle. He knew its bitter edge was caused by adrenalin. Adrenalin was produced by the adrenal glands, it stimulated the nerves and the production of insulin and other endocrines. That was one of the bits of information he had accumulated from books. All his life he had only read about things, never experienced them. Now knowing such esoteric facts did him no good whatsoever.

The cars drove on. Above the lake, on their left, the sky lightened almost imperceptibly. The streets of the Loop were strangely empty, the streetlights shining down onto gleaming trolley tracks, shop windows, parked cars, occasional walkers shuffling to or from the job, head down, thoughts elsewhere. If they noticed the brief parade of cars and vans passing through, they ignored them. Wisely.

The people of Chicago knew when to look away.

**

It was very quiet when the men had left the house.

Ellie sat in one chair, Mrs. Logie in another, both lost in their own thoughts. Five minutes passed. Ten. They heard the engines of the cars as Moran's men arrived. Then they heard them leave, going away down the drive, one by one.

Suddenly Mrs. Logie stood up and went to the desk. She opened a drawer and looked down into it silently. Then she took a deep breath. "Can you drive?" she asked Ellie.

"Um . . . sort of." Hugh had given her exactly two lessons the previous summer.

Mrs. Logie reached into the drawer and drew out a gun. "That street they're going to can't be very long. We can find that warehouse."

Ellie was dumfounded. "Are you serious?"

"Never more so. Chang wants Harry to live. I don't." Her words were bitter.

"But he's your son."

"He's a stranger. My son died a long time ago."

"Mr. Lee – "

"I know. I know." She closed the drawer, and closed her

270

eyes for a moment. When she opened them again, there was resignation behind the glitter of tears. "A good housekeeper can always find work, even in these days."

"But he's your husband."

A faint flicker of a smile passed over the older woman's thin mouth. "That died a long time ago, too. Perhaps one day you'll understand."

Ellie didn't think she ever would understand. How could a woman want to kill her own child? Even one as evil as Harry Lee? "Can't you drive?" she asked.

"No. I was never allowed to learn. If there was shopping to be done, I was driven, waited for, returned home. There have been many chauffeurs, but the rules never changed. Lately, Helen would drive me."

Ellie understood. Helen Chou had taken Mrs. Logie's place as mistress. And Helen Chou had betrayed Mr. Lee as Mrs. Logie never had. Mrs. Logie saw the realization in Ellie's face.

"In China, only sons count. Women are useful bystanders."

"But he must still love you."

"I love him. That's enough. Now – " She paused, then rushed on. "Don't you see? The other sons, the sons he had with the wife he did love, are good men. Harry is – " She paused again, and her mouth twisted. "Misbegotten. The runt of the litter. Every evil that Lee and I deny in ourselves came out in him."

"You're not evil." Ellie wanted to weep for this woman, and yet the resolve that was now apparent in her was frightening, unnatural.

"Everyone is evil and good. Yin and Yang. Cold and hot. Hard and soft. The Chinese understand that. Sometimes, in a child, in a person, evil triumphs. And when it does, it's strong and it spreads. You have to cut it at the root. Lee sees only a son. I see a cancer."

"I won't drive you to kill your son."

Mrs. Logie raised the gun. "I think you will. I wouldn't kill you, you know. But I would cripple you, make you spend the rest of your life in a wheelchair."

"You're that determined?" Elodie was appalled.

Mrs. Logie nodded. "I am."

There seemed to be no alternative.

There were three cars in Mr. Lee's garage. The big black limousine, a more modest sedan, and a small black van, probably used for transporting large art objects such as the red and gold altar Ellie had seen in the treasure house. She saw that the guard had returned to his post there, and was sitting peacefully on his chair. She wondered what he thought about, if he had ever seen what he guarded. Nobody had said anything to him. Moran's men had arrived at the front of the house, so he hadn't seen them. She wondered if he fell asleep out there, or whether the lights in the passage kept him awake. She wondered if he expected to be relieved, soon. When he would begin to realize something was wrong. She wanted to think about anything except what she was being forced to do.

Mrs. Logie didn't hesitate. "The van," she said.

Ellie got behind the wheel. Mrs. Logie produced the keys she had taken from a board in the kitchen, and handed them to Ellie. "Hurry up. We have to get there first."

"They're way ahead of us."

"Even so – "

Ellie stalled the engine twice before jerkily backing the van out of the garage. She had never driven anything but Hugh's little sedan, and then only on country roads. She couldn't see very well going backwards, but managed not to hit anything.

"You can go faster than they can if you put your foot down." Mrs. Logie was calm, now, but still held the gun. Ellie briefly considered trying to take it from her, but decided it would be easier when they got out. Meanwhile she could take wrong turns, go slow, even run the van into something on the way. Or when they got there, perhaps she could alert the others.

By driving Mrs. Logie to confront her son, she was going to be an accessory to a killing. Everything she had been brought up to believe and live by said that was wrong. Killing was wrong.

And yet, and yet –

She thought of Harry Lee. His sneering face, his vile beliefs, his willingness to commit any sin to advance those beliefs, and his craven desire to shame his father.

She wondered if Mrs. Logie was right.

She turned onto Lakeshore Drive.

She put her foot down.

The van jerked, balked, then moved forward.

**

Hugh Murphy was in the back of a van with four of Moran's men and Archie Deacon. Mr. Lee was in front with the driver. The van moved smoothly, occasionally turning, bumping over unseen trolley tracks, once bumping a curb. Hugh felt sick with fear and excitement. He had always arrived after a crime. Saw the scene when everything was over. He had seen corpses, he had seen destruction, he had interviewed terrified witnesses and stoic policemen.

He had heard gunshots in the movies but he had never heard a shot fired in real life until Archie had let off his gun in Manotta's office. He hadn't realized that it would be so loud, so stunning. He looked around.

Four guns were visible. Archie had one somewhere. And Hugh had been given one himself. He took it out and looked at it. So heavy in his hand. What was it that Ellie had said? Point and pull? Where had she learned that? He supposed it was common sense. How complicated could it be?

Each of Moran's four men had machine guns. They held them as they would hold a baby, cradled in their arms. Dull black, the smell of the oil on them was strong, reminded him of the smell of the garage at 2122 North Clark Street, two years back, on St. Valentine's Day. Oil and gasoline fumes overlaid with the smell of blood and the stink of bodies fouled by the betrayal of their bowels as they screamed and died or bled to death. It had been quiet when he got there. It was always quiet when he got there.

It wasn't going to be quiet this time.

**

As Ellie drove down the street lined with warehouses, they saw Moran's cars drawn up in front of one of them. Men were getting out.

"Drive past," Mrs. Logie hissed in her ear. "To the alley."

"They've seen us." Ellie was sure they had. She was tempted to blow the horn.

Mrs. Logie twisted around to look out of the small windows in the rear doors. "No. They took no notice. Go around the corner and turn into the alley."

"They'll be covering the alley."

"In a minute, in a minute. Do you recognize the door you went through?"

Ellie bent down and peered through the windshield at the silhouettes of buildings against the skyline, then looked along the alley itself. "Yes. But it will be guarded."

"Go to the far end of the alley and stop the car." Ellie did as she was told. "Turn off the engine. Now, get out."

Ellie did, hoping for a moment when she could perhaps tackle Mrs. Logie and take the gun from her. But Mrs. Logie gave her no opportunity, coming around the van and staying behind her. "We'll go along and hide as close to the door as we can. When Moran's men go in, we'll follow them."

"But – "

"Most of the noise will be at the front, the men at the back are just going to be there to stop anyone escaping. Here – duck down behind that pile of crates."

Again, Ellie did as she was told, and felt Mrs. Logie crouch down behind her. She still had the gun – Ellie could feel its hard little snout pressing into her back. I should have run away when I got out, she thought. She wouldn't shoot me. The others would have heard . . .

But she hadn't run away, and she knew why. Somewhere on the long drive she had felt her anger start to grow. Her fault? She'd started 'all this'? Well, if she'd started it then she should help finish it. Leave her behind, would he? Damn Hugh. Damn Archie Deacon. Damn them all.

**

Archie sent three men to the rear of the warehouse, to watch both the entry and the loading doors. In front there was just a single door, presumably leading to an office where business would normally be conducted. One of Moran's men easily picked the lock, and they went in silently. It was dark and empty, even of furniture. Moran's men piled in behind them and waited silently.

Archie sniffed. Ellie had been right. Ether and pickles and something of the barnyard. So they were not only processing opium into heroin, but still turning out cocaine.

It was a big place. Ellie had only seen a small part of it, and the priest and Cohen could have been moved from where they had been to anywhere in the building.

If they were still alive.

When he inched open the rear door of the 'office', light flooded in. The space beyond was well-lit and huge. In it he could see at least six men, but there could easily be more out of his line of sight. Four of the men were playing cards at a small table. The other two were lounging against the far wall. All but one were Chinese. The odd one out looked Italian, swarthy and scowling. He sat apart from the rest, and looked very bored. He had a gun in a shoulder holster, but none of the Chinese looked armed. At least, not with guns.

There was almost no cover in the room. What packing cases and boxes were there were scattered, few and low. When they went in through the narrow door, it could be only one at a time, so they would have to move fast. They had one moment when the element of surprise would help them. After that all hell would break loose.

Archie turned back to the group of men behind him and gestured one forward. He stepped back so Moran's man could get a look at the situation beyond.

"You see who to go for first?" he whispered.

Moran's man nodded.

The moment had arrived.

**

The three men in the alley stiffened as the sound of machine gun fire came from within the building.

"They're in." The man who had spoken went forward and tried the entry door beside the loading dock. It was locked. "Our turn," he said, and kicked the door in with one hefty thud. The men piled through the door and disappeared.

"Count to ten, then we go in." Mrs. Logie's whisper was tense, and Ellie knew she, too, was frightened by the noise of firing and shouting, but still determined. "They won't expect anyone to be behind them."

Ellie hesitated. Being angry and wanting to take part in all this was one thing, actually doing it quite another. All that noise was from real guns, real bullets hitting home. Moran's men didn't expect anyone to be behind them, so if they were detected they would undoubtedly shoot automatically. Suddenly she thought of her family sitting at home, unaware of where she was and what she was doing. Archie had pointed out that Harry's threats to them were sham because he had no idea where the Browne house was, nor who Ellie really was. So she didn't have to worry about them anymore.

But if she was hurt, or killed ...

"Now!" Mrs. Logie pushed at her, took her by the upper arm, forced her up and forward. Stiff and resisting, Ellie was propelled toward the open door and the sound of mayhem beyond. They stepped into the light from the hallway beyond.

Could they be seen?

Would they be seen?

**

Hugh Murphy was throwing up in a corner of the big open space. The Chinese men and what was obviously one of Capone's men lay dead on the concrete floor. He had thought, he had assumed, they would simply round up the people in the warehouse, not kill them. He wondered whether Archie had thought the same thing. But the Italian guy had fired, and then there was no stopping Moran's men. To them, killing was just an efficient way of dealing with opposition, no moral questions involved. Now they were swarming up the two staircases that led up to the next floor, Archie was behind them, gun out, shield out, but white-faced with shock. Hugh knew then that Moran's men meant to go on killing because as far as they were concerned it was all part of the vendetta against Capone. Shining Sword meant nothing to them. He retched again, and went down on his knees. What was the saying – he who rides the tiger cannot dismount? They had certainly loosed a tiger in here.

Drew stood still, undecided. Stay here? Help Hugh? Go up

the stairs – left? Right? Get the hell out of it?

Archie looked back down at him. Their eyes met briefly. The message was clear – they were part of the horror, whether they wanted it or not. All they could do was hope they found the General and the priest before they got caught in the cross-fire.

Drew went for the caged elevator he had just spotted in one corner. It had to lead somewhere. As he moved, he took out his flask one more time.

Hugh stood up and avoided looking at the dead men. He had seen dead men before. But he had not seen men stand up suddenly, terrified, seen blood spurt from chests and heads, seen them fall, twitching. He had not fired his gun. He knew that. He hadn't needed to.

Moran's men had done it all.

He didn't feel any better for it. He had been there. If there was ever a trial, he would be a witness. Would have to admit that he was part of it. Shaking, he took out his handkerchief and wiped his mouth and forehead.

Then he heard a woman scream.

**

Moran's men had kicked open doors as they went along the back hall, up the stairs, down the corridors. As Ellie and Mrs. Logie followed them, they passed the door behind which Ellie had last seen Father Anselm and General Two-Gun Cohen.

There was one dead Chinese man on the floor, almost under the table.

Nobody else.

"They were in there. Maybe Moran's men have them." Ellie was still resisting Mrs. Logie every step of the way. She had lost her anger, lost her bravado, lost her self-control. When she had seen the dead man she had screamed and would have gone on screaming if Mrs. Logie hadn't shaken her, hard. That was a real man, lying there. A real, dead man. Blood seeped from beneath his head, part of his face was torn away. Hideous, horrible. She retched, but her stomach was empty. Only sour bile rose in her throat.

"I don't care about them. You know what I want." Mrs.

Logie pushed and finally pulled Ellie along the hall toward the stairs at the end. "I want it over with. I want him dead. I want all this to stop, now." It ocurred to Ellie that the woman was hysterical, impelled by something she could not, chose not, to control.

There was shouting and shooting from everywhere, it seemed. The noise was tremendous, echoing, re-echoing through the building. Ellie imagined Moran's men moving like a scythe, cutting down everything in their path. 'Cleaning up'.

Mrs. Logie pulled her up the stairs. Another corridor, more open doors. "He's here, he must be here." She was panting, grunting with the effort of keeping Ellie with her. How can she do this? Ellie wondered as she was dragged along.

How can she possibly do this?

**

Drew stared as the elevator came to a halt. Beneath him was the noise. Here was silence. No, not silence. Whispers and the sound of dripping, liquid flowing, a hissing, a bubbling, a stink so strong it almost made his eyes water.

The top floor of the warehouse was filled with laboratory apparatus. Nobody was there. He stepped out of the elevator and looked around. Where had they gone, the men who worked here? He recognized a bunsen burner, still alight. Overhead lights were reflected in large vats of water, in glass tubes and vessels of all sorts that twinkled and shone.

He was fascinated.

They must have heard the shooting, he decided. They must have always had a plan for escape. His shoes crunched on some broken glass on the floor between the long tables. They had left in a hurry, that was clear. Were they hired hands, or dedicated members of Ming Dao? Had they fled for their lives or joined the fight downstairs?

He felt for his flask and held it to his lips, head thrown back to catch the last few drops. He staggered, lurched to one side, grabbed for the top of the table, dislodged the flaming bunsen burner. Fire licked along some spilled fluid, ran away from him like a child, fleeing, leapt to an overturned flask that hissed and exploded with a small pop. The fire leapt higher.

"Oops," said Drew.

**

Moran's men had been ruthless, shooting every man they met. The bodies lay in log jams in the corridors, mostly Chinese, but not all. The Chinese only had knives, and they had been easily picked off. It had ended here, in a large room decorated in the Chinese manner, but sparsely. Symbols painted on the walls were in Chinese, writ large, emphatic. One large decorative sword, highly polished, hung above a low table on which were candles and other objects, like an altar.

Here, too, were Harry Lee, two other Chinese men, Father Anselm and General Two-Gun Cohen. Harry appeared icy calm, but his eyes glittered with a kind of cornered madness, and he actually snarled as his father came through the door of his lair.

One of Moran's men, the one who had been first into the big ground floor area, turned to Archie. "That him?"

"Yes." It was Mr. Lee who spoke.

"Then we're done." Moran's man gestured to the others and one by one they left the room, silent when before they had borne the thunder of machine guns before them.

Harry Lee's face was twisted in fury. "You will die for this, Father. I will see to it."

"No." Mr. Lee's voice was soft, sad. He seemed to have grown older with every step he had moved further into the warehouse, following the killers, stepping over the dead.

Harry hissed vituperatively in Chinese, words obviously meant to wound. Mr. Lee's face remained impassive.

Archie and Hugh, who were holding guns on Harry and his henchmen, waited. Eventually Harry simply ran out of breath. Hugh thought he was an ugly little snipe and felt the hatred emanating from him like some kind of smell. Hugh was almost deafened from the noise of the guns, dazed by the killing and the inexorable advance of Moran's men. His legs were weak, his vision blurred by sweat and tears of despair. He held his gun as a threat he knew he could never carry out. But Archie Deacon was in control. Archie would fire long

279

before he did.

Where the hell was Drew?

**

Ellie and Mrs. Logie ducked into a room when they heard Moran's men coming back toward them. They stood behind the door and listened to the shuffle of their feet passing. Nearly all of them had gone by when one of them grunted.

"This ought to put a spoke in Capone's Chinese cart-wheels."

There was a general mutter of agreement and some laughter.

Then they were gone, clattering down the stairs and out into the dawn. The room the two women were in faced the street, and they heard the engines of the cars starting below them, heard them driving away one by one. For a moment there was silence.

And then, far far away, the sound of sirens.

Chicago music.

Again, Mrs. Logie pushed Ellie ahead of her. They followed the sound of voices. They came to the room where the others stood. When they entered, Archie and Hugh turned, but Archie quickly returned his attention to Harry Lee. Ellie could see he was angry, but he wasted no time expressing what he felt to see her there.

Hugh did.

"God dammit, Ellie – " he began. Then he saw Mrs. Logie behind her, saw the gun in her hand, and was silent.

Mr. Lee saw her, too, and stepped forward as if to protest, for he recognized the look on her face.

Harry did not. "Mother," he said, as if pleased to see her, looking for a distraction, hoping for a way out. Only two guns against three, he saw there was still a chance.

"No." Mr. Lee said, loudly.

"Yes," Mrs. Logie said, and fired before anyone could move or stop her.

She missed.

Ellie had known in her heart that she would.

But Harry, enraged by the situation, the noise, the betrayal, jumped onto the low altar and wrenched the sword from the wall – the Shining Sword. He raised it above his head and prepared to charge. Archie's finger tightened on the trigger, but before he could fire a short sharp shot rang out. Harry Lee stood there for a moment, poised like a ballet dancer, the sword high over his head, and then he crumpled and fell, the sword clattering uselessly onto the floor beside him.

General Cohen straightened up from where he had bent over to retrieve a ridiculously small revolver from his ankle. A thin spiral of smoke rose from its barrel. He smiled shyly at their startled expressions.

"Three-Gun Cohen," he said.

Father Anselm crossed himself.

Mrs. Logie dropped her own gun and covered her face, weeping. Mr. Lee stared at her and them moved to her side, awkwardly patting her shoulder, offering what comfort he could. Father Anselm came over to her, too. He glanced at Ellie, horror and dismay in his eyes. "I knew you would think of something, but . . . " He gestured toward the open door through which could be seen some bodies, bleeding still.

"Not her decision," Archie said, quickly. He would have said more, but there was the sound of running footsteps. Drew leapt over the last body in his path and stopped in the open doorway. His eyes were wild and he was stone cold sober. One lens of his glasses was spiderwebbed with cracks, and there were ashes in his hair.

"I think everybody should leave right – "

Above their heads there was a brief explosion, followed by another. Cracks appeared in the ceiling and some plaster fell. There was a strong smell of burning.

" – now," Drew panted, gesturing them out.

The two Chinese man who remained looked up, suddenly terrified, and gabbled something desperate to one another. A whoosh like dragon's breath was heard, and sounds of windows breaking and glass falling to the street below. They gabbled faster, and then, totally ignoring Archie's gun, which was still aimed their way, they bolted for the door.

"I think they agree," Drew said.

**

All Moran's cars were gone. No trace of their presence remained. Flame poured like liquid down the sides of the burning warehouse, licking and sucking its way through each successive floor. The roof had blown off in one massive burst, and black viscous smoke rose into the pink dawn sky.

The fire engines arrived a few minutes after the police cars, but there was little they could do. Firemen and policemen milled around the street, watching the show. People had arrived, seemingly from nowhere. Although it was not a residential area, quite a crowd had gathered, a rich mixture of Chinese, Italian, and American chatter rose with the smoke. Many of them were in robes and slippers, excited enough by the spectacle to ignore convention.

"What the hell was in that place?" one fireman asked another, who shrugged.

"Beats me. Supposed to belong to a tea importer."

"That don't smell like tea to me. Don't burn like it, either."

In a doorway opposite, Archie, Hugh and Drew stood beside Ellie. Mr. Lee and Mrs. Logie had disappeared, as had the two remaining Chinese men – hopefully all that were left of the Ming Dao. Buried in the blazing rubble, the dreadful sword was no longer shining.

Father Anselm and General Cohen had stayed awhile, then bid them goodbye. There was nothing to say, nothing more to do. T'zu Hsi's treasure was still for sale. They would continue their activities on behalf of Chiang Kai Shek, and who could tell whether they would or would not make a difference? But China was far away, and that was up to them. What Mr. Capone would make of his lost investment was yet to be discovered. No doubt he would suspect Bugs Moran's involvement, but there was no proof. None at all. The fire was too hot for that.

"Mrs. Logie made me come." Ellie shivered despite the heat radiating from the burning building.

"Sure she did." Drew believed her. Hugh scowled.

Ellie was silent for a while, then spoke again.

"At least we don't have to worry about heroin getting Americans hooked. It's all going up in smoke."

Archie did look at her, then.

"Is it?" he asked.

She met his eyes and saw no triumph there.

He gestured toward the fire. "You think that's all there was? We've slowed it down, but we haven't stopped it, Ellie. The Syndicates won't stop because one shipment or even twenty were burned up. They've got the idea. They're bound to run with it."

"You have to do something, then."

He sighed. "What do you suggest?"

Tears came into her eyes. Just the smoke, she thought. It's just the smoke.

"You're an idiot," Archie said, affecting a stern voice. "You let your curiosity get the better of you, you didn't think ahead, you risked lives – especially your own." Then he smiled, took her chin in his hand, and kissed her, gently. "Just the kind of girl I like."

"But – "

"Go home, Ellie. Go home now. I have work to do."

She considered him; his red hair, his soot-streaked face, his green eyes, his weariness, the sound of his voice, the weight of his responsibility.

For the first time in a long time, Elodie did as she was told.

26

Elodie slept all that day and all the following night, rising very early the next morning. Only Marie was awake, as usual, getting breakfast in the kitchen.

"The coffee's ready, but you'll have to wait for oatmeal and there are muffins in the oven, out in five minutes." Marie poured her a cup from the percolator and watched as Elodie sank down beside the big kitchen table. "You look a lot better."

"I'd have to." Elodie had caught sight of herself in a mirror on her arrival home, just before she fell into bed. In her mother's distraught words, she looked like she'd 'been dragged through a knothole backwards'. They'd all been waiting for her.

Drew took Sal home in a taxi, Hugh had fallen asleep on the living room couch, and her family had had to be content with a few quick words of explanation. Archie – she still did not know what had happened to Archie. A patrol car had brought her home. After that it had pretty much been a blur.

Now, one by one, the family appeared, eyeing her with great relief and some apprehension. It was clear whatever Ellie had been through, it had changed her a lot. Even Alyce was subdued and seemed almost afraid to speak, but eventually she did.

"You have to tell us what happened. You have to."

"If Ellie doesn't want to talk about it – " Mrs. Browne began, protectively, but Ellie raised her hand.

"I waited until you were all here. I only wanted to tell it once because . . . " She stopped. Images poured through her mind: Webster being shot, the jade butterflies, Bernice's big eyes and quick smile, Mr. Lee and Mrs. Logie, Father Anselm and General Two-Gun Cohen, the dreadful Harry Lee, the sound of the machine guns, the explosions and fire, the running ...

" ... because I want to forget it."

She looked at each one in turn. Her family – still innocent, still kindly and real, still worried about her, still uncomprehending of the evil and wickedness outside their contented little world. Even Maybelle, more sophisticated than the others, didn't realize how terrible it could be. If she had even glimpsed Moran's men with their impassive faces, most of them spattered with the blood of their victims, talking to Archie as if what they had done, the sheer slaughter of it, was no more than a company outing, a Fourth of July picnic, fun and games with the guys – even Maybelle might not understand. A lot of it Ellie didn't understand herself, because it had seemed so simple in the beginning, and then things happened faster and faster –

"It all started with Mr. Webster," she finally began. She told it in an even and fairly steady voice. They listened without interrupting her, as if they were standing around someone being sick, waiting for it to be over, waiting for the fever to break.

She stumbled over telling them about Mrs. Logie. "She . . . was so . . . "

"Wicked?" Alyce burst out.

"No!" Ellie protested. "So sad. So very sad."

"But she made you drive her, made you take her to kill her son ... her only son." Mrs. Browne's voice cracked a little. The concept of *wanting* to kill your own child was anathema to her, even though, in the end, the housekeeper had been unable to do it.

"You didn't see him." Ellie tried to encompass Harry Lee's viciousness. "He was nobody's son anymore. She said he was a cancer and she was right. He was the driving force behind Ming Dao. It was his idea to come to Chicago after the jade, because he knew it would be his father who would probably be selling it. He wanted to destroy his father, first, and then the rest of America. I think he actually believed he could do it. A man like that, a personality like that – " She shook her head. "It's amazing what they can make other people do. They can talk the weak and poor into believing anything by just stirring up hate, encouraging them to blame someone else – anyone else – for their troubles. And they can convince the intelligentsia with their so-called ideals, because ideals are a perfect cover for viciousness. If he'd gone back to China with the money from T'zu Hsi's jade there's no knowing what he could have brought about."

"I hope nobody like that ever happens to America or anywhere else." Marie put a plate of hot blueberry muffins in the center of the table, went around and topped up their coffee cups, and then sat down to join them. She had been listening as she moved around the kitchen. Quiet Marie, who saw so much and said so little. Ellie drew in the sweet rich scent of the muffins and felt herself begin to relax. Marie's magic, she sometimes called it.

"So then Drew set the lab on fire – "

"I don't understand about the lab," Maybelle said.

Ellie explained what Drew had told them about how cocaine was processed and how he thought the heroin was being distilled from the opium. "It was the ether and other inflammable stuff used for the cocaine that exploded. Processing heroin needs just mostly water ... and anyway, he didn't set it on fire deliberately. I'm afraid Drew was a bit . . . "

"Tipsy?" Maybelle was amused. She had liked Drew. His fear had dissipated on the drive to the Browne home, but the alcohol had remained in his blood, and she had recognized its return in his blurred eyes and shaking hands. "He's an interesting man."

Mrs. Browne scowled. "He obviously drinks to excess," she said, giving Maybelle a reproving look. Maybelle just grinned. She had a penchant for lame ducks.

"And we all got out before the roof fell in and that's all." For a moment Elodie felt it all sweep over her again, felt tears burn behind her eyes, and she quickly reached for a hot muffin and broke it open.

"Your clothes are ruined," Marie observed. "All that smoke and soot will never come out."

Ellie kept her eyes on her hands as she buttered the steaming muffin. Butter dripped onto her thumb and she licked it off, biting into the muffin at the same time. She spoke around it, tried for a jaunty tone. "I never liked that dress anyway."

Marie sighed. "I'll make you another one."

"No. I am going to buy a dress." Elodie licked more butter off her fingers, and glanced around. They were all staring at her, aghast. Buy a dress? None of them had had a store-bought dress since October, 1929.

"With what?" demanded Alyce.

Ellie smiled. Marie never bothered about the morning mail or paper. By coming down early, Ellie had been the one to pick up what lay outside the front door. The morning paper, with – she noticed – a picture of the fire on the front page. The mail. And a small box with her name on it. Mrs. Logie couldn't drive, so Mr. Lee must have brought it himself, or sent the guard from the vault.

She put the box on the table and opened it. Inside was a cheque for a ridiculous amount with a note suggesting she could use it to 'replace her burned clothing'. More like get the roof fixed, she thought. Beneath the note was a small translucent carving that seemed to have an inner glow – a delicate white jade figure of a young girl bending to pick up a lotus blossom.

"With my ill-gotten gains," Elodie said.

**

Elodie was late for work, having gone to the bank and then to Marshall Fields where she bought two new dresses and a hat. Encumbered by her packages, she stepped out of the elevator and looked around the tenth floor reception lobby.

Today the blonde girl with the marcelled waves was at the central desk. Men were sitting in the leather chairs with briefcases on their laps while others passed to and fro carrying papers or talking to one another. Secretaries hurried past on errands for their bosses.

Normal.

Smiling to herself, Elodie went down the long marble hallway to the familiar glass door, and opened it. Sal looked over her shoulder from where she was filling the percolator. Today her dress was white and patterned all over with huge red peonies. Her shoes matched, and her stocking seams were slightly crooked. Drew looked over the toes of his shoes from where he lay on the sofa, looking hung-over and still a little red-eyed and sooty. The table in the middle of the room was filled with papers, both handwritten and typed. A box of doughnuts had been dropped on top of them.

Normal.

Elodie came in, closed the door behind her, dropped her packages under the hatstand and grinned at them.

"Hey," she said. "Have I ever got a great idea for a new show."

**

Announcer: There are a thousand stories in the big city. Bix Benedict, ace Crime Reporter, knows them all – the secret sorrows, the lies, the dangers, the cruelty and the kindness, the hatred and the love that fills these streets. And he reports them all.